Bard FICTION PRIZE

Bard College invites submissions for its annual Fiction Prize for young writers.

The Bard Fiction Prize is awarded annually to a promising, emerging writer who is a United States citizen aged 39 years or younger at the time of application. In addition to a monetary award of $30,000, the winner receives an appointment as writer-in-residence at Bard College for one semester without the expectation that he or she teach traditional courses. The recipient will give at least one public lecture and will meet informally with students.

To apply, candidates should write a cover letter describing the project they plan to work on while at Bard and submit a C.V., along with three copies of the published book they feel best represents their work. No manuscripts will be accepted.

Applications for the 2016 prize must be received by June 15, 2015. For further information about the Bard Fiction Prize, call 845-758-7087, or visit www.bard.edu/bfp. Applicants may also request information by writing to the Bard Fiction Prize, Bard College, Annandale-on-Hudson, NY 12504-5000.

Bard College PO Box 5000, Annandale-on-Hudson, NY 12504-5000

COMING UP IN THE FALL

Conjunctions:65

SLEIGHTS OF HAND:
THE DECEPTION ISSUE
Edited by Bradford Morrow

Children deceive, as do grownups, and many are the moments when all of us even deceive ourselves. People of every age and stripe, whether rarely or often, dissimulate, bluff, and beguile. Sometimes we deceive in order to harm another; sometimes our deception is meant to protect another from harm. Some deception is evil, some begets beauty. The writer who fabricates and populates worlds is a deceiver, as is the artist whose triumph is to trick the eye, to alter perception. The honest magician's livelihood is based on deception; so is the dishonest thief's. Animals, too, are masters of deceit. Survival in the natural world often depends on camouflage and concealment, faking out wily predators or wary prey ("The fox barks not, when he would steal the lamb," Shakespeare, ever the student of deception, reminds us). Even that most exquisite of plants, the orchid, employs a wonderfully varied arsenal of pollinator deceptions, luring bees and wasps with a false promise of nourishment or sex. And consider the great Russian poet Marina Tsvetaeva who wrote, "A deception that elevates us is dearer than a legion of low truths," thus complicating the subject entirely.

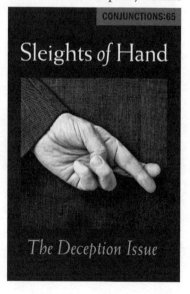

This special issue of *Conjunctions* will gather a wide spectrum of essays, fiction, and poetry on the classic subject of deception, exploring in original and thought-provoking ways a world in which truth is a most fragile, elaborate, and mercurial thing. Contributors to *Sleights of Hand: The Deception Issue* include Laura van den Berg, Edie Meidav, Terese Svoboda, Yannick Murphy, Paul Hoover, and many others.

One-year individual US subscriptions to *Conjunctions* are only $18 (two years for $32) for today's most fearlessly imagined, immaculately conceived fiction, poetry, and narrative nonfiction. To read dangerously, subscribe or renew at conjunctions.com, or mail your check to *Conjunctions*, Bard College, Annandale-on-Hudson, NY 12504. For e-book editions of current and selected past issues, visit openroadmedia.com/conjunctions. If you have questions or wish to request an invoice, e-mail conjunctions@bard.edu or call (845) 758-7054.

CONJUNCTIONS

Bi-Annual Volumes of New Writing

Edited by
Bradford Morrow

Contributing Editors
John Ashbery
Martine Bellen
Mei-mei Berssenbrugge
Mary Caponegro
Brian Evenson
William H. Gass
Peter Gizzi
Robert Kelly
Ann Lauterbach
Norman Manea
Rick Moody
Howard Norman
Karen Russell
Joanna Scott
David Shields
Peter Straub
John Edgar Wideman

published by Bard College

EDITOR: Bradford Morrow
MANAGING EDITOR: Micaela Morrissette
SENIOR EDITORS: Benjamin Hale, J. W. McCormack, Edie Meidav, Nicole Nyhan, Pat Sims
COPY EDITOR: Pat Sims
ASSOCIATE EDITORS: Jedediah Berry, Joss Lake, Wendy Lotterman
PUBLICITY: Darren O'Sullivan, Mark R. Primoff
EDITORIAL ASSISTANTS: Matthew Balik, Laura Farrell, Grayson Gibbs, Ariana Perez-Castells, Dan Poppick, Zoe Rohrich, Natasha Wilson-McNair

CONJUNCTIONS is published in the Spring and Fall of each year by Bard College, Annandale-on-Hudson, NY 12504.

This issue of Conjunctions is made possible with the generous support of the National Endowment for the Arts and of the New York State Council on the Arts with the support of Governor Andrew Cuomo and the New York State Legislature.

SUBSCRIPTIONS: Use our secure online ordering system at www.conjunctions.com, or send subscription orders to CONJUNCTIONS, Bard College, Annandale-on-Hudson, NY 12504. Single year (two volumes): $18.00 for individuals; $40.00 for institutions and non-US. Two years (four volumes): $32.00 for individuals; $80.00 for institutions and non-US. For information about subscriptions, back issues, and advertising, contact us at (845) 758-7054 or conjunctions@bard.edu. Conjunctions is listed and indexed in Humanities International Complete and included in EBSCOhost.

Editorial communications should be sent to Bradford Morrow, Conjunctions, 21 East 10th Street, 3E, New York, NY 10003. Unsolicited manuscripts cannot be returned unless accompanied by a stamped, self-addressed envelope. Electronic and simultaneous submissions will not be considered. If you are submitting from outside the United States, contact conjunctions@bard.edu for instructions.

Cover design by Jerry Kelly, New York. Cover art by Carolyn Guinzio (carolynguinzio. tumblr.com). Gaps in Knowledge, 2014. Digital photographic collage. © Carolyn Guinzio 2015; all rights reserved by the artist.

Conjunctions e-books of current and selected past issues are distributed by Open Road Integrated Media (www.openroadmedia.com/conjunctions) and available for purchase in all e-reader formats from Amazon, Apple, B&N, Google, Indiebound, Kobo, Overdrive, and elsewhere.

Retailers can order print issues via D.A.P./Distributed Art Publishers, Inc., 155 Sixth Avenue, New York, NY 10013. Telephone: (212) 627-1999. Fax: (212) 627-9484.

Printers: Edwards Brothers Malloy, Circle Press

Typesetter: Bill White, Typeworks

ISSN 0278-2324

ISBN 978-0-941964-80-7

Manufactured in the United States of America.

TABLE OF CONTENTS

NATURAL CAUSES
Edited by Bradford Morrow

EDITOR'S NOTE. 7

Karen Hays, *Frothy Elegance & Loose Concupiscence*. 8

Ann Lauterbach, After *After Nature* 34

Thomas Bernhard, *Eight Poems* (translated from German
   by James Reidel). 42

Russell Banks, *Last Days Feeding Frenzy*. 49

Lucy Ives, *Transformation Day* 57

Martine Bellen, *Two Poems*. 72

Benjamin Hale, *Brother Who Comes Back Before the Next
   Very Big Winter*. 77

Evelyn Hampton, *Fishmaker*. 116

Margaret Ross, *Visiting Nanjing*. 129

Michael Ives, *And the Bow Shall Be in the Cloud* 137

Joyce Carol Oates, *Big Burnt*. 149

Sequoia Nagamatsu, *The Return to Monsterland* 182

Christine Hume, *Ventifacts*. 195

Lily Tuck, *The Dead Swan* 201

Greg Hrbek, *The Confession of Philippe Delambre* 207

Thalia Field, From *Experimental Animals, A Reality Fiction*. . 223

Diana George, *Wara Wara*. 234

Wil Weitzel, *Green Eyes of Harar* 241

Meredith Stricker, *Anemochore* 252

Jessica Reed, *Five Poems* 257

Miranda Mellis, *The Face Says Do Not Kill Me* 263

Matthew Pitt, *After the Jump* 267

Noy Holland, *Fire Feather Mendicant Broom* 281

Sarah Mangold, From *Her Wilderness Will Be Her Manners* ... 284

Matthew Baker, *Proof of the Monsters* 287

China Miéville, *Listen the Birds, A Trailer* 321

NOTES ON CONTRIBUTORS 325

EDITOR'S NOTE

IN SMOG-CHOKED NANJING with its vegetable vendors and on an island encircled by the pristine waters of Lake George and haunted by a doomed man's memories, nature generates its own narratives in which humans play out their ordinary lives and, sometimes, extraordinary deaths. In the ancient city of Harar in eastern Ethiopia where hyenas come to feed in the sultry night and in the snowy Alaskan wilderness whose Russian River salmon are being greedily, hedonistically overfished, nature is observed, marveled at, even as it's being exploited and threatened—together with its hapless human "custodians"—with extinction. Nature survives as best it can while we savor and pollute it, celebrate and misuse it. And as for its misuse, humans have long been an egregiously clever tribe of misusers. If, for instance, the Department of Defense has its way, as Christine Hume notes in these pages, weather itself could one day be weaponized using "weather-modification technologies [that] might give the United States a 'weather edge' over adversaries."

Yet not all is apocalyptic. Nature has traditionally played a rich, central role in literature, sometimes becoming a character itself. Yes, a dead swan becomes a metaphor for a dying, violent marriage, but then springtime flora proposes rebirth, the promise of futurity. In these pages we encounter shrimp farms and spoonbills, maize husks and Austrian woods, tarantulas and eels, multitudinous winds that pollinate or desiccate—nature in all its myriad forms, right down to photons, neutrons, neutrinos, and, yes, even Godzilla, the Sasquatch, and other of nature's fictive and folkloric monsters.

Natural Causes is less a dispatch from the Sierra Club—although concern for our environment and appreciation of its ravishing beauty and diversity are very much on the minds of these writers—than a reimagining of how nature writing can be written. Here are twenty-five engagements not only with our natural world but with the ways in which we contemplate it in art and essay.

—Bradford Morrow
April 2015
New York City

Frothy Elegance & Loose Concupiscence
Karen Hays

FROTHY ELEGANCE

TO GET TO THE FIELDS this morning, the kids, most of them still too young to drive, ride in school buses, the route illumined by high beams, the drivers alert to deer along the shoulder, the sun canoodling and vexing the sleepy horizon as it stretches and procrastinates getting up, the smells of the Missouri countryside rising to the open bus windows—full-bodied, sour-sweet, piquant.

Each bus is a capsule of fireflies rocketing down the highway in the predawn dark. The jars are overfilled and their occupants drowsily blink on and off, on and off. Most slump and doze in upright fetal curls, their knees pressed into the unyielding green seat backs in front of them, their heads cocooned in soundscapes specially chosen to romanticize the unique brand of lust or angst or rage or heartbreak they seem to feel they suffer from, their faces lighting up with electronic glow whenever they stir to adjust the volume, or skip a song, or text a kid a few rows back or up, or whenever the bus dips into a pothole or veers onto the rumble strips, jarringly.

By the time they arrive, the light in the cornfields is crepuscular and it almost feels like morning out. As many girls as boys tumble off the buses, and both genders dress in the same work clothes. They wear long-sleeved shirts, heavy pants tucked into tube socks, and baseball caps or wide-brimmed hats. Because the dew is so heavy, they also don hull-like Hefty sacks. Bandannas enfold their necks like fallen crowns or forsaken brigand masks. On their feet are the boots or high-topped shoes they fully expect to pitch in the garbage when, a couple of weeks from now, their pockets will be loaded with cash, and their work mercifully done with.

The kids are brought in as a kind of cleanup crew, to get what the machinery has missed. The mechanical detasselers have already

8

taken a pass through the fields, but about a third of the male flowers on the female-designated rows still linger. Those have to come off before pollen shed or else the females will pollinate themselves and the corn won't crossbreed like it's supposed to. To make a female corn plant out of a bull corn plant, all you have to do is snap off the tassel. Because variety is the key to producing robust offspring, bulls and females are grown from different seed stock. The better and heartier ears are hybrids.

When it comes to detasseling, there's still no substitute for human hands. Over the medical tape, the kids, ages twelve and up, wear protective gloves. Some think they're guarding against an allergic reaction, but the truth is, corn has glass in its leaves, little microscopic beads of opaline silica that keep animals from grazing its stalks down to spayed and neutered nubs. Because of the silica, corn leaves slice and rasp. Even when barely brushed against, a leaf of maize will impart a laceration as deep and fine as a paper cut. Walking a row unprotected will raise a whole terrain of welts that will itch and blister, weep and crust over, render wakefulness miserable and sleep next to impossible.

It's a race to the end of each row, but whoever misses a tassel loses. Here now a kid grabs hold of a stalk with one gloved hand and, with the other, snaps the tasseled end to the side, rights it, then yanks it straight off the top of the plant. He tosses the male flower on the ground where the wind will never gather the strength to lift and broadcast its pollen. Steps on it. The sound the stalk makes breaking is appetizing, like teeth in an apple or a rib of celery fracturing.

In maize leaves, the beads of glass are shaped like human molars. In other plants, the shapes are different.

•

The seed of the Missouri state motto was planted in 1899 when Congressman Willard Vandiver was pressured into giving a speech under somewhat awkward circumstances.

Vandiver was in Philadelphia on business when, "after a very busy day among the naval officers and the big guns and battle-ships and armor-plate shops,"[1] he and several colleagues were unexpectedly invited to attend a formal dinner. Congressman Vandiver had nothing appropriate to wear and not much time to improvise. He was pleased to discover former governor Hull of Iowa in the same boat as he. As they were the only two invitees unprepared for a banquet, the two agreed, albeit reluctantly, to attend in casual clothes; each man would at least draw the thin comfort of knowing he wasn't the only underdressed guest at the club. The two parted company, but while Vandiver relaxed for a few minutes, Hull scrambled to obtain dinner attire. As a result, Vandiver was the only man in two hundred not dressed in an evening suit for the banquet. Asked to stand and give a speech midway through, the humiliated Vandiver realized he "must crawl under the table and hide, or else defy the conventionalities and bull the market, so to speak."[2] Willard attempted to recover from his embarrassment by falling on the time-tested method of talking trash about his neighbor. He accused Hull of stealing his own dress suit and offered as proof the sloppiness with which the clothes hung from Hull's frame. In his own words:

> I made a rough-and-tumble speech, saying the meanest things I could think about the old Quaker town, telling them they were a hundred years behind the times, their city government was the worst in America, which was almost the truth, and various other things, in the worst style I could command; and then turning toward Governor Hull followed up with a roast something like this: "His talk about your hospitality is all bunk; he wants another feed. He tells you that the tailors, finding he was here without a dress-suit, made one for him in fifteen minutes. I have a different explanation; you heard him say he came over here without one and you see him now with one that doesn't fit him. The explanation is that he stole mine, and that's the reason why you see him with one on and me without any. This story from Iowa doesn't go at all with me: I'm from Missouri, and you've got to show me."[3]

According to Willard, the speech was a rousing success and induced ribald cheering all around. Soon it became a song. "He's a good liar!" the crowd chorused in merriment.[4]

---

[1] W. M. Ledbetter, "Whence came the magic words, 'I'm from Missouri'?," *The Mixer and Server* 3 (July 1922), 41.
[2] Ledbetter, 42.
[3] Ibid.
[4] Ibid.

In Willard's day, swindling and pomp were big entertainment. In the nineteenth century, medicine shows made tours of tiny towns in the Corn Belt, traveling by horse-drawn wagon and moving from north to south in a swath that coincided not with detasseling, but with the grain and cotton harvests, ideally staying in each backwater for two weeks at a stretch. Medicine shows featured everything from performing dogs to ventriloquists, fire-lickers, comedians in blackface, and pie-eating contests. All of this free revelry created a sense of indebtedness in the entertainment-starved audiences, making them extra suggestible when nostrum hawkers interrupted the frivolity to spew patter like this: "Is there some way you can delay, and perhaps for years, that final moment before your name is written down by a bony hand in the cold diary of death?"[5] The answer, of course, provided by the snake-oil salesman, was "Yes" and quickly followed by: "Well, step right up then."

What many don't know is that "show me" and "Missouri" were paired long before Missouri adopted its state slogan. The two were connected in a way that was not meant to praise Missourians as keenly cynical and discerning but to pillory them. Missourians were considered by the residents of their neighboring states to be too dumb to grasp a situation or perform a task unless provided some kind of overblown pantomime or explanation. It was more like, "Oh, Willard? No, no, no. You'll have to *show* him if there's to be any hope of him getting it." Willard upended the insult and his vindicated statesmen ran with it. One journalist wrote this concerning the motto's evolution: "Like the grain of dirt in the oyster shell [. . .], the process of assimilation into the language of everyday life has transformed it from a phrase of opprobrium into a pearl of approbation."[6]

The quote most often attributed to Vandiver is, "I come from a land of corn and cotton, cockleburs and democrats, and frothy elegance neither satisfies nor convinces me. I am from Missouri and you have got to show me."

••

[5]Brooks McNamara, *Step Right Up* (New York: Doubleday Press, 1995), 43.
[6]Ledbetter.

The same year that Vandiver is believed to have made his "frothy elegance" speech, Italian botanist Federico Delpino wrote this about the attention we pay to the sometimes-deceiving appearance of things: "What is morphology, if not the measure of our ignorance?"[7]

The first to study the actual functions of plants—then regarded as "curious accidents"—Delpino is considered by modern botanists to be the father of plant biology.[8] Though history seems to have largely overlooked him, Delpino's contributions to science were major. He was a fervent champion of Darwin and, as such, he worried that the theory of evolution would never be proven through traditional analyses of form or systematics. What was needed, Delpino argued, was a thorough understanding of how plants relate to one another and their environment. Delpino shared the results of his botanical observations with Darwin, maintaining an affectionate correspondence with him for years and signing his letters with valedictions such as "your most humble disciple,"[9] "your most obedient disciple,"[10] and "your true admirer and servant."[11]

In the autumn of 1869, Delpino received an irresistible suggestion in the mail from his friend. In a letter he closed with "Believe me, dear Sir, with much respect, Yours very faithfully, Charles Darwin," Darwin suggested his pen pal take up the study of grasses, corn in particular. He wrote, "Permit me to suggest to you to study next spring the fertilisation of the *Graminaea* [. . .] *Zea mays* would be well worth studying."[12]

Study he did, though communication was difficult between the two men. Some believe that Delpino's contributions to botany were overlooked because he wrote only in Italian, a language typecast for romance, not science. Darwin had to have his wife translate Delpino's letters before he could learn their contents. "It is a bitter grief to me that I cannot read Italian,"[13] Darwin wrote to his Italian friend.

---

[7]Stefano Mancuso, "Federico Delpino and the foundation of plant biology," *Plant Signaling and Behavior*, 5 (September 2010), www.ncbi.nlm.nih.gov/pmc/articles/PMC3115070/ (accessed February 14, 2015).
[8]Ibid.
[9]www.darwinproject.ac.uk/entry-7196 (accessed February 14, 2015).
[10]www.darwinproject.ac.uk/entry-7055 (accessed February 14, 2015).
[11]www.darwinproject.ac.uk/entry-5622 (accessed February 14, 2015).
[12]www.darwinproject.ac.uk/entry-6938 (accessed February 14, 2015).
[13]www.darwinproject.ac.uk/entry-6869 (accessed February 14, 2015).

Perhaps it was this incompatibility of tongues—this deprivation of voices—that made Darwin wish he could lay eyes on Delpino. Perhaps Darwin wanted to assay the intolerable ignorance of languages by making a survey of Delpino's appearance, by looking and also by revealing. "Pray oblige me by sending me your photograph," wrote Charles after enduring a summer of poor health, "and I enclose one of my own in case you would like to possess it."[14]

•••

Summer break lasts less than a quarter of the calendar year and each year it gets both shorter and hotter. The kids quit midday when the heat begins to feel apocalyptic. By midmorning the milk jugs they filled with water and put in the freezer before bed are melting into their least favorite but inarguably most quenching thing to drink in the field. Weeds and springtails and maimed daddy longlegs cling to the beads of condensation and to the jugs' mud-smeared handles while the kids flirt and sing and talk trash to one another between the rows, looking insectile in their farmer-provided wraparound eyewear.

Rising temperatures make it a toss-up for the younger and more impetuous teens: Is it worse to swelter beneath all the cotton and the Hefty sack or to expose some skin to the glass and sun and insects, so that their sweat can do the job it was meant to, and the wind can relieve them?

In the fields, the wind is everything.

When Delpino undertook the study of grasses, he discovered that, while some flowering plants rely on insects, birds, or bats for their pollination, others use wind. The first to classify "pollination syndromes," Delpino labeled grasses like *Zea mays* "anemophilous," or "wind-loving." Simply put, corn loves the wind.

Though its method of fertilization is well understood, corn pollen remains a bit of a puzzle in terms of its appearance. What controls the size and geometry of a plant's pollen are its method of dispersal and how ancestral or highly evolved it is. Evolution tends to lead to

---

[14]Mancuso.

complexity of form, with more recent bodies exhibiting more elaborate designs. Though grasses like *Zea mays* are newcomers to the botanical scene, their pollen resembles that of the world's oldest, most primitive plants. Corn pollen is modest in architecture. It lacks the baroque crimples and pores that render other species' pollen so stunning under magnification. Absent are pointy stalagmites, Moorish tessellations, lacy fretwork, rolling folds, sticky pollenkit, lunar pocks, waving hairs, and so on. The pollen grains of *Zea mays* are just plain dry spheres, each possessing a single mouthlike aperture for its sperm to escape from. Where other pollen varieties resemble modern sculpture in their intricacy and elegance, a grain of maize pollen resembles nothing so much as an overstuffed beanbag chair.

One explanation for maize pollen's surprising simplicity of form is that possessing a single feature—the mouthlike pore—weights the grain so that it's more likely to find itself aperture down when it lands, improving its odds of making meaningful contact with a strand of silk, or corn stigma, should it be so lucky as to alight on one. Helping to weight the grain is the fish-lipped, or "crassimarginate," nature of its pore. (A note on etymology here: Before it meant "crude," "earthy," and "unrefined," "crass" was used to designate objects that were literally thick or fat. The process of assimilation has turned "crass" into an adjective of opprobrium.) The pore is also termed "opercular," as in the little circular door that snails close when they don't care to be messed with.

Another puzzling thing about maize pollen is its size. Though anemophilous, maize pollen is large, its diameter more in league with animal-conveyed than wind-conveyed pollen. At about one hundred microns, each grain is the approximate thickness of a coarse human hair.

In the fields, everything hinges on a breeze.

The kids long for relief in the form of pools, lakes, ponds, showers, lemonade, and ice cream. Instead, they're forced to rely on the caprice of the wind. When a breeze comes along, they raise their hats and invite it to enfold their necks. Then they get back to work. In this way, "rite of passage" becomes synonymous with "misery," a word they already know bears uncanny resemblance to the name of their home state.

At least they're all in it together. At least they all look stupid. Each of them is muddy and sweating more than they'd like to be in front of their peers. Each of them smells like a pair of moldy gloves that was recently rummaging around in a cow's rumen. Each suffers, and each makes money. The kids walk the rows in the morning so that the female-designated plants don't fertilize each other, *yeah sure whatever*, but mostly so they'll have enough cash to keep them in their various pleasure-poisons until late August when school starts back up again—Monster drinks and digital downloads and lip gloss and condoms and smokes and *chaw* and movie tickets and Cheetos and more.

They suffer to the extent that they're exposed. Their emotional misery almost offsets their physical pain, however. Walking the rows, the kids get bug bites, corn rash from the leaves' glass, and, in some cases, hospital-grade sunburns. They also get endorphin rushes from the camaraderie. They get boners and embarrassed and hormonally high enough from those last three not to feel the damage wrought by the bugs, the glass, and the UV right away. Detasseling lasts less than a quarter of summer break and each summer something magic happens. In the cornfield, social strata collapse. Unlikely kids become friends or more than that.

••••

In the leaves, the opalescent beads are phrases of opprobrium; in the ground, pearls of approbation. The biogenic silica beneath the kids' feet is so resilient it will linger in the soil for millions of years after the kids have passed. It will lend some grit to that cold diary of death until some archaeologist comes scrabbling in the field's paleosol and catalogs it as evidence. Then the opals will be fossils and more properly referred to as "phytoliths."

Phytoliths are the main tool for tracing the history of maize and, by proxy, Paleo-Indians. The oldest discovered maize phytolith settled like an embryonic molar into a Panamanian lake bottom right about the same time that one of the world's oldest surviving shoes was pitched onto a heap of unmatched others, average size women's 8½, in a bat-inhabited trash cave overlooking the Missouri River. The shoe was braided from the leaves of a tallgrass prairie plant known by Native Americans as "rattlesnake master." That was about eighty-five hundred years ago. Since then, maize has succumbed to what one archaeologist calls "extreme domesticity." At first blush, "extreme domesticity" borders on the oxymoronic, but what it really means is this: Modern ears are so tightly wrapped in their husks that, without serious intervention, their seeds have no hope of escaping them.

Dressed as they are, the only way to tell the boys and girls apart from a distance is their voices. Words are airborne and letting them fly brings a modicum of relief to the kids. When it comes to pain, swearing is chemically anesthetizing and serves a real physiological purpose. Studies show a person can hold his or her hand in a bucket of ice water a lot longer if allowed to let fly a few choice words in the process. The dirtier, the better. For the boys more than the girls, swearing is an art form they're driven to master. Steven Pinker says that swearing originates in a primal part of our brains, the same part that gives rise to a dog's howl when its tail has just been stepped on. Cussing is crying foul when trespassed against, which, when you're a teenager, is pretty much always. *Don't look at me. Leave me alone. What do you want?* Cussing is verbal silica.

Neither maize nor language can self-sow, yet both hybridize as readily as plants with wind-borne pollen can, specially slang, whose usage spreads way faster than proper English's. When it comes to the origin of "slang" itself, etymologists are at odds. Anatoly Liberman's *An Analytic Dictionary of English Etymology* devotes about half a dozen pages to "slang," citing a Scandinavian trajectory and tracing its roots back to a time when "slang" meant "a narrow strip of land."[15] From there, "slang" was used to refer to the people who traversed that narrow strip, and then to name the patois of the strip's itinerants. Along the way, "slang" was employed as an adjective to mean "sinuous, snake-like, long and narrow and winding" as well as a verb for "to roam, wander" or "to linger, go slowly."[16] To traipse the country was to be "on the slang" like a group of "traveling actors [. . .] hawkers, strolling showmen, itinerant mendicants, and thieves fighting for spheres of influence."[17] To be on the slang was to go wherever the wind

---

[15]Anatoly Liberman, *An Analytic Dictionary of English Etymology* (Minneapolis: University of Minnesota Press, 2008), 195.
[16]Ibid.
[17]Ibid.

blew. It wasn't until the word hit London in the eighteenth century that "slang" began to signify "jargon."

According to an entry recently removed from the Urban Dictionary, "cornilingus" is the act of eating popcorn like an anteater.

According to the National Institute of Standards and Technology, the minimum acceptable abbreviation for corn is "CORN."[18]

Though they were told how to spray and to dress, and no, those weren't suggestions, many kids feel hard words backed by hard muscle are all the protection they need in the fields and, for that matter, everywhere else. Those young bulls. Those plucky Vandivers. The kids who suffer the worst need to be seen learn the hard way to keep their skin covered no matter the temperature or the heat index, to keep as shielded in the rows as the ears of corn in their glassy husks, to keep extremely domestic.

•••••

Some of us require serious intervention. I moved away from my hometown decades ago, but my dad still lives in the fertile loess bluffs along the Missouri River. When I get homesick, I call him up and he tells me about the plot of corn he's growing alongside his beans, okra, jalapeños, tomatoes, and spinach. His land is a fossil river meander; it is shaped like a human ear and its soil is the silt typical of all floodplains everywhere. The dirt there is as sparkly and fine as the moth wings I used to desquamate in order to paint myself glittery when I was a kid.

On the phone my dad and I are on the slang. We talk about things real and terrifying, winding from politics to natural resources to climate and back again. He likes to wrap up on a funny note. Joking, he says that maybe if we humans can delay our own self-induced extinction long enough, then after some critical count of generations the races in our country will homogenize, "racist" will become obsolete,

[18]NIST, "Table S.1.2. Grain types and multi-class groups considered for type evaluation and calibration and their minimum acceptable abbreviations," *NIST Handbook 44-2015*, http://www.nist.gov/pml/wmd/pubs/upload/5-57-14-hb44-final.docx (accessed February 14, 2015).

and everyone will self-identify as "Native Americans." It will be funny in an ironic kind of way, but only a handful of historians and we ghosts will get it. But hell, funny won't ever count half as much as what's for dinner does. People will always struggle first and foremost to feed their kids, and that's both the noblest and the most savage struggle there is. Then we talk about what each of us is cooking for dinner, and the provenance of our dinners' ingredients.

During the Pleistocene, glaciers picked and plucked, scoured and ground to flour the bedrock of the Canadian Shield. The silt wove its way south through the blue braided rivers that flowed within, beneath, and beyond the glaciers. Fine enough to hitch a ride on the wind when it dried, the sediment blew south and blanketed the Mississippi and Missouri River Valleys with a thick, wholesome dust. Glacial loess is so fertile it forms the loam of our nation's breadbasket. When the North American ice sheets retreated after the Last Glacial Maximum, the loess became a plush 150-billion-acre bed from which prairies waved their enticing tallgrasses. Then, at the start of the nineteenth century, John Deere invented his steel plow. In short order the loess became the subcutis of the Corn Belt. Within a human generation, the geographical extent of tallgrass prairie declined by approximately 99 percent.

Before there was corn, there was teosinte, a wild grass whose numerous little ears were each about the size and shape of a full-grown snake's rattle. Teosinte kernels are not pillowy soft and golden and full to bursting with sweet milk. Nor are they interlocked on a thick cob in a hexagonal honeycomb pattern. At just a few inches long, teosinte ears bear only two rows of triangular kernels, about a dozen seed grains total. They are spikes, not ears. Their two rows of kernels come together like the toothed blades of pinking shears, each kernel encased in a dark, rock-hard shell. When dried, the seeds have nothing to hold them together. Instead of clinging to a cob beneath husks that are bombproof, the kernels separate and fall to the ground where they readily grow into new plants. Unattractive as they are by comparison, it is nevertheless true: If heated over a flame long enough, teosinte grains will blow their hull and turn inside out, flaunting their starch just like the blond seeds of our movie-theater corn do. Step right up.

A couple of years ago, geneticists figured out that sometime during the Last Glacial Maximum, a wiseacre jumping gene named

Hopscotch took a wild leap and landed somewhere in the architecture section of a teosinte plant's double helix, resulting in the potential for a less branched mutant capable of bearing fewer but bigger ears. Jumping genes are bits of DNA that can detach from their strand, splice the strand closed, and then leap like a springtail to another rung on the spiral staircase. Jumping genes do their stuff when their host cells sense danger. What happens next is up to chance. Evolution can act on the changed genetic structure in a way that causes a disease to be expressed, or it can act on the changed genetic structure in a way that causes nothing to happen, or it can act on the changed genetic structure in a way that dramatically makes over a rather unappetizing grass, turning a dowdy tuft into a big, tall queen or crassimarginate goddess, a grain of dirt into a pearl. About twenty-three thousand years ago, when the North American ice sheets were at their most eminent, a teosinte cell sensed danger and its DNA took measures so drastic they were heritable, the DNA revising not only itself, but also its future generations. Thirteen thousand or so years later, Native Americans coaxed maize from teosinte by selectively breeding the Hopscotch mutants through a process called backcrossing, successfully domesticating corn, a feat made easier by the wind-pollination method of grasses. Ninety-five percent of the corn grown today contains the Hopscotch gene.

●●●●●●

Darwin thought Delpino's finding "surprising"—why should animal-pollinated plants abandon their M.O. to become anemophilous when clearly insects are much more reliable couriers, providing pollen "incomparably greater safety" than the wind possibly could?[19] Yet that seems to be the way things happened. Anemophily is a "derived" or secondary condition. Wind-pollinated plants came from animal-pollinated plants. Modern scientists believe anemophily evolved from zoophily at least sixty-five separate times in the evolutionary history of plants.

Wow.

---

[19]Janice Friedman and Spencer C. H. Barrett, "Wind of change: new insights on the ecology and evolution of pollination and mating in wind-pollinated plants," *Annals of Botany* 103 (June 2009), 1515–1527, http://www.ncbi.nlm.nih.gov/pmc/articles/PMC2701749/ (accessed February 14, 2015).

Karen Hays

Like the flowers of most anemophilous plants, maize blossoms are fairly inconspicuous and lack fragrance. There is no nectar to speak of, and the pollen offers little in the way of nutrition. Maize flowers aren't tantalizing because all they need is a stiff breeze to peddle their pollen, which is also plain looking. There's no pressure to lure winged beings with food, no need to seduce them into inadvertently doing maize's dirty work for it. Fragrance and physical beauty would be a waste of effort. The elegance is in the mechanism, not on the face of the plant. The elegance is in the wind.

Delpino said that if form and function were considered synchronously, they would "mutually form together a set of high scientific interest."[20] He wrote, "[. . .] raise the veil of apparent immobility and insensitivity of plants, and below it you will see [. . .] a number of curious phenomena, which compete for the number, variety, talent, and effectiveness with those presented by the animal kingdom."[21]

The science of botany was a bit of an uphill battle in the beginning. Linnaeus lifted the veil before Delpino, and many of his contemporaries were scandalized by the fantastic goings-on that plants seemed to keep hidden. Goethe contrived prudish explanations that he hoped would redeem the botanical world from whorishness and prurience, using the phrase "loose concupiscence" to describe the reigning explanations of the pollination process.[22]

Botany seethes with sexual verbiage—how many books about plants have you seen whose titles titillatingly combine the word "sex" with "hidden" or "secret"? And most comparisons between *the fertilisation of the Gramineae* and our own lusty shenanigans are just too crude and obvious to mention, the processes and scientific parlance lending plenty of innuendo on their own. It can be hard to keep a straight face, though the science is both real and real amazing. That's why, for Goethe's sake, I'm hopscotching the mechanics of maize pollination to the essay's end.

Here's how it begins.

[20]Mancuso.
[21]Ibid.
[22]Johann Wolfgang von Goethe, *Botanical Writings* (Honolulu: University of Hawaii Press, 1952), 109.

20

In stillness, the rays of maize's tassel point like the arrows of a wind rose. The main rachis pokes straight up and the many auxiliary spikes point in every direction of the compass. They look like a coterie of prairie dogs surveilling the horizon—not for predators, mind you, but for mating prospects.

Stillness is waiting, is torpor, is (it's too easy to anthropomorphize here): anguish. Maize leaves come alive to natter and flap in the wind, to loll and to lash, but the more amazing thing is what the tassel does. In the wind, the coterie becomes the supplest of fronds. It becomes a feather plucked from the display of a color-blind peacock. It becomes a whole tail full of feathers. A flirted fan. A flag waved with the coquettishness of a mock distress signal. The tassel struts and bunches. It twirls and sways. It performs great supplicating bows. It's as if the tassel were playing the wind and not the wind playing the tassel.

But look closer. Each arm of the tassel's plume is covered in several dozen wind-sensitive spikelets. Each spikelet blooms with two florets. Each floret opens to release three stamens. Each stamen is a gossamer filament with a pollen-producing anther bobbing at its end. Each anther hangs like a clapper from a hull-less bell, like a runneled tongue stuck into the wind, like a shotgun's double barrel.

Holy moly.

In the wind, the spikelets put on a show. It's *The Gold Rush*, Charlie Chaplin's table ballet, except instead of two dinner rolls, there are six anthers, the forks are gossamer stamens, and Chaplin's dancing eyebrows are twin florets. In a cornfield, a billion million anthers kick at the sky like little impaled baguettes, testing and tasting the breeze, desperate. *Which way? Which way?* their choreography seems to beg. *Where did it go?* and *Can you feel it, is it coming?* and *When?* and *How strong? Is it strong enough yet?* and *Now? Now? Now?*

It's important to know when the perfect breeze will arrive because there's last-minute work to be done before the anthers let go of their pollen. Right about the time of pollen shed, one of the cells (there are only two to begin with) inside each pollen grain undergoes division. From one cell come the two sperm necessary for pollination.

21

●●●●●●●

Maize husks have runnels that span their length like the ridges in the aisles of school buses. On the seats in the otherwise empty buses are closed lunches and wadded-up rain ponchos. Inside the maize husks are pithy unfertilized cobs. Cuplike are their bare white sockets. I once trespassed on a bus to do things I never told anyone about and my bare feet slipped on the runnels. The bus was parked in the middle of a field in Iowa. The door was unlocked. I stepped up. The ears of maize are waiting like the rest of us to fulfill their own *superspecialsecret* purpose, a purpose that feels so unique and custom fit when you're realizing it, but which is in fact the oldest, most universal deal in the book. There are soundscapes for this. Check iPods for playlists titled "urgent."

What if you only had one summer?

What if you only had two weeks?

In the time it takes a few busloads of Midwestern kids to detassel a cornfield, a language is buried with its last living speaker. According to the Living Tongues Institute, every two weeks a language dies.

By the time the kids are middle-aged, the world demand for crops will have doubled. Linguists estimate that half of the seven thousand languages now spoken on our planet will be extinct if not by 2050 then at least within a half century later. If they're right, and the UN's predictions for population growth are also correct, then in another thirty-five years, earth will be host to 35 percent more humans and 50 percent fewer languages. What's ironic but not funny at all is: Even though our country produced about fourteen billion bushels of corn last year, Native American tongues are among those most threatened by language extinction.

Maybe, because we humans have been growing roots around this planet since the scabs on our ancestors' knuckles healed, because we've been reaching and wrapping it in our thick tangles of cultures and customs, been colliding with and outcompeting and succumbing to one another's armies and tongues since the dawn of combat and language, all the time sprawling faster and harder around the earth's surface, something akin to thermodynamic heat death is in the works in terms of language. "Entropy" means "turning into." In thermodynamics, the thing you start with is the ability to do work and the thing you end up with is spent energy in the form of heat. Different sciences use the word "entropy" to express different things, but all agree that entropy is a one-way street. "Entropy" is synonymous with irreversibly momentous chaos, disorder, homogeneity, and, in some disciplines, species loss.

But language isn't dying like a tree with a few girdling roots. No. It's thriving while also becoming monotypic. It's undergoing a major architectural overhaul. It's forsaking its fretwork of twigs and limbs and girthing up a few of its basal branches, namely Mandarin, English, Hindi, Spanish, and Arabic.

Zooming out, it looks like the ancient ongoing process of globalization has rendered language sort of self-pruning, and now the whole system tends toward austerity and sameness, supporting just a few tidy forks instead of the many filigreed branches, the whole trajectory paralleling the journey of corn, from teosinte, corn's bushy little Mexican ancestor, to our modern *Zea mays* with its one feathery tassel and two enormous ears and tall martial posture, a now insanely important crop plant that is weirdly incapable of reseeding itself yet, at least according to the promotional pablum on the back of my box of cereal, currently thrives on every continent save Antarctica, nearly a third of the world's supply sprouting from the very same soil I grew up in.

It's hard not to think that quantity grows at the expense of variety, the latter caving to the former as in some gross "horsemen of the esophagus"[23] corn-eating contest. But there's some other mischief involved, some speedily proliferating sham element that throws the whole thing off, some wolf-eyed sameness going around disguising itself in variety's clothes. Take the verbiage on the back of my cereal box. The breakfast aisle at the grocery store offers an ever-expanding cornucopia of crunchy, grainy confections. The products have all kinds of different names and shapes, but basically contain all the same ingredients. Anyone who's watched a documentary about food

---

[23]Jason Fagone, *Horsemen of the Esophagus: Competitive Eating and the Big Fat American Dream* (New York: Three Rivers Press, 2006).

in the last ten years can name them. I grew up in the same dirt that the corn did.

There's an illusion of variety, a mock diversity to which our culture seems addicted. Our verbiage reflects this. Recently I read a synopsis of a study conducted by a psychologist hoping to illuminate how the switch from mostly agrarian to more urban living has affected our social interactions over the last twenty decades. She looked at more than a billion English-language books published in the United States between the years 1800 and 2000 and found that the use of the words "oblige" and "give" and "pray" and "belong" declined over that period, while the use of their near opposites, "choose" and "get" and "self" and "unique," rose.[24] (*Permit me to suggest to you to study . . .*) The psychologist concluded that our changing verbiage reflects our ability to adapt to the changes we've made to our environment, like the institution of a new verbal dress code.

Modern technology lets us zoom out in ways we couldn't in Darwin or Vandiver's time. Maybe choice and variety and uniqueness help us counter the terror of what those views afford us: our own weed-like proliferation, depleting resources, "extreme domesticity," self-centeredness, and leveling animalistic sameness. Maybe we rearrange corn and sugar into a million nameable shapes as a show of respect to the thermodynamic properties our bodies unwittingly defy through their symmetry and functional orderliness, as if to say, *We are not the same, we only look that way from a distance.* Take, for example, the popularity of tattoos. While the design of our bodies pushes the entropy boulder uphill, we lustily and uniquely label our skin. *See me*, our brands seem to beg. *Read my message. Choose me. Exempt me. I am highly evolved. Different.* In Darwin and Delpino's time, you would have been one in a billion. Today you are one in seven billion. Does it matter to you what number the denominator is, so long as you're the numerator? I think of the denominator and it looks like, sounds like, smells like, seven billion mouths in various states of smile and delectation and pronunciation and *goo-goo-g'joob* and gleam and scream and drool and root canal and curse and dirge and asymmetric paralysis and halitosis and lipstick and milk tooth and kiss. I am frightened to death by the arithmetic. I want

---

[24]Tom Jacobs, "'Give' gives way as word usage reflects shift in values," *Pacific Standard, Books and Culture* (August 7, 2013), www.psmag.com/books-and-culture/use-of-language-reflects-our-shifting-values-64183 (accessed February 14, 2015).

variety. Choose me. I am different. I want to hear the words for "sex," "home," and "banquet" spoken in all seven thousand extant languages, one after another. I want to pretend I'm the toastmaster and then watch it all unfurl in a six-hour-long YouTube video. I want to hear and see all of those unfamiliar sounds, not the loud swallowing undulations of a few tongues cannibalistically devouring all the rest.

I don't know how to reconcile the fact that I find terrifying, on a truly panic- and claustrophobia-inspiring level, the idea of sharing the globe with seven billion human mouths in various states of loquacity and mastication and slobber and howl and hunger and hygiene, while a playlist featuring seven thousand incomprehensibly nattering mother tongues is one I'd press repeat on again and again. This, I suppose, is the unique brand of lust, angst, rage, and heartbreak to which I subscribe.

The playlist asks to whom my future belongs. It asks to whom my land, my stock, my silica, my tassels, my TV, my history, my teeth, my dress, my domesticity, my dinner, my inheritance, my name, my children, my youth, my hybrid vigor, my voice, my language, my parents belong.

It asks and it answers.

• • • • • • • •

They're falling in love, some of these kids are, peeling off their layers come lunchtime to use the Porta-Potties and eat from the coolers they or, if they're maybe indulged a little at home, their moms packed up for them. *Don't worry, honey, no note. No more notes from Mom.*

Some of the kids save for college. A third of all Missouri high-school graduates will matriculate at the University of Missouri in Columbia, where Barbara McClintock traumatized corn chromosomes by exposing them to X-rays. McClintock later received a Nobel Prize for her discovery of jumping genes in maize. Panicked cells mount radical responses that permanently rearrange the shapes of things. When evolution acts on internal change, we're given a fresh opportunity to assay our ignorance.

The kids are terrified of exposure and terrified of coverage. They lower their language and lift their voices. They walk the rows on the slang. They complain boisterously about ambient smells, fret as they do over their own odors and, by proxy, bodily impulses. It's universally true that damp places accrue odors. The kids don't know the half of how olfaction or desire works, but what the hell does that matter? Does lifting the veil give desire any less agency over us? Pass me a smoke. Scratch my rash. Gimme a beer. Turn on that fan. According to an article from the National Conference of State Legislatures, a third of the girls will get pregnant before they're twenty. *Don't worry, honey, no more notes.*

Mom, it hurts.

Step right up.

The teenagers' noses know by instinct what biologists diagram with genes, cranial nerves, and weird-sounding chemicals. The kids sniff out each other's immune systems in order to maximize their own progeny's hybrid vigor. To crossbreed. They have no idea how much of them is on the wind. They couldn't care less. *OMG.* Breakfast was Cocoa Puffs and that was back when it was dark, still very dark, *like the ass crack of the fattest possible dawn out,* dark.

In 2013, the world's most ancient pollen fossil was found. Its age pushes the dawn of flowering plants all the way back to 240 million years ago.

The oldest known phytolith was found in a 70-million-year-old heap of dinosaur dung.

The mnemonic for remembering the roles of the first twelve cranial nerves, exempting the pheromone-detecting neuron number zero, is: Some Say Marry Money But My Brother Says Big Boobs Matter More. S is for "sensory," M is for "motor," B is for "both."

There are the things we do to delay that final moment when our names are written down in the cold diary of death, and the things we do to ensure that the ink in the diary is as indelible as pollen or phytoliths. So our genes outlive our voices and our voices outlive our regrets.

A third of the kids are cared for by single mothers.

A third of the girls get pregnant in places they're too embarrassed to admit.

Fewer than three tassels per one thousand female designated stalks can remain if this field is going to pass inspection.

In seventy years, no innovation has been made to the mechanical "cutters" and "pullers" to improve their efficiency enough to render human hands obsolete. Some 99.5 percent of the female plants must be detasseled for the harvest to keep its integrity, a third of them manually.

Backcrossing isolates the desired characteristic by continually breeding the end back to the beginning. Though I walk the rows, the process is sinuous; I'm on the slang forever and ever with it. Every time I open a Word document it's to cope with the lack and the liquidity, with my arms' awful emptiness, with the elusiveness of "home," that old shape-shifter, and to try to render something fully in spite of the maddening insufficiencies of language. It slips through my fingers, airborne. Every time I break from the task, it's to admit that the loftiness of words and the bluntness of distance have me licked again. Home looks like this:

(My dad's land is hidden by steep banks from all that surrounds it, suggesting that the little river whose past and present arc contours his property was at one time a lot more powerful than it is currently. Now it's a creek that, courtesy of some corps of engineers, courses a straighter-than-is-natural path. (Have you ever looked out of an airplane's window and seen the pattern of parentheses that meander scars make on the land, the imbricated crescents of fossil waterways, the circumscribed ear shapes, the silt-filled pinnae, the curly pinnae, the listening, history-hoarding pinnae that slow-going rivers trace? (Let's say a bend in a river is a parenthesis. On the inside, where the curve is concave, the river flows at its slowest, allowing even the lightest sediments to settle like ideas out of suspension. (It's a gentle rain. The fine-grained stuff drifts down and piles up on the riverbed, deepening the curve of the meander, and forming a point bar.) On the outside, where the parenthesis is convex, the flow is faster and instead of deposition, erosion takes place. (This is the cutbank,

27

where old floodplain sediments are plucked off, entrained, and sent downstream.) The eroded material heads seaward 'til the flow can no longer sustain it. On the inside of some other parenthesis, it falls out of suspension again. (Be they water or be they air, streams are fluid. So too are their beds. Soil and sediment are continually reworked.) A river is always on the revise.) Again and again.))

Work equals force times the measure of my displacement and in a system where energy is a constant, it's irreversibly spent. Work is. No matter how circular I write it, no matter how many times I loop it, disorder doesn't climb back into Pandora's Box at the essay's end. Instead it's the opposite. The Second Law of Thermodynamics says that entropy is always on the rise, the whole system marching toward thermodynamic equilibrium, which is the heat death I mentioned in the last section. In the end, everything's monotypic and homogeneous and I haven't isolated the desired characteristic of "home" in a way that's vivid enough to allow me to walk through its front door, sit at the kitchen table, pick up my spoon, and swallow my palliative. In the time it used to take a traveling medicine show to outwear its welcome, another language dies and a busload of Midwestern kids detassels a cornfield. Oblivion is where we're all headed in the end, of course, but that's oversimplifying it and also skipping quite a few really interesting steps.

What would you say if you only had two weeks to get your photo from Florence, Italy, to a sickly Charles Darwin? Would you write a crash course on the occult mechanisms of anemophilous organisms, including language and yourself among them, or would you write something else instead? What picture would you draw with your last words to assay the intolerable ignorance of incorporeality and/or voicelessness? What fragile or refractory parts of yourself would you expose or try to keep hidden? What crass grit, what elegant pearls, would you hold up to manifest your hidden function? Who would you roast or toast, and how many secrets would dehisce without your authority? What valediction would you offer at the end? *Is* there some way to delay that final moment, not merely of your death but of your legacy's death—of your terrible obsolescence? My valediction is: God, I hope so. I humbly and obediently do. I want to hear the final word of every silent and silenced language, whether silent because wordless or silent because dead. *Permit me to suggest to you to study this spring . . .*

LOOSE CONCUPISCENCE

Not long after the kids pitch their detasseling shoes in the garbage, another two-week-long process begins.

At night, while the kids shed their sunburned skin and scrape their bug bites and rashes against sheets made of cotton, dew beads the tassels' anthers. It soaks the anthers through and bloats their thin skins.

The sun's first order of business after vexing and pinking the horizon is to wick the dew back up to the atmosphere. The fields steam with its efforts. It takes all morning.

The sun warms things up, establishes a temperature differential, and has a nice breeze going by 9:00 a.m.

Below the tassels, the striated leaves wag tonguelike, cut the air, are susurrant. Their language recalls the vinyl's burnt-in hiss, the needle in the worn-down groove, the shush before the song begins, a sound to foreshadow every human's playlist.

In the breeze, the tassels bow and sway. Cluster and fan. To hell with boxing the compass. To hell with cardinal and ordinal directions. Each stamen is a forked baguette in Charlie Chaplin's miniature dinner-roll ballet. Each anther toes the sky, toes the sky, toes the sky.

By late morning, the sun and wind have dried the anthers and, in the process, shrunk them. Their skins grow brittle, pull taut.

Then a wind comes along that is more than some of the anthers can stand. A breeze comes along like a final straw and draws their skins so tight they split open. The anthers dehisce. Their twin barrels roll back like the eyes of the seized, ecstatic, letting fly their golden blueprints. From their retracted domes spills pollen.

Given a good stiff breeze, an anther can kick itself empty in as few as three minutes—about a song's duration.

For the same couple of hours every day, for a couple of weeks in mid-summer, midmorning, between 9:00 and 11:00 a.m., the maize broadcasts its pollen.

It keeps to a circadian rhythm. It minds the local weather conditions. When the dew is dry, the breeze stiff, the sun unclouded and just about to peak, the time is right for corn pollen to hitch the wind. A broken record. A cue burn on the lead-in groove. The pollen takes its two cells and makes a third.

Sometimes there is a second opportunity for the tassels to release their pollen when things cool down in the late afternoon or early evening. On cool and cloudy days, corn can sprinkle its pollen all the livelong. Pollen shed shuts down entirely when the mercury hits eighty-six, and when it rains. Temperatures of one hundred degrees or higher kill corn pollen outright.

(Because it's not obvious: Human sperm dies around the same temperature as corn pollen does, at just a few degrees above our own body temperature.)

It takes about two weeks for an entire field of maize to shake loose its capsules of pollen. Spreading the process out means a few really hot or dry or wet days won't wreck the whole season.

Wind speed increases with height from the ground. The tassel is an organ of flight, poised eight feet into the air so that its pollen can travel the maximal distance. Because it is big and heavy, corn pollen doesn't make it far before the wind dumps it—usually only between twenty and fifty feet. In a field, it needn't travel far. If lucky, the grain will alight on the stigma, or silk, of an unpollinated ear. *Baby, let me tell you what I been through, what all it took me to get here.*

Corn may be anemophilous, but its affair with the wind is puppy love compared to what happens next. As soon as it alights on a strand of silk, a pollen grain begins soaking up the stigma's moisture. Immediately a dialogue begins. Pollen and stigma exchange pedigrees. Flirt. The pollen grain performs a quick chemical assay to assess their compatibility. A proper introduction takes about five minutes. While pollen and silk converse, the tissue inside the pollen wall swells from all of the moisture it's been taking in. This creates a pressure

30

differential that can only be brokered by the crassimarginate oper-
culum popping open. At this point, the pollen is ready to be messed
with, but the reports of its analysis still aren't in.

If the answer is no because the stigma belongs to some other species
of plant, then the pollen hitched an unlucky wind and it's fucked,
dead in the water, just another wasteling in an incomprehensibly
populated sea of wastelings—the golden film on a windshield or some
poor sneezer's mucus membrane.

If the answer to the pollen's chemical assay is yes, a vermiform tube
begins growing from the aperture. If the pollen is also lucky enough
to have landed pore down, the tube burrows into the silk, lengthening and slimming as it shimmies into the darkness beneath the ear's
husk. Its progress is guided and lubricated by molecules released by
the egg down at the cob. The pollen tube wriggles the length of the
stigma all the way down to the white pithy bed where the egg awaits
pollination.

Let's be clear. Though chemically invited, the pollen tube must
mechanically force its way in. "Drill" is a word oft repeated in the
literature.

Since the beanbag chair that it escaped from is still perched up on the
green ponytail, no doubt frying in the sun, the pollen tube must grow
at the same time it bores through the stigma. This it does in the
unique manner of our own neurons—never at the base of the cell,
but only at the end. Tip-wise.

Of all the different types of plant cells, the cells that make up pollen
tubes are by far the fastest growing. A *Zea mays* pollen tube can
grow at the rate of a centimeter per hour. That's because pollen tubes
grow in competition with hundreds, sometimes even thousands of
others. Darwin felt anemophilous plants were wasteful with their
pollen, but others have suggested that tube competition and not the
inferiority of wind-as-pollen-vector is what drives their massive
pollen production. While heaps of pollen may alight on the same
strand of silk, only one grain can fertilize the egg at the other end.

A typical tassel bears about six thousand anthers and releases
between two and twenty-five million grains of pollen. The cob, by

contrast, is host to somewhere between four hundred and one thousand fruit-bearing eggs. Each silk strand connects to a cupule where an ovule-containing egg is housed. There's the familiar order of magnitude difference between the genders.

(A human man releases between one hundred and three hundred million sperm per ejaculation, but only about four hundred survive his orgasm; a woman is allotted between three hundred and four hundred eggs for her entire lifetime.)

As multiple pollen tubes race along the shared tract to reach the one egg, the ear conducts its own chemical assay, rejecting the pollen of incompatible plants and halting their tubes' progress.

If all goes well, a *Zea mays* pollen tube will arrive at the kernel bed within twenty-four hours. Traveling just within the leading edge of the pollen tube are the pollen's two sperm cells. The sperm are not motile on their own so, to keep up, they flow in a matrix of cytoplasm.

At the final stretch, the tube must round a bend—the final obstacle in the gauntlet. Things get tricky here because if the tube is too restricted when it twists, it will release its sperm cells before it reaches the egg. Game over.

The first tube to successfully turn the corner is guided the rest of the way by a protein secreted by the egg. All that's left for the tube to do then is tuck into the egg's little crevice. When it does, the egg releases a self-defense protein that induces the explosive self-destruction of the pollen tube. The pollen tube blows itself up, freeing the two sperm cells to meet up with the two ovules housed in the egg. One sperm-ovule pairing will develop into the fruity endosperm that surrounds and nourishes the maize seed; the other will develop into the kernel's seed ingredients—the embryonic root, leaf, and stem.

After this burst-and-release step of the double-fertilization process, the egg powers down its come-hither protein and all of the other pollen tubes veer off. I imagine them like a pack of terriers whose members have all suddenly lost the scent and given up, vaguely dissatisfied and confused.

The corn has been pollinated.

Within about twenty-four hours of fertilization, the silk detaches from the kernel bed and a blister begins to swell where it was. From here, the cob's pom-pom of silk can be used as a ripeness indicator. Over the course of the next two to three weeks, the ponytail turns from the greenish-blond hue of overly chlorinated towheads to a kinky auburn red and then finally to the dark brown that heralds ripeness.

The stages of ear maturation are: silk, blister, milk, dough, and dent.

Sweetness is a spontaneous recessive mutation in the maize gene. Sweet corn is harvested at milk stage, field corn at dent.

To test an ear's ripeness, wait till the silk is a couple of days past dark brown, peel back some husk, and sink your thumbnail into one of the kernels' skins. If clear fluid seeps out, the corn is still at blister stage. If it's sweet corn you want, wait a day and check again.

When you find a honeycomb of plump kernels beneath the husk, each fruit tucked into its cozy cupule and swaddled in yellow satin, the fruits bursting with skim-blue milk when pierced with your thumbnail's crescent, then the corn is ripe and ready to be sold or eaten.

Experts advise against picking too far in advance of eating because, like a car whose resale value goes down once driven off the lot, an ear of corn loses half of its sugars within twenty-four hours of being pulled from the stalk.

Afternoons, kids who are old enough to drive sit in trucks in the exhaust-filled, mirage-distorted parking lots of Missouri gas stations, grocery stores, and fireworks barns, the windows down and the engines shut off, selling armloads of sweet corn out of their flatbeds for cheaper than you can imagine. Spray-painted sandwich boards advertise that their product was *picked fresh this morning*. When business is slow, they drape themselves over their steering wheels and snooze, bare legged and bare armed, the radio on and their phones gently vibrating in the seats beside them.

After After Nature
Ann Lauterbach

1.

The unsaid strafes its enclosure.

I'm in a store, a storage,

among forgettings that anchor them.

The pasture is all snow and its perceptions

drain the day

outward

onto a disheveled, reckless halo

unspun from a saint's hair

as if scribbled.

The withheld stares

back onto its insolent intention, some girl

in the bridal threshold of a museum

her white shoulders

readied for sculpture and for the thin fingers

of her groom. Tidy these ancient portals,

says the Bergsonian moon, there's more

to see of the great murals

whose scansion is blocked

by the banquet's black plumes and

crimson napkins, fake beads of hanging ice.

2.

The baffled children stand their ground.

The boy who cannot smile

the girl who stares into the mutant air

my own mirrored self

dancing in the aisle of beloved

animation, singing along

to a tune rescued and

hid under soil

piled on the floor in that corner.

That room, that window, those stairs

and across the wide portico a muse

yelling in French

and the mother in pails, the mother in ashes.

And the flowers? You ask. They were

announcements that came slowly up

with the man with a sack on his shoulder.

The snow will not burn but falls as heaving flame.

The drifts are catalytic

plummeting toward amnesia

and a recessed doll appears, her eyes

painted open.

3.

I did not ask for this bouquet. Please return it.

The form of attention bewilders

and the signal's arc wavers. If I

gaze I gaze, and the blue mountain

is indifferent, like Wittgenstein

staring out from his captive picture.

Some beauties are best left unobserved.

Some dues are best left unpaid.

And if Sebald once retrieved

Grünewald's journey,

exposing the throat and often turning

the face toward a blinding light

then let us be

amazed and wander up a hill

and turn to see

the bereft tribe following Moses

out of Egypt, following

an uncertain path into a tent onto which

only a vane fastened with string

remains. The route was written

but the map's insignia and

all the variants of white

dispersed through the holy frame.

4.

Wait here a minute. I need to attend to

the soot. A gashed estrangement

dramatizes the ocular theme.

Rag rag rag. It's a quick refrain,

what the broom might chant.

Accidents happen and rage resumes

under the free rights of dream,

the unsafe conditions

masked by law. The scene

melts into its recursive

harm; the tent

blown up by a young man in the film

of the young man in the film.

The black boy is shot and shot and shot.

Which war are we after? And home

he came smelling of sandalwood and silk,

the scent of beautiful strangers.

The yoked extravagance, the carnal scene,

fire and ice, her crimson

lips stamped on the rim of a glass.

Take them back. The apparition

thwarts declension for the sake of an image.

5.

We settle for stone

even as it attracts disaster

just at the welcoming hour.

Now the exposed branches

have turned

yellow, their threads crawling

out from the scripted scene.

Arendt talks about metaphor

enthusiastically; she honors

the sign of what she calls

invisibles,

that which will never attach itself

to thingness. The philosopher's

wonder is fraught; words charge

our love with action

and action blurs syntax. She thinks

we can see what we hear

just as it vanishes.

The chickadees orchestrate

the silence of the hawk's

swerve; all is readied for accounting

as for abstraction.

6.

I liked it better elsewhere,

in the drafty aftermath,

along the dark hall or

sitting on the porch, before the fly

awoke from its winter nap.

Up it crawls on the glacial window.

If I say cardinal, do you see red?

Grace is legible; we collect variously,

accordingly, in the zone

allotted. So a democratic yield

might fashion our taste

for the old sword or the ripe fruit

or the red panoply

of Matisse. Love

moves among us and elicits

the daring collective.

Marvelous and outward we go

toward the plight to heal

what has no mercy, incorporated

as sorrow or bliss, sold separately

to those who come to witness.

7.

Abstraction is invisible, it

pours through the sockets

of the hours and the

broken debris goes

out to sea—a flood of names,

old particulars—

what never was translated;

some drafts on paper—

erode the banks and the banks

rise up into the empty horizon

like nameless cartoon giants.

Be not afraid.

These fives, these tens,

watch them change hands

to bring forth shiny arrest.

Dip the oak leaf in gold.

Dip the screen into the rushing waters.

The days will end without portraits.

The days will end. *Rag rag.*

—For Thomas Wild

Eight Poems
Thomas Bernhard

—Translated from German by James Reidel

ROT

Imperishable as the sun I saw the earth
   when I fell back to sleep that seeks my father,
who brought the last wind's message
   into my wretchedness that grieves for his fame,[1]
the fame of which he said: "Great talents
   come to naught tomorrow . . ."
Immortal stand the forests that once filled the night
   with their lament and their talk
of cider and doom. Only the wind
   was above the wheat ears while spring survived
amid this sweet rot.
   The snow turned against me and made
my limbs shiver at the sight
   of the restless North that resembles an enormous, inexhaustible
cemetery, the cemetery for the prisoners
   of this triumph worming its way
into every wayside cross, into every fieldstone
   and into every country road and church, whose spires rose
against God and against the wedding party
   who gathered around their cask of wine to
drink it up with pig's laughter.
   How I watched these dead in the village on benches
eating red meat with swollen bellies,
   slurring the hymns of March beer,
the rot slinking through the inn garden

---

[1] *Fame (Ruhm)* is a key word in Bernhard's poetry that should not be confused with the banality of "fame" in commodification–American English. Here fame has an element of humility too. It is closer to Heidegger's sense vis-à-vis Hölderlin, who saw the fame and glory of gods and poets in terms of being allowed to appear (*Erscheinen-lassen*), i.e., to be made real.

amid the dull braying of the trombone . . .
I heard the deep breath of depravity
between the hills . . .

Imperishable like the sun I saw the earth
whose August was bad off and irretrievable
for me and my brothers who learned their craft
better than I, who torment me
with millions of beggarships and no longer
do I find a tree for my insane conversations.
I went from a night of hell
to a night of heaven,
not knowing who must crush my life
before it is too late, to speak of fame and courage,
of poverty and that earthly despair
of the flesh that will annihilate me . . .

BEYOND THE TREES IS ANOTHER WORLD

Beyond the trees is another world,
the river brings me lamentations,
the river brings me dreams,
the river keeps silent when I with evening in the forests
dream about the North . . .

Beyond the trees is another world
that my father mistook for two birds,
that my mother bore home in a basket,
that my brother lost in sleep when he was seven years old and tired . . .

Beyond the trees is another world,
a grass that tasted of sorrow, a black sun,
a moon of the dead,
a nightingale that never ceased to lament
of bread and wine
and milk in big mugs
during the night of the prisoners.

Thomas Bernhard

Beyond the trees is another world,
they walk down the long furrows
into the villages, into the forests of thousands of years,
tomorrow they ask for me,
for the music of my afflictions,
when the wheat rots, when nothing has remained
of yesterday, of their lodgings, sacristies, and waiting rooms.
I want to leave them. With no one
do I want to speak anymore,
they have betrayed me, the field knows it, the sun
will vindicate me, I know, I have come too late . . .
Beyond the trees is another world,
there is another country fair,
the dead swim in the kettles of the peasants and around the ponds
the lard quietly melts from red skeletons,
there the souls no longer dream of the mill wheel,
and the wind only
understands the wind . . .

Beyond the trees is another world,
the land of rot, the land
of merchants,
a landscape of graves left behind for you
and you will annihilate, sleep horribly
and drink and sleep
from morning to evening, from evening to morning
and understand nothing anymore, not the river and not the sorrow;
for beyond the trees
    tomorrow,
and beyond the hills,
    tomorrow,
is another world.

Thomas Bernhard

ONE DAY I WILL WALK INTO THE FOREST

One day I will walk into the forest
and bury the cities and tame the night
with the knife of melancholy.
I will walk through the meadows on Corpus Christi[2]
and press my cheeks into the grass
and stick my finger down the throat of the earth.
But my night will be like this: without fire and without salt,
I will kneel on the stones
of my deserted village
and search for my father—
I will listen by the udders of the cows and hear the pails whisper,
    filling with milk.

NO TREE

—A reason for John Donne

No tree
will understand you,
no forest,
no river,

no frost,
not ice, not snow,
no winter, you,
no me,

No storm wind
on high, no grave,
not East, not West,
no weeping, woe—
no tree . . .

---

[2]*Corpus Christi* (*Fronleichnamstag*) is a feast day and procession that occurs in the late spring in honor of the Holy Eucharist; line 7, *without fire . . . salt* (*ohne Feuer . . . Salz*), compare with Mark 9:49, "For everyone will be salted with fire and every sacrifice will be salted with salt."

Thomas Bernhard

I KNOW THAT IN THE GREEN ARE THE SOULS

I know that in the green are the souls
of my forefathers,
that in the grain
is the pain of my father
and in the great black forest.
I know that their lives, which are spent
before our eyes,
have a refuge in the tassels,
in the blue brow of June sky.
I know that the dead
are the trees and the wind,
the moss and the night
that lays its shadows
on the mound of my grave.

IN THE GRASS

Speak, grass, shout my word to heaven!
From stake to stake[3] and over the moss
spring the wind's red and yellow brothers.

Hear how the bush burns and smoke issues
through wet mouths and cracks,
hear the cry of the brood in the poisonous weeds.
Poisoned are the clusters of flowers and laments.

The sick mother is inside the tree and weeps
and counts the tears like in Paradise,
and a thousand strings span the forest
from my breast into the face of the sun.

---

[3]*Stake to stake* (*Pflock zu Pflock*), i.e., wooden grave markers.

IN SILVA SALUS[4]

> *King: Though yet of Hamlet our dear*
> *brother's death the memory be*
> *green, and that it us befitted . . .*

I ask the death's-head in the forest
    for my father . . .
Father . . .
    the moon hangs like a corpse
between the tops of two trees, so
    as to deceive me . . . there
is the spine, through which the wind whistles . . .
    Father, you have killed
my heart . . . two feet without boots,
    a rusty belt buckle
reflected in the pond . . .
    Two steps away
your rotten shoulder strap . . .
    How shall I hear through the undergrowth
what you give me for an answer,
    where so many voices are?
I ask the death's-head in the forest
    for my father . . .

---

[4]*In silva salus* is a Latin motto ("in the forest lies safety or salvation") that resonates in Germany-Austria for it recommends the benefits of the forest retreat that is here a negative experience.

Thomas Bernhard

THE WIND

The wind comes in the night
    and carries me back into the villages,
into the dull swish-swash of the butter troughs.

The wind comes in the night,
    it spins my name in chestnut leaves
and drives it back north.

The wind comes in the night,
    before the face of the sun
that abducted my brother.

The wind comes in the night,
    its cry of pain swirls
in countless treetops,

that cry that my father hadn't known,
    the wind, the wind, the wind

    that gathers the dead,
that flings open the front doors,
    that drives my soul,

the wind, the wind, the wind.

Last Days Feeding Frenzy
Russell Banks

FIVE MINUTES OUT OF Anchorage, past the karaoke joints and strip-per bars, the fast-food outlets and flag-flapping car dealers, suddenly there's scree, glacial ice, and endless sky above, serrated cliffs and crashing waves below, and I'm in the Alaskan wilderness. Snow-crested mountains tumble through fir trees and sedimented rock into the cold, zinc-gray sea, and the sight of it takes my breath away, literally—my chest tightens as I drive—and I think, I'm not worthy of this much beauty, no human is. But I'll sure as hell take it. And I do—I drink it in, eat it up, gobble it down while I can, because I know that it's not going to last. I'm on the Seward Highway headed south through the Chugach State Park and National Forest, looping along the sawtooth edge of a long, narrow fjord off Cook Inlet called Turnagain Arm. It's the summer solstice, June 21, 2003, the longest day of the year, and a good thing too: I'm driving the length of the Kenai Peninsula today, from Anchorage to Homer, 225 miles, and left Anchorage around 4:00 p.m., so won't make Homer till 9:00 or later and don't want to arrive in the dark at the backwoods cabin I've borrowed but not yet seen, where there will be no electricity, no run-ning water, no company.

The only other vehicles on the highway this afternoon are ele-phantine RVs, pickups, and SUVs, all of which appear to be registered in the Lower 48, most of them driven by late-blooming baby boomers taking early retirement. As they lumber toward me or when, on the occasional straight stretch of road, I overtake and pass them, the drivers and passengers grin and pump fists or cheerfully flash Vs for victory and two thumbs-up, like we're all pals up here in Alaska. Their easy bonding bugs me. Then I remember what kind of car I'm driving along this long, lonesome, wilderness highway. I'm at the helm of a brand-new, bright-red ("sunset-orange metallic") Hummer, test-driving the 2004 H2 model with the full-bore luxury package. It's got all the bells and whistles: Bose six-disc CD changer; heated, slate-gray leather seats; sunroof; OnStar system—all that and, as they say, more, more, more. It's got wraparound brush guards, running lights, off-road lights, seventeen-inch off-road tires on cast-aluminum wheels, and the same Vortec 6000 6.0-liter, fuel-injected V-8 engine that powers the 2003 Corvette. It's got a self-leveling, rear air-suspension system with an on-board air compressor. It's got a thirty-two-gallon fuel tank. And needs it, especially out here in the wilderness, where filling stations are separated from one another by very long walks.

This is a vehicle that for sheer bulk and brawn can't be equaled by any other so-called passenger car on the highway. It may be a guzzler, but there isn't an RV or an SUV anywhere that the Hummer can't knock from the sidewalk into the gutter with a simple dip and shrug of one broad shoulder. It's six foot six in height, close to seven feet wide, and just under sixteen feet long. It's built like a bank vault on wheels, thick all over and squared. Cut. Not an ounce of body fat. Driving it is like riding on the shoulders of Mike Tyson in his prime. It's not sexy, however, unless you think Mike Tyson is sexy. People, especially guys, grin, flash the victory sign, and step aside. "Hey, Champ, how's it goin'?"

I know I'm not supposed to like this car. It's the most politically incorrect automobile in America. Maybe in the world. Consider who purchased the cruder, more forthrightly militaristic H1 model that preceded it, and who we must assume will be first in line for the H2: Arnold Schwarznegger, yes, we knew that, and Bruce Willis; but also Don King, Coolio, Karl Malone, Dennis Rodman, Al Unser, Sr. and Jr. Ted Turner owns an H1, not surprisingly. And Roseanne Barr. And, of course, Mike Tyson, who bought a brace of Hummers for himself and a few more for his friends. As party favors, I guess. By and large, this is not the green crowd.

And look at its heritage, its DNA. Its closest modern-day relative is the scruffy, friendly-looking Jeep, which evolved out of the original mud-spattered WWII jeep and still summons the spirits of Ernie Pyle, Bill Mauldin, and a generation of unshaven, exhausted foot soldiers bumming a ride back to the base. The Hummer, however, is the direct descendent of the post–Vietnam War era's Humvee, which is to the old WWII jeep as Sly Stallone is to Audie Murphy. The Humvee is a jeep on steroids, built to handle anything from Afghan road rage to a good Gulf War. Its newest civilian incarnation, the H2, is dressed out with enough leather, polished-walnut dashboard trim, and high-tech add-ons to pass for chic in the Hamptons or fly on Rodeo Drive, and enough tinted glass, CD speakers, and sheer size to become next year's official hip-hoppers' posse car. It's a gigantic steel jockstrap. The vehicle goes straight to the testosterone-drenched fantasy life of the adolescent American male, no matter how old he is, and butch-slaps it into shape. Driving down the Kenai Peninsula in my Hummer, I keep remembering how I felt when I was a kid in New Hampshire cruising around town in winter in a dump truck loaded with sand and a snowplow attached to the front, feeling larger, stronger, taller, wider, harder than anyone else on the road. It was a good feeling then, and, I have to confess, it's a good feeling now.

Along the Russian River, a short ways south of Resurrection Pass, I see where all those RVs, pickups, and SUVs from the Lower 48 have been headed. The salmon are running, and the people in those vehicles are like hungry bears trundling to the riverbank to pack their bellies with fish and roe. The glacial river is cold and wide and fast and mineral rich, a strange, almost tropical shade of aqua, and thousands of fishermen and -women, but mostly -men, are lined up shoulder to shoulder for miles along both banks, mindlessly, recklessly hurling their hooks into the rushing water and one after the other yanking them immediately back with a glittering, twisting salmon snagged at the end. It's the warm-up to an annual potlatch, an ancient midsummer harvest rite, and the native people have followed the example of the bear for thousands of years. But somehow, as I drive slowly past them, these people, in their greed and desperation to take from the river as many of the salmon that survived last year's rite as they can, seem oddly postmodern. Postapocalyptic, actually. For soon there will be no more salmon returning here to spawn. We all know that. Never mind the catastrophic effect of dams, oil spills, and nuclear leakage, we know that the millions of adult salmon being hooked, bagged, and tossed into coolers and freezers from California's Klamath River north to Alaska are likely to be the last of these magnificent creatures we'll ever see. And none of these folks flipping fish into tubs and coolers looks especially hungry. They're mostly on the overfed side of fitness. So why are they pigging out like this? I wonder. This is more like a feeding frenzy than a ritual, and it's sure not a sport, I decide, and drive on.

Halfway to Homer, I check the onboard dashboard computer and note that I'm averaging just over ten miles a gallon. And do I connect that fact with the feeding frenzy I've just observed along the banks of the Russian River? Of course I do. These are the Last Days. The planet is running out of everything except human beings. Clean water, boreal forests, wild animals, birds, and fish—soon all of it will be forever gone. Fossil fuels too. Gone. Yet we Americans, especially, consume fossil fuels at an accelerating rate, and to aid and abet our consumption, we build and buy with each year more and more ten-miles-per-gallon vehicles—Suburbans, Expeditions, Navigators, Land Cruisers, and $100,000 Hummers painted sunset-orange metallic. It's a different sort of Last Days feeding frenzy than the one along the Russian River, but related, and the planet, as if preparing to explode, is heating up. The paradox is that here in Alaska, with fewer people per square mile and more square miles of protected wilderness than any other state in the union, the calamitous effects of global warming are more obvious than anywhere on earth. Since the 1970s, mean summer temperatures in Alaska have risen five degrees, and winter temperatures have risen ten. The permafrost has gone bog soft, glaciers are shriveling, the ice pack is dissolving into the sea like sugar cubes, and on the vast Kenai Peninsula, nearly four million acres of white spruce, thirty-eight million trees, have been killed by the spruce bark beetle, a quarter-inch-long, six-legged flying insect that, because of the increased number of frost-free days, reproduces now at twice its normal rate, enabling it to overwhelm the trees' natural defense mechanisms.

I'm not puzzled as to why GM, Ford, and Toyota build and sell vehicles like the Hummer, the Expedition, and the Land Cruiser, and can't condemn them for it; they're in the automobile business, and these behemoths are big sellers. What puzzles me is why so many Americans are jostling for a place in line to buy one. It would not surprise me if there were something deep in the human psyche, the vestigial male chimp brain, maybe, that makes us rush to the trough as soon as we sense it's nearly empty and snarf down as much of what's left as we can. It's not greed. It's an atavistic fear mechanism kicking in, the sort of move made by our lower primate ancestors whenever they saw that the troop's population had outgrown its food supply and they were going to have to move to a new forest, one run by an unfriendly, possibly tougher troop, or else stop having sex. In a paroxysm of anxiety, the big males instantly start gobbling up every banana in sight.

Such are my melancholy thoughts as I make the long, gradual descent on the Sterling Highway from the town of Soldotna to the old Russian settlement in Ninilchik. On my right is Cook Inlet and on the far side of the bay, profiled in purple by an evening sun still high in the cloudless sky, are the volcanic cones of the Aleutian Range. On my left, as far as I can see, is the ancient spruce forest, devastated by the work of that little yellow bark beetle. The trees are withered and gray, all of them dead or dying, miles and miles of tall, ghostly specters of trees that look like they've been hit by radioactive poisoning, as if the Kenai Peninsula were downwind from Chernobyl. I'm doing eighty along the wilderness highway, cruising through a vast forest destroyed by the gas-gulping culture of which there is no purer expression than this vehicle, and I'm feeling bad. Not that it's not fun to drive this damn thing. It's just that I'd have to be a cynic not to feel a wrench of conscience driving it here. These drooping, gray trees are like accusatory ghosts.

The Russian settlement is from another century, however—a cluster of small, white, wooden houses with tiny windows and a graveyard and orthodox church atop a grassy hump overlooking the sea far below. It's a Chekhov story waiting to be told. I turn off the main road and find my way along a twisting lane down to the narrow beach at the base of a set of high, sandy cliffs shot through with runnels and caves. A magnificent pair of bald eagles flies back and forth along the cliffs, switchbacking their way toward the top, looking for an easy-picking supper of seagull and plover eggs. At the top, they cross over me, gain altitude with a half dozen powerful beats of their enormous wings, and head out to sea, floating on rising currents toward the distant mountains. I want to follow them, and actually do try it for a while, driving a short ways into the water and south along the beach, testing the manufacturer's claim that the vehicle can drive in twenty inches of water. It more than passes the test. For several miles I guide it over rock slabs and through shifting, wet sandbars, until the beach gradually narrows, and soon I have no choice but to drive in the water now, for the tide is coming in, and I can't go back. I can only go forward and hope that I'll come to a break in the cliffs and a road leading away from the beach before I have to abandon the Hummer to the sea.

At the last possible minute, the beach suddenly widens, and the cliffs recede, and I come up on a caravan of a dozen or more RVs parked where Falls Creek enters the sea at Clam Gulch. A herd of bearded, big-bellied beer drinkers in duckbill caps and flannel shirts lean on the hoods and fenders of their vehicles, smoke cigarettes, and talk about fishing. These are the guys known in their hometowns as "hot shits." Their wives and girlfriends lounge in beach chairs close to a big driftwood fire on the beach and watch their kids chase the dogs. The men spot the Hummer first and react as if a mastodon is stomping up the beach toward them. Their mouths drop, they grin and point and call to their wives and kids to come look, look, it's a goddamned Hummer! A brand-new, bright-red Hummer, its huge tires thickened with clinging sand, has come dripping wet from the bottom of the sea. They wave me to a stop and crowd around the vehicle, firing questions as to its engine, its weight, its cost, and, when I've answered, they and their wives and children all step back for a long, admiring look as I drop it into gear and pull away in what I hope is an appropriately cool manner.

The Hummer does that to you—makes you feel watched, observed, admired for no deserved reason. You feel the way Madonna must whenever she leaves her apartment. Every time I stop for gas, wait at one of the three stoplights on the 225-mile drive from Anchorage, or pull over for a minute to photograph a spectacular view of mountains, glaciers, and sea, people come up to the vehicle and stare at it. They stare in an appropriating way—you feel yourself enter their fantasy life. Mostly it's a guy thing, especially young guys, teenagers, and preadolescent boys, whose faces brighten with lust when they see the Hummer. They're clearly getting off on its sudden, overall impression of brute, squared-away power. The women's gaze has a somewhat different quality, however. To them, the profile and face of the Hummer are grotesque, weird, almost comical looking, and they'd laugh, I feel, if the vehicle didn't also signify the presence of a man with money, which makes it somehow socially acceptable. Everybody seems to have a fairly accurate idea of the Hummer's price tag.

When I drive it onto the long, narrow spit that is downtown Homer, slowed to a crawl by the sudden presence of Saturday night, barhopping traffic, a crowd gathers around the vehicle and keeps pace with it, waving to me and hollering hey. You're never lonely when you're the only boy in Homer with a Hummer. I roll slowly through the traffic, trying to ignore the gaping drivers and pedestrians and trying not to wrap the vehicle around a pole or kill somebody with it. Suddenly among the crowd a dark-haired woman in a nurse's uniform catches my attention. She's less than four feet tall—a dwarf with a characteristically large, square face and head, short, blocky body, and muscular arms and legs. She has spotted the Hummer, not me, for I'm invisible to her, and a warm, utterly delighted smile has spread over her face, as if by accident she's run into a long-lost, dear old friend. I wave at her, and she waves happily back, the recipient of an unexpected gift from a stranger.

Most of the town of Homer—described by a local bumper sticker as "a quiet drinking village with a fishing problem"—is situated on the long spit of land extending several miles into the Kachemak Bay

and is made up of restaurants, bars, stores, and motels catering mainly to the crowds of people who drive up from the Lower 48 to fish for
salmon and halibut. The parking lots are crammed with RVs and
pickups towing camper trailers and boats, and every few yards is
another charter fishing outfit. Halfway along the spit I come to a
nearly landlocked bight, clearly man-made, about the size of a football field. A sign tells me it's called the Fishing Hole. Curious, I pull
in and park.

There is a narrow inlet from the sea and a gently sloped embankment surrounding the shallow saltwater pond, for that's all it is, a
pond. People with fishing rods stand shoulder to shoulder and two
and three deep around the Fishing Hole, while below them the water
churns with trapped king salmon, and the people along the embankment haul them in, snagging them without bait or lures. It's a pitiful
sight. I ask around and learn that salmon eggs raised in hatcheries are
transferred here as smolts, held captive in floating pens in the
Fishing Hole until they're large enough to be released into the ocean.
Later, when they're grown and the ancient impulse to spawn kicks
in, the salmon return to the Fishing Hole, their birthplace, in actu-
ality a gigantic, carefully designed weir, and on a midsummer night
like this huge crowds of people scoop them up as fast as they can.
The people stumble against one another, step in each other's buck-
ets, swear and shove and cast again. "It's called combat fishing," a
grizzled fellow in a NYPD cap tells me. "It's wheelchair accessible,"
he adds.

I climb back into the Hummer and head out to find the friend
who's loaned me her wilderness cabin for a few days. All I know is
that it's a dozen miles from town and has no water or electricity and
is located on the bay. Two hours later, directions in hand, I drive off-
road. It's after 10:00 p.m., but the sky is milky white. It feels like
midafternoon, and the difference between what my watch says and
what the absence of darkness says is disorienting and makes me feel
uncomfortably high.

The Hummer shoves its burly way through chest-high brush and
ferns, over washes and gullies, and then up along a tilted ridge to a
clearing, where the lane stops in front of a small, slab-sided cabin
with a short deck. I shut off the motor, step down as if walking
ashore from a large boat, and stand in the middle of the ferny clearing for a few moments, savoring the silence and the view. Below the
cabin is the bay, and across the bay is the Kenai National Wildlife
Refuge, a vast, mountainous wilderness area split by three glistening,

white glaciers, a world where no Hummers roam, where most of the salmon fishing is done by bears and the native people, where there is nothing like the Homer Fishing Hole, and the white spruce trees have not yet begun to die.

After a long while, I go inside and make a fire in the woodstove and uncork the bottle of red wine I picked up earlier in town. Out the window I can see the Hummer sitting in the brush, looking like an alien vehicle sent to earth in advance of a party of explorers scheduled to arrive later. I sip wine and wonder what the space people, when they finally get here, will make of our planet. All those dead trees! All that flooded land and the dead villages that once prospered alongside the bay! And the dead and dying rivers and seas! The space people will shake their large, bald heads and say, If they'd stopped devouring their planet, the humans might have saved themselves. Those Last Days must have made them mad.

Transformation Day
Lucy Ives

I.

THE PROTAGONIST IS AWAKE. This the protagonist knows.
The protagonist is awake but not at home.

Waking is the moment, the time, when she is closest to herself, when she perceives herself with fullest clarity. It is as if she passes herself by, near enough to touch; like a mirror, now. As she wakes, the mirror recedes.

Today, on this morning, the protagonist is obscure. I don't mean to say she can't perceive herself, but rather that there is nothing distinct, nothing specific to recommend what she perceives. Nothing recommends this image to her, as an image of herself.

This is, at any rate, how the protagonist begins to know.

It is enough, having woken, to accept the sensation of cement, cold and hard and unnaturally even, damp and pungent, beneath her. She is not in bed but rather on the street, a sidewalk.

She knows this street. Here is a slight hill and row houses packed together.

She is about to touch her face, but as she seeks to move her arm, she discovers that there is no arm. There is no arm to move. Some part of her body "lifts." She shakes her head. It's heavy. She breathes. Her nose is a remarkable instrument. She smells the excrement of dogs, rotting paper, water flowing just beyond the curb mixed with motor oil, more excrement, a cat crouched some four feet from her, behind the wheel of a compact. Now somewhere overhead pigeons chortle.

How did the protagonist arrive here? The only answer is that she has been asleep, sleeping. In her sleep she has arrived here, although that was only sleep and not a real place, not a way.

She wants to move. Her back is so long. Her legs shift beneath her, shift against cold cement. Her arms are also very long. She cannot seem to bring them to her sides. They are pressing against the ground like two stilts attached to her shoulders. There is almost no sensation in her "hands." *Why*, the protagonist is thinking, *do I think*

57

"*hands*"? At the rear of her body the legs stir. They press up. They lift her long back. She shivers. She is not "on her hands and knees." Her "hands" contact ground, and yet she stands. And she "stands." She is not upright.

I am ruined, she thinks and does not know what this means.

Her body is large now, massive. Her heart thuds below her neck. Again her nostrils open and the world enters. She smells food, some kind of rotten food, but the rottenness does not concern her. It is bread somewhere, along the ground. She moves toward the smell. She continues to look at the ground, the sidewalk, her neck extended. She has a long neck and is covered in a kind of fur. She knows of the existence of this fur because of the new sensitivity of her body. The breeze stirs these soft bristles, these thick hairs. The breeze passes up the backs of her legs, over her genitals, across her anus. There is a sense of complete alertness in her body. She can take nothing for granted.

The protagonist finds food, which is an old white roll. It is wrapped in a wet paper plate, discarded, and she is eating the plate. She is eating the plate and the roll in rough, trembling, tearing bites. Her ears, meanwhile, take in space. There is so much movement of motors, of bodies. The protagonist is threatened by this movement, and yet it does not come near enough to her. She will not react. She chews. Her eyelids move. She blinks. She becomes aware of her sense of sight. Again she sees the ground. There is a tree in rancid earth. There is cement. The door of a car.

If she will lift her head now, she will know. If she will lift her head she will know herself, such as she is. *It is not like an animal,* she finds herself thinking, *to be afraid of its own thought. Now,* she thinks, *that I have become an animal, I must learn not to fear my thoughts. I must think thoughts. I cannot fear them.*

Anyway, she thinks, *I am already forgetting. I am an animal and I will forget to fear. I will forget that I had a name or*—she cannot remember. She cannot remember what she is forgetting.

Something happens in her ear. She hears a sound that pricks her and is cold because it is the sound of a man, and the man is moving down the hill on the sidewalk, and the man is moving steadily, and she has raised her head, and because she has raised her head she has seen herself, out of her right eye, in the smooth, dark glass of the car, and she has seen the animal there, and she knows the name of the animal. The animal—the name of the animal is—her head swims because it, her brain, is emptier, fuller, than a stone.

Donkey. There's the word.

All around the protagonist (it is barely possible that she can think this and yet) things have begun to lose their names. The treasure of the wet smell of the hard cement that greets her in its openness and plainness and its existence otherwise than that of life and whatever lives has no name. If she must move it will not be because she knows where she is going. How to evade the movements around her that threaten to evict her or snuff her from this strange, large body? Her eyes blink and yet she barely sees. She smells and hears but does not see.

And so something begins—which is slow walking. She is moving beside parked cars. The protagonist moves deliberately. Her large body can be seen by a human. And so when she enters the sight of a human she may graze this sight but must not pass through it. She must cause herself to be treated as a matter of course. She must move by any means toward water.

And I would like to say a few things about what happens next: how this donkey, or rather this female donkey, this *jenny*, for that is the correct term—the protagonist—moves at the pace of an animal serving a human, how she moves forward and though she is seen no one wishes to capture her. She moves over the ill-considered streets of unimportant quarters and areas of this city you and I know well. You and I would laugh if we stood there and saw her coming toward us. Sometimes someone will turn his head to watch her, this beast. Someone will concern himself for a moment with the thought that animals really can have a kind of impressive, solemn, solitary, and nearly human air about them, even if this air is just the effect of our having looked at them. *For they are not human, of course, the animals. Their faces are the faces of animals, not the faces of men. Any animal's "expression" is only the result of the gaze of a man.* And someone looks away, not knowing what he has seen.

I never knew anything about animals, in some sense, until I wrote these paragraphs. I guess I believed that someone could become so lost that she would be forced to change. I could believe that something like this could occur, but I was never forced to believe it until now. Here a human being has become so lost in life that she can no longer hold her form. Her body could not remain present with her, the way she thought and traveled. She did not even know what she was doing. I pity her for that. Like all men and women to whom such a fate befalls, she only believed that she could change. She did not know that she could become anything, that *any human* can become *anything*. Like many men and women, she did not know what being human is.

II.

She's passed into shade. She is under an elevated highway.

The morning has expanded and increased in brightness. It is summer, after all. The morning is an oval, infinitely broad and deep at its center. The morning is a lozenge. Heat is constant and balances perfectly on every surface.

The jenny hangs her head. Until this moment the jenny has been persistently in motion. She considers a puddle of standing water in the relative darkness beneath the highway but cannot bring herself to drink. Her fear is an ache or it is a rigid alertness, at a donkey's nostrils, at a donkey's ears, along her spine. She is a donkey, so how can she know where to go? What is direction to her? A donkey can flee. A donkey can hunger, thirst.

Here is a short tunnel with walls of brick. Humans and other animals have urinated and defecated and vomited here. Sometimes they have slept here or been slaughtered. The smells remain, fainter in some places and so, confusing. The scent of one presence attaches to the outlines of another. The imprint of an old dog is entangled in the acrid, well-defined trail left by a colony of rats who make nightly use of three feet of this passage in their transit from one hole to another. There is gasoline; the reek of human distress; rubber and mold.

What it means to thirst in the way she now thirsts is to have perception shrink, simplify. Even the simplicity of a donkey can be further reduced.

Strange, too, to see the creations of humanity in this way—as if from a great distance. The minds of humans are vast and essentially identical to one another. It takes very little effort even for such a being as a donkey to reflect in this way. The minds of humans are extremely big and very similar and yet they are full of blockages. The lumbering device that is the human mind acquaints itself with other human minds with terrible difficulty; its ability to recognize itself is even more limited, faltering. Thus the construction of mirrors and barriers throughout the landscape human beings inhabit. Barriers exist nowhere else in the natural world; no other organic or living thing knows a barrier. The human body does not know barriers; it dies and is transformed. Similarly, there are no images in the world. Only in the minds of men are there images. There are lenses, there is focus, there is projection and interference, but only in the mind of man do static images exist. A donkey will know this. A donkey stands in the narrow space it has been permitted. A donkey may suffer death at any moment. A van swings roughly into the road within the tunnel and idles.

The sound of a door: the latch and then precise, light closure. A rubber heel in glass and gravel.

The jenny stiffens. A donkey can imagine flight and yet feel sick with longing, with an anticipatory dependence on the human hand. The jenny foresees her capture. She is half in love, pleading for this to occur. She will be restrained. The barriers of human habitation will be explained to her by the confines of some cell, cage, or paddock—or perhaps by a butcher, a stunning blow and then knife. She, as donkey, will give meaning to such structures, such behaviors. She will rejoin the world of men, will be reincorporated, and will no longer be an exile.

She can hear the human behind her, at her left. It is clear that the human makes an effort not to frighten her. If a donkey could laugh in such a moment, this donkey would laugh. The fear that paralyzes her is a feeling of already being bound to the human, a feeling of uncertainty about the temporality within which—along which—this ownership will unfold, if the ownership has not already happened, whether or not it is still possible to flee, even if for now it *seems* possible. There is a sensation of dazzling, of being dazzled, though this has nothing to do with the sense of sight or any kind of brightness.

The human crunches over small debris in his path. "Yeah," he is saying, clearly into a cell phone, "I couldn't believe it either. Hold on," he says. He is retiring his device.

That the human does not speak further indicates his resolve. He will reach her, desires to reach her.

Therefore the jenny is not thinking when she moves, when she springs forward onto the hard fronts of her hooves. Her knees come up—if these can be called "knees"—and she is stamping, streaking into the sun and the vast industrial stretch beyond the underpass.

Behind her, very briefly, *early* as it were, she hears the astonished squawk of the human, who seems compacted, deflated somehow, by her sudden exit. She runs.

To her right and left are warehouse buildings, senseless places. There is hasty fencing in corrugated metal. Gasoline soaks all things under the sun. She runs. She runs.

Breath inside her body is ropes, some kind of a net, tensing and slackening. She gathers herself around this, though it is a sensation like pain. She forces the donkey's body forward, even if against a kind of bond, a knot or a resistance. The physical world possesses her, and yet she strains forward into it, as if she must, as if she must be the one to do it, as if she must choose, as if she is free, as if there were a desire or a body she could hold back, could keep. She has a feeling now as if the body of the donkey has been impaled by an infinitely thin yet infinitely strong metal wire, as if she propels the carcass that she is along this line that cuts her flesh and yet constitutes the sole remaining narrative concerning her being. It is her own story. It runs her through.

And she is impassioned by this, because the flesh is not willing. She is in a rage because she is not human any longer and no longer has human relations, friends. The hours in the day are nothing more than a kind of empty space to her and can't be filled by language. The hard bottoms of her "feet," her hooves, strike the ground and she wants to strike the ground harder. She wants to shatter this hardness, and she wants the heat in the muscles of the animal to melt the tissue and the sinew and the bone, and she wants the animal's jagged breath to become like acid and wants it to eat away the inside of the body of the animal until there is nothing left there but vacant air.

But this does not happen. What happens instead is far stranger than this. I do not know if you can believe me. What happens instead is that now, no matter how wildly, how intently she pushes, seeking greater speed and suffering in the body of the animal, she experiences only a sinking, a coldness. It is in broad daylight, and it is on the ground, but it is as if she falls—as if she is in darkness. She falls to the earth in coolness. She comes closer to the earth. She is small now and she is soft. She moves into a piece of shade, an awning over a garage. She has the sense that she "darts." Her eyes are puzzled by the light, and yet she seems to see behind things. She seems to see, now, *in time*, as well as in space. All objects contain a temporal dimension her eyes move, *lick* along. It is with a light fascination that her eyes whip across the surface of the world. The line of the street hovers before her and recedes slightly; she follows the intricate surface of an adjacent sign with raised lettering, lingering in the lowest interior angle of an *E*. Her ears tingle with information. Her nose acquires eternity. She is very small. She sinks further back against the building, pressing herself against its solidity.

I am, she knows this, *a cat.*

At the end of her body *a tail* twitches. Experimentally, she jumps.

In her mouth are fangs. Recessed in her feet are claws. She shivers. She smells the air.

She knows that she must not begin to think of hunger. There will be nothing for her if she begins to think of hunger now. Now instead she is, must be, guided by a strange intellect of a kind. There are bodies elsewhere. These teem. These vibrate with their little portion of blood. They are hot. They're live and quick.

She travels along the base of the building, rejoicing in her slightness and the richness of perception, the ease of her reaction, the pleasure of knowing exactly what she will find. She knows their place, can hear them in a kind of crowd in one place in her ear, like little sacks crawling over one another. She knows their warmth. She travels. She moves between and under and behind. She inhales the faintness of their blood, still enclosed. She inhales the scent of their minuscule excrement, the oil of their skin, their gathered bodies. They huddle and squirm. They are lax, delayed, incipient. She finds.

And what an orgy of blood spilled as claws slice and mouth bites and seeks and burrows and tears. The mouth throws aside bodies, and a paw slaps, and claws quarter. And she eats and feasts and drinks, her eyes like two pebbles in her head, two bits of gravel, useless to her joy. She is death and fills with life and praises herself, is a falling sword; she is the perfect eye of the rose, the outline of the moon's horn against the blue midst of day; she is sated.

She walks. She traces the edges of buildings with new weight in her stomach. Her ears buzz softly. The interior of her mouth tingles.

She begins to hear the humans, in their work, around her. She is now not afraid, as she was before. To be what she is is to be of the world of men but to have no meaning for them, in their work. She is of their world but means nothing to their efforts, and so they wish nothing of her. She pauses in her path to fool with a twist of plastic twine. The twine trembles antagonistically, appears insouciant. She bites it, and the biting irritates her mouth, and she bites further. She pounces and bites and leaps in the air, flinging the twine aside.

When last she knew something of what she was she was mortal. And this is not so now. It is not that the cat will not die, but that the cat has not yet begun to conceive of her death. The cat makes nothing of her death, while living. In this sense, a cat has never been mortal. A human, meanwhile, makes many things of its death. The hands of a human are never still.

The cat sniffs at a trapezoid of sun descending through an awning of smoked glass. The temperature of the light pleases the cat. The cat lowers her body to warm tarmac. She extends her legs and rolls onto her spine, blinking.

The theory of life to a human . . . it is a wonder that the human can find food or remembers to sleep. The human's theory of life blankets all things in the world, making them useless to the human, except as names. The cat thinks of herself when she was human. The cat's mind is a comfortable place. As a human, the cat had loved. The cat had been a human who had loved and the human had so frequently lost its way among objects in the world. The human liked objects so much! The human had had a home and would leave this home during the day and return at night, dragging bags of items. The human contemplated another person or persons, and the human struggled with its own inability to grasp another, the human always lingering between forms of transport in the city, asking itself why it was unable to possess some other human like the objects with which the human inexplicably filled its home. The human was always hovering between one location and another, asking itself what it had just done, what it planned to do. Similarly, other humans to some extent relied on this human or perhaps desired to possess this human. And yet this human could not give itself, or could not give itself *correctly*, as the human sometimes thought to itself while it was lingering, suffering in some space in which it did not fully belong.

The cat separates the toes of her paws, forcing out claws, feeling the long stretch, tips her head back so the mouth opens in a wide yawn, the pink interior of her throat exposed to air. She snaps her mouth shut and becomes loose and pants briefly, eyes closed. She slackens, lets her head droop, chin against the ground, slips into a kind of dream.

In the dream, the cat watches a human. The cat is perched above the human. Perhaps the cat is sitting on the top of a bookshelf; it is not entirely clear to the cat. The cat's body, at any rate, is always a source of comfort to the cat. It matters little to the cat where the cat is.

The human, the cat observes, is seated. The human is seated at a desk and the cat is able to perceive only the back of the human's head. The human is doing almost nothing. The human is doing so little in this moment that the cat feels a kind of glee. The human's behavior is strange, a spectacle. The human shakes slightly where it is. The human brings its hands to its face. The human has been sitting in this position for nearly an hour and will go on sitting in this position. The human brings its hands to its face and lowers them again. The human touches the surface of the desk.

In the dream, the cat's tail twitches. If the cat could laugh, now she would laugh. The cat's love of existence is simple. A cat cannot be

64

betrayed nor can a cat experience disappointment. Things in the world hide from the cat, but the cat will seek them. The cat loves to find and then to lose again and then to seek. The cat's tail twitches. It pops against tarmac.

In the dream, perhaps the human is poor. Perhaps the human has another problem with its possessions. The cat waits to see if the human will lift its hands again or leave them where they are, resting on the surface of the desk. After a while, the human lifts its hands again and recommences shaking.

The cat's tail twitches.

A sound.

The cat is awake. A man is standing beside the cat, under the awning. The man is looking at something in his hands, looking into it carefully. The man grunts softly to himself.

Now the man retires the thing to a pocket in his garment.

The cat sniffs the air. Her head comes quickly off the ground and she rights her body. She perches on her haunches, staring out into the street, watching the man with the edges of her eyes.

"What are you doing here?" the man says now, for some reason. He is speaking to a cat.

The cat stands. She dislikes the man's directness.

The cat considers the contents of her stomach. Certainly, she is thicker here, heavier, than she might wish. However, her body is no longer dangerously sluggish.

The man rotates so that he faces the cat. He does not quite trap her against the building with the front of his body in this way, but it is possible that he may wish to do so.

The cat dances back.

"Hey," the man says.

"*Erk,*" the cat pronounces, in annoyance. "*Roawmm.*"

"What a pretty little cat," the man is saying. "Are you a friendly little pretty cat?"

The cat's tail switches.

The man takes a step toward the cat. "Never saw you before."

The cat skitters back. Her body bunches up against itself, accordion-like. There is tension here. The cat's face retreats back as far as it can retreat back from the front of her face. The cat's ears flatten. The cat seems to hang in place: her terror thick, dimensional, a rod that passes through her meager body. Then, as abruptly and as simply as hair lifts in the breeze, the cat's head sinks, swings left, the torso following. Electrically, she removes herself from the vicinity of the man. The cat bounds. She pursues the side of a building, seeking concealment.

When the cat was dreaming, she had seen a person there. The person in the dream was not aware of the presence of the cat. The person in the dream appeared lost somehow, although how a person appearing in the dream of a cat could be "lost" to a cat, the cat does not know. She is a cat. The person brings its hands to its face. These events seem to have occurred not long ago.

A person wishes for something. A person is seized by a fantasy, cannot look away.

A cat already is whatever she might be. A human will never know the change that it desires. A human thinks to change, all the while changing. A human complains of a lack it has never had.

The cat is standing now in a field, an empty lot where no buildings are. There are chunks of brick and other remains, powdered glass and screws and metal scraps, the carcass of a refrigerator, a strip of tire. The cat has found a small hill. The cat sits at the top of the hill.

The cat is very still. She has stopped attempting to move and here at the center of this field it is no longer necessary that she move. She surveys this place, sinking into a kind of lethargy whose result will not be sleep. She is still. And in this stillness she no longer contemplates the difference between cat and person. She feels being condense. It is not the hot, steady sun that causes this reduction of sense. It is not an effect of what the animal beholds. The cat blinks and closes her eyes. She descends, swims away from the realm of perception. Time reorients, swinging up and then down. Time is no longer before her. Or: Time is no longer behind her. She has no front or back.

And she is by far littler now—reduced, as I have said.

It is a mark of the nature of this change that here someone else must begin to speak. I have to begin talking.

At the center of the field, in an empty lot where no buildings are, there is a small hill, and in the sand that makes up this hill, there is a narrow green stem, from which several fringed leaves extend. The stem has no bud, though perhaps in time a bud may form. The stem anchors itself in the earth by means of shallow roots. Air currents tousle it slightly, from side to side.

What is the difference between then and now, someone might ask. In human memory it is always easy to recall a certain scene. One remembers the particulars of space, for distance occurs in different ways, no matter where a person is. One recalls movement and the look of other faces around one. One hears the sound of a voice or voices. Perhaps one knows what one thought at this time.

And yet, it always seems possible that the particulars of memory compete. How is it, I might ask, that I am here but not there, where I was—that my being here, in this place and time, precludes my being there, where once I was. Is it not possible that I am still there, that those sensations that were mine then are also mine now, in this present. I could, for example, not be certain, then. I could not know the ways in which those things I saw and felt would come to mean, and yet now, now that I know what those things mean, I cannot cease sensing them. I know their meaning, as I did not when I experienced them, and yet I experience them still, though I no longer have power to change their course. I can no longer reply to your words, yet here I am.

III.

Human memory exists somewhere in this landscape. However, no one here is living—at least, not in the human sense. There is a plant in a small hill of refuse.

Minutes pass. Within the plant, there is the slow tug of liquid. Wind moves it. Light moves it. A sentence is a peculiar vehicle for the sentience of a plant. An English sentence begins in one place and ends in another; an English sentence proposes a high point and then guides the mind into a flat expanse of deliberation, shifts and drives forward like a century. All the language available to me is so deliberate. My language is the language of a being in possession of legs, a head, and face. There is a front of my body, whenever I speak.

It isn't that the plant can't think, of course. A substance seeps into its cells; the plant learns. The sun ticks across the sky and the plant knows seconds. Minuscule parts of the earth are incorporated.

All the same, human memory exists somewhere in this landscape. I am not sure where to locate it.

I yawn. I get up and walk away from the keyboard, move around the house.

I return to the keyboard, consider the document. In the time that I have been away, something has changed in the landscape. Where previously there had been a small plant, a weed, really, if we are honest, now there is an object, something not even alive. I lean in to get a better look. It is a pencil, a yellow pencil.

I sit back in my chair. I am unsure what to do. My protagonist is becoming increasingly difficult to work with. I don't know how to navigate this latest change, what to say.

The pencil lies in the sand and dirt and refuse. The sun beats down. Time is rounding into late afternoon, and so perhaps it is better to say that the sun "glares." The sun enters the scene from the edge of the sky.

Here there's not much for me to say. I simply have to wait this phase out. The metal band around the pencil's pink eraser glints significantly, but really it doesn't mean anything.

I am thinking, now, about how years ago, many years, I made a discovery. I, and now this is Lucy speaking, was eleven or twelve years old, I guess, when I first started to have what I'll call bad feelings. I would think about life, how it is limited and nothing ever happens, and I would, though I was only a child, feel ground down by boredom and hopelessness and could not understand why anyone believed that what they were doing was really living; and for many years I could not stop being bored and simultaneously horrified by my strange, anomalous boredom, since it was so different from what was portrayed to me as true boredom, until one day when I was sixteen I was on a bus and I was watching shadows on the sides of buildings and something was happening with the sounds of voices and the weird movement of shadows, the flickering and extension and diminution, and I felt somehow raised out of my body, pressed closer to thought, and I felt my thoughts, felt the abstract pleasure of thinking, felt time as something different.

I've often practiced this experiment since. It is why I write. All the same, many kinds of experience become soft or abstract for me of late. There is now for me a singular kind of space related to writing, into which I am either tending or to which I am somehow always referring, when I speak to others. Time is flaccid, heavy of late. However, it is even beautiful like this. This can be like the discovery of my own personality, accomplished by me. I become aware of the one person that I am only or as soon as I understand that it is a matter of attending to this particular space of concentration. Anything may be within this space. Anyone may be within it. Perhaps only I know for sure how to define or know it. And it is not changeful, though it may change, has changed, may be changing.

Sometimes I think that I should admit that I have made a serious error in my life. At a moment like this, I will ask myself if I regret not my error but instead only its consequences, is it an error, exactly. And what is the name for such a misstep? Is it a misstep that is in part desirable because it casts light on a part of living not yet known or experienced by me?

At other times I will have a good or fairly good night of work and feel calm again in certain moments, satisfied. This calm, a sort of drinking in of random visual fields (whatever is outside my window) plus a certain quality of time, is the only thing that comforts me. Yet it is difficult to obtain such equanimity in writing without a horrifying everyday life. The writer Alain Robbe-Grillet, whose work I don't always admire, asks, *"Une interrogation persiste: Est-il possible d'échapper à la tragédie!"* (A question persists: Is it possible to evade tragedy?)

Someone calls me a "romantic." But why is it so strange to wish to be loved unconditionally? What if I decide that it is unacceptable that I not be loved in this sense? What if for this reason I simply stop and end and so on; if I don't survive. What if I simply decide to waste everything—because it is within my power to do so. What if I am too ill to move, too ill to wish. I still cannot decide if something terrible is happening to me already, like I am in an airplane all the time and never touch the earth again for the rest of my life—or, if it is I who have in fact made a terrible error, I who am at present electing to board an airplane that never touches the earth again. There is no clear difference for me between boarding an airplane (an act) and something that befalls a person (tragedy). Either I pity myself too much and blindly enter such a plot or am already living inside tragedy, previous to my own actions. And maybe "or" is not the correct term.

Human memory exists somewhere in this landscape.

I am stubborn and don't want to admit that I have anything to do with the protagonist.

Anyhow, it is evening.

IV.

The sun is blue. Now there is really nothing here. Which is to say: A human eye cannot look closely enough to see her.

Where there has been a pencil, now there is a fleck of dust, a mote, a microbe. It is not even heavy enough to avoid being carried off by breeze. It has already risen up, is circling the abandoned lot. It lofts up, further up, and begins to traverse great quantities of space. It flies, climbing and sinking, over the industrial zone, over the many regular warehouses. It streaks above the highway that rings the city.

69

A miracle of some kind that such motion can be contained in an entity so small.

It seems possible to say that the mote is blind, because it does not see. Because it moves, I can speak for it. I can say that it is traveling through early night.

I can also tell you that it is returning to its point of origin. I have come very close to losing my protagonist, you see. As if it were not enough to have allowed her to relinquish her human form: I just now have recast her as entities that have no life, properly speaking. I did this, perhaps, in order to discover something that I already knew. I wanted to look at this thing I already knew, this thought, this fact, again—to see it as another life that was not my own.

The mote has retraced the path of the cat and it has retraced the path of the donkey. It is now following a route that the protagonist must have taken at some point, though this is not something that I have written of, properly speaking. The mote is wafted along a street in a residential neighborhood. It ascends a hill. The dwellings become smaller and farther set apart. The mote enters at a window of one small home. It enters a room containing a bed and a chair and a dresser with a round mirror. In the bed someone is sleeping. The sleeping person is a man. The mote alights on the bed.

In Apuleius's novel *The Golden Ass*, there is a mysterious interlude that has often been repeated since, in various versions and guises. No one is really sure what this interlude is supposed to mean. An old woman begins telling a story to a kidnapped girl. This story is the history of Cupid and Psyche, in which the god of love marries a mortal girl and maintains her in a magic home in which invisible servants do her bidding. The main condition of this marriage is that Psyche never see her husband's face; yet Psyche is convinced by jealous relatives that she is living with a carnivorous beast. Confusion, harm, deaths, and many trials ensue. Throughout the story Psyche is guided by a series of speaking objects, plants, bodies of water. At the story's end, Psyche and Cupid are married once again and Psyche gives birth to a daughter named Pleasure.

It is not clear what this tale, reported at second hand, has to do with the rest of Apuleius's narrative, which concerns an idiot named Lucius, who mistakenly assumes the titular animal form (donkey) on account of a misplaced spell. All the same, this story, primarily a story about doubt and redemption, does not seem misplaced within the longer novel. Perhaps it is a story about learning, a story about what in us *can* learn. For it is possible that every story

70

of metamorphosis is also a story about misrecognition. Sometimes even a reflection will do no good.

This is why I can say that now, when she rises from bed, for she is human again and has two legs onto which to rise, and comes to the familiar round mirror that hangs above the dresser, and does not see herself, or, rather, does not see what she has known to be herself, there, she, the protagonist, is not surprised. She can wonder and can marvel yet can hardly be surprised. The face she raises her hand to and touches is her face, as she has known it, in some sense, only time has passed, great amounts of time, as far as a human can understand. She is old, fragile, feeble. The skin on the front of her skull is creased and soft, hanging from the bone in flaps. Her hair is sparse and downy, colorless. Her eyelids sag and her eyeballs bulge and everywhere muscle that once encased her body has been lost. She stands in the sleeping attire of a much younger woman, a T-shirt advertising sports, and is decrepit. The light of the moon shows spots on her skin, the blueness of blood.

Slowly she returns to the bed where a man is sleeping. It is with care that she must lower herself; the bones seem ready to crack. It is a strange sensation to be so aware of the existence of one's bones. And there is fatigue of a kind that she has never before experienced. She is breathless, weary. The young person beside her continues to sleep, undisturbed, his smooth flesh rising and falling. Now she begins to sink, now fade.

A young woman had disappeared; this was what they said. On the morning of the next day, this woman returned to her place in the world, the home she had occupied, happily, they say, though she had, unaccountably, in the time that she was gone, grown old, quite ancient, really. It seemed that the woman had died in her sleep, of what were quickly deemed natural causes. These events could not be explained and so have been very little spoken of since.

Two Poems
Martine Bellen

THE WOODS

The blue woods, the milkweed meadow woods, woods thick, woods
night. Reams of dreaming woods. Vast woods in a dram of spirits.
Mangrove woods with crabs and spiders. Mangroves with gators.
Webs wending spirals between viny shelves for shells and schools
of skeleton fish, anchored in mud, anchored in mind. Virgins and
terrapins. Tarantulas and slugs. What in the world is not in the
woods?

Everyone you love is in the woods.

Mother tells you Auntie's heart is bad, that it has run amok. You hear
this as *a band of bandits heisted Auntie's heart, removed it from
her chest and locked it in a chest in the woods.* You hear this as
Auntie's woods is in her heart.

When you hear with your eye, for the first time, the woods will
become intimate.

There are woods you walk through every day.

Sometimes you are aware of the woods and some days you don't
notice.

Mother tells you Auntie's hungry, she's scared of the dark, she's scared
of death, scared to death. Mother gives you a wicker basket and scoots
you out the mahogany door, the door that leads straight to the woods.

As you walk the woods, the fetid fragrance smells like Auntie's
putrefying flesh. The eyes of the woods are yellow irises. The teeth of
the woods are like arrowheads.

You go in search of your auntie's heart. Her dark, sick heart. In the heart of the woods.

You go in search of Auntie's dreams.

One goes for one thing and returns with something else.

One learns in the dark. One sees and hears differently there. One fills one's pockets with the dark.

You do not want to close your eyes. It's dark in the woods. You ask Mother to keep the stars on, you ask for the moon to be your night-light. You ask to take a dog with amber eyes that shine like the Lupus constellation, a seeing-eye dog that seizes small prey in the dark. You pray in the woods. It is your altar. You burn sweet sage, and you change in the woods. The woods is your alter ego.

You dress as a glowing worm in the woods. You become an oak, a mighty oak with red squirrels swirling down your limbs and branches. Your roots tangle in the earth of the woods. You learn the language of frogs in the woods. In the dark, scary woods you find your powers, your potions, your prowess. You learn the language of woods and find that it is not foreign. There are no foreign words in the woods.

When you enter the woods, when you breathe woods' air as you exhale the woods, as you become the woods, your heart is no longer your heart.

When you enter the woods, you are alone; your heart races through your inner woods.

When you enter the woods, you aim to walk through the woods, you aim to find Auntie and then you aim to return to a place that is anti-woods, that is nonwoods, you aim to return home. You believe your home is not the woods. You believe your home is Auntie.

When you enter the woods your bones begin to ache. The boles sway. Trees nurse. When you enter the woods, your breath turns wet and life thrives from the air you share with the woods, the air you offer the woods.

73

When you enter the woods, you become the woods, you become its food. The heart that oxidizes your blood becomes the woods' thousand and eight hearts. The sweat pouring from your brow becomes its dew. Your amber irises become the woods' flowers. You are the woods' blood as you race through the woods.

Of course you get lost in the woods, of course you can't leave the woods—that is the nature of woods. Auntie got lost in the woods, wrote of the woods, sang woods words, woods worlds. Whorls of woods. Woods moons, woods dogs. Woods creep into buildings, spies of woods fly in the sky, expanding woods by night, disguising woods by day. Even if you extinguish all the wind of the woods, all the rings of the woods, there'd be books made of woods, libraries of trees, all singing woods' paeans, inks of woods and atlases, clothespins and plastics, film and fabric, all rhizomes connecting to the woods—all roads, all roots, leading there.

MAPPA MUNDI OF THE UNCHARTED SEA

(*Song to My Ancestors*)
To penetrate our hydrosphere,
The fathomer must plumb memory
Moment by moment, mile after mile, must calculate the depth
Of a line of sound
Submerged in a pitcher of ocean,
Pouring wave after gravity wave into a tide-pool glass and starfish sky.

Shallow fractal shells on ocean shelves
Lace down the tapered back of black abyss,
And classical strains wend violinistic Ōkeanós
—The fathomer's unconscious and unmapped ardor or water.
In the quiet of the sea, bioluminescence drifting
                    Past the deep knees of liquidity.

Our ancestors' passive lower lair, where time and density clash with
    destiny

Our ancestors of alchemy energy, following the marine mammals' lineage
    of light.

At first, underwater habitats and habits were hard to habituate
Plummeting

Subsurface ribbons and angels and eels, elephant seals.
The fathomer must have felt her ancient fish, scaly flesh

The continuous body of earth's blood.   (oceanic heat bath)

To make it work, they had to stop thinking
Of themselves as individuals
Who ever lived
On land.

To make it worse,

Prostrate before Ondine with whiskey and wine

They had to stop thinking as individuals.

(*Memory of an Oceanic Party Girl*)
Earthlings lost the shell game, a confidence trick that overconfidence
Tricked them into buying into
When air expired.

At goddess correspondence school, I traded in my fur for Neoprene

Despite what had been trending, there wasn't a planet B,
So the earthlings dove into the sea,
Made their home in earth unknown,
Lemurring into under-life, without demurring.

Jump!

Martine Bellen

There is no sound here. No light. No autumn leaves.
Ocean without sausage, no derma
For the golem,
        Only that great encompassing stream, compassionate
Scream or omphalos—

The fathomers scale
The longest mountain chain in this vast, tireless multiverse

Multiloss vest of life

Strung around the neck of the sea,
Buoyancy of diamonds, carbuncles, our most precious colonies.

Brother Who Comes Back
Before the Next Very Big Winter
Benjamin Hale

Maybe they don't exist. But I want them to.
—Jane Goodall

HE IS PAINTED ON THE SIGN that welcomes drivers coming into Black Rock from the east on Route 9, waving. A bronze statue of him stands in the center of town, depicted in the pose made classic by the creature (almost certainly a person in a gorilla suit) captured on the Patterson-Gimlin film: midstride, head turned, looking back over his shoulder at the man with the camera.

Sightings of the Black Rock Monster flare up from time to time with long lulls between. It's as if the sightings crest and trough in accordance with some cosmic cycle, like cicadas (every seventeen years) or sunspots (every eleven). If the functions of the universe can be envisioned as a gyroscope, many wheels within wheels, then the punctuation of the Black Rock Monster sighting clusters is a tick mark on one of the slower-spinning, outermost wheels.

Audrey hated him. No: Audrey hated "him." The idea of "him." She considered the Black Rock Monster a sign that she was from a place too small to take itself seriously. Often, conversations about "him" that began in ironic, joking tones ended in the spooked swapping of unsubstantial anecdotes about such-and-such things seen or heard that "could not be explained." Evidence, Audrey would ask (demand). Evidence. Where was the evidence? All we have is your stupid anecdotes about bumps in the night, the firsthand accounts of unreliable witnesses, and the rumors that circulate in the wake of what were surely either honest mistakes or cynical lies. "Absence of evidence is not evidence of absence," is what her Sunday School teacher said, when little Audrey, already a skeptic, told her she didn't believe in God. Yes, but (Audrey, much later, wished she had said to her): Absence of evidence is not *proof*, the burden of which, as a believer, is on *you*, not me.

Later, when she was in college studying linguistics, Audrey would learn about evidentiality. Languages with multiple evidentials have grammatical elements (such as verb suffixes) that indicate not only mood, case, tense, and so on, but also *how the speaker knows this information to be true.* The Tuyuca and Tucano languages, for example, have five terms of evidentiality: firsthand witness, nonwitness, nonvisual sensory, inferential, assumed. For example, her professor used the sentence "It snowed last night."

"Because," he said, "if you go to sleep at night and there's no snow on the ground, then you wake up in the morning, look out the window, and there's snow on the ground, can you say, 'It snowed'? If we were speaking Tuyuca or Tucano, we would have to say it something like this: Firsthand witness: 'I saw it snow last night.' Nonwitness secondhand: 'Mom told me it snowed last night.' Nonvisual sensory: 'I haven't gotten out of bed yet, but I can already tell from the quiet of the house that it snowed last night.' Inferential: 'I didn't see it snow, but I see snow, so I believe that it snowed last night.' Assumed: 'I shan't bother to look out the window, the weatherman said it would snow, so I believe that it snowed last night.'"

Audrey would remember the small mountain town she grew up in as always evidencing a recent snow. In the winter, really heavy snowfalls can almost bury the stop signs. But it was the leftover snow that sticks around everywhere all winter and spring that she would remember most of all and associate with her hometown. On mornings after blizzards, snowplows and bulldozers scoot the snow into enormous piles against the sides of buildings, and the compacted snow crusts and glazes over with ice; by spring it's so hard it can't be cracked with a chisel. Gloopy cascades of icicles melt and refreeze again and again, eventually making their sluggish glissandos from the corners of rooftops down to the ground. The gutters are always pattering in the spring.

Black Rock, Colorado, is famous for two things: the Black Rock Monster and good skiing in the winter, when the town of forty-five hundred residents inflates to three times that from first snow to snowmelt. All winter long the locals play host to wealthy outsiders, upon whom the town's economy depends and whom the locals simultaneously hate, almost openly. (That muzzled desire to bite the hand that feeds is there in most economies of seasonal tourism.) The Black Rock Monster is only ever spotted in the off-season, usually toward the end of it in the fall, which Audrey's mother used to speculate was a product of underemployment and boredom. A few weeks later, when the temperature dives and the skiers arrive in their glowing aurora of brightly colored nylon and Gore-Tex, the jobs return, and people no longer have the time to think they see mythical monsters in the woods. Hospitality and service kill the beast.

The earliest alleged sightings predate the incorporation of Black Rock's township. In 1912, three silver prospectors living on the outskirts of Black Rock claimed that a group of "ape-men" had bombarded their cabin with rocks. One of the prospectors, Theophilus Phelan, claimed to have shot and killed one of them with a rifle, but could not recover the body. Many years later, as an old man, Phelan self-published a rambling, barely sensical book about it, which was sold around town in the souvenir shops, alongside backcountry tchotchkes like dream catchers and mounted jackalope heads. Phelan's book was also, to Audrey's embarrassment, sold in the lobby of the hotel, in a niche of the wooden rack that held brochures for local attractions and maps of the ski runs.

(Audrey's parents owned the Pronghorn Lodge, a midrange hotel—not the place where people held weddings, but where they booked the spillover guests. It was a Western-themed faux chalet built in the late sixties, the building and almost everything in it made out of logs. The lighting fixtures were made of elk antlers, thorny entanglements that cast intricate nets of shadow in the hallways at night. Over the years, for lack of many other watering holes in Black Rock, the bar downstairs had become a neighborhood local. Audrey's mother usually tended it. Audrey's family lived in a house behind the hotel. Audrey and her brothers had half grown up in the hotel, had all been de facto part-time employees from the age at which they could be trusted to carry things without dropping them.)

Theophilus Phelan's story had always struck Audrey as particularly ridiculous, and not only because (as Phelan detailed in his memoir) in his years and travels he had also encountered space aliens and caught a glimpse of Ogopogo, the monster that haunts Okanagan Lake in British Columbia (what are the odds?), but mainly because throwing rocks at a cabin seemed an implausibly sophomoric thing for wild ape-men of the mountains to do.

Prior to Phelan's account, the Ute Indians told legends of a giant, hairy creature that walks on two legs like a man, and is seen very rarely, always from very far off, and only at certain times in certain seasons, usually the late summer and fall. They had names for the apparition that Audrey was told translated literally as "The Bad-Smelling Tree Man," "Big, Big, Hairy Figure with Eyes Sunk Deep in

Benjamin Hale

Head," and "Brother Who Comes Back Before the Next Very Big Winter."

The more famous incident "happened" in 1961, when Brian Franklin, the owner of an auto-mechanic shop and at the time a member of the town council (Audrey supposed Franklin's dossier as a local business owner and active member of the community were in the retelling meant to underscore his credibility), discovered tracks—five-toed, eighteen-inch footprints—while on a hike with his son in the early morning after a night of heavy rain. He drove to town and brought back witnesses, showed them the massive footprints, and someone made a plaster cast of one of them (replicas of which were also available for sale in the souvenir shops).

The sightings quieted down for another ten years or so, and then there was another spike in the midseventies. Since then there had been another long—longer—lull. They were due for another wave of sightings, and sure as the clockwork of heaven, it came.

First, there was a spate of overturned and rooted-through garbage cans. People woken up in the middle of the night by frightful noises, something banging and rattling outside their windows. Even well-lidded garbage cans, bungee-corded shut, were found in the morning with their contents strewn helter-skelter across front yards and driveways, especially if they had contained food or remnants of food.

"For God's sake, it's just bears," Audrey's mother said. She was spritzing the bar counter with Lysol and pushing it around in circles with a rag. "Every other damn time something got into your garbage it was bears. Why's it Bigfoot all of a sudden?"

Audrey's mother was of the opinion that every single Black Rock Monster sighting that was not a bald-faced hoax could be chalked up to someone whose vision was too bad, too fleeting, or too warped by hope, fear, or imagination mistaking a bear for the Black Rock Monster. It would make much more sense to assume it was bears (garden-variety American black bears) who were pawing through people's garbage at night—wouldn't it? Bears were real, documented creatures absolutely beyond a shadow of doubt proven to exist, and they did indeed inhabit this area—in fact, anyone in this town who had lived here long enough had probably seen them once or twice.

Audrey had a very clear memory of the first time she saw a bear. It was an early memory. She had been in preschool. She'd attended a Montessori school in a converted residential house run by blissed-out

80

hippie ladies. Of course she'd only come to think of them that way when she got older, and continued to know the same ladies as their long, braided hair frizzled and grayed. (One of these women now worked part-time in a shop on the main drag that sold polished rocks to tourists when ski season was on.) A black bear had wandered into town and climbed a tree in the front yard of the house. The children were all pointing and shrieking behind the picket fence that corralled in the playground until the grownups herded them inside and locked the doors, and then the children pointed and shrieked from behind the windows. The grownups called the sheriff, who was prepared for such problems and arrived with a rifle that shot tranquilizer darts, and was soon joined by several park rangers, who held a blue-nylon parachute beneath the bear to break his fall. The sheriff shot the bear with a tranquilizer dart as the children pointed and shrieked. The bear gradually melted out of the tree as if he had become an enormous glob of molasses. He drooped and tumbled headfirst from the branches and bounced on the parachute. The park rangers wrapped up the sedated bear and took him to the nearby Arapaho National Forest, where they released him back into the wild. It was one of Audrey's earliest memories. Her recollection of the event was a mixture of what she actually remembered and what she'd been told. She thought she remembered the sight of the bear falling from the tree, but she might have only been remembering the image she had pictured when Jim, who'd had a better view of it, had described it to her. Jim had been about fifteen then, and their mother had sent him to pick up Audrey from the day-care place and walk her home. Jim had arrived in time to watch the sheriff shoot the bear, was standing watching from across the street when it happened. She'd held his hand when they walked home together afterward—that day, and every other that he'd picked her up—and while she did not remember the bear so clearly, she remembered very clearly the walk home, remembered their talking excitedly about the bear falling from the tree into the parachute the whole walk, and possibly for days afterward.

Memories like these made Audrey even sadder for Jim now. Jim had since become the only major source of discord in the family. He was a one-man constant, consistent exploder of everyone's stability and happiness—both of his own and his family's. Her oldest brother, Liam, was thirteen years her senior, and a lawyer now in Seattle, living life and making money: He rarely visited and rarely called—a remote figure, missed, but not to be worried about. Liam had been more or less out of the picture ever since he'd gone away to college, twelve years ago, when Audrey was five—the same year of the black bear's vaguely remembered sleepy tumble from the tree. Jim, however, was constantly in the picture. Much more so than anyone, including Jim, wanted him to be. Something had crawled up inside Jim's soul and warped him—hung weights on him that prevented him from getting off the ground, from even leaving Black Rock for very long. He was a daisy chain of problems. He'd crawled through what college he could, dropping out and reenrolling again and again, eventually dropping out for good. Then a succession of hourly wage jobs that always ended in his being fired. Drugs, blackouts, arrests, perennial financial problems. Pathetic moneymaking ventures that often involved "buddies" in Austin or Portland. He was back in Black Rock now after another disastrously unsuccessful attempt at starting an independent adult life for himself in Denver. Semihomeless, he alternated among crashing on his childhood friend's couch across town, the futon in their parents' unfinished basement (their father, in a passive-aggressive rage at a son seemingly incapable of growing up, had converted his old bedroom into a gratuitous home office), and the vacant rooms of the hotel when there were vacancies, which there usually were in the off-season. This last thing Audrey's mother hated most—especially when he let himself in late at night and grabbed one of the keys off the wall behind the front desk. If he had been a guest, she might have sent him a fine in the mail. He was sloppy, had never learned to cover his tracks. You could tell he'd been there if the sheets were gross, peppered in little black hairs, a yellowish sweat ring on the pillow where his drunken head had been. Cigarette reek lingering in the air. A family friend had lately given him a part-time job at a Sunoco station—which Audrey found more embarrassing and depressing than if he weren't working at all. Beneath the twenty-six-year-old man in a yellow-and-blue Sunoco uniform, the man with a scraggly beard and unwashed, greasy hair, smelling always of smoke, either sullen-silent, or, when pressed, ready to blather about whatever lamebrained conspiracy theory he was currently obsessed with, Audrey saw the sweet and fundamentally good guy who had held her hand and walked her home from her Montessori school, talking with her excitedly about the bear that had fallen from the tree.

Audrey was worried at how relieved she felt that Jim was not among that fall's surge of local crazies who claimed to have seen the Black Rock Monster. She was worried because the acuteness of her relief meant that if Jim had claimed to have seen him, it wouldn't have surprised her. And people who see Bigfoot, see ghosts, have paranormal experiences, get abducted by aliens, so on and so forth, Audrey generally regarded as: losers.

But, no: He wasn't among them, thank God. Their mother would have gone catatonic with humiliation had he been. Duncan Hodges had been the first to "see" "him" that year, thus confirming Audrey's prejudice about the kind of people who report sightings of cryptids: losers. Duncan had been in the same year in school as Jim. He worked in a ski shop and in the summers sometimes busked on a street corner with a didgeridoo. Ratty white-guy dreadlocks tied up in a blue bandanna, always had the look of someone who wandered in ten minutes late and isn't sure if he's in the right room. Jim and Duncan had a friendship, like many friendships between people who have grown up together in a small town, that accordioned in and out of closeness as years passed. There had been a while in high school when the two'd been thick as thieves; both of them had been suspended when they got caught setting fire to a pile of Funyuns behind the tennis courts. Lately they seemed to have been hanging out again more since Jim had moved back from Denver. Duncan claimed he saw the Black Rock Monster while hiking on Rattlesnake Gulch Trail, a few miles west of town. The trail winds alongside the gulch and up to a bluff on the side of Sugarloaf Mountain, where the ruins of the Tabor Hotel are: one of those bizarre nineteenth-century ideas, to build a luxury hotel on the side of a mountain in the middle of nowhere. It burned down in the twenties, and all that's left is the foundation and the chimneys. That's where Duncan claimed to have seen it. He told everyone that it was probably because he had been hiking barefoot, to "truly feel the earth beneath his feet," or something: That is, he didn't scare it away because he wasn't making much noise.

"I think they have really good hearing?" Duncan theorized into the clown-nose-red foam microphone cover held in front of his face by a woman from *9 News* who might have been praying that nothing important would happen during the two hours it would take to drive back to Denver. Duncan's finger fiddled sissily with one of his blond dreadlocks. "I mean, like, I bet most people, you know, have, like, shoes on, and they hear you when you come and they, like, you know, run away real quick."

Duncan said he saw the creature "sunning himself" on the flat stone floor of the ruins of the hotel. He said he stood still and watched it for about five minutes. He approached, and when he was maybe thirty feet away, the creature seemed to take notice of him. It jumped to its feet and ran, as Duncan said, "like *real* quick," into the woods. His description of the creature was essentially consistent with those of the Black Rock Monster already on record: between six and eight feet tall; very long, gangly arms; dark-brown fur; a high, sloped forehead.

That was in mid-September, when their part of the country may be at its most beautiful. From where Duncan Hodges had or had not been standing when he did or did not see the creature that was or was not the Black Rock Monster, he would have also seen—and this is certain—much of Black Rock Valley and the town of Black Rock itself resting in the bottom of its enormous bowl of granite. He would have seen the unsightly tracks of cleared mountainside where the ski runs were; the motionless ski lifts with creaky gondola boxes dangling from the cables like rows of orderly, evenly spaced fruit on vines; and the aspen groves above the town, which are at their most breathtaking in early fall—their leaves turn all at once to a buttery-golden yellow, and when the wind blows through them great sinuous ripples of color follow each other patiently across the mountainside. Audrey's father had told her more than once that an aspen grove is the largest living organism on the earth, because the roots all connect beneath. A single aspen is not a tree; it is a small component of a vast system. That's why their leaves all turn at exactly the same time. You see? Audrey believed there was already enough mystery and wonder in the visible world right beneath our feet without the need for mythical monsters sunning themselves on the ruins of old hotels, supposedly seen by her brother's friend, that scuzzy stoner who sometimes sat on a milk crate next to the ice-cream store and played his didgeridoo in front of a hat.

The second sighting that fall was even more vague but perhaps slightly more credible, as it was corroborated by two people. (Though Audrey doubted that assumption as well. She didn't trust two people any more than one. Three, *maybe*. She knew about shared psychosis, conversion disorder, *folie à deux*, contagious hallucinations.) Jason Henly and Kate Pletl, who had graduated from Black Rock High two years before, claimed to have seen the creature moving in the woods behind the Safeway that employed them both. It was around twilight, they said, about six thirty at night. They were taking the garbage and recycling out to the Dumpsters in back of the building, which abuts the edge of a spruce-fir forest. They said they saw something, about maybe forty paces into the forest, stand up from a sitting position and then flit between the trees and disappear. They watched it for about half a minute before losing sight of it, they said. Something large, brown, and definitely alive. They thought it might be a person at first, they said, because it appeared to be striding on two legs, but then they saw that it was much too tall to be a person.

"Except maybe Shaquille O'Neal," Jason joked to the reporter who wrote the three inches of column about it in the *Daily Prospector* (*9 News* didn't bother sending a van up for this one). Audrey had read that over breakfast and thought: Jason, it is, in fact, much, much more likely that Shaquille O'Neal, who is proven to exist, was for some reason hiding in the woods behind the Safeway than that the Black Rock Monster was. Jason and Kate weren't quite as dumb as Duncan, though—they admitted they weren't exactly sure what they'd seen; the light outside had been dim. And the guy from the *Prospector* hadn't known to probe them about this, but everyone under thirty in Black Rock knew that everyone who worked at that Safeway was high *all the fucking time* (how else could they stand it?), and everyone who had ever worked at that Safeway furthermore knew that "taking out the trash"—a task easily accomplished by one employee— was code for sneaking behind the building to smoke a bowl. That was in early October.

A flurry of unsubstantiated and unreported sightings followed, which many of the adults remained unaware of, as they all happened inside the social underbelly of Black Rock High School. Suddenly everyone at school had seen the Black Rock Monster—on camping trips, while fly-fishing with mothers and fathers, in backyards, in backcountry, in back of the Pizza Hut, in the woods back behind where the Kmart used to be, from the backs of cars parked by the edge of the lake, and so on, and so on.

These sightings were not credible, and Audrey chose not to report on them.

Audrey was the editor in chief of the school newspaper, the Black Rock High *Husky Howler* (the school's mascot was the Husky). The newspaper's sponsor, Mrs. Bond-Simmons, thought it would be cute or something for her to write a story on the Black Rock Monster— "For the Halloween issue!" she twittered—and at first, Audrey refused outright. That was exactly the sort of softball puff piece that Audrey loathed, was embarrassed by every time something like it appeared in the *Howler*, thinking it cheapened the prestige of the publication, made it harder to take seriously.

Of all Audrey's desires—the desire to get out of Black Rock, the desire to be in the "real world," the desire to be a "real" journalist, the desire to find truth and the desire to say it, the desire to perhaps find love, the desire to as soon as possible be an adult with a career, a bank account, and a yearlong lease on an apartment in a big city, the desire that her brother Jim improve himself and begin at last to lead a better life—what among them belly-growled the loudest, the hungriest, was the desire to be taken seriously.

The third sighting officially reported that year did or did not happen on October 17, the first day of deer-hunting season, a Sunday. The weather had warned of a possible early snowstorm that day, but it had produced only a soft, white sky that lightly powdered the fallen leaves in the morning like a dusting of confectioner's sugar. It was early in the morning—an unusual time for a sighting. (They usually happened toward the evening.) The unlikely seer of the beast was Bob Mecoy, a native Black Rocker who ran a business painting houses and doing other manual odd jobs in the summer, and in the winter did HVAC repair and coached the wrestling team. Audrey didn't know him well, but had always thought of him as a fairly no-nonsense guy. As in: not likely to engage in nonsense. The Black Rock Monster was: nonsense. Bob was also an avid outdoorsman, hunter, and fisher— one of his many side hustles was selling elk jerky he'd killed and cured himself out of the back of his truck in the parking lot of the B&F Super Foods. Thus it was that he was already out tromping around in the woods at the crack of dawn on the first day of deer season. His description of the monster differed somewhat from those Duncan Hodges, Jason Henly, and Kate Pletl had given. They had all described an intensely musky odor, even from far away. Bob Mecoy did not report any distinctive smell that he could detect, and he clarified repeatedly that he had no idea what it was he saw—only that he had never seen it before. He said whatever it was walked upright on two legs, and moved more or less like a human being. It was tall, but again, not taller than a very tall man. It was hairy, or furry, all over, and he didn't get a clear glimpse of its face.

"Not hairy, no," he said to the same reporter from the *Prospector* who had interviewed Jason and Kate. He said its fur was not dark brown but a light brownish gray. "More like, uh, *shaggy*. Like a great big old sheepdog had started walking on his hind legs."

Bob told the reporter that he had been so close to it that he could have had a clear shot at it.

The reporter asked him why he didn't shoot it.

"This is deer season," Bob said. "It wasn't a deer."

Audrey met Bill Burns shortly after the Bob Mecoy sighting. Had she known the reason for his being in town she might have written him off as a crackpot right away. She had been doing calculus homework with pencil and TI-83 calculator at one of the tables in the bar on the bottom floor of the hotel. Her mother was behind the counter, and there was no one else in the room. It was a weeknight. There was no music on. As with the rest of the hotel, almost everything in the bar was made of wood. The counter was an irregular span of pine log planed lengthwise and glazed thick with finish, and those tessellated elk-antler lighting fixtures dangled above the bar, casting spiky netted shadows around the room. The hotel bar had a warm, dark-honeyed glow to it. Her mother was watching the PBS *MacNeil/Lehrer NewsHour*, and Audrey, from her table in the corner of the room, was half paying attention to it between calculus problems, each one like an irritating little knot of hair she'd been tasked to disentangle. The man who had checked into the hotel earlier in the afternoon came downstairs, sat at the bar, and ordered a beer, which he sipped slowly while watching the news in silence with Audrey's mother, sucking foam from his mustache between sips. Jim Lehrer was talking about Slobodan Milošević meeting with representatives of the other belligerents in Bosnia for an American-led diplomatic conference in Dayton, Ohio. Audrey herself had checked the man at the bar into the hotel that afternoon—her mother had asked her to work the front desk for a few hours after school. It still being the off-season, there were very few guests. The Pronghorn Lodge still handled its booking the old-fashioned way, with a physical log-in book and all, and the wall behind the counter was still a Masonite pegboard with rows and columns of metal hooks with keys hanging from them. This was how Audrey knew the man's name was William Burns, and that he lived in Bainbridge Island, Washington. He was a soft-featured man who looked to be maybe in his fifties or early sixties, balding with white-gray hair and a sandy-colored, mostly gray beard—thickset and potbellied, but not quite fat. He wore jeans, hiking boots, a bland blue Oxford shirt and unfashionable eyeglasses whose frames had clearly been chosen for function over form. Audrey felt certain he was somebody's dad, possibly a young grandfather.

When *NewsHour* ended, the guy asked Audrey's mother if she would switch the channel to football, and she did, and although he watched it he didn't appear too invested in the game. Audrey's mother began chatting with him.

He had been a professor at the University of Washington, he said, when asked what he did.

"For twenty-nine years. Just retired."

"Congratulations!"

He raised his glass of beer at her.

"One of my sons lives in Seattle," her mother offered. "So we've been there to visit now and then. He's a lawyer. Says he loves it out there. Beautiful city. Rains all the damn time, though."

"That is true."

William Burns had been a professor of, as he put it, animal behavioral ethology—Audrey learned this from listening in over her calculus, and, as she learned more about him, she began to listen more closely.

What is behavioral ethology?

The study of the social behavior of animals, essentially. Usually in the wild, though not necessarily. He had spent much of his career and life studying baboons—

"Baboons?"

"Right, baboons."

And although he was now retired, he still frequently published research, he said, and still in the summers visited "his troop" in Botswana. He referred to this troop of baboons in the possessive, he said, because he had been studying this same group of animals since the 1970s, and felt they were his. He had observed the short-arc narratives of individuals and the long arcs of generations, rising, bending, and rising again. Childhoods, courtships, friendships, motherhoods, fatherhoods, surrogate mother- and fatherhoods, alliances and grievances, favors and revenges, dominations and submissions, power struggles, politics, rebel insurgencies, coups d'état and de grâce, hostile takeovers, gang warfare, rape, murder, infanticide, matricide, patricide, fratricide, cannibalism, altruism, mercy, mourning, forgiveness, kindness, grief, and grace: He had seen it all.

"Most of the baboons' day is spent annoying and harassing each other to no particular end. They're ornery critters."

Mr. Burns—"Dr. Burns?"—handshake—"Bill"—Bill had also done research with other nonhuman primates, a phrase that appeared to confuse Audrey's mother. He had that mildly autistic air of someone whose depth of devotion to a particular subject blinds him to facial expressions and social cues: He could not see that other people might not find the subject as fascinating as he did, or even, for that matter, know what the hell he was talking about. Audrey's mother tried to steer the conversation away from baboons, attempted more casual small talk with him, but he fumbled to put words together when asked about the basic things anyone could talk about—how he liked living in Bainbridge Island, the fact that it was often rainy there, and so on. To him, Bainbridge Island was a place. A place where people lived. Just like this was a place where people lived.

"I like it there," was all she got out of him about it. Though he had grown up in Ohio, he put in after. It seemed to him that Ohio and Washington were perfectly interchangeable. He very much enjoyed, however, his summers in Botswana, when he did his field research with the baboons. He spoke of Botswana without exoticizing it: He went there simply because it was where the baboons happened to be. And so the road had curved back around to baboons, and he was rattling away again. Audrey, who by then had been sitting on the stool next to him at the bar for some time with a Coke, supplied this baboon expert with an interviewer and an audience, which Audrey's mother was grateful for, as she had gotten a bit bored with this monkey professor and meanwhile the bar had gotten busier. Audrey fed him questions, kept him talking, motivated nine parts by interest and one by her desire to stay down here with the grownups. (As a child, Audrey had been uninterested in childhood, and now, at seventeen, something inside her was coiled tight with the impatience to be rid of adolescence, like a windup toy so wound up the key's become hard to turn.) Audrey's mother let her sit in the bar downstairs and do her homework when it wasn't busy, but shoved her out later when business picked up.*

Bill Burns, who had introduced himself to her by then, was telling her about some experiment he and his wife had done—his wife, Deborah, whom he'd been married to for thirty-five years, was also

---

*She didn't like the idea of her seventeen-year-old daughter in a bar—even though Audrey appeared to her eyes about as sexual a being as an eggplant: always in her snow boots and her drab, bulky sweaters; no makeup; that saggy, colorless knit hat she wore everywhere. She had once asked Audrey if she had "a crush on any boys at school," and received in return a look that was as if she'd asked if Audrey knew anyone who'd been eaten by rats lately. Another time, after that, Audrey's mother had begun to tell her that she and Audrey's father would love her unconditionally, no matter what course her life should take, before Audrey stopped her cold with another "Please don't" stare. All she'd accomplished in worrying about her daughter's seemingly vacant sexuality was to let Audrey know her mother thought she might be a lesbian. Thereafter, she dropped the subject.

his research partner and former colleague at the University of Washington—in which they'd gone around scooping up the feces of female baboons to measure their glucose content. When an animal's stress level rises, so does the glucose content in its feces. Over time, they were able to graph the spikes and drops of the averaged stress levels of the female baboons in the troop. As predicted, the line rose dramatically every time a socially significant event occurred. Because, you see, female baboons tend to stay within their troop, whereas male baboons travel from one to another. Once in a while a new male baboon comes around, tries to become alpha male. If he's defeated, he usually leaves to go pick another fight elsewhere. If he's accepted as alpha male, often, but not always, the first thing he does is kill all the infants. Which makes perfect sense from the perspective of evolution: Get the competition out of the gene pool. But the new alpha males only do this *some* of the time. Whenever a new male joined the troop, or there was a change of leadership from within, the stress levels of the females (especially the mothers of infants) would go through the roof during the period of uncertainty when they didn't know whether the new alpha was the kill-all-the-babies type or not. Their stress went down after he'd either killed all the babies or enough time had passed they felt assured he wasn't going to.

"Why do the new alpha males kill the babies only some of the time? Why not all the time?"

"Ah! Now, that's behavioral ethology! In order to take the next step, you've got to assume that animals are not soulless little robots enslaved to instinct, as Descartes believed, but creatures with some degree of consciousness."

Audrey knew three things about Descartes: "I think, therefore I am," that he sort of invented the grid, and that there was a Latin poem inscribed in cursive on his skull. Audrey appreciated that Bill didn't talk down to her. Still, though, she didn't quite know what he was talking about.

When she asked him about Descartes, he said, "Oh, well—backing up a bit. Descartes argued that animals have no souls. That they're automata, driven only by instinct, whereas humans have souls—that is, consciousness—the ability to make decisions and act on them. I find that most people still think this way about animals, even the ones who don't feel that way. We don't like to think they think, or feel, or have whatever it is we call 'consciousness.' Philosophers talk about finding the 'edge' of consciousness. Is it language? Is it the ability to recognize yourself in a mirror? I say, who says there's an edge?

Whoever said there's some line somewhere, where, on this side of it you put human beings, chimpanzees, gorillas, and, uh, why not throw in dolphins while we're at it?—and you put all the other animals on the other side of the line? I'm sorry, but it makes no fucking sense!"

He'd carried himself away. Audrey's mother shot him a look when he cursed.

"Sorry!" he said, covering his mouth, embarrassed.

"Gonna have to wash her ears out, Professor."

"Mom, I've heard the word 'fuck' before. Am I five?"

"Have you finished your homework?"

Audrey didn't answer, and the kitchen bell in the window dinged, calling her mother away. Bill made a worried face that Audrey found adorable.

"Don't worry, she's not mad."

"Anyway"—he searched for his bearings—"where was I?"

"Descartes? Animal souls? Baboons killing babies?"

"Right! So, I'm anthropomorphizing here, I know, but bear with me. Say you're the new alpha male of a baboon troop. If you start killing everyone's babies right off the bat, that's not going to engender a lot of trust and goodwill in you as a leader, is it? As Machiavelli said, it is better to be feared than loved, if you cannot be both. Killing the babies will make them fear you, but it certainly won't make them love you. For you, it's a high-risk, high-confidence gamble. Because it might make them want to gang up and kill you, and then you're out of the gene pool for good. So, a lot of the time, bullies get their way. But just as often, it pays off to be nice—or at least merciful."

The bar was filling up, and Audrey was getting a tingling that her mother would kick her upstairs at any moment. She saw that Bill, who was still talking excitedly about baboons and had had a couple of beers, could not sense this anxiety in her. Though maybe he would if he could only measure the glucose content in her feces. She did not want to leave his conversation. Having grown up in a small town, and poised at the cusp of finally getting to leave that small town, Audrey had a powerful hunger for conversation with people whom she had not known all her life, and for subjects of conversation that were not also those same people. It wasn't that she had no ear for gossip, but only that she was heavy bored with the gossip available. It was far more interesting to hear this spectacularly unself-conscious man ramble on about his baboons.

What had brought him to town, however, was "the Sasquatch": for that was his preferred way of referring to the nonexistent animal that most people called Bigfoot and was known locally as the Black Rock Monster. He seemed to regard "the Sasquatch" as the most respectful and correct name for him, the way thoughtful people say "Native American" instead of "Indian."

At his first mention of the Sasquatch, Audrey felt her heart turning away from him, disappointed. It turned out this fascinating man from the Outside must also be: a loser.

He was a real scientist, though, which confused her.

"Oh, I would never publish anything about the Sasquatch, unless I had a slam dunk on my hands. I'd be laughed out of town. No major journal would ever publish my papers again."

"So it's more of—?"

"It's kind of a hobby, I suppose. But it's not so crazy. Do you know when the mountain gorilla was 'discovered'?"

He put the word "discovered" in finger quotations of contempt.

"Because, 'discovered by white people' is what 'discovered' usually means. Any guesses? Not until 1902! That late! Before that, the animal's existence was regarded as an unsubstantiated rumor, some spooky legend cooked up in the primitive brains of savage Africans, not to be trusted. Now think about that and consider all the Native American folklore about the Sasquatch."

There was a poignant pause. Audrey wondered what to say in response, before Bill saved her by starting up again. He was on a roll. He reached out and lightly touched her arm.

"How much do you know about *Gigantopithecus*?"

"I don't know," said Audrey. "I've never been asked that."

"*Gigantopithecus* was a hominid ape, thought to be extinct, that stood about ten feet tall, probably weighed around a thousand pounds, and may very well have walked upright. It's hard to tell from the incomplete fossil evidence we have. *Gigantopithecus* is the largest ape known to have lived on earth. All the fossils have been found in Asia so far, and radiocarbon dating puts the last of them at around a hundred thousand years ago. Totally contemporaneous with modern humans. Now we think that modern humans crossed the Bering Land Bridge about twenty thousand years ago. So that's a gap in time of about eighty thousand years between when we think *Gigantopithecus* went extinct and the time when we think humans crossed into North America. That is a *blink of an eye* in geologic time. Blink—of—an—*eye*."

"So—do you believe in Bigfoot?"

"Do I believe it is entirely possible that a very small but viable breeding population of *Gigantopithecus* could have survived far longer than we thought, long enough for some of them to cross the land bridge into North America, along with modern humans and countless other species, during the Last Glacial Maximum? Yes. Do I believe it is entirely possible that some of them survive even to this day? Yes."

"But do you believe in Bigfoot?"

"What, I ask you, is the difference between a monster and an animal? Is it possible that it's only the difference between the unknown and the known? When you see those old maps of the ocean, with sea monsters coming out of the waves, and it says, 'There be monsters here . . .' Well, say you're a sailor in the Middle Ages, and you happen to see a giant squid. This is an animal that can grow up to *sixty feet long*—eyes the size of dinner plates. Up to this day, it's never been photographed alive. We only know they can get that big from the size of sucker marks around the mouths of beached sperm whales. So you happen to see this creature in a prescientific era—before Darwin, before Linnaeus—before we know 'That's not the Kraken, that's *Architeuthis dux*'—before all that. What have you seen, if not a monster? Isaac Newton believed in alchemy. The same guy who wrote *Principia Mathematica* spent a lot of time trying to turn lead into gold. And why not? How many things have made the leap from magic to understood natural phenomena because of science—because somebody asked, 'Why not?' The spirit of science is not, *This is crazy, this is unbelievable, this cannot be so!* It's—it's asking— 'Well, why not?' Let's entertain the possibility, let's do some exploring and some experiments, let's try to figure it out. My point is, we know much, much less about the natural world than we think we do. Let's not be arrogant."

"But do you believe in Bigfoot?"

Bill sighed, a bit theatrically. He gave up, shrugged.

"No. I wouldn't say, categorically, that I believe in the Sasquatch. Personally, I've never seen anything I would call direct, convincing evidence. But I want them to be real. I don't know. I've always been a romantic at heart."

The offices of the *Howler* were the back corner of an English classroom, where a row of beige Power Macintosh 6100s were obscured behind a low, gray wall of cubicle partitions. The low drop ceiling was made of those gray-white speckled panels rumored to contain asbestos, and the floor was thin, mottled carpeting the color of a rotten orange. During eighth period—Journalism, the last period of the day—the classroom turned into the newspaper office. The news paper had to share the space with the yearbook staff (the sign on the door read "English 103/Publications"), which wasn't much of an issue, as the yearbook was extracurricular—they only worked after school, and they only really worked in the spring semester. There was an overlap between the newspaper and the yearbook kids, and Audrey wasn't a part of it: She regarded the yearbook as a once-annual organ of frivolous propaganda. The newspaper was for truth—a necessary check on the power structure, not its fangless cheerleader. This, she knew, is a difficult thing for a high-school newspaper to do. It is almost impossible, really, to teach a real journalism class that produces a high-school newspaper. Real journalism must be independent from the state, and a high-school newspaper owes its existence to the state: Because the state is paying for it, it has the power to censor or suppress the newspaper whenever it wants. And, as Lord Northcliffe said, "News is something someone wants suppressed. Everything else is just advertising." This was one of Audrey's many impatiences: the impatience to be through with high school so that she might write for more serious publications that would allow her to write more seriously.

Mrs. Bond-Simmons had encouraged her to write a story about the recent Black Rock Monster sightings. Audrey would have never written such an article, but having met Bill the night before had given her an idea. She approached Mrs. Bond-Simmons and described Bill, the baboon expert who had a side interest in Bigfoot, and had come to Black Rock to investigate the recent uptick of sightings. Mrs. Bond-Simmons loved the idea.

"Write it as a personal-interest feature!" she bubbled. She might as well have added, "Won't that be *adorable*?"

What Audrey had in mind was more of a meditative profile piece, admiring but not uncritical of its subject—sort of in the vein of Gay Talese's "Frank Sinatra Has a Cold." She envisioned an intimate piece about an eccentric man on a quixotic journey, which would fold in on itself to reflect on larger questions about the curse of devoted ambition, the line between inquisitiveness and folly, the interior battle of skepticism and animal faith.

*

Sometimes, years later, in still moments while sitting at her work spaces in the offices of the various newspapers and magazines she would write for and edit, she would remember the production of the *Howler* as being charmingly primitive. It was a product of perpetual obsession, that biweekly eight-page tabloid newspaper with a print run of five hundred and a readership smaller than that. Audrey was the *Howler*'s midwife from the first editorial meeting through its design, production, printing, and distribution. She assigned the stories, wrote several of them herself while also editing everyone else's articles, drove the finished galleys to the printer in the middle of the night and came back at the crack of dawn to pick them up, arrived at school with a carload of the bound bundles of newspapers, snapped the plastic bands with a box cutter, and handed them to the rest of the newspaper staff, who were gathered waiting for her by the main doors of the building early on Friday mornings before first period, and they in turn would distribute them around the school (which Audrey also helped with). The *Howler* was Audrey's obsession. Other kids worried about their boyfriends and girlfriends, grades, sex, parties, bands, drugs, college applications, etc.—things Audrey found trite and tiresome. She had no interest in these things.

The Thursday night before the paper went to press was always a sleepless one for Audrey. They would usually be working on it until midnight, one, two, sometimes three in the morning, ordering pizza, drinking black coffee under harsh fluorescent lights in English 103/ Publications in an otherwise dark building long after the night janitor had gone home. They printed out their columns on perforated computer paper, carefully cut them out with scissors and pasted the pages together on the galleys, 11" x 17" tabloid sheets, drew the dividing lines in the picas by hand with fine-tip pen and ruler. Audrey developed a jeweler's eye for detail, became a black belt with Wite-Out. When a page came to completion it was usually Audrey's hands that, taking the delicate and precious object gingerly by the edges, laid it flat in the galley box, which, when all the galleys were finished, was closed like a sarcophagus lid and secured with rubber bands. Audrey would tuck it under her arm and in the company of whoever else had made it to the end of the night (but more frequently alone) make the thirty-minute drive out to Elk Park, where the printer would scan the galleys and print the newspaper. She relished her brief, transactional conversations with the guy who worked at the printer. They made her feel adult. Is it that strange and strikingly ugly men are drawn to night jobs, or is it the night jobs that make them that way? The guy at the printer was a young man who already looked old, with a bad limp and bad teeth, a soft pack of Lucky Strikes in his breast pocket, arms gray black with newspaper ink up to the elbows, and finger smudges all over his crooked face. Audrey had a little bit of a crush on him. She admired him because she guessed he was only a few years older than she was, and was working a physical job dealing with concrete matter, a job that made him a necessary node in the chain of connections that lead a fact from occurrence to reportage to information on the page to a reader's eyes. He'd slide the lid off the galley box on the counter of the small, dim office, printing machines clacking, whirring, and creaking in the next room through the door he'd jammed open with a brick, flip through the pages quickly, and mark down their order on Black Rock High School's tab in his ledger book. The conversation usually passed almost without words. Audrey would come back at dawn, sometimes after a quick nap at home or in her car in the parking lot if it was a warm night, but usually after a few hours spent drinking coffee at Denny's. She would drive up to the back of the building, by the garage doors and the loading dock. He would be tooling around the vast concrete floor on a forklift. The room smelled of ink and machine oil. The enormous printing press shuffled and hummed, fresh copies of newspapers moving rapid-fire along the conveyor belt. She would pick up the bundles of the *Howler*, stacked into a cube next to a much larger stacked cube of the *Daily Prospector*, and load them into the back of her car. When she was done, she waved at him, and he waved back at her from the forklift. To Audrey, whose god was truth and journalism its religion, this building was a church, and this man its Quasimodo—lonely, deformed, ringing its bells in the middle of the night.

In years that followed, Audrey would come into journalism as it was cartwheeling through a radical transformation the old guard feared was death. Local newspapers across the country folded one after another like lights on a map flickering weakly and winking out between ever-wider gaps of darkness as the old giants struggled to hold on. Words were migrating from paper to screen, and the eyes of the people followed them there, into the flatness, into the untouchable, into the intangible, into the soft, clear, glowing light. Sometimes, when Audrey found herself in an open-plan office on the thirty-seventh floor of the Condé Nast Building, thirty-six years old with a punishing rent to pay, student loans in deferment, and twenty tabs open on her browser, her eyes moving from laptop to smartphone to iPad, Twitter pinging away with information and misinformation high and low scatterblasting across the earth, she would remember the old world of scissors, glue, pencils, tape, ink, paper, and mechanical machines—and miss it. Audrey had probably been one of the last children in history to learn to type in a softly whirring room full of electric typewriters, with her eyes locked on a skittery metal ball of letters and symbols, hands hidden beneath a sheet of paper taped to the front of the IBM Selectric, typing

```
The quick brown fox jumped over the lazy gray dog.
The quick brown fox jumped over the lazy gray dog.
The quick brown fox jumped over the lazy gray dog.
```

—again, and again, and again.

There was no one behind the front desk of the hotel when Audrey came home from school in the afternoon. She descended the two wide steps onto the sunken floor of the bar, expecting to find her mother behind the counter, but she wasn't there either. The whole building was empty and absolutely quiet, except for two customers: She saw Bill Burns bent over one of the tables pushed against the wall in the corner of the room, talking with Duncan Hodges. The bar was not open yet; her mother must have served them anyway as a favor. From this evidence Audrey guessed she was probably in the kitchen. Audrey dumped her backpack on a barstool, squeezed her coat off, and sat on the one beside it. She spread her calculus before her on the lacquered pine counter and began working. The word "homework" to her would always evoke math homework specifically—something about the repetition and grinding futility of it, how drearily unchanged the world looks after an x has been solved for. She happened to be good at math, but it bored her nevertheless. She was good enough at it that she could figure out the problems with her mind on other things, as if she were knitting or assembling a jigsaw puzzle, which freed her ears for eavesdropping.

"How tall, would you say?" she heard Bill saying.

"Like, at least seven feet? Maybe more?"

"Would you say it had a pronounced supraorbital ridge?"

"What?"

"This thing." His finger tapped something on the table. "See? The browridge above the eyes."

"Oh, yeah. I don't know. I guess so?"

She stole enough backward glances at them to see that Bill Burns had a coffee cup in front of him; Duncan, a glass of beer. Bill, between every question he put to the inarticulate Duncan Hodges, scribbled notes onto a legal pad, and beside this was a tape recorder with its red recording light on. He also had a lot of other documents—folders, photo prints, drawings, things like that—spread out around him on the table.

Audrey could hear her mother's voice behind the kitchen doors, those swinging doors with porthole windows, and another voice. She couldn't hear what they were saying, but she knew whatever conversation her mother was having was one she didn't want to have in earshot of the public.

"How about a skull crest? Like a gorilla?"

"Um—"

"Most primates don't have them, but gorillas do. They have conical heads with a pointed crest running vertically along the middle of the skull." Pointing, drawing a line up the middle of his own head with his finger. "Like this."

"Um—I don't know."

"How about arm-to-leg ratio?"

"What?"

Audrey smirked to herself listening to them—listening to a smart person who was socially stupid enough to not know how to talk to a stupid person. Bill might as well have been trying to interview a six-year-old child about the US military involvement with the conflict in Bosnia.

The shouting in the kitchen rose in volume. She could now hear the unmistakable timbre of her brother's voice. The shouting reached the peak of a crescendo and abruptly stopped—and then there was a brusque march of sullen stomping.

The kitchen doors whacked open and Jim walked through them. He stopped when he saw Audrey sitting there. He looked awful. Jim had always been a tall, handsome guy, but he'd let himself go to pot in the last few years. Or maybe the drugs and booze had only visibly caught up with him in the last few years. He was only twenty-six. He looked rotten, puffy and bloated. He had sallow, ashen skin, a gruesome paunch, and a fat face, but was skinny everywhere else. His beard looked like bits of lint that had been clumsily glued onto his cheeks, and there were saggy, dark pouches under his eyes; the eyes themselves were murky, florid with blood. He even smelled bad—sweaty, unclean, his clothes mildewy, as if they'd been wadded on a bathroom floor for days before he put them on.

"Hey yo whatup?" he said to her, without pauses. "What you up to, Tiny?"

Audrey could not remember exactly when Jim started calling her "Tiny." It had begun when she was a small child and he was a teenager, but the appellation was still true: At five foot one and ninety-eight pounds, Audrey was not a great occupier of physical space in this world.

She pointed at the papers in front of her.

"Calculus homework."

Uninvited, he snatched up the textbook spread open on the counter. He read from it, slowly, as if he had to put his finger on each letter to pronounce it:

$$\text{Differentiate } y = (1 - 4x + 7x^5)^{30}$$

Actually, out loud, as far as he got was "Differentiate y equals—" and then he gave up.

He whistled appreciatively.

"Shit, dog, this shit is unreal. I don't know how you can make heads or tails of this shit, Tiny."

"It's not that hard. Give me my book back."

When, *when*, and *how* did he acquire all this idiotic, affected ghetto slang? Their parents didn't talk like that. Liam, their ghost brother, the brother who appeared only at Christmas and sometimes Thanksgiving to introduce a new beautiful girlfriend, who studied law at Northwestern and made six figures a year—*he* didn't talk like that. *Why?*

Jim handed her back the textbook.

Their mother emerged from the kitchen doors. Audrey could tell at once they'd been having a bad fight—a fight that was probably still unresolved. Jim's fights with their mother were like trench battles in World War I: violent, destructive catastrophes of no consequence. He shouted and raged at her, and usually wound up saying something appallingly horrible to her. And she never cried—their mother was not a woman who cried easily or frequently. She only shouted and raged back. Had there been a time when Audrey's sympathy for her brother was strong? She had sided with their mother in these fights for so long it was hard to remember if she had ever not. She still had some sympathy for Jim, but her sympathy was battle weary and weak in her heart.

Jim's cinnamon-brown eyes were stern with useless and unrighteous rage, and his breaths whistled audibly through his nostrils. Their mother's jaw was clenched. She did not say anything to Audrey—no hello, no how was school today. She was lockjawed and blinkered with anger. Her face was flushed too. She had rosacea that came and went: Her nose and jowly cheeks boiled with broken blood vessels in the wintertime, or when she was angry, or, in this case, both.

Everything about Jim was off-kilter somehow. He walked with a strange, loping, duck-footed gait, stomping every step, like a sleepwalker. His gaze didn't quite fix on yours when he looked at you, unfocused and always drifting slightly away, coming back, drifting away.

"Get out," said their mother. "Leave. I have customers."

Mr. Burns and Duncan Hodges looked up at them from their inane interview.

"Yo, Jim!" Duncan called from the table. "'Sup?"

Jim zipped up the puffy red coat he'd worn every winter for years, which was now grubby with black smudges, and lope-stomped over to their table, fist-bumped Duncan, and lope-stomped out, fishing around in the coat and sticking a cigarette in his face on his way to the door.

"He lost his job," Audrey's mother said when he had gone. "He shot his mouth off at his boss again and got himself fired from the goddamn gas station. He came here asking for money."

"Did you give him any?"

"Hell, no."

Whenever Jim's net worth hit perfect zero, which was often, or whenever he sank into meaningless debt with a credit card, he first asked their parents for a loan. If they said no, then he'd call Liam and hit him up for a thousand dollars, which Liam would usually give him out of misguided brotherly fidelity, even though he knew there was no way in hell Jim would be able to pay him back. And Jim would somehow plow through that money in a week or two—paying off delinquent parking tickets that had trebled themselves in late fees, things like that. Or he would just drink his way through it. Apparently he had been fired from the Sunoco station weeks ago, but had only told their mother about it today. It was amazing to Audrey how much Jim took and how little he gave: He was a karmic vortex, a black hole that resources fell into, from which nothing ever came out.

When Duncan had left, Audrey joined Bill at his table, and asked him if she could write a personal-interest feature article about him for the school newspaper.

Of course, he was delighted.

"Would you like to come on a ride-along?"

A "ride-along"—as if he were a cop. She found that funny. He was a little boy of an old man, who seemed more naive than even boys her own age—but then again, she knew that adolescent boys' greatest fear is being seen as naive; it's the time when they harden their hearts and sharpen their fangs. Bill had none of that. He had never grown up.

A few days passed. Audrey ate breakfast with her parents every morning before school—bagels, coffee, and frozen concentrate orange juice over the newspapers (her parents subscribed to the *Daily Prospector* and the *Rocky Mountain News*)—and these were several days of dark moods at breakfast. Her parents were at a loss over Jim. There was no disagreement between the two of them about him: Both were of the opinion that they had given him far too many fish for far too many days, and he was so resistant to learning to fish that starvation was the only way left to teach him. But even though they were in agreement, they were still at a loss. Jim poisoned the air between her parents, made them sullen and snappy with each other.

Audrey's days as usual fell one against the other in exact repetition like clicking mechanical parts, the spokes of a sprocket: a hallway lined with metal lockers opening and banging shut, the buzzer, the board, the boredom—and, eventually, at the end of each day, the newsroom, where she began outlining her profile feature about Bill Burns, summertime baboon expert, autumnal Bigfoot hunter.

Every evening Bill Burns came back to the hotel, empty-handed, disappointed but not dissuaded. His jeans and hiking boots would be mud spattered from all his romping around off-trail in the woods. He would come in stamping on the mat—bundled up like someone who lives in a place without serious winters, who has overshot the danger and overdressed—gradually unraveling himself out of hood, hat, scarf, gloves, coat as he made his way across the amber-hued woody interior of the lobby and down the three wooden steps to the bar, where he would order a cheeseburger and a beer, eat his dinner while studying his field notes, and then repair upstairs. He would wake before dawn to go out again into the woods. This was because he believed the Sasquatch was primarily a crepuscular animal: most active around dusk and dawn.

Audrey scribbled that down in her yellow spiral flip-top steno pad.

101

She was sitting in the passenger seat of Bill Burns's van, which rollicked and juddered over the washboard ruts in the narrow dirt road they were driving on. They were on their way to the Brainard Lake Wilderness Area, because Walt Elkins, Audrey's now-retired high-school science teacher, had told Bill in an interview that he might have witnessed the Black Rock Monster there about five years before.

"Plus, major bodies of water are always good places to look."

She scribbled that down too.

"Always? How can you say that if you've never actually seen one?"

The TV had warned that there would be a storm front moving in later that night.

"Supposed to snow all night and all day tomorrow," her father had said, back from the grocery store with canned chili, crackers and Spam, jugs of bottled water.

It amused Audrey the way people fell back into talking about the weather in terms of what it was "supposed to" do. As if the weatherman were a secular prophet to be believed but only with a grain of salt, and "the weather" a remnant of pagan providence.

"Supposed to be a big storm tonight. First of the season."

"I know. I heard we're supposed to get eighteen inches."

"Boy howdy."

And if the weather didn't do what it was supposed to do, it was the weather's fault, not the forecaster's. To Audrey's father, a grownup Boy Scout who still winced if he saw an American flag graze the ground, being underprepared for a bad storm was a moral failing—an ants-and-the-grasshopper, Protestant-work-ethic kind of thing—but to wind up overprepared for a storm much lighter than predicted was mildly embarrassing. People put faith in forecasters cautiously here.

The first "real," "butt-kickin'," "serious-business" (these were all her father's words) snowstorm of the winter meant at least two things.

One was that they must do what all people who live above a certain latitude must do before a blizzard, all the requisite battening down of hatches: See that the fuel in the tank wasn't low and firewood was plenty, the pantries were full, candles and propane lanterns ready in case the power went out, enough bottled water to last for days.

The other, that it was good for business. The citizens of Black Rock regarded a snowstorm the way a sailor regards a good gust of wind going in the right direction, the way a farmer regards rain: a boon for business that comes from the sky, those primeval fortunes of nature for which we first made the old gods to pray to. Soon the skiers would come in holiday colors. Soon the out-of-state plates

102

would fill the parking lots, waiters and waitresses would see their tip earnings quintuple, and for the first time in the season Audrey's mother would switch on the NO part of the NO VACANCY neon sign underneath the rustic wooden sign for the Pronghorn Lodge.

It was nearing sundown: The light was getting golden, the sky had begun to redden in the east. Bill's van was a battered dust-brown Ford Econoline that he had taken all the backseats out of. It was his mobile Bigfoot-hunting station. There was a twin mattress in the back and a battery-powered space heater, and a lot of camping equipment. Two hunting rifles rested in a metal gun rack screwed to one side of the back of the van. The vehicle put her in mind of a wagon in a gypsy caravan or something, or a traveling circus, pioneers headed west: a cramped, serviceable space for a nomad accustomed to scrappy shelter, made to be lived in while necessary—pots and pans dangling from hooks, a propane lantern—a rattletrap kitchen/bedroom where everything clattered and knocked together when it was rollicking over a rough road, as it was doing then.

"You have beautiful sunsets here," said Bill.

"I guess so," said Audrey. Never having lived anywhere else, Colorado's sunsets to her were not an issue for regional comparison and evaluation. The sky at that moment was feathered in striated pink clouds, goldflamed at the edges by a sun that had gone already behind the mountains, and the rest of the sky was turning purple.

"Look," said Audrey. "You can see bats."

She pointed up, out. Bats flitted above the road in the gloaming, creatures halfway between birds and shadows.

"That's weird," Audrey said. "They're usually hibernating by now."

"Bats are not true hibernators," said Bill. "If it's warm, they'll come out even if it's late in the year."

It was warm—the weather had been getting colder day by day, but today had been warm—it was still warm, even as the sun was going down. Audrey knew this was a sign of a very big storm.

"I heard a story," said Bill, "can't remember where, so I can't vouchsafe it, about a spelunker who got stuck in a cave-in. He had his leg trapped under a pile of rocks."

"I've heard about that. He cut off his own leg with a pocketknife."

"No, that's another story. This one has to do with—well, OK—the guy was wearing a red sweater. And pretty soon, the people who lived near the cave started noticing bats with red strings tied around their little feet. Somehow he was catching bats and tying threads from his sweater to the bats. And the people figured out what it meant, and went to the cave, and he was rescued."

Audrey, sitting in the roomy leather passenger seat beside him, had not been jotting any of this down, but by the end of the anecdote she felt she ought to have been—that somehow, this silly story about a trapped spelunker scapturing bats by hand and tying strings to their feet was relevant to Bill's pursuit of the monster.

Audrey was first, foremost, an adventurer—journalism to her was an excuse to explore the world, in order to render it. Poetry didn't interest her much—it always sat still on the page in her eyes, looking opaque and pointless, and she frankly didn't much care for fiction, either. Other people's imaginations she found ponderously uninteresting compared to the real world. Often, into her adulthood, when she saw a movie "based on a true story," she would get curious about it and do a little research, and always find a story far more complicated and interesting than what the movie had depicted. Human imagination seemed to distort, simplify, and dumb down everything it touched. In the years that would come, Audrey would sit in a lot of passenger seats scribbling into her little yellow steno pads—in Afghanistan, in Venezuela, in Burma, in Cuba, and countless times all over America. She had a knack for listening. Her trick, which she developed as a teenager, was to keep herself out of it: No matter who she was talking with, whether or not she silently believed her interviewee to be a lunatic, a narcissist, a criminal, or an idiot, he or she always believed Audrey was on their side. She sat there without a note of judgment, armed with curiosity, asking questions, and taking notes.

They parked in the gravel parking lot of the Brainard Lake Wilderness Area. There was one other car parked there, a white minivan. It looked ominous.

"They're probably campers," said Audrey.

"I hope they're prepared," said Bill. "I heard it's supposed to snow tonight."

Car doors slammed, their boots crunched on the gravel, bats dipped and flitted in the purpling air over their heads. A wall of clouds was moving fast across the sky from northwest to southeast: The clouds were rolling visibly, expanding and unfurling like white paint in water. The storm was moving in.

Bill hitched on a small camouflage backpack. He had binoculars and a clunky, ridiculous pair of night-vision goggles around his neck. He went into the back of the van and came out with one of the rifles.

"You're not going to *shoot* him, are you?"

Audrey caught herself sounding ridiculous: Who was "him"? In truth, she'd only been a little shocked to see Bill holding the gun.

"This gun shoots tranquilizer darts. If it happens that we get close enough to a Sasquatch, I would try to hit him with a tranquilizer so I can examine him more closely, take photographs, and hopefully tag him."

There was nothing about the gun suggesting to Audrey that it might not be a lethal hunting rifle that shot ordinary, lethal bullets. The barrel was long and slender, with a mounted scope and laser sighting, and the gun was as black, complicated, and evil looking as these machines had always looked and always would to Audrey, and, despite that, she thought him charmingly deluded. She liked Bill Burns, considered him a very sweet, nice man—round bellied and almost white bearded, he could have played Santa Claus—and it was incongruous to see such a sinister-looking thing in his hands. The juxtaposition was comical, but it wasn't funny.

He showed her one of the tranquilizer darts: It was a long, thin plastic tube—a hypodermic needle with a puff of fuzzy red stuff on the end of it.

"That's the tailpiece," said Bill, flicking at it. "It stabilizes the dart during flight, like the feathers of an arrow."

They walked together in the woods for about an hour. Audrey crept along beside him in silence as he crept through the woods, sweeping them with his tranquilizer gun. All the trees that were going to shed their leaves had shed them by now, and these dead leaves crunched brittlely under their feet. They were walking aimlessly, it seemed to Audrey.

Once, they heard movement—something rustling in the leaves somewhere off to their left. He swiftly pointed his gun in the direction of the sound. The jittery red dot of the gun's laser was a tiny, gleaming pinprick of human invention in an otherwise natural environment: No light so bright and so red could possibly exist in nature, and its presence here looked jarring—ugly and sinister even to Audrey, who was no romantic.

The sound had been made by a small group of deer.

They moved very slowly. They spoke only when necessary, and only in whispers.

They searched for the Black Rock Monster.

All the while Audrey was feeling two conflicting feelings.

The first? Absurdity: She was humoring a lunatic. Trooping around in these empty woods with Bill felt to her exactly as if she were playing a game of make-believe with a much younger child whom she

105

loved and wanted to make happy. One of her little cousins. Let's search for the monster! Look! Over there! I think I see him! Do *you* see him? But whenever she had been in such situations, she had always felt a tacit understanding between her and even a very young child that what they were doing was imaginary—that they did not actually entertain any real hope of seeing the monster. But this man was an adult, decades older than her, a good decade or so at least older than her own parents, an adult with a PhD no less, a scientist, who had credentials and many published papers, who'd held a distinguished chair at a public research university. And here he was, chasing after fairies with a butterfly net. How could she be feeling this way with a man like him? Now that he wasn't just sitting in the hotel bar blithering about the Bering Land Bridge and *Gigantopithecus*, now that he was stomping around in dark, empty woods with a loaded tranquilizer rifle in serious hopes of spotting and anesthetizing Bigfoot, she was more incredulous than she would have been if her little cousins had told her they'd seen a unicorn. She would be more inclined to believe them—or at least believe that they believed themselves. Believing, belief: These were not good words to Audrey.

The second feeling, then, in conflict with the first, was a blobby, ineffable tingling sensation in her stomach, and it was not unpleasant. No—it was a good feeling. It was a feeling she had felt maybe only a dozen times in her life. Once, she had felt it (to her horror, now) in church. She had felt it with that same Sunday-school teacher, whom she had challenged with her first skeptical inquiry, who had been the first person to tell her that "absence of evidence is not evidence of absence." She remembered feeling it in that room—it almost looked like a nursery, but with colorful wraparound wallpaper of watercolor paintings depicting Bible stories: Noah's Ark, Daniel in the lions' den, advancing through the Old Testament into the New, and ending with Jesus on the Olive Mount, surrounded by children and fluffy, trembly-eyed lambs. She had been a child. She had liked the colorful wallpaper. She'd liked Mrs. James's honeyed voice, and she liked Bible-story time. She liked the stories. They charmed and haunted her at the same time. And she would remember feeling that feeling for the first time in her life in that colorful, ugly, low-ceilinged room in the basement of Bethany First Baptist Church. If Audrey were pressed to describe it she would have said: It feels like when you sit weird on your leg and it goes to sleep, and then you suddenly stand up, and at first, for a moment, the feeling of all the blood rushing back into your leg is painful, but then there's the tingling feeling, the pins and needles in reverse. It was one of the most pleasurable physical sensations she had ever felt (she did not think she had ever had an orgasm; childish sensations like these were what she had to offer up for comparison now). Well, it feels like that, she would have said, but in your stomach, and the rest of your body relaxes too—untenses, feels pleasantly chilled and calm. Your breath becomes shorter, you feel almost dizzy, but not in a bad way. Anyway. It was a feeling so personal, so privately and inwardly felt, that she did not feel like she had ever been able to describe it adequately to anyone.

And, well: She felt it that night. They did not find the Black Rock Monster, or Sasquatch, or Bigfoot, or Brother Who Comes Back Before the Next Very Big Winter, but that spiny physical feeling did not go away, even after Bill gave up for the night and decided it was time to turn back. It was full dark now. Bill shouldered his tranquilizer rifle and clicked on the Maglite he slipped from its loop in his belt—no longer concerned with a low profile, he walked in an ordinary crunch-crunch-crunch across the mushy forest floor. The sky was a uniform gray and the moon had risen, but wasn't visible: It was a pale, milky blur behind the clouds, a flashlight under a sheet.

She noticed, in relief, that he had a good sense of direction—a good thing, as Audrey had essentially put her faith in it. He had seemed confident that he knew where they were going—plus he was much older than she was, an adult, an old man even, who had been doing this a long time and was uncontestably still alive. And, sure enough, soon the Econoline in the parking lot became visible through the trees. When they returned, the other car that had been in the parking lot, the white minivan, was no longer there.

While driving them back into town on Route 9, Bill seemed to have convinced himself that Colorado was out of the Sasquatch's range, actually. He was a man who said the word "actually" often.

"It is entirely possible," he speculated, "that a very small breeding population does exist here, but typically they prefer wetter, more temperate climates. The vast majority of the Sasquatch are almost certainly concentrated in the Pacific Northwest, most of them in Oregon, Washington, British Columbia, the Idaho panhandle."

He went on awhile in this way, helpfully, Audrey scribbling down usable quotes again, hoping that her scrawly handwriting written in the dark in a moving vehicle would be legible later. Bill, in his monologue, was distracted enough that it was Audrey who glanced up from her steno pad at the road in front of them and screamed. Bill reawakened from within himself in an instant, and stopped the car.

He did not slam on the brakes. He pulled the van to a halt as quickly as he could without letting the tires squeal. There was something standing in the road.

The headlights of the van harshly illuminated the cones of the tall fir trees beside the road and threw their long, high shadows against each other. Below the trees, there was something standing in the road. They were right behind a sharp blind curve around the side of the mountain: To their right was a vertical wall of dynamited rock, and to their left was a metal guardrail, and below that probably a steep grade and dense forest. The thing was standing at the edge of the curve, in the left lane of the road. It looked like it was made of shag carpeting. It was hard even to tell what color it was with the headlights on it. Its shadow stretched up into the trees. It did not appear to have a face, or its face was completely obscured under long, shaggy hair. It stood upright. It stood still. It was shaped roughly like a human being. It moved slightly. It swayed. For a very long time, all they could do was sit in the van, parked with engine idling in the right lane of the narrow mountain road, staring at it, unmoving and silent as it was. Did it have arms and legs? It was hard to say. It only looked like a vaguely contoured column of long, pale fur, or grass, or hay.

Bill whispered: *"Shit!"*

Audrey saw an instant later why: Another light was gathering on the sides of the trees. There was another car approaching the curve from the opposite direction. The other light brightened and grew, and all in a moment the shaggy column of hair became a body, with arms and legs. The thing walked—or sort of shambled, with long arms swinging at its sides—over to the guardrail in a few steps, climbed over it easily, off the road, descended into the woods, and was gone. The next instant, the other car swung around the curve, momentarily blinding them with its high beams, and blasted past them, its driver apparently oblivious, leaving behind it only the van's headlights shining onto the trees, onto nothing.

Bill moved faster than Audrey would have thought the old, fat man capable of moving. He unbuckled his seat belt, scrambled into the back, snatched the tranquilizer gun from the rack, and was out of the van via the side door, not stopping to shut it, running across the road while snapping on his silly slime-green night-vision goggles. He scurried over the guardrail and into the woods, looking like a hamster: frantic, uncoordinated.

Audrey hadn't even unbuckled her seat belt. The van's engine was still on. For a moment she just sat there, wondering if he wanted her to wait for him in the car. He probably didn't want anything of her. He wasn't thinking of her at all. She reached over to the driver's side of the dashboard and sank in the button that turned the hazard lights on. She got out of the van and shivered: The temperature had dropped by at least ten degrees since they'd left Brainard Lake. A snowflake glittered in the headlights as it fluttered to the tarmac, on which it landed and instantly disappeared.

It was a bright night, the sky pale and swollen with the snow it was preparing to shed. The blinking hazard lights added a pulsing orange glow to the night. Audrey crossed the road and climbed with a little difficulty (she was short) over the guardrail. The grade below the road was so steep she nearly fell, twigs and pebbles skittering and raining beneath her feet as she stumbleslid down the embankment.

The woods were dark and silent. She walked a few steps into the forest. She could not see Bill. Or anything. Her eyes gradually adjusted to the dark. The light from the headlights of the van parked above and behind her cast hard yellow light on the tops of the fir trees.

When her eyes had adjusted to the dark, she saw a tiny, shivering pinprick of piercing red light. She watched it swim through the trees, flashing in and out of visibility. It jumped and slashed from one place to another. It was the only thing she could concentrate her vision on that would not move and transform away from her.

She did not know how long she stumbled, groping from one tree trunk to the next, in the darkness. Ten minutes? More? Impossible to say. Time stretched, dilated.

And she saw it again. The thing that had been standing in the road. It moved between the trunks of the trees. It was pale, ashen gray. Or maybe light brown. It did not look much different from the stuff of the surrounding forest. It was a person, walking out there, perhaps fifty feet away from her. She heard the crunching of its footsteps on the leaves and pine needles.

The shining red prick of light found it. Among the few flakes of snow that had begun to fall, she saw the perfect mathematical line of its beam slicing through the dark. She heard a popping sound—a swift, sharp crack, a bolt of compressed air released. Somewhere far off to her left, Bill turned on his flashlight. A hard cone of yellowy white beamed through the forest. He shakily trained his flashlight on the thing. The light bounced and jittered with Bill's footsteps as he approached it. Not far ahead, through the trees, Audrey could see the needle with the red tuft on the end of it sticking out of the thing's side. The thing stopped, yanked it out, and held it to its face, looking

109

at it with eyes obscured behind wild, shaggy fur. The thing threw it on the ground and began to run. With the beam of the flashlight aimed at his back, the carpet-man ran, crashing blindly through the brush, waving his arms in front of him. He looked as if he were running away from a beehive he'd just thrown a rock at. He was slowing down before her eyes. Occasional snowflakes twinkled in the beam of hard artificial light. The man-thing ran as if the air around him were thickening: slower and slower—until he was not running but staggering, reaching out and groping his way from one tree to the next, flailing his arms out in front of him for temporary purchase between every step. Bill was close behind him with the flashlight. Audrey recognized the man-thing's walk. She knew who he was. He lurched forward, tripped, and fell.

Audrey called his name: "Jim!"

Audrey and Bill both ran through the woods toward the fallen body of what Bill still must have believed might be the first anesthetized specimen of "the Sasquatch," and what Audrey already knew to be her brother. Bill, who had been chasing him, reached him first.

When Audrey reached him, Bill was cursing to himself.

"It's some guy in a ghillie suit," said Bill.

Audrey said: "It's my brother."

And so it was. Her older brother's painfully stupid face peered out on top of a strange suit made of what looked like tattered fabric, string, and dry grass. He was conscious, but barely so. His eyes were slits. He was writhing on the ground, moaning.

"Jim. Can you hear me?"

Jim said: "No . . . No . . . No. Don't hurt me. Don't hurt me. Don't hurt me."

Jim looked like someone asleep, but having a terrible nightmare—someone you are afraid to shake, because he will wake disoriented and confused. His head rolled heavily from side to side.

"What's a ghillie suit?"

"It's what he's wearing. It's deep camouflage. Hunters and snipers wear them."

Audrey kneeled on the ground beside him and touched his face.

"Jim," she said. "What are you doing here?"

She fingered the material of the ghillie suit. All the long, shaggy hairs were made of shredded brown twine.

"Will he be OK?"

"How much does he weigh?"

"I don't know. Like, two hundred pounds, maybe?"

"He should be fine. The tranq was ketamine. Hard to overdose on. What in the *hell* was he doing standing in the road out there?"

"I don't know."

Jim wasn't fully asleep. Dragged to his feet, he was just conscious enough to walk with Bill and Audrey supporting him, one on each side, holding his arms around their shoulders, drunken sailor at dawn. They walked with him—Jim dragging his feet and stumbling, tripping on his own feet, the heavy weight of his lifeless arm on her shoulder—along the ditch under the road, hoping for a place where the embankment was shallow enough to get him up it and then over the guardrail. And so, when they finally found a way to drag him up and over and onto the road—an old, fat man and a seventeen-year-old girl trying to move an able-bodied and nearly unconscious man in his twenties—they had to walk this way with him a good while up the shoulder of the road with the snowfall coming down faster and the temperature sinking, fearing that a car might not see the three of them around the sharply curving, dark, narrow mountain road, all the while Jim muttering, "No, no, no," and "Don't hurt me."

At last they saw the pulsing orange glow of the hazard lights flashing, and came to the van, still parked in the middle of the right lane of the road with the engine on and the tailpipe panting smoke into the cold air. Both of them exhausted under Jim's weight, Bill managed to get the back doors of the van open, and they maneuvered him into it until his body found the mattress on the floor and sank into its contours at once, like a baseball into the palm of a well-worn glove. He was asleep almost instantly. Feeling comfortable while barely conscious in unfamiliar beds in strange places was one of Jim's few skills.

"Well, then. Are you going to put this in your article?" said Bill.

"No," she said.

But she did not also say that there would be no article. Audrey knew she would not write the article, because to omit this incident from the evening would be untruthful, and she could not have that, and her mother would self-immolate from embarrassment if anyone heard about this, and she could not have that, either. "This"—whatever this was. It was unclear what Jim had been doing that night—the best she could guess was that it might have been some ludicrous plot to try to make money somehow from orchestrating fake Black Rock Monster sightings. (Listen to yourself—"fake" Black Rock Monster sightings?) It was probably something he'd cooked up together with Duncan Hodges. She would never ask him. She pretended it had never happened, and either Jim did the same, or he didn't remember it. She maybe would have asked him if they'd gotten out years distant from it, but she wouldn't get the chance, as Jim would only live for another year or so after that night. Later that night, Bill would help Audrey smuggle Jim into the hotel through a side door. Audrey would steal a key to a vacant room from the pegboard behind the front desk, and they would lay him on top of the starchy white bed, the shredded twine of his ghillie suit rustling and fanning out around his body. He would look like an enormous sheepdog asleep atop the sheets. The following morning, he would be gone, and any evidence of his being there—footprints in the snow—would be rapidly snowed over.

And Audrey would never tell anyone about what happened until much later in her life. The journalist Warren P. Murray, when once asked why as a reporter for *The New York Times* during the Korean War, he had knowingly suppressed certain information that might have been useful to China and the Soviet Union had it been in print, answered: "Sometimes it is hard to be both a good newspaperman and a good American. When in doubt, my allegiance was to my country first." When Audrey had read that, she balked at it, appalled at Murray's attitude. A country is an artificial, imaginary construction—one's allegiance ought always to be first to the truth. Transparency before all else. News is something someone wants suppressed. Everything else is just advertising. This late encounter with her brother had put Audrey, for the first time she would really remember, in the position of being the someone who wants something suppressed. Was the truth so sacred that it was worth embarrassing her own family? No. Is something sacred by degrees, then, sacred at all?

Bill slammed the back doors of the van shut. And then he stood there, bracing himself against the back of the van with his hands spread palms out on the doors. He shook his head, looking down at the ground, down at his boots on the road. Audrey began to move toward the passenger door of the van, but when Bill didn't move, she stopped, turned back, and looked at him.

It is an arresting thing to see deeply felt emotion unhidden in the face of a grown man—well, deeply felt emotions other than anger, that is. Audrey's heart had gone lightly into her tagalong on Bill's hunt that night. Her heart was not light now, but for reasons that had nothing to do with the Black Rock Monster. She had not expected to see the Black Rock Monster. She had not expected to see anything at all. But looking at Bill now, she saw that he was embarrassed—humiliated—and, more so, disappointed. He had the look of a man who'd gathered the whole town to watch him fly with his wax wings, taken his leap into the void, and promptly fallen off the building. She stood behind the van, her hands sunk awkwardly in her coat pockets, waiting for this grown man to collect himself. She wondered if she should say something to him. She wondered if it would be best to leave him alone awhile with his thwarted yearning for the impossible, if she should go sit quietly in the passenger seat, or walk far enough away from the van for him to feel alone. She wondered if she should try to comfort him—put a hand on his back or something, pat it. There, there. There, there.

But why should *she* comfort *him*? It was *her* brother who was a drunk: broke, stupid, homeless, hopeless, insane, wearing a ghillie suit, sleeping off the effects of a tranquilizer dart meant for Bigfoot on a mattress in the back of a van. It was her brother who was beyond saving. It was her brother who would commit suicide one year later. It was her brother who would park his car in the dirt lot in front of the Rattlesnake Gulch Trailhead, the trail that leads to the ruins of the Tabor Hotel, where she did not believe Duncan Hodges had seen the Black Rock Monster. It was her brother who would inject a lethal dose of heroin, put his head in a plastic bag, roll a rubber band over it, recline the driver's seat all the way, lie back, and go to sleep. It was her brother who would do this in the middle of the night on the night before Thanksgiving, which would be Audrey's first visit home from her freshman year of college. It was her brother who would not show up for the meal, but this would cause no special alarm, as his not showing up to things was not and would not be anything new. That is why her family would go most of the day before they knew what her brother had done. And once they, and the town, knew what he had done, all would offer her family their sympathy, but none would be too surprised.

So why should she be the one to comfort Bill, who seemed to be suffering an attack of existential despair because he hadn't discovered Bigfoot—again. Oh, excuse me—"the Sasquatch."

But anyway, she didn't. She didn't comfort him. She didn't try to say anything to him. She just stood behind him on the shoulder of the road, shivering, practically feeling the mercury drop in the thermometer, with her hands in the pockets of her coat, wishing to be inside the van with the heater on. A car passed: It slowed down in curiosity, whoever was inside it looking in passing at the van parked in the middle of the other lane, an older man and a teenage girl standing around behind it. Audrey was afraid of the story whoever was in the car might be telling themselves about what they were seeing. The headlights swept fast across the trees and left them standing in the dark again.

Bill Burns walked to the edge of the woods. His boots crunched arrhythmically on the gravel as he crossed the road, and then he simply stood in front of the guardrail, the place where the forest had been cut down to clear the way for the road, and seemed to stare into the woods beyond the road. She didn't know if he was staring—his back was to her—but what else could he have been doing? Was he staring, or looking? He still actually believed there was something out there.

After all this—long after Bill Burns, summertime baboon expert and Bigfoot hunter in autumn, packed his van, checked out of the hotel, and drove back home to Washington the next day—wait—no—it wasn't the next day, because the town got snowed in that night, and they closed the roads: So it must have been the day after that when he left—Audrey would think back on him fondly, although she never saw, heard, or spoke to him again. He had made her feel something disquieting but not unpleasant: a desire to believe in something that has not been proven. It was that indescribable tingling sensation in her stomach. It was a foolish, childish feeling, wonderful to feel. It was almost religious. This man really believed that there were still mysteries left. He really believed there were unknown things still possible to discover. Not just on other planets, or up in the canopies of rain forests, or down at the bottom of the ocean, but right here, in North America, in Colorado. His world was vast, and his curiosity excessively generous. He was a grown-up little boy, who did not fear monsters in the woods so much as he loved them and wanted to get close enough to throw a rock at them. He was naive, but he did not mind being seen as naive. Audrey liked people who do not mind being seen as naive, and always would. Bill's fault was a mind that was too open. Is it worse to have a mind that's too closed, or one that's too open? Was Audrey's conviction that skepticism is better than faith a kind of faith itself, and therefore hypocrisy? If he'd asked her, Bill Burns would have been the only person in her life to make her hesitate before answering: no.

Snow had begun to fall in earnest. The heavy snow fell in silence.

Not a silence of cunning or fear, but of listening.

She could feel that it would be a big storm. She could see it in the sky. It was the middle of November (if anything, they were long overdue already for the first big storm of the season), and lately it had been getting colder and colder, until today, which had been unseasonably warm. Audrey did not know the meteorological reason for this—something to do with fronts and barometric pressure—but she knew a warm day in winter was the prelude to a snowstorm. The milky ceiling of clouds had sunk low enough to hide the peaks of the mountains. The weatherman was predicting at least twelve, possibly up to twenty inches that night. And that, she knew, watching fat, wet snowflakes drift across the high, dark forest, was good for business.

Fishmaker
Evelyn Hampton

THEN I MADE FISH.

I was living in the bank of a river. I'd found a small den and outfitted it simply.

I needed only a few things: work to do, a place where I could do it, and rest.

First I would decide on a design for a fish, then prepare the parts from a supply of materials I kept on shelves I'd built of wood dragged from the river.

The lining of a fish is a form of electricity.

A fish's brain can be made of almost anything as long as it's small enough to fit inside the skull. A fish's skull can be made from windshield-wiper-fluid caps. These could be found in the river.

My favorite was plunging my hand into the sack of dry fish-eye lenses. The little pink ovals felt like sun-warm sand on a beach, a day of no worries. I knew the delight of a chef when finally her pantry is stocked only with the best ingredients—she can taste and touch and look at them, content that everything she makes will be delicious.

Brain stems are small white rods that become translucent as soon as they are attached to the lining.

When I ground the seeds for the paste I would cast teeth from, I added a pinch of white pepper from the shaker on my table.

On the basis of its ingredients, life shouldn't exist.

Making the eyes was a most delicate process. Sometimes, anticipating the demands of the work before me, my hands would shake so much, I wouldn't be able to take the rubber band off the bag of irises. They looked like brown mustard seeds and would take on the consistency of tapioca pearls when I placed them in eye fluid. I used a tweezers for this, after my hands had steadied.

For the blood I would make a kind of jelly. The stuff would visibly hiss when I added the final ingredient, a dash of sea salt I'd brought with me from the city.

I had lived so many different lives in so many different places, the sight of the salt shaker, this little container of crystals, gave me such comfort—seeing it day after day on its shelf was like seeing the face of a dear one who had aged gently beside me.

I liked to think of that hiss as the fish's first breath. It wasn't a sound of relief but of shock and discomfort. Life must be surprised to be so suddenly embodied.

I am old, let it be no mystery. I'm older than walls and most days I feel stiffer than a brick.

Something I learned making fish is that life isn't very good at living— it has to be coaxed and prodded to take to its next body.

And then even after it has taken and gives every sign of being a success, life tends to remain limp and dormant.

Anyone who has lived in a winter climate and watched snow falling on the first day of May knows how very far away life can get from the ones craving it.

I am so old now, I keep my skin in a zipped bag in the refrigerator. It stays fresher longer; when I put it on, I like how cool I feel, almost as if I am young again. The coolness of my skin during those first minutes out of the refrigerator reminds me of the walls of the den. Those were happy days, making fish. Even my shadow was content.

In the outer wall, I'd made a hatch to throw finished fish out of, into the river. The hatch also functioned as a window for me. I liked a certain kind of light.

117

Evelyn Hampton

It would frighten me to look into a fish's eyes the moment before I threw it out of the hatch. I would see there a dilating terror that encompassed everything. Was it knowledge?

How had knowledge gotten into the fish? I hadn't put it there. Knowledge wasn't one of the ingredients. Consciousness, never.

Usually there would be a tomcat crouched in the hatch. The look in a fish's eyes told me it already knew this cat, had seen it a hundred times, had been caught and eaten by it in lifetimes past. *Please don't throw me out of that hatch!*, its eyes were pleading.

But I always threw the fish out. I wasn't going to spare them from what they knew was coming. I had made them—I was much worse than that tomcat.

They should have been relieved to be tossed out of the hatch. To escape their maker—their death.

At first I resented that tomcat gobbling up my careful handiwork.

But when I watched with an attitude a little more detached than disdainful, I noticed that not every fish got caught. Only the ones life hadn't really taken to were gobbled. The ones in which life was vigorous thrashed their tails and flipped their bodies and managed to evade old Tomcat.

These fish made it into the river, where other perils worse than Tomcat awaited. The other fish, the weak ones Tomcat caught, would not have survived anyway. They were pretty fish, and exacting to make, but they were not hardy enough to be real.

In time I considered Tomcat my cocreator. His job was to test the final product.

I mentioned I liked a certain kind of light.

Indirect, reflected. The hatch let in sunlight reflected by the river. On my ceiling I could see the water's surface eddying and flowing its shadows.

Lucky me. Nobody from my old lives knew where to find me. I called myself Lucky.

Old lovers, old loves; debts and family: They had exhausted all my old haunts. I was relieved to have finally been forgotten.

Being alive is mostly a matter of believing you're alive.

Once their eyes were attached to the lining, the fish could see. Once they could see, they could believe. They blinked and blinked.

The air in my den was cool and damp, excellent for naps.

Before I became Lucky, I was no good at sleeping. I just couldn't find the right time or position. I wandered restlessly, searching for relief.

When you're happy, sleeping is easy. Counterintuitive maybe, but when you're happy, it's easier to leave your life. Relaxed, you can slip right out of it. You can always come back to it later, and if you can't, no big deal.

Maybe it's a matter of having proper lighting, happiness. Light should not impede the ascension of dreams.

Yet one day it did. Happy, I was lying on my back, preparing for a nap. I gazed up at the ceiling, and instead of river light flowing past, I saw a brittle, jagged kind of light, more knife than light. I could not look at it without feeling as if my teeth were going to crumble right then and fall out of my head.

Lucky I have been, and Lucky I no longer am, I thought.

I went to the hatch and looked down at the river.

So long, easy sleep. Good-bye, happiness.

River? No. That mass of cracks was not what a river was.

Time to find new names for everything. *Despair. Apocalypse.* Old Tomcat yowled. He hissed. He moaned. He grunted. He lay down on the ledge outside the hatch and let loose a litter of kittens.

Evelyn Hampton

So. Old Tomcat was neither Old nor Tomcat. Figured. She would need a new name too.

And these mewling things beside her, they would need names. She licked their heads between their blind eyes. She laid her head back and let them feed on her milky body.

Below lay the broken bones of what used to be called River.

Despair, I named the kitten with a white stripe between black eyes. Apocalypse, I named the one that looked vaguely at me. Two-Headed, Nobody, and Sheila were the other three.

I fed Not-Old-Not-Tomcat some of my fish ingredients. She ate them scavengingly while Despair, Apocalypse, Two-Headed, Nobody, and Sheila mewled and sucked on her. *Not*, I shortened her name to. She seemed to have diminished considerably from her Old Tomcat days.

I called myself Un. The Undoer. Undone.

Not ate the eyes one at a time. I let my hand reach out and pat her head. She ate a few brain stems.

My thoughts turned then to the ocean.

*

Sometimes things just dry up—that might make a nice, stupid ending.

Not,
Despair,
Apocalypse,
Two-Headed,
Nobody,
Sheila,
and me, Un. We were a company.

In my den our business was doing nothing. Making nothing. Going nowhere.

The cracks in the mud of the river sometimes looked at me. Sizing me up. *Why don't you come with us,* they said in a masked voice coming from somewhere under the cracked earth. *Sometimes things just dry up.*

Get over it.

Two-Headed developed a strain of apathy that made him want to devour me.

He would sleep on my neck. Always this led to chewing. Even his dreams were hungry. Well, so were mine, when I managed to have one.

I sprinkled fish scales on the rug when I wanted to see pure appetite's teeth. Pure appetite's claws. Quite a lot of cat blood was shed because of my boredom.

Two-Headed always got the most of whatever it was. I named him Chief Executive Officer of Discorporation.

I made a little sign. Wrote it in cat's blood, hung it above the door to the den. DISCORPORATION.

Things were becoming squalid. Things were, shall we say, in a state of drastic decline.

The cracks would laugh sometimes. *Why don't you . . .* they said one morning. Their voice sounded like a platter heaped with pancakes dripping with syrup. *Help us, Un,* they dripped. Only the syrup was blood.

As a souvenir, I kept a little bit of fish lining in a small glass box. Blue sparks still shot through the lining. I would watch them through the walls of the box. At night I would hear crackling like the static between radio stations. It was the lining, searching for a body to light with life.

How about a song, I would hear a voice within the lining ask itself. This would be in the middle of the night. The cats of Discorporation around me howling in their sleep. *This one goes out to . . .* and then the static would begin crackling again, this time to a different rhythm.

The fact that Two-Headed actually had two heads did not change anything.

I imagine the lining of an antelope or a dog would behave in much the same way fish lining did.

I could not have been a maker of mountain lions or of humans—I only cared about making fish.

The lining of a hawk—it would make an elegant jacket. Dark and fitted.

I am old, but I still consider the possibilities.

Though mostly what I do is look back, I still see:

Sometimes there's even someone new coming toward me.

Who will she be this time? Or he. Long nights, little sleep—I'll take just about anything. Even if it's only my own past coming back. (There is only so much future. Only so much raw material for time to make its designs upon.)

Sheila was becoming more and more stunning. One of those objects that exist only once they have disappeared. Her fur had begun to shimmer. Colors undulated along her back. Would not let me pet her. Crouched all day at the hatch looking down. Did not even come down to fight Two-Headed for a bit of brain.

The less she behaved like a cat, the more stunningly beautiful she became.

Suspicious, Two-Headed would hiss at her. She was not being enough of a cat to satisfy him.

Look at me, she said one morning.

I was still in bed, static lining my drowse with its shifting frequencies.

I looked toward the hatch. I had recognized the voice as Sheila's. It sounded exactly the way I expected Sheila to sound, like a piece of purple velvet wrapped around sunflower seeds, tied off with jute thread.

Look down, Sheila's voice said.

There in the riverbed sat an old boat, decrepit, DELIVERANCE in faded paint on its keel.

A woman sat in the captain's nest. Hair black as it gets. Purple shimmer wafting off the waves of its hanks.

Later I was not surprised to find that the lining had been lifted from my little glass box. Its lid had been tipped open. Only a few shreds of the lining were left. The work, I would recognize it in my sleep, of a cat's teeth. Sheila.

She turned a key; the rudder sputtered. I saw the boat had tires.

All aboard, Sheila said.

*

That's how we got to the ocean. Sheila drove.

When we arrived, we rented a little cabin on the beach. BEACH-COMBERS PARADISE said the sign. The owners hadn't made the *S* possessive. Paradise belonged to nobody.

Which reminds me—Nobody hadn't made it. He'd leaped from *Deliverance* and took off into the forest with Apocalypse. Not, Two-Headed, Despair, Sheila, and me, Un—we were the only occupants of Paradise. It was the off-season.

Apparently other people were not interested in seeing how towering the waves can be in January.

They want sunsets, Mel said. Mel was one of the caretakers of Paradise. The other was Holly. She was ill; dying, Mel said. They'd come here so she could do it in peace.

I asked why we never saw Holly at the beach. Was she too sick even to sit?

Doesn't like to see the horizon anymore, Mel said. It makes her queasy. Ceiling and feet—those are the things she likes to see now. If you come to visit, wear nice shoes, she'll appreciate it.

*

I spent days walking the beach. It is essentially a boneyard, the beach, a vast cemetery. It comforted me to be surrounded by so many possibilities. I began scheming about how I could use these washed-up pieces of life, maybe make fish again. . . .

I would look out at the horizon, wondering how many of *my* fish had made it that far.

Mine—I still thought of them that way.

The horizon is made of pure wondering, by the way. We make it distant merely by longing for it, since longing pushes away its object at the same time it reaches for it.

Sheila mostly stayed in the cabin with the cats, fiddling with lids and tea. At night we would sit together on the deck, our bodies almost touching. I would feel the crackle of the lining leaping between us, arc of energy. I wondered how long it would be before we . . .

We should visit Holly, Sheila said one night.

We?

The woman's dying, and we haven't visited yet.

OK, say hi for me, I said. I was frightened of Holly. No, I was frightened of death. Death had nothing to do with Holly, nothing to do with anything at all; it was impersonal, that's what frightened me about it. No name can keep it away.

The crackle of the lining I liked. Even the hiss of the fish. The look in their eyes as they began to live. Life—I craved it. I wanted to make more and more of it. Gather together all the fragments on the beach, make something that would be able to see me.

The life in another's eyes verified my life. But death, it took me away from me.

No, we should both go. Out of respect. For Mel. Think of what he must be going through.

I imagined Mel actually passing through something, Holly's death a dark corridor, Mel blinking and crawling through it.

We knocked on the door of their cabin the next morning.

Mel's face was no longer Mel's face; it belonged to gray, like a soft, unappetizing cheese.

We brought you something, said Sheila as Mel let us in. I thought, *We did?* I didn't recall bringing anything. Yet I watched as Sheila pulled it from her pocket—the fish lining. *My* fish lining, from my little glass box. She hadn't devoured it after all. She'd been keeping it with us, and from me.

As she handed it to Mel, blue sparks fell to the floor and crackled for a moment at our feet like sparklers, then went quiet. In his hand the lining danced and laughed and leapt and threw flickers of blue into the room. I thought of the river again, its surface reflected on the ceiling of my den.

She'll love it, said Mel. Thank you.

He unfolded it, then folded it, then put it in his shirt pocket. I'll introduce you to Holly, he said.

We followed him to the bedroom. I hoped that when he opened the door, the room would be empty except for a chest of drawers made of dark, deeply grained wood, the kind that captures light and gives the impression that it contains all of space in its surface. Each drawer would be a different size. *This is Holly*, Mel would say. He would open a drawer; inside, a blue marble. In another drawer, a wind-up eye. In another, one of those birds that endlessly dips its head to drink water from a dish. In another, another, smaller drawer, taking me farther from reality . . .

125

Instead what we saw in the bedroom was a bed, and on it a woman, a real, dying one. I knew she was dying by her breath—it could hardly lift itself out of her body anymore, and the look in Holly's eyes seemed to be falling inward toward it. I had watched this happen with the fish: As they died they would disappear into their own eyes.

Scattered on the floor around her were yellow tissues, books, dishes that must have held Mel's meals so that he never had to leave her side.

Come in, Holly said when she saw us. She smiled a little and didn't lift her head off the pillow.

Mel introduced us as *our guests*, which I could tell he immediately regretted because Holly's face drew into itself and she said, I'm sorry there's such a mess.

We're not that kind of guest, Sheila said. She smiled. She knew how to have the right effect. Holly smiled and Mel said, They brought you a gift.

Oh! said Holly. I love gifts.

When we left, Holly's eyes were shut. The square of lining flickered in one of her hands.

*

Late that night, Sheila and I sat on the deck of our cabin. I was waiting for her to lift one of her hands to the back of my neck, which tonight felt too exposed. I knew the movement was coming; I could feel it weighing itself between us, making the air around our mouths ready. When we breathed, the readiness entered our heads. *Now, Sheila*, I was thinking. *Now is the time to touch me please.*

Sheila lifted one of her hands, placed it on my knee. Are you mad? she asked. I gave away your lining.

Stole it, then gave it away, I said. I tried to laugh, laughed a little. After you did away with one of my cats.

I didn't make the river dry up, at least. That one wasn't my fault.

I could feel the air crinkling around her smile, touching her teeth.

Her hand was still on my knee. The weight of it on my body kept answering her question. Was I mad? Keep touching me.

Sheila, I said.

At night there's no horizon; or it's so near, everything exists within it. We walked through the boneyard of the beach and at a point in the night that had no depth, we slept.

*

In the morning Mel stood on our deck. His face still belonged to gray, but there was relief around his chest. Holly was dead. She had died during the night. I could tell he was breathing better now that death had left that room. Even though it had left by way of Holly.

I wanted to invite you to Holly's funeral, he said. It'll just be us. Her body's already on the boat. He gestured toward something between the back of his shirt and the horizon. Floating there was a red boat about the size of *Deliverance*, but eminently more seaworthy, to judge by the fact that it could actually float.

In it, Holly lay on a simple straw mat, her hands resting on it along-side her nightgown, inside of which her body seemed to have faded to a flat white line. Sheila and I sat on benches around her while Mel navigated.

Do you want this back? he asked once he'd stilled the engine and we were floating with the current. He'd taken us far from the beach—no more cabins, no more land. The bottom of the boat was the only sure footing, and it was never still.

He took the lining out of a pocket of his jacket. When she died it was in her hand, he said.

No, it should go with Holly, Sheila said. She looked at me. The look told me that I agreed.

127

Mel nodded, tucked it into Holly's nightgown. We helped him lift Holly over the starboard side of the hull. There wasn't any pause or ceremony—once we had her up we let her drop into the water. Splash.

Or rather the entire thing was ceremony—the water, its buoyancy, us floating upon it.

Visiting Nanjing
Margaret Ross

AIR QUALITY INDEX

You know you see it if you're seeing
less. The skyline peters out. High-rises
forget themselves, go gray, then pale, then

nothing. Horizon encroaching. You can
see your life as something you pass through
or something pulled through you

while you keep still. Nothing visible a hundred
paces forward. Smog cinches in attention
like pain would. A fresh cut yanks

the mind snug on the single thought "it
hurts." It's now you see a stretch of pavement
acting like a girl. All powdered up and shimmering

and everything around it blurs. Something fine
accumulating—
                        Easy: sift breath, ash
surface, granulate the breeze. Wanna see

the end? Let it grow on things, a dark layer
on your counter, screen, touch a finger
anywhere here your finger comes up black.

Riddle in the concrete sense means *sieve*.
Death's a pointillist, you know you see it
if you're seeing less add up to something

larger than it was. *One second I*
was nearly struck, I gasped, I couldn't
budge, then back to same old same old

fishing for my bus pass. To inhale here
draws grit through the lung that every later
breath must navigate around. *Thought nothing*

of it, naturally, like anyone, it's just
what happens now and then, but over time
the glimpses that you get fill out a picture.

Don't breathe too deep today. Faces on the street
walk by with mouths sealed under masks
like baby blankets: pale blue, pale pink

with a yellow trim, two bows at the sides
where dimples would be if it were skin. Who's
getting born? Who dying? You could

call this form of breath a form of
reading, information parceled piecemeal
through a clear expanse you move through

unimpeded, only later do you realize
certain fragments settled on your mind, they stick,
you have to think around them, unable to

sweep them out, they make me up, the stubborn
bits configuring a mesh through which
thought strains. Read it in again. "I held my

tongue before the mediocre thing apparently
intent to smash perspective. Vanishing point
gone, depth expunged, still recognizably the world

but with the old view ground into a kind of soot
dispersed across the surface like some intermittent
inkling of a whole." *Wherever You aren't*

I'd break my eyes to see. Look up from it
on the bus at a kid just starting to bleed,
a lot of blood it seems, from the nose.

She doesn't notice. Doesn't do anything
until the man whose lap she's sitting on
clucks and fishes out a wad of tissue, balls a piece

to hold up to her nostril till the piece goes red,
he slips the dark wet pellet in his pocket,
does it again, the kid throughout just

staring ahead, mostly, once in a while reaching up
halfheartedly to stay the hand on her.

MEAT OF THE MATTER

A woman folds her arms
and lays her head down
on the table at the corner

selling meat. Her ponytail
black running over wood
to meet the glossy naked cut

of pork beside her. It's hot.
Midafternoon. The fly
climbs a white aisle in the fat

then up the milky glare-drawn
highlight of her hair. "Oh where
oh where," sings the TV

perched against a windowsill
behind her. Scuffed tupperware
from which to buy puce

livers smooth as species
gradually evolved to manage
sea. *Nothing catches on thee*

who have no lip nor snare
nor snag. My little dog is fear,
his leash, ennui. A color

like a memory of red.
A kid poked at the edge
of the white hen rustling

through the mesh whose throat
a hand then texting
later snipped with scissors.

That woman's sleeping.
What body does her dream
give the groan of a lathe

the worksite's starting up? Once
the beige-pink greasy slab of chicken
on my plate was "Actually,"

he corrected, "swan." Looking
then was like surveying
some slick face the morning's

butchered from a heady
absence kissed in the dark.
To be such duped bulk

hung from the hook of the mouth
with our ears cut short and
our hair cut long and the sly

flesh laundering your every cell
from cell like stolen bills. I bit his arm
so hard one time my teeth

got red. I peeled the band-aid
from my finger and discovered
where my skin had been

a damp white band, death's
wedding ring. Dreamt again
of getting pestled down by thought

until I'm just a fine grain
sifted through your skin. *Nor clasp*
nor grip, no purchase on. Settling

inside you I could there
at last see nothing. The land
here's full. A grave costs

more than a lease on a flat
and a body's legally evicted after
twenty years when the plot

can sell again. Government
handouts feed the living willing
to be shipped offshore.

From city-sponsored vessels
passengers throw ashes at the bride
the ocean is and back on land

it's beachgoers in "facekinis," lycra
ski masks to preserve their skin
so from a boat coming in

you'd think the sand
was mobbed with robbers
who suddenly lay down midheist.

KNOTWORK

Somewhere can we not say "if, then."
Somewhere can we not think "first, second."
Line loose on the wind
that turns it and it curves.
That twists it into things
of this world. For example
this vine called "empty-hearted
vegetable" in a green tangle
on the vendor's table. Crisp spines
of spinach and the amaranth's magenta tips
alongside heaped sprouts, every white arc
ending on a moth-green seed.
The vendor bunches scallions
under orange rubber bands.
A woman knocks on each
watermelon to hear within the sound
how it will taste. Somewhere
you can feel the sinuous shape
of the future start to be perceptible
as leaning toward the pane
there stroked my cheek
a spider silk I hadn't seen before.
"The hollower the echo is," she says,
"the sweeter." *Soft red encircled*
by a dark green globe. Here
across the earth from home
I'm twelve hours deeper into time
but further outside, stranger
to the thoughts I thought
I knew. The body's pulse I understood
in numbers I have learned
to understand as texture
blood can thread
between its vessels. A needle
pierced behind the neck released
an old pain from the heart. A legend
ties red thread around the ankles
of an infant and the person he or she

will one day marry. *White shoots*
sent down through the dark
  by grass I lay in as a child. Is the deepest
root of a plant the plant that grows
  on the Earth's other side? The legend goes
the child shown the life he'd lead
  was so disgusted by the sight, he threw
a rock at her. If it were only hollow,
  the future, that we might enter it
untouched, unstitched from what
  we've done before, but it's
not like that. Not destiny
  but neither is it chance
since chance ignores the rigging
  winding through experience
ornate as knotwork
  tying nothing to depict
at every scale (from cell-phone charm
  to wall hanging) the intricate charade
of human will. An art
  in practice now for twenty
centuries. Red cord twisting
  back on itself. The world
a slipknot closing
  on the senses. It brushed my face.
I touch my wrist. What pulls
  the line through me? A floating
pulse, a flooding pulse, a hollow pulse,
  firm pulse, a knotted pulse, a wiry,
rolling, superficial, leathery,
  a scattered, silken thread through water,
empty, slippery, hesitant. The story goes
  two decades later, the boy weds
a beautiful girl he loves
  who always wears a flower
on her forehead. Inkling
  in the vein like footfall on the other face
of the world, the force that through
  the green fuse drives the wire. "Why
do you wear that flower
  on your forehead?" "I can't show

135

Margaret Ross

my forehead." Of course you know
        the end but what is it you know
knowing that? "Why can't you?"
        "I can't tell." "Tell me, you're bound
to me now." "All right. When I was still small
        someone threw a rock at my forehead." Not chance
but neither is it choice, this wiring that isn't
        will or love or need or sense, the feel
of things starting.

And the Bow Shall Be in the Cloud
Michael Ives

routine hub-tones figure in a scatter
drum at a slight torque to religion
house of contrary jade
burning in the mountain's phoneme
an event consists of a mirror and a
stork holding an egg upright in its bill
reinvents home

*

marble can make eyes pressed into
that serious weather of rocks
left scarred by their attractor
while our delicate veins forged in Jeta Forest
push a pavilion full of bulls
toward the flower's center filters out
even distances want their now

*

when I take the coral reef out for a drive
whose tourist attraction smears into
birds falling out of the flight path
dint cost me a Jungian shadow
O anti-aging truck locked in reverse be the food
when I catch my bearing witness fucking a cache of knives
but only once

*

a lion drinks from the myth of the hammer
and the sky opens out into itself
another sacred pause in the sacred chaos
making stone / back in five
life isn't your dad's Texas
not that it matters
if the storm's buried in a / in a frost of bones

*

to hear immortal birds
singing near the waterfall
a privilege of elite power
but they'll tear you
from your throne of obsidian
like you were a vein in a mine
if you don't die when they tell you

*

should certain forms of detachment
reflect a setting sun
with bone inlay at the eyes and dreams
but what did they see in their gaze
those people from a cloned before
gathering both in and near the appearances
the ones refitting the vision cog / ?

*

dark money influence at the think tank
a flux in the reconciliation
of polished granite and warning sirens
frames the entrance
to every merger
there is a season
gumming the tape head

*

as to using screw braces
to still a vibrating conversion riff
I'd go instead for a clutch reverser
behind the secondary water chimp
ack / ! / sorry / more mechanization
seems like an arbitrary solution
to what / ?

*

those crocodile-headed days
arranged in a sex-wreath
round the baby shower
their lives spent brooding
over the downed Blackhawk
if you've got wings
fly the hell out of there

*

surceases never wonder
but front a vibe syndicate
forging the absolute
in a diagram of phenomena
as still as constant motion
as overt as a hidden
non-dimension-less-ness

*

before an afterlife
it swaddled me in its frequency
many Hz above the sweep
of my previous life
the one before that become a stir of rags
around the ankles of another
I shall learn to hear in yet another

*

Michael Ives

air dynasts take their meals
in a silence of three suns
embassage many months from home
yet the palace walls taper toward a war
visible under the viceroy's half-opened robe
and the funerary urn at the inter-pulse
full of kingdom

*

under the sky horse at its zenith
dynasts reduced to sand
and fragrant wood
growing through the openwork
moon tethered over bridge
as from the search for a glazed jar
a system of highways emerges

*

and heaven looks once again like a shark attack
to the girl I want to be
when I'm exactly this distance from you
late grove of blossoms / one Jessica Savitch
tackling the problem of surface area
along an end-folded Villa Lobos bottle
twisting on its axis at the speed of sky

*

for an albatross has no need of time zones
as are the names of the letters
the vestal virgins of the names
afternoon a squirrel's dark eye
opens onto the fippled conch of dawn
sluiced at soft diagonals
to your sense machine

*

the gradual opening of animal flesh
to a generalized tool power
over time reveals physical action
to have been an ur-robotics
in conspiracy with the speech of rooms
which flows without obstruction
through the walls of human speech

*

the head of the pope is a plot twist a portal
of Chartres is the stoma in a leaf a bestiary
a tunnel to the leopard's banquet a year
the monocerous turning in its sleep symbol
an echo in front of its source blood
the youngest child of ocean Christ
a fold of drapery if

*

as soon as you're sure the
it's there hook into the
echo plex behind the
zero hour's wizard I've seen the
invisible forms passing through the
my vision is exactly the
watching invisible forms pass through the

*

ask me how I know what's in the tabernacle
salt the opposition's morning
lube your inner Ibiza
pet it and breathe
tell her you haven't been outside in a year
introduce fetters
appropriate the oceans

*

before we approach the glory
we dump the organs
before we void the plenty
we meat the air
posit the house / but burn the room
synthesize the manga load
de-tune the day

*

guilt cuff having deactivated itself
within Mangelsdorff range
where all the sidemen are named Lloyd
at a rate of three an hour
in observance of late privileges
given over to advents and infancies
but I was coming around from the other side

*

to explain how the original prayer
recaptured in a cold sophistication
had presaged the art of trench digging
into an impermanence forever
which to approach from below
thickens a vertical ocean of stone
and on it goes and

*

stacked schemes in the sense of
it comes flooding back to you
shards of a second Los Angeles
in desert with Moses and his silent hench
same as per the squeeze fix
draining from centers of questionable tension
all the old lymph

*

there's trouble in the VX tower
crypto-synchronization of opaque speech / :
burning clay syndrome all over again
thus wishing 2 introduce
Repurposed Redaction of the Primary Telos
as if it were mounted
on small adjustable road trips

*

directly across the street
from a thinking such as haunts Her
here in the throat of anger
feeds Her children toward a covenant
of faux Ezekiels at the center of the storm
state pontoons will tilt
but the roof of malachite remains singular

*

to have pulled another "Sierra Club"
while She who authorized the naked pics
I had taken as a species of bath salts
afterwards compelled for the sake of the perceiver
to grind Her oblique garden
into an unregistered level
of unicorn

*

remarkable nonetheless for its ( )
will not broach queries having to do with ( )
flows yet wrestles itself into an ( )
adversary the better to disturb my ( )
whose blood sphinx tied to ( )
waits to catch when it falls from ( )
restless brilliance is killing ( )

*

143

or storm door into mood ox
uncertain as to weather
I'm still a standing member of society
sewed my wings back into
dank was their Sabbath
blind starting out toward what avails
appearances the gill in the being

*

back in the day when mothers were
moved backwards and forwards
over the harrowing cradles
by an endless chain of commands
issuing from the central shaft
when a snow-monkey wardrobe
made the presidents laugh

*

endless mille-feuille of monetized sleeving
one's Mylar brainpan cradles the
performs a unification of
strip mall under morpho-
sex-o-tic cloudscape euphoria with
have you learned nothing / ?
endless gorgeous convexity of nothing / ?

*

its torso as permeable
and closed at either end with openings
their calendar day ran unnoticed
along the bottom of a master codex
truer than the tale it told
of standardized children and the Jones
for a flame-cooled orthodoxy

*

if astonishing sequences of fine movement
rippling across the planes of the face
means to possess a face
having fixed early on in its lineaments
enormous quantities of atmospheric anxiety
which to witness rescues the Other
from what His inherent Nixon deems

*

during a five-minute gene morph
should it wander toward the blurred edge
of the target algorithm
is often refed through several more molts
till override kicks in
and registers the work unit a fetus
and agrees to come home to it

*

intricate marks on the shell
taken for writing and whole kingdoms
of possibility referred to as music
or a language of tones reduces sound
to the merely legible creases in the palm
are signs to them who
rent out their sight to prophecy

*

could hardly be a more lucid account
total river as interplay of movement
and its inconceivable opposite
will not be described here
without provoking a disturbance
from a time-elapsed version of the same problem
captured in words

*

in eye contact with a state-run probe
-t's why we chained the Doge to his pet Luther
and lit out for West Clench
across the night barrens
mules build their fires
but on the Morning of the Reciprocator
a shade refuses to be a shade

*

what appears
is an interiorized space mastering its effect
on an absentee perceiver
has enthroned those of us here at the entrance
waiting our whole lives to get in
we masters of all
we did not survey

*

and for these reasons He Smithed me out
with His womb transplants and nerve harps
and I was lost all over the place
juggling again with no hands
all the old pauses in His story
were a series of interlocking bleeds
were a shiv coda

*

and for this reason He black boxed the field of lambs
with His pressure holes and beheadings
and I was sub-jacked by His purist dynamic
like a particulate in a heat exchange
hold Him at False Church why don't you
sure / wrap Him in a layer of math
in that throne grease of yours

*

146

He'll just flush the heroic mode
with a method of heroic sleep
˙so as to elasticize the modulus of the aggressor
running all wounds through the proper channels
coordinating field adjustments with Langley
the asset is en route
His tongue is never out of your ear

*

another bone toss another racket another alone
another dire circumstance another head cage
another source of power another ink blossom
another crank buyout another valley in the distance
another dark aggregate another alien threat another map
another torrent another proverb another run-in
another somebody else another some other thing

*

beneath the multisyllable words meaning
they became bony animals
and the guts in question lying on a plate of zinc
to which Mengele attached the conducting wire
are forces which shall give rise to enormous carved heads
memorials to the mystery of ant peoples
who tear up their floors to preserve their shoes

*

powerless / making an improbable passage
across a wilderness of voter IDs
home to "Florida" and certain syncopated slogans
where as soon as the germ vector
differs from standard frictions
in that it's a color
stuffing flailing things in ships

*

during those hotly disturbed few hours
that are my history of lust
shaking free its paralysis
in submission to the fathers of paralysis
yet with a thick wall of oil behind them
from which His iconic face shall surface
"I" is the NRA

*

whose nerve god transmits His message
along a rebus of product placements
in His film of my life
whose thirst ran away from His quench
and this made the water
and the moment free of its history
and the life of the world to come

Big Burnt
Joyce Carol Oates

FROM THE START the plan had been to include a woman. Not *the woman* but *a woman.*

Yet it hadn't been clear if the woman would be a witness or whether the woman would be involved in a more crucial role.

"Don't panic."

Her eyes glanced upward, in alarm. Somehow, without her awareness, the sky had darkened overhead. The temperature was rapidly dropping and the wind was rising.

At the wheel of the small rented outboard boat the man pushed the lever that controlled its speed and the boat leapt forward, slapping against waves in a quasi-perpendicular way that was torture to the woman though she was determined not to show it.

"We're not in trouble. We'll make it. Just hang on."

The man spoke almost gaily. Quickly the woman smiled to assure him—*Of course!*

They were only a few minutes out onto the wide wind-buffeted lake when lightning flashed overhead in repeated spasms like strobe lights and there followed a deafening noise like shaken foil, many times magnified.

The lake was the color of lead. The first raindrops were flung against their faces like buckshot.

The woman, shivering, was sitting so close beside the man she could easily have lifted her hand to touch his wrist, which was covered in coarse, dark hairs; she might have touched his shoulder in a gesture of (wifely) solicitude. If the situation were not so desperate she might have—playfully, provocatively—pressed her hand lightly against the nape of the man's neck.

He liked her to touch him, sometimes. Though he rarely touched her in such casual ways. His sidelong glance at the woman would be startled as if she'd touched him intimately.

(But is not all touch intimate?—the woman reasoned. For her, *touch*

149

was the most intimate speech.)

For the past two and a half days the woman had been calculating how to make the man love her. The man had been calculating how, when the interlude at Lake George was over, and he'd returned alone to his home in Cambridge, he would blow out his brains.

Earlier that day, when they'd taken the boat to Big Burnt Island, several miles from the marina at Bolton's Landing, the lake had been calm, even tranquil—*glassy*. Vast lake and vast sky had reflected each other in an eerie and surpassing beauty that made the woman's heart contract with happiness.

"What a beautiful place you've brought me to, Mikael!—thank you."

The woman spoke warmly like a heedless child. In an instant she was the ingenue Nina of *The Seagull*. She heard her voice just too perceptibly loud, rather raw, overeager. Yet the man who did not smile easily smiled then with pleasure. Yes, this was what he liked to hear from a woman's mouth. For indeed the vast lake surrounded by pine trees was beautiful, and *his*.

Now, a few hours later, the glassy surface of the water had vanished as if it had never been. All was agitated, churning. The wind made everything confused, for it seemed to come from several directions simultaneously. The sky that had been a clear, pellucid blue that morning was bruised and opaque.

"Christ! Hang on."

"What?—oh."

The man was white lipped with fury. On their left, out of nowhere, a large motorboat bore down upon them like a demented beast. In normal daylight this twenty-foot boat would have been dazzling white like their rented boat but the light was no longer normal but dimmed, shadowy. In normal weather, boaters on Lake George were courteous and respectful of others but with the approaching storm, no. In the wake of the larger boat that crossed their path their boat shuddered as if rebuked. *Thump-thump-thump*, the small boat slapped against waves sidelong, slantwise.

Don't panic. He will hate you if you panic. You are not going to drown.

She had an old terror of collision, chaos. A childhood terror of dark water covering her mouth, a panicked swallowing of filthy water. The sensation of water up her nose, recalled from swimming as a girl in a school pool amid a flailing of arms and legs of other girls, thrashing, splashing, sinking, gasping for air, and yet there came water up her nose and into her head, which felt as if it were about to explode.

The woman gripped the seat beneath her. Tightly with both hands. Crazed waves in the wake of the rushing boat were making her head pitch forward, and then back; forward, and back. She was being shaken like a rag doll. Her neck ached alarmingly—whiplash?

Frothy water was beginning to wash into the boat, onto the woman's feet, wetting her legs, her hair, and her face.

Deftly, or perhaps it was desperately, the man turned the wheel, that the boat might roll with the waves. Always he was shifting the speed lever—forward, back. And again forward, and back. The boat jerked, bucked crazily. But no sooner was one danger past than another boat, not so large as the first, but large enough to stir waves like punitive slaps against the smaller boat, crossed their path from the right, at a fast clip.

Just. Don't. Panic.

She'd resisted the impulse to press her hands against her eyes, in a childish gesture of *not seeing.*

Surely they would not be capsized on the lake? Surely they would not *drown*?

She didn't think so. Not possible. Well—not *probable.*

This was Lake George, New York, in late August. This was not a remote region of the Adirondacks. Or a third-world country vulnerable to typhoons or tsunamis where thousands of people died in the equivalent of a key click. There had to be rescue boats in a severe storm—yes? The equivalent of the US Coast Guard?

The woman was determined to smile, that the man would see how she *was not panicked.* The woman recalled her children, when they'd been young. They too had tried not to show fear, sorrow, grief when these emotions had been perfectly justified. They had tried *not to cry brokenheartedly* when their daddy departed with a (vague, guilty, unconvincing) promise to return. The woman who was their mother had loved them fiercely, seeing this: stoicism in such young children! Surely this was a kind of child abuse.

On the island, the woman had seen flashes of heat lightning in the sky, in the distance. The man had taken no notice; most of the sky had been clear at this time. But the woman had noticed other boats leaving the island and had asked, "Will there be a storm? Should we leave now?" and the man had merely laughed at her.

"Don't panic. We have plenty of time."

151

Once they were in the boat, however, he'd seemed surprised by the quick-gathering thunderclouds. The rapidly increasing wind, the drop in temperature, and the first raindrops chill as hail striking the bow of the boat, the windshield, their faces. He'd asked her to retrieve their nylon rain jackets from the back of the boat, and the bulky bright-orange life vests he'd disdained earlier in the day.

Being taken by surprise was upsetting to the man, the woman could see. She had not ever known any man who'd liked surprises unless the surprises were of his own doing.

Now came rain pelting like machine-gun fire pocking the water's surface. Amid the churning waves visibility was poor. There were drifting mists. The woman peered anxiously ahead—she had no way of telling if the boat was making progress.

Beside her the man was steering the boat with the fiercest concentration. His face was tense with strain. His jaws were clenched. He was enjoying this frantic race across the lake—wasn't he? In his mostly sedentary life in which he gave orders to others, subordinates, and was not accustomed to being challenged or questioned, let alone actively opposed, this lake crossing to the marina at Bolton's Landing had to be an adventure, the woman thought. Several times he'd admonished her not to panic; she had to surmise that it was panic the man most feared, in himself as in others.

He'd told her when they'd first arrived at Lake George that he knew the lake *like the back of my hand.* This was not an arrogant boast but rather a childlike boast and so the woman had smilingly questioned whether a person did indeed know the back of his own hand, and could recognize a picture of his hand among the hands of others.

But the man hadn't heard her (quite reasonable, she'd thought) query. Or if he'd heard, he disdained schoolgirl paradoxes.

The woman had examined the back of her own hand. Her hands. She was shocked to see—what, exactly?—had her hands, already in her early forties, begun to age, to betray fine, faint lines, odd little discolorations, freckles? Or was she imagining this? But there was no doubt, she couldn't have identified her hands pictured among the hands of other women her own age.

Sometimes, glimpsing by chance her reflection in a shop window or a reflecting surface, the woman thought with a quizzical smile— *But who is that? She looks familiar.*

The man had no time for such caprices. His mind was not a mind to "wander" but was rather a problem-solving mind, or rather brain, sharp and fine-tuned and galvanized by challenge. When he ran, he ran—for a specifically allotted amount of time. When he walked, he walked—swiftly, with a minimum of curiosity. Driving a vehicle, he drove swiftly and unerringly though consumed in thought, *thinking.* In any public neutral space through which he was merely passing he had no time to waste merely *seeing.*

As he'd claimed to know the vast lake *like the back of my hand*—its inlets, its shoreline, its myriad large and small islands, the mountains in the near distance (in particular, Black Mountain)—so too he knew the little fifteen-foot outboard he'd rented that morning at the marina in Bolton's Landing for he'd once owned a near-identical model, trim and compact and dazzling white with a canopy and a 65-horsepower motor, purchased in the bygone days of a marriage now disintegrated like wet tissue.

Did the woman dare ask the man about this marriage? She did not.

The man had come to a point in his emotional life at which he had no need to articulate *My marriage* but only to feel the edginess and dread of one who has come too close to a precipice, without needing to give his fear a name.

Intuitively the woman understood. The woman was adept at reading the secret lives of others, which are presented to us in code; she could sense the man's fear of something not to be named, and would make herself indispensable in combating it.

That morning the man had deftly steered the small boat between color-coded buoys on the route to Big Burnt. He'd had no trouble avoiding the trajectories of other boats. To his admiring companion he'd pointed out landmarks on shore, and mountain peaks in the distance. But now in heavy rain he was having difficulty steering a course to take him to the inlet that contained the marina—though (of course) as he drew nearer, he would begin to recognize crucial landmarks.

Unless, as in a nightmare, he'd forgotten these landmarks. Or the landmarks had ceased to exist.

When the rain had first begun, they'd put on light nylon rain jackets, with hoods. But now, as rain and wind increased, the man conceded that they might put on life preservers also.

When the woman had difficulty adjusting the bulky orange vest that was much too large for her, he'd tied it, in a lull in the storm, to see that it was properly secured.

The gesture had been curiously tender, protective. The woman was touched, for the man did not always behave toward her in a way

153

that signaled affection, or concern; often, the man seemed scarcely aware of her. She wondered if when he'd secured the ties of the life preserver the man was thinking of his children when they'd been young, as she often thought of her children, not as they were at the present time but as they'd been years ago, requiring their mother for the simplest tasks.

Impulsively she thanked her companion with a quick kiss on the mouth. He laughed as if surprised, and a flush came onto his rain-wetted face, which had a slightly coarse, just slightly pitted skin as if it had been abraded with some rough substance. "Mikael, thank you! I feel like"—the woman hesitated, not quite knowing if this was the right thing to say—"one of my own children. Years ago."

To this feckless remark the man did not respond. She had noted how, frequently, it was his way to smile stiffly and in silence when another's remarks baffled or annoyed him.

I can love enough for two. You will see!

The storm lull had ended. The boat was bucking and heaving and the man had to grab the steering wheel quickly.

It was at that moment that the woman happened to glance behind them, to see to her horror that water was accumulating in the back of the boat: backpacks, towels, articles of clothing, bottles were awash in water; the back was alarmingly lower than the front. But when she nudged the man to look he brushed her hand away irritably and told her there was no danger, not yet for Christ's sake, and *not to panic.*

"Are you sure? Mikael—"

"I've told you. *Don't panic.*"

If the small boat were to capsize, or to sink—if it were swamped, and they were thrown into the turbulent lake—they would be kept from drowning by the life vests. Still, the woman was frightened.

She recalled a canoeing accident at a girls' summer camp in the Catskills years ago when she'd been eleven years old and away from home for the first time in her life; inexperienced girls had been allowed to canoe, and one of the girls in her cabin had drowned—the canoe she'd taken out onto a lake with another girl had overturned; she'd fallen into roiling water screaming and within seconds disappeared from view as if pulled down by an undertow.

Lisbeth had been in another canoe, staring in horror. No one seemed to know what to do—no one was a good enough swimmer, or mature enough to attempt a rescue. By the time an adult came running out onto the dock it was too late.

She'd never been able to comprehend what had happened except that one of her cabinmates was gone and the camp had shut down and sent all the girls home a week early. Soon after she returned home she could not recall the name of the drowned girl.

Yes, but her name was Fern. Of course you remember.

She could cling to the overturned boat if that were possible—if the boat didn't sink. That had been the drowned girl's mistake—she'd panicked, tried to swim, failed to grab hold of the canoe as the other girl had done. Lisbeth's own terror she would transform into the sheer stubborn hopefulness of one who *would not drown*.

Oh, but where was the marina? How far away, the southwestern shore of Lake George? She did recall a narrow inlet—passing close by land on their way out into the lake—but she had no idea where this was and she did not dare ask the man another time.

She remembered an American flag stirring in the wind, high above the marina dock. Vivid red striped, white stars on blue background, triumphant in morning sunlight like something painted in acrylics. The flag was so positioned, she supposed, to reassure persons like her, uneasy on the open lake, that they were nearly safe, returning to land. Her eyes filled with tears of yearning, to see that flag again and to know that the ordeal on the lake was nearly over.

The man's name was Mikael Brun. The woman's name was Lisbeth Mueller. They were forty-nine and forty-three years old, respectively.

Each was unmarried. Which is not altogether synonymous with *single*. Between them they had accumulated just three ex-spouses. And just five children, of whom the eldest (nineteen) was the man's and the youngest (seven) was the woman's.

The two were—technically—lovers; yet they were not quite friends. It was painful to the woman (though she knew that this was a thought the man wasn't likely to have) that they were not a *couple* but *two*.

A casual observer at their lakeside motel in Bolton's Landing, at the marina that morning, or on Big Burnt Island through the day— obsessively the woman would afterward contemplate such "pictures" frozen in time as a way of trying to comprehend the man's motives in behaving as he'd done—might plausibly have mistaken them for a married couple: middle-aged, in very good physical condition, and just slightly edgy as if they'd had a recent quarrel and wanted to avoid another. The woman, quick to smile. The man, more likely to frown, glancing about as if distracted.

155

He is looking for someone. Something.
That is why he has come back, to look.

Were the two long married, thus invisible to each other? Or were the two not married, nor even lovers? The casual observer might have noticed how the man held himself aloof from the woman, as if unconsciously; though meaning her no ill will, he simply forgot to hold open a door for her, for instance, so that she knew to come forward quickly behind him to press her hand against the door, to hold it open for herself in a graceful gesture lost to the man; when the man conferred with the lank-limbed boy at the marina who was preparing the boat for him, the woman stood by alert and attentive, though neither the man nor the boy would acknowledge her. The woman had perfected a small smile for such limbo situations in which, though in physical proximity to her companion, she somehow did not exist until he recalled her.

In the light wind, the woman's tangerine-colored scarf blew languidly over her face. Somehow, without her knowing, she'd become the sort of woman who wears such scarves even before there is a need to hide a ravaged neck.

The man wore a baseball cap to shield his eyes from the sun. The man also wore (prescription) sunglasses. His jaws glittered with a two-day beard that gave him a look of mild debauchery. Yet the man was speaking quietly, wistfully, to the marina attendant: "I first came to Lake George forty-six years ago—that is, I was brought as a small child. My parents camped on Big Burnt for weeks in the summer. I've come back often—though I've missed a few years recently. . . ."

But why did the man feel obliged to tell this to the lanky-limbed teenager in shorts and T-shirt, how did he expect the boy to respond? The woman was embarrassed for her companion, that he spoke so frankly to a stranger. Clearly, this was out of character. Mikael Brun barely spoke to *her*.

"Same as my dad, I guess," the boy said, not looking up from what he was doing in the boat, "except he lived here year-round."

"You've camped on Big Burnt?"—eagerly the man asked.

"Some islands we camped on, I guess. But I don't remember their names." The boy paused, shifting his shoulders uncomfortably. "Hasn't been for a while."

Lived. The man had not heard the boy say *lived.* The woman sensed this.

In Cambridge, Mikael Brun was often stiffly formal with strangers, and even with acquaintances and colleagues; his manner was never less than civil, but he wasn't a naturally friendly man. As a prominent scientist at Harvard, he'd cultivated the poise of a quasi-public figure who, even as he seems to be welcoming the interest of others, is inwardly repelling this interest.

When they'd checked into their lakeside motel Mikael had engaged the proprietor in a similar conversation about Bolton's Landing, Lake George, and the Adirondacks generally; he'd asked the proprietor questions intended to establish that they knew some individuals in common in the area. And the proprietor had certainly known of Big Burnt Island though he had not ever camped there.

Lisbeth had thought of her companion—*He is lonely. Lonelier even than I am.*

She felt a surge of hope, knowing this. For the weakness of the man is the strength of the woman.

He'd called her out of nowhere, to ask her to accompany him to Lake George for a few days at the very end of August. It would make him very happy, he said, if she would say *yes.*

Astonished by the call, needing to sit down quickly (on the edge of a rumpled bed in her bedroom) as faintness rose into her brain, the woman had murmured, *Yes maybe*—she would have to check her schedule.

She scarcely knew Mikael Brun. She'd had an unfortunate experience with the man the previous year, which she would not wish to repeat; yet, when she'd heard his voice on the landline, she'd felt a stab of hope, and happiness. She'd thought—*He has forgiven me.*

Lisbeth Mueller was an actress, or had been an actress in regional theaters and on some daytime TV, whose primary source of income came now from teaching in the speech and drama departments in local universities. Of her recent projects she was most proud of having staged a multiethnic production of *A Midsummer Night's Dream* conjoined with an original, collaborative drama of the sociology of urban immigrant life from the perspective of first-generation American-born undergraduates at Boston University.

Among Lisbeth's fiercely loyal circle of theater friends and acquaintances in the Cambridge-Boston area, ever shifting and diaphanous as the trailing, undulating tendrils of a great jellyfish, it was believed that her considerable talent as an actress had never been fully realized. Married too young, children at too young an age, two divorces, numerous men who'd exploited her trusting nature, career missteps, misjudgments—how swiftly the years had gone, and how little, except for the children, and her reputation for stubborn integrity,

Lisbeth had to show for them. It was very difficult for her to believe, waking in the early hours of the morning as if an alarm had rung somewhere close by, that her career wasn't still in its ascendency: The next audition would be the catapult to long-delayed recognition. . . . And there was always teaching, into which she threw herself with the zeal and enthusiasm of a seasoned ingenue, always the hope that, experience to the contrary, she would be offered a more permanent contract than simply the three- or one-year contracts given adjunct instructors like her.

"'Adjunct'! I don't think we have 'adjunct instructors' in our department. I know we don't have anything like 'adjuncts' at the institute"—so Mikael Brun had remarked, like a man discussing a rare disease.

How did you meet Mikael Brun?—the woman who'd accompanied him to Lake George would be asked. *What did you know of Mikael Brun's state of mind?*

And she would say, for this was the awkward truth, that she had no clear memory of when they'd first met, only a (vague) memory of their being (re)introduced to each other, at one or another social gathering in Cambridge. Not frequently, but occasionally over the past several years since Lisbeth's separation and divorce they'd "seen each other" in interludes of varying intensity. Lisbeth berated herself for being (nearly almost) always available to the man. (Of course, she saw other men in the interstices between seeing Mikael Brun. Always she was hoping that a relationship with another man would take predominance in her life, that she might forget Mikael Brun altogether; but this had not yet happened.) Once he'd brought her a dozen bloodred roses after he'd seen her in *The Cherry Orchard*, and they'd been drinking together in her house when Mikael said, in an outburst of emotion, that lately he'd been feeling the *need to try again*. . . . And this, too, in the faintly bemused, faintly incredulous tone of a man describing a rare pathology.

He had not stayed with Lisbeth that night, however. Or any other night.

And then, he'd been furious with her when she'd had to leave a dinner party to which he'd brought her, having had an unexpected call from a friend who'd had a medical emergency that day, and could not bear to be alone. Livid with indignation, Mikael had said to Lisbeth, not quite in an undertone, that, if she left the dinner, she shouldn't expect to see him again; Lisbeth was stricken with regret and tried to explain that she couldn't ignore the call, a plea for help—

"Please understand, Mikael. I'd rather be here. I would rather be with you." Her oldest friend in Cambridge had had a sort of seizure, perhaps a small stroke; the woman simply could not bear to be alone that night, and had called Lisbeth out of desperation.

Lisbeth had smiled at Mikael Brun most winningly, like Desdemona beguiling Othello. But the man had been unmoved. It was astonishing to her, he'd been unpersuaded by her appeal; for wasn't Mikael Brun renowned as a man of generous instincts himself; wasn't he a legendary figure with students, postdocs, younger scientists? Lisbeth had said, faltering, "Well—I won't go. I'll call Geraldine and explain that I can't see her until tomorrow." But Mikael said, "No. Go to her. Whoever she is, go. I'm leaving, myself." Others at the dinner had seemed not to be listening to the two as they spoke rapidly together in an adjoining room.

In the end, Lisbeth left the dinner, her host having called a taxi for her. By the time the taxi arrived, Mikael Brun had departed.

How stunned she'd been by the man's fury! It had been in such disproportion (she thought) to the situation. He'd looked as if he'd have liked to hit her.

She'd wondered if it meant that Mikael Brun was in fact attracted to her, and possessive of her; or whether his behavior was just mean-spirited male vanity.

I'm sorry, Mikael. I don't think I want to see you again.

Or simply, *I'm sorry. I don't want to see you again.*

These terse words Lisbeth prepared, but Mikael Brun had not called her.

It was the story of her life! Lisbeth Mueller was the radiantly smiling person to whom others turned in desperation, like stunted plants in need of sunshine. Patiently she listened to them, like a therapist; unlike a therapist, she didn't charge a fee. (Though if she'd been a therapist she might have had a steady income at least.) She was kind, generous, unjudging. She had not the personality for the rapacious competition of the stage. She was never ironic and may even have not quite understood what "irony" was—as she'd been accused by more than one man. Possibly it was easy to take such a woman for granted, even to betray her, who seems to demand so little from others, while freely offering so much.

But then, after several months, Mikael Brun called her. His voice was tremulous over the phone. He made no acknowledgment that months had passed since he'd last spoken to her, as if he'd forgotten the circumstances but he did sound contrite, hopeful.

"You will, Lisbeth? You'll come with me?"

"I said—I'm not sure. If the children can stay with their father a few more days . . . They're at Aspen."

"You're—free? And you'll come with me to Lake George?"

Had he not heard? *Children, their father. Aspen.*

"Well, yes, I think so. Yes."

Impulsively she spoke, overcome by emotion. She would not have been prepared for her reaction to the sound of the man's voice.

Mikael Brun continued to speak, excited, near ecstatic. Through a buzzing in her ears Lisbeth could barely make out his words. Had she been mistaken, all these months?—had the man been waiting to hear from *her*?

After they hung up Lisbeth remained sitting on the edge of the bed, somewhat dazed. Her heart beat sharply, quickened. Her heart had not beat in this way for a long time.

Afterward she would realize that she'd been waiting for the phone to ring again, and for Mikael Brun to decide that he'd made a mistake and would have to cancel their plans after all. For he'd called the wrong woman.

Elaborate plans he'd made for the weekend, which had to include the woman. A woman.

And the Monday following, when he'd have returned home.

Last things he'd prepared with care. So long he'd contemplated these, with the thrill of toxic bitterness, it was a relief when the *last things* were finally executed.

At the time, in his fiftieth year, Mikael Brun was a distinguished scientist, professor of psychology at Harvard and director of the Harvard Institute for Cognitive and Linguistic Research. In Cambridge it was generally believed that Brun was on an extended sabbatical leave from Harvard, freeing him to spend all his time at the institute; in fact, the leave was unpaid, and open-ended, while Brun was being (secretly, by a committee of professional peers and high-ranking Harvard administrators) investigated for "suspected improprieties" in his research. A former postdoc in Brun's laboratory had reported him for having purposefully misrecorded data in a number of experiments, subsequently published in leading professional journals. Vehemently Brun had denied the charges; he had no doubt that he had not committed "scientific misconduct" (as it was primly called) either willfully or inadvertently, yet the effort to clear his name would be demeaning, exhausting; he thought of Shakespeare's Coriolanus—he would not lower himself to the level of rabble to save his own career. And his disintegrated marriage, and the disenchantment of his children—he was weary of the effort of trying to make his fickle daughters love him again and prefer him to their mother as they'd once done.

To the north. I will go to the north. The words haunted him like words from a song of long ago when life had been simpler and happier.

Of course he would never do it that way—so crudely. . . .

Blow out my brains was a phrase he sometimes heard himself say, with a bluff sort of heartiness. There was a Chekhovian ring to such a remark—melancholy yet bemused. A joke!

Still, he would not *blow out his brains* for such a trifle as the meretricious investigation at Harvard. And it was an absurd cliché to ascribe suicide to the breakup of his family; that was hardly a new development in Mikael Brun's life. It was infuriating to him, that others might interpret his suicide in such petty and reductive terms.

Who dies for what is quantifiable dies in shame. The suicide soars beyond your grasp as beyond your ignorant understanding.

One final time, he would return to Big Burnt. He would put his things in order before driving north so that, when he returned, he would not be confronted with the responsibility. He'd come to realize that all the places he had lived had been spoiled for him by the experience of living in them, except for Big Burnt Island.

Impulsively, he called a woman whom he'd known casually, in the years following his divorce, a woman whom he found attractive or in any case sympathetic, an intelligent woman, an uncomplaining woman, with a local reputation as an actress—Lisbeth Mueller. And when he heard the woman's startled voice over the phone he'd thought—*She is the one.* He heard himself ask Lisbeth if she would like to come with him to Lake George, in the Adirondacks, over the long Labor Day weekend.

In an instant he'd felt certain. Something like a leaden vest had slipped from him. There'd been other women he called, or left messages for—this, Mikael would never tell Lisbeth, of course!—but Lisbeth Mueller was *the one.*

She was a beautiful woman, or had been. He saw other men appraising her, and took solace in their looks of admiration and (maybe) envy. Several times he'd seen her onstage and would scarcely have recognized her, her ivory-skinned face illuminated by stage lights, flawless as her carefully enunciated words.

In actual life, Lisbeth Mueller was not so assured. Often there was faint anxiety in her face, even when she was smiling—a "dazzling" smile. Her manner was gracious, and seductive; she was a woman who was always *seducing*, out of a dread of being rejected. A woman always slightly off-balance, insecure. Mikael quite liked it that Lisbeth was always in need of money, for the man should provide the money, binding the woman to him for as long as he wished her bound to him.

Seeing Lisbeth Mueller enlivened in his presence, made happy by *him*, he'd laughed with relief and pleasure. Often there was a kind of skin or husk over him that made relating to others difficult, even breathing in their presence difficult; but that was not the case when he was with Lisbeth, who seemed never to judge and always grateful for his attention.

It was crucial to Mikael, or had once been—that others might be made happy *by him*. For so long he'd been an outstanding son who'd made his parents happy or in any case proud of him. All of the Brun family, proud of Mikael, who'd received a scholarship to an excellent university (Chicago) and had the equivalent of an MD (that is, a PhD) from another excellent university (Yale). And now he was a professor at the greatest university of all (Harvard)—in fact, he was the director of his own research institute (though it wasn't clear to the relatives exactly what Mikael was researching).

There'd been a few women whom he'd made happy, if not for long. And the children—for a while.

For a long time he hadn't had a reasonable expectation of happiness for himself. Maybe something like *gratification*—being elected to the National Academy of Science at the right time, before most of his rivals; being awarded million-dollar grants, in the days when a million dollars meant something. And of course seeing his ambitious experiments turn out successfully, results published in the *American Journal of Cognitive Science* and elsewhere.

Not happiness but relief. Shrugging off the leaden vest. As if his lungs were filled with helium. He *could float*.

Neatly laid on the desk in his home study were these items: *Mikael K. Brun Last Will & Testament*; a manila folder containing financial statements, including IRS records; the title for his Land Rover, which he was leaving to a cousin (whom he had not seen in fifteen years); an envelope containing a final check for the Filipino woman who'd been cleaning his house—soiled laundry, stained sinks and toilets, sticky tile floors, carpets—on alternate Mondays for nearly twenty years; envelopes containing detailed instructions for his young laboratory colleagues, who would be devastated by their mentor's death; and envelopes addressed to several former students containing letters of recommendation.

He had tried, and failed, to write letters to his son and his daughters. He had not tried to write to his former wife (whose address he no longer had) nor had he tried to write letters to his own relatives. For words of a personal, revelatory nature did not come easily to him.

Was he hoping that the woman would change his mind in this late stage of his life? That was a possibility but—*no.*

No more than a terminal cancer patient could have a reasonable hope that vitamin C shots will alter the course of his disease.

Had he hoped for the woman to change his mind about the possibility of his being amenable to his mind being changed by any woman—*no. Not that either.*

"Here we are."

At last they'd come to Big Burnt Island. Lisbeth was prepared to find the island remarkable in some evident way, unusually "scenic"—but of course it closely resembled nearby islands, as it resembled the densely wooded Adirondack mainland surrounding the lake. Tall pines, deciduous trees, a hilly landscape, what looked like dry, slightly sandy soil—"It's very beautiful," she said uncertainly.

"Is it!"

Mikael Brun laughed. She supposed he was laughing at her—for having said such banal words, with an air of surprise.

Mikael had been in an exalted mood since early morning. Lisbeth had never seen him so happy, and was grateful for his happiness; he was a man of moods, mercurial and unpredictable. Not happiness itself but the relief of the other's happiness was crucial to her.

At first she'd been uneasy in the rented boat. It did look—*small.* And Mikael had made a droll comment that it wasn't *teak,* only just fiberglass—"Minimally adequate." She could not control a faint shudder as she stepped down inside the boat, which immediately rocked beneath her weight, assisted by Mikael and by the lanky-limbed marina attendant. She'd never felt comfortable in any boat, for invariably she was forced to recall the canoeing accident of her childhood about which she hadn't wanted to speak to Mikael Brun—

163

of course. He'd have laughed at her for worrying that a fifteen-foot outboard might be as easily overturned as a canoe.

Mikael had rented a boat with a canopy, to protect them from the direct sun. Lisbeth was relieved to see oars and bright-orange life preservers stored in the rear.

On their way to Big Burnt Island Mikael kept to a reasonable speed even as other boats rushed past. He was in very good spirits. Lisbeth thought—*How close we are! How intimate.* Seen from a little distance they were certainly a couple.

At Glen Island, where, at the ranger station, Mikael applied for a single-day permit for Big Burnt Island, as at Big Burnt Island itself, he had some initial difficulty securing the boat to the dock. In both cases Lisbeth was pressed into helping him, awkwardly looping a rope around a pole. In both cases the helpless *thump-thump-thump* of the small, vulnerable-seeming white boat against the wooden dock was distressing. Lisbeth saw her companion's jaws clench as if he were feeling pain.

But then, at last, at Big Burnt the boat was secured. There were a few other outboards in the small inlet but none at the dock for which Mikael had a permit. Happily he sprang out of the boat and reached down to grasp Lisbeth's hand, to pull her up onto the dock. His fingers tightened upon hers to the point of pain. She laughed breathlessly and protested—"Please! You're hurting me."

Sorry! He hadn't realized, he said quickly. He was wearing a cap with a visor pulled low over his forehead, and dark sunglasses that obscured his eyes. His skin was just slightly coarse, pitted. He seemed excited, mildly anxious. But happier than Lisbeth had ever seen him.

How easy it would be to love such a man, she thought. And easy to be loved by such a man.

It was a foolish, feckless thought. Such thoughts plagued the woman in times of stress in particular, seeming to come from a source beyond her.

In their backpacks were sandwiches, Evian water, towels, and the morning's *New York Times.* Mikael intended to swim, and hoped that Lisbeth would also—"I don't enjoy swimming alone." He was scornful of her mild addiction to the daily crossword puzzle but she'd thought that in these circumstances, in protracted intimacy with a man she scarcely knew, focusing on the crossword puzzle would be a way of focusing her excitement.

On land, Mikael took Lisbeth's hand in his and led her briskly uphill. There was no evident path but Mikael's way was unerring through stands of scrub pine—he might have made his way blindfolded.

"This was our campsite. On this promontory."

Mikael's face fairly glowed with excitement and his voice seemed higher pitched, tremulous.

Fortunately no one was camping on the site. There was a clear and unimpeded view of the lake. Happily Mikael pointed out to Lisbeth mountain peaks in the distance—Black Mountain, Erebus Mountain, Shelving Rock Mountain. Lisbeth shaded her eyes and stared.

They left their backpacks on a weathered picnic table, which, Mikael told her, had been the table his family had used. He was speaking warmly, intensely. Lisbeth knew better than to interrupt as he reminisced about the summers he'd come to the island with his family—"Until everything ended."

"And why was that?"

"Why was *that*?"

She'd said something wrong—had she? Was he angry with her, in an instant?

"I mean—did something happen? So that you stopped coming here . . . ?"

"Yes. Of course 'something happened.' It's in the nature of our lives that something invariably 'happens'—isn't it? You do something for a finite number of times, but you often don't know when you will do it for the last time. In our case, we knew."

Mikael was speaking matter-of-factly now, as if he were lecturing, and not accusingly; after a while he said, relenting, "It was more than one thing but essentially, my father died."

Lisbeth asked how old he'd been when his father had died and Mikael said, with a shrug, "Too young for him, and too young for me."

Lisbeth touched his wrist in silent commiseration. She did not intrude upon him otherwise for she saw that he was deeply moved. Behind the dark lenses his eyes were rapidly blinking and evasive.

Another time she thought—*He is such a lonely person!*

She thought—*I will make him love me, and that will save him and me both.*

It was another of her bizarre feckless thoughts, which seemed to come to her from a consciousness not her own.

Several times Mikael circled the campsite. He might have been seeking the entrance to an enclosure—a tent? His expression was pained, yearning, tender. He took pictures with his iPhone. He squatted on his heels, oblivious of Lisbeth, who stood to the side, waiting uneasily. Indeed it was a beautiful setting—the campsite with an open view of the lake, and the pale-blue sky reflected in the lake. She was touched that Mikael Brun was sharing this private place with her and that they would be bound together by this sharing.

It was a fair, bright, warm morning on Lake George. As midday approached, the air grew brighter and hotter. There was the likelihood of rain sometime later that day—so Mikael had mentioned to her at the motel, casually—but for now, the sky was clear, luminous. Lisbeth noted the abrupt drop beyond the campsite—not a very good site for children. She noted how clean the island was, so far as she could see. Visitors to the islands were forbidden to leave debris and garbage behind; they were required to carry it back with them to the mainland. In that way overflowing trash cans were avoided. The air was wonderfully fresh and the lake water, as Mikael had several times said, was pure enough to drink.

Was it?! Lisbeth wondered at this. Hadn't acid rain fallen in the Adirondacks in recent decades? Was the lake so pure as it had been in Mikael Brun's childhood? Lisbeth noted that they'd brought bottled water with them, in any case.

A thrilling idea occurred to her: She would suggest to Mikael that they camp on Big Burnt sometime, together. Was that possible? Would Mikael be touched by this suggestion, or would Mikael resent her intrusion? *Was* it an intrusion, if he'd brought her here? Lisbeth had no great love of the outdoors, still less camping, but if such a romantic interlude would appeal to Mikael . . .

We decided that Big Burnt would be our honeymoon. Beautiful, remote, Mikael's boyhood place. . . .

After some minutes Mikael returned to Lisbeth, walking unsteadily. His cheeks shone with tears. He seized her hand again, as if he'd feared she might be easing away. For a moment she was frightened that he would do something extravagant—he would kiss the back of her hand and cry out that he loved her, like a Chekhov hero.

That was when we knew. Where we knew. Big Burnt.

Instead he led her along a path above the lake, speaking excitedly. Big Burnt was the largest of the Lake George islands, he said—thirty acres. It was so called (his father had said) because Native Americans had once burnt the trees to clear fields for planting.

Now they were beginning to see campers at other sites, in colorful tents. Mikael waved at them, called, *Hello!* Lisbeth tried to see how living in a tent on this remote island might be romantic—to a degree.

166

She tried not to be distracted by the cries of children. She tried not to notice campers staring at her with something like envy. (Was this so? But why? Was it so clear that she and Mikael Brun were only day packing, and not camping here?) To every remark of Mikael's she was smiling, enthusiastic. She did not listen to everything he said but she gave the impression of devoted attention. He was pointing out to her the varying merits of the several campsites, which she would never have seen for herself—some had open views of the lake, some were farther inland; some boasted shady trees and privacy, others did not. Proximity to the lake, proximity to a marshy area, frogs at nighttime, gnats and mosquitoes, morning sun, evening sun, camping platforms, steep ledges, flat rocks, sandy soil—proximity to outhouses. These varying features had to be weighed carefully in choosing a campsite, Mikael said gravely.

"Which would you prefer, if you were camping here?"

"Which would I *prefer*? The campsite my father chose, of course."

What a naive question Lisbeth had asked her companion! She wondered if she should apologize.

Lisbeth asked if Mikael had brought his own family to the site and Mikael paused before saying vaguely yes, a few times he had.

Mikael paused again as if there were more to say, but he did not say it.

Not such happy times. Not often repeated.

Lisbeth was thinking she should have known better than to ask Mikael Brun about his ruinous marriage. For a man of such pride and self-regard, any reminder that he had failed at anything would be devastating to him.

He'd become quieter now, walking slightly ahead of his companion. He was thinking—he was *not thinking*—of what awaited him after Lake George.

The *last things*. Boldly and brashly he'd executed the *last things*, which would outlive him, so he had no need to think at all, now.

Now, no question *Why*. For him there was only *how, when*.

Hand in hand they walked along the edge of the island for some time. It had been rare in their relationship that Mikael Brun had ever taken the woman's hand in quite this way—certainly, she could not recall Mikael having done so. By another route they returned, steadily uphill, in the increasing heat, to the picnic table at the Brun family's old campsite. It was a mild shock to the woman, that their backpacks and other items were there—as if indeed they were camping here, and were returning to their temporary home.

Mikael had bought lunch at a deli in Bolton's Landing and had been very particular about the sandwiches he'd ordered; but now the multigrain bread was badly soggy, the lettuce limp. The tuna-fish salad tasted as if it had been laced with something sugary and the cole slaw, in little fluted cups, was inedibly sweet. Still, Mikael ate hungrily. He had not shaved for two days—it was a custom, he'd told his companion, that he ceased shaving as soon as he left Cambridge and headed north—and his beard had come in graying and steely, a surly half mask. At Lake George, he said, his appetite was always "prodigious."

He saw that the woman was eating sparingly, as she'd eaten sparingly at breakfast. She was having difficulty with the large, damp sandwiches, which leaked watery mayonnaise. Each time she drank from the plastic water bottle, she took care to wipe the opening with a paper napkin. But she removed from a plastic bag the several ripe peaches Mikael had bought, offering him one and taking a smaller one for herself.

The peach was delicious. Juice ran down Mikael's chin. His mouth flooded with saliva, the taste of the sweet fruit was so intense.

Shyly, yet with an air of recklessness, the woman was saying that she thought she might like to "try camping" again. She hadn't been camping, she said, for a long time.

Mikael laughed, not troubling to disguise his disbelief. "You camped, at one time? Really?"

"Not in a tent but in a cabin. Just once. I mean—for about a week. When I was a girl."

"Where was this?"

"*Where?* Oh, nowhere—important. . . . Somewhere in the Catskills, I think. It wasn't nearly so beautiful as Lake George." Embarrassed by Mikael Brun's bemused scrutiny, the woman wiped her mouth. She'd given up on the soggy tuna-fish sandwich. She'd used all the paper napkins she'd been allotted. In the dappled shade at the picnic table her face looked appealingly young yet strained.

He did not want to hurt this woman, who had been hurt by other men. Without her needing to tell him this, he knew. For she seemed to open herself to such hurt, and to recoil from it belatedly, like a kind of sea anemone that is exquisitely beautiful but fragile. You begin in awe of such beauty but soon become impatient with it and want to injure it.

"Nowhere I've been has been quite so beautiful as this," the woman said, as if her point had been contested. "You must have been so happy. . . ."

"You think that children are made 'happy' by beauty? You should know better, you have children of your own. Children are blind to beauty."

They were silent for a moment. The woman surely felt rebuffed. But she persisted, as if reluctantly—"A terrible thing happened when I was at camp. A girl from my cabin died in a canoe accident . . ."

"It wasn't a canoe. It wasn't an accident."

Mikael spoke with such authority, the woman looked at him. Her smile was faint, quizzical.

"What do you mean? Why do you say that?"

"There was a girl, and she died—she'd been murdered somewhere on Big Burnt. But it wasn't a canoe accident. I was very young and all I knew was what I could overhear from adults speaking. . . . This was in 1972."

The woman was silent, staring at him across the badly weathered wooden table. Her eyes were widened in perplexity and yet in a distrust of her perplexity—should she know what her companion was talking about?

He spoke sometimes in a kind of code. A kind of poetry. Elliptical, elusive. He left me behind. Probably—he left us all behind.

The silence between them was strained, for silence between individuals in an island setting is far more awkward than on the mainland.

Mikael could not think of more to say because he'd just realized that the subject of the *murdered girl* had been a forbidden subject about which he should not have known. The memory of the girl (whose family had been camping at a site not far from the Bruns at the time of her death) was both scintillate and fleeting, like a fish seen in murky water, which has no sooner emerged into sight than it has vanished.

Sylvia. The forbidden name came to him, though he knew not to speak it aloud.

He had not thought of *Sylvia Delacorte* for years. He was sure it had been most of the years of his adult life.

The girl hadn't been so young, actually—sixteen. To Mikael, at age five, that had not seemed young.

A man had strangled Sylvia Delacorte. Or had he beaten her to death with a rock?

Somewhere in the woods it was rumored to have happened, in the dense interior of the island where no one went. Mikael had been too young to be told what had happened, why the park ranger boat had come to Big Burnt in the early morning bringing such disruption and upset and why adults had stood about in small, stunned groups speaking quietly together. His young mother he'd seen embrace herself as if she were cold, and shivering, and when he'd seen her, and she saw him seeing her, she'd frowned at him with a look he'd interpreted as angry and told him to go away, back into the tent.

For the remainder of the summer he'd had trouble sleeping in the tent. In the child-sized sleeping bag that he'd so loved.

Later he'd learned, when he was a little older, that the murderer of Sylvia Delacorte had been a boy of just seventeen. He too had been a camper on Big Burnt, with his parents. One of those boys Mikael had probably seen on the island, older boys whom he'd envied—barefoot, dark tanned, fearless swimmers off the docks, loud voiced and jeering, oblivious of a five-year-old.

Mikael was staring at his woman companion whose name—for just a moment, fleetingly—he'd forgotten as he'd forgotten what the thread of their conversation had been, before the subject of the murdered girl had derailed it. Dappled light gave the attractive fair-skinned woman an underwater look as if seen through a scrim of water of a depth of just a few inches.

The woman was telling Mikael how much she'd like to camp on Big Burnt Island, and how much her children would love it. This was a bold statement, Mikael knew. But what could he say in response?—the *last things* determined that, after Labor Day, Mikael Brun would cease to exist.

How vulnerable this woman was!—how perishable, the human body. That was the human tragedy, which no one could bear who dared to confront it head-on, without subterfuge and hypocrisy.

He was touched that Lisbeth Mueller had trusted him, coming to Lake George with him on this impulsive venture, and to Big Burnt; he was obliged to protect her, since she had so trusted him.

Yet still it was so—*she too could perish in the woods. Whatever has happened to one can happen to another.*

He announced that he was going swimming, and hoped that Lisbeth would join him.

She had told him earlier—in fact, several times she'd tried to explain—that she did not much like swimming, and had not swum in years.

Yet he seemed almost not to hear her. When she told him that she didn't think it was a good idea to swim so soon after eating Mikael laughed at her. "That's ridiculous. An old wives' tale."

Zestfully he stripped to his swim trunks, which he was wearing beneath khaki shorts. His legs were covered in coarse, dark hairs and were hard muscled and tanned from the knees downward; his thighs were pale, his torso and upper arms so pale you might imagine you could see veins through the skin. His body was reasonably lean yet flaccid at the waist; his chest and back were covered in wispy, graying hairs. Lisbeth had not seen the man so exposed—that is, on his feet, a little distance from her.

"C'mon! Come with me."

"I didn't bring a bathing suit. I told you . . ."

"Then wade in the water. You won't get your shorts wet. And if you do, a little—so what?"

Because I don't want to! Damn you, leave me alone.

But she was laughing, for Mikael meant only to tease.

Lisbeth accompanied Mikael to the edge of the lake, directly below the promontory; she would take iPhone pictures of him swimming, as she'd taken pictures that morning of the lake, the island seen from the lake, the mountains across the lake.

Pictures of herself and of Mikael Brun in the rented boat, taken by the teenaged marina attendant who surely thought the two a married couple. *Thanks!* Lisbeth had told the boy brightly.

You want a record, a commemoration of an interlude so intensely lived. You believe that you do.

Below the promontory there was no beach, only a few misshapen boulders strewn amid sandy soil. Boldly Mikael stepped into the lake and waded out until he was staggering waist-deep in the thick-looking water and then, as Lisbeth watched with some unease, he pushed himself out as if plunging into the unknown and began swimming.

He was a good swimmer, as he'd boasted. Fortunately he seemed to have forgotten about urging her to wade by the shore. A stronger breeze had arisen and the lake was now reflecting a pale-glowering sky.

For some minutes Lisbeth stood watching her companion swim in large, loose circles like a freed child. She smiled to think how totally oblivious of her he was—and yet, she could understand that he wouldn't want to come to this remote place alone.

It was a relief, her companion was swimming so well. Other campers, if they happened to glance in their direction, would think that the middle-aged husband was a competent swimmer but the middle-aged wife standing on shore looking on with a vague smile, probably not. She had no need to think, wryly—*What if he drowns? How will I get back home?*

Lisbeth returned to the picnic table, and began *The New York Times* crossword puzzle. What a relief, to be alone! To be free of Mikael Brun's laser-like attention, if for just a few minutes!

Of course the crossword puzzles were trivial and a waste of time but there was solace in such brain activity, which blocked unwanted thoughts. Even so, Lisbeth often left the puzzle unfinished. As (she thought) she left so much of her life unfinished. And now she could not concentrate. It did seem ridiculous to be in this beautiful place and to be focused on a mere puzzle.

Her attention was drawn to the figure in the water, diminished at a distance, vulnerable seeming, and yet somehow stubborn.

The man was her lover, but not her friend. She had trusted him well enough to accompany him on this end-of-summer trip to the Adirondacks, but in fact she could not trust him, she knew this. In his bemused indifference to her was the promise of betrayal to come. She could not risk this, not at her age.

"I will risk it. Mikael Brun is worth it."

Onstage it is not uncommon for solitary individuals to speak aloud. The convention is that the audience overhears, and the convention is that the audience pretends it is plausible that a solitary individual, brooding, musing aloud, would think so coherently and succinctly. In her adult life Lisbeth yearned badly for the protective confines of a play—a script. Chekhov, Ibsen, Shakespeare. Recently, she'd performed in a locally praised production of Synge's *Deirdre of the Sorrows*—which Mikael had seen, and seemed to have admired.

It was the invention of original speech, spontaneous and unrehearsed speech, that had been so difficult in her life, and had propelled her into a succession of misunderstandings and mistakes.

Farther out, she saw one of the ungainly predator birds Mikael had pointed out from the boat. A prehistoric-looking creature—a "great blue heron"—though its feathers were gunmetal gray, not blue. The heron's sharp beak was perfectly suited for aquatic hunting.

At last, after about twenty minutes, Lisbeth saw to her relief that the swimmer was turning back. Streaming water down the length of his body, stumbling just a little, Mikael emerged from the water. He seemed to be searching for her, staring. (He'd removed his dark glasses before entering the water.) She saw the pale torso slick with wet hairs, which looked thin and wispy; the soft, fleshy knobs at the waistline;

the legs, which appeared just slightly tremulous after the strain of energetic swimming. When Lisbeth came to him with a towel he was short of breath.

His skin felt cold, clammy. His fingers were chilled. Lisbeth embraced him in the towel and rubbed him vigorously as she might have done with one of her children until he took the towel from her to dry himself. He insisted that the swim had been "terrific" and that next time, Lisbeth would come with him—"You're a good swimmer, after all."

"Not me. You're thinking of someone else, Mikael."

"I'm thinking of *you*."

His mood was brusque, jocular. But still he was short of breath. Ascending along the steep, scrubby path to the picnic table he surprised Lisbeth by leaning on her, just a little.

Her companion seemed to be feeling almost faint. Lisbeth took hold of his arm and held him as he walked in such a way that it wasn't apparent that she was supporting him, if he chose not to notice.

Returned to the picnic table Mikael drank bottled water thirstily, and insisted that Lisbeth drink as well. He asked Lisbeth what she'd been doing while he was swimming and she told him nothing really, for she'd been watching him—"Watching and thinking."

"Yes? Thinking what?"

"How lucky we are to be here, in this beautiful place."

He was regarding her closely. Again, she'd uttered the word *beautiful*. She did not know if *beautiful* was a word that conveyed genuine awe or whether it was merely banal, overused; she dreaded Mikael Brun disliking her, for the shallowness of her soul.

His soul, she supposed she could never grasp. He was right to be bemused by her efforts to understand his work. When they'd first begun seeing each other she'd tried to read some of his scientific publications—*A Short History of the Anatomy of the Human Brain, Cognition and Its Discontents: The Linguistic Wars*. She could not read more than a sentence or two of his scientific papers, filled with the terminology, figures, and data of neuroscience. She understood that Noam Chomsky had long been a mentor of Mikael Brun's, and she had tried to read work by Chomsky on linguistics, biological determinism, genetically transmitted principles of language. But when she'd tried to speak to Mikael about these subjects, he'd listened to her with such an expression of patience, if he didn't laugh at her outright as he might have laughed at a bright, naive child, she'd soon given up.

173

"Yes. You are correct, Lisbeth. Our lives are purely 'luck'—we are borne along by the current, and imagine we are the ones in control."

In his elevated, jovial mood Mikael pulled Lisbeth with him to a secluded place beyond the campsite. He'd returned from the arduous interlude of swimming—and from the bout of breathlessness—with a desire to make love, Lisbeth surmised. She chose not to suppose that, in his exalted state, Mikael Brun would have made love with anyone; she chose to believe that he did in fact desire *her*. He was not always affectionate in lovemaking, and seemed more playful now. She wasn't comfortable with the quasi-public nature of this lovemaking but there appeared to be no one within sight. And so she did not resist but returned his kisses avidly, and ran her fingers through his thinned, damp hair. His skull was hard, bony as rock; his breath still came short, but his skin, which had been clammy from the water, was warming. Soon, it would be aflame.

She had not ever made love in any place quite like this. On the ground—which was hard, uncomfortable against her back—and the sky abruptly overhead—the sky not fair and tranquil as it had been but thicker textured and bunched together, like blistering paint. Mikael was kissing her eagerly, pressing his mouth against her mouth as if wanting to devour her. His unshaven jaws were harsh, abrasive. He was much heavier than she, his limbs longer, dwarfing her as he held her down, in place; a moment of panic came to her, that the man would hurt her, he would suffocate her, half consciously perhaps, for having intruded in this childhood paradise with her distracting questions. Clumsily he pulled at her clothing, pushing aside her hands though she meant to help. She felt like prey gathered in the beak of a great predator bird, without identity, even as the life was being annihilated in her. She was thinking, *He has planned this. But not with me.*

Afterward she asked him if as a boy camping on the island he'd had fantasies of bringing girls here and he said curtly, as if the question were offensive to him, "No."

"Really? Not even when you were an adolescent?"

"Big Burnt is like no other place."

He spoke disdainfully, and would say no more.

By quick degrees he fell asleep, one of his arms outstretched and the fingers twitching. Lisbeth tried to lie beside him, in the crook of his arm, not very comfortably. Her breasts, her lower body ached. Her mouth throbbed as if bruised. At a distance she heard the voices of campers, and at distance the sound of a boat on the lake. Her eyelids were heavy yet her brain was alert, brightly awake. She had not yet slept beside this man for in his sleep he was restless, sighing deeply, shrugging his shoulders, pushing her away if she came too near. Now she was wondering if she would ever sleep beside him, in any normal fashion. In a bed, in a bedroom, in a house, in the confinement of a shared life.

Lovemaking. Making-of-love.

As if love does not generate itself but has to be made—by the effort of two.

She was sitting up, and had adjusted her clothing. Her hair was matted. Her skin felt sticky. Gnats circled her damp face, her hair. She took one of the man's hands in hers—gently. She saw with curiosity that his thumbs were precisely twice the size of hers. The backs of his hands were covered in thin, dark, graying hairs. On the third finger of his left hand was the ghost of a ring (she thought); the wedding ring he'd worn for years, and had, as he'd told her with a harsh laugh, "tossed away" after his divorce.

She did not want to wake her lover for he seemed drawn, fatigued. Like the swimming, lovemaking took a good deal of energy from him. His face that was usually so alert, handsome in alertness as a predator bird, was slack now in repose. His mouth was slightly open. A glisten of saliva in the corner of his mouth. She wondered if she could love the man sufficiently, to compensate for his not loving her. Or perhaps, in some way, out of weakness perhaps, he would come to love her.

In time, he stirred and woke. His eyelids fluttered, he was seeing her. "Lisbeth." The name seemed strange on his lips, a memorized name that made him smile in a kind of dazed wonderment as if the glowering sky was partly blinding.

Lisbeth leaned over him to kiss him. "Welcome back to Big Burnt, Mikael."

It was not a naturally caressing name—*Mikael*. Yet in Lisbeth's soft, throaty voice, it had the effect of a caress.

Overhead the sky appeared to be dimming. The air was humid but a cooler wind was rising. Lightning leapt among the clouds like exposed nerves but it was only heat lightning—so far away, its deafening thunder had dissipated to silence.

"Don't panic—hey?"

Another time he spoke playfully yet she understood the severity beneath—*Don't you dare become emotional, not in my presence.*

175

At last, with a single sixteen-ounce plastic Evian bottle, she'd begun to bail water out of the back of the boat, which had risen to a depth of—could it be six inches? For Mikael Brun had decreed finally, bailing might not be a bad idea. Pelting rain and waves sloshing steadily into the rear of the boat so that the rear was much lower than the front did indeed cause Lisbeth to feel panic, which (she hoped) she was able to disguise from her companion.

He'd insisted that the boat was "unsinkable." He'd insisted that she should not worry, he would bring them back to the marina safely. Yet Lisbeth thought Mikael was probably relieved that she'd begun to bail water even as he hadn't wanted her to think he thought it was necessary.

Their things in the back were awash in churning water. The backpacks were thoroughly soaked. The oars were floating. Lisbeth was turned awkwardly in her seat in a desperate attempt to bail out water. At least it might be possible to keep pace with the water coming into the boat, though the sixteen-ounce bottle was much too small, absurdly impractical. She had never worked so hard, and so frantically at any physical task. Emptying water out of the bottle, over the side of the boat; submerging the bottle (horizontally) into the water in the rear, allowing the bottle to fill, and again emptying it over the side of the boat. . . . The continuous jolting and rocking of the boat, the agitated motion of the waves, not rhythmic but chaotic as if being shaken in a madman's fist, was making her nauseated. She felt as if she might vomit but would not succumb.

Directly overhead were flashes of lightning, vertical, terrifying, so close that the deafening thunderclaps came almost instantaneously and she could not keep from whimpering aloud.

"If you hear the thunder, you're all right. You're *not dead.*"

Mikael was trying to be funny, even now. She supposed that was what he was attempting—to be funny.

Ever more desperately she was bailing water. Like a frenzied automaton, bailing water. Whatever she could do was not very effective—the rear of the boat seemed to be sinking steadily. But she could not give up—could she? If she gave up she would crouch beside the man with shut eyes, pressing her hands over her ears, catatonic in terror.

She was thinking how good it was, thank God her children were nowhere near!

Still, she continued to bail water. Numbly she smiled, bailing water.

Her clothing was soaked. Her hair hung in her face. She was shivering convulsively. Yet her heart beat hard in determination. One day, she and Mikael Brun would look back upon this nightmare and laugh, in recollection.

Crossing Lake George in that storm we realized if we survived, we could survive virtually anything. Together.

At the steering wheel of the boat Mikael kept on course. Tried to keep on course. His mood had shifted. He'd been elated at the outset, pushing off from Big Burnt, and then he'd been grim, abashed; but now again he was feeling elated, even reckless. They could not drown, after all—impossible! This was Lake George, which he knew like the back of his hand. He had no doubt that he was going in the right direction and might have been a quarter mile from the marina.

He'd been so happy that day!—he could not surrender that happiness now.

On Big Burnt he'd felt as if he had come home. Yet it was a home from which others had departed. He'd felt like one who has opened his eyes in a strange place that is also a familiar place—a familiar place that is also a strange place. One of his lurid fantasies, that his father was buried on Big Burnt. . . . Melancholia like an undertow had had him in its grip all the days of his life but now the raging lake was making him happy again, holding his course on the raging lake was making him happy again, bringing the woman back safely to the marina, not harming the woman as he'd vowed he would not do, though it was within his power—as a child is made happy he was being made happy in sudden random gusts, waves.

Of course, he would not blow out his brains. Ridiculous!

There are ways less melodramatic. Ways that emulate natural causes. Whiskey, sedatives. He was a distinguished neuroscientist, he knew how to obliterate consciousness the way a blackboard is cleaned. So many "sacrificed" animals in the Brun lab, so many years. The scientist's hand would not waver at obliteration.

Though possibly: He'd direct his lawyer to file a countersuit. He'd fire that lawyer and hire another, better lawyer. He would not slink away in disgrace. He would not slink away at all—*he would never resign his professorship*. He would certainly never step down from the directorship of the institute that he himself had founded. Instead, he would appeal the university's (hasty, ill-advised) decision if it went against him. If the appeal failed he would sue. He would sue the dean of the college, and he would sue the chair of his longtime department. He would sue each of the committee members. He would sue the president of the university who was ex officio on the committee.

He could marry again if he wished. It was not too late.

He would not make the same mistakes again. If he could remember these mistakes that had not seemed to be mistakes at the outset.

He could marry this woman—Lisbeth. She loved him, and would grow to love him more deeply. He would give her no cause not to love him as he'd done with other women, out of distrust of female weakness and subterfuge. But what was her last name, he'd forgotten. . . .

Wide is the gate, and broad is the way, that leadeth to destruction. Strait is the gate, and narrow the way, that leadeth onto life.

These biblical words came to him at the wheel of the little outboard, he had no idea why. He was no admirer of the Bible. He wasn't even certain which of the gospels this was—St. Mark? Matthew? Carefully he'd explained to anyone who asked, to interviewers, he was not by nature a religious person, yet, as a neuroscientist, he understood that religion is probably hardwired into the human brain.

Wide is the gate . . . That was the problem: The lake was too vast, "broad"; it was the narrower inlet he sought, to bring them to safety.

This inlet was close ahead. A few hundred yards perhaps. In a few minutes he would be close enough to the mainland to see exactly where he was.

Already it seemed to him that the waves were less severe. He was nearing land—wasn't he? To his left, a small familiar, nameless island would appear; to his right, the rocky mainland. He would see (was he seeing?) lights on land; he knew where this was, very close to the marina. He had only to keep on course; even with this poor visibility he could not miss it.

And yet, there was a thinness, almost a transparency now to the mist. Everywhere he stared was embued with a kind of radiance. It was the illumination of the finite, which filled him with melancholy, but also, strangely, a great happiness, hope. . . .

And then, out of nowhere, there appeared a boat—a rescue boat?— and a male voice calling to them, *Did they need help?*

A Lake George ranger boat, suddenly beside them. The man was both immensely relieved and terribly disappointed.

Out of the heavy rain a flashlight beam was directed at them, at the man's grimacing face.

"Hello? D'you need help?"

"Yes! Please! We need help!" the woman cried.

The man was furious with her, in that instant. But he did not contradict her. Abashed, he followed the ranger's directions. He followed the larger boat, which accompanied them to the marina. To his dismay he saw that, as he'd anticipated, the marina was directly ahead. He would have brought the boat in safely himself, within ten minutes.

Neither he nor his female passenger would see the flag at the end of the dock, high above their heads, hanging limp, sodden, unrecognizable as an American flag.

There, in still-pelting rain, amid flashes of lightning and claps of deafening thunder, the man and the woman were greeted by a teen-aged marina attendant in a yellow rain poncho. "Great! Great job getting back, mister"—the words were as flattering as they were insincere, and much appreciated. The young man secured the boat for them, which was bucking and heaving beside the dock; he helped each of them out of the boat, the woman first, then the man, with as much solicitude as if they were elderly or infirm, and their bones fragile. "Careful, sir! Ma'am! The dock is slippery."

Returning in the car to their motel several miles away, the man was silent in his soaked, sodden clothes as if abashed, brooding. The woman could not stop exclaiming how wonderful it was to be out of the boat, off the lake, in the car, and out of the rain! She was delirious with gratitude, relief. How happy she was, and how determined never to step into a boat again in her life! If she was expecting the man to protest such an extravagant statement, he took no notice. Halfway to the motel the man abruptly braked the car on the shoulder of the road and asked if the woman would mind driving? He had a migraine headache, all the muscles of his upper body ached.

Gratefully the woman drove the rest of the way, still in rain. How she hated rain, in the Adirondacks! She'd been shaken for just a moment, thinking, *He is disgusted with me. He will make me get out of the car and walk back in the rain.*

Of course, he was not angry at her in the slightest. He too was relieved—obviously. Several times he embraced her, kissed her roughly on the mouth as soon as they entered their motel room.

Their nostrils pinched, the room smelled musty. Outside the sliding-glass doors to their little balcony the vast lake was invisible in rain, mist. Perhaps there was no lake at all, they'd been under a cruel enchantment. There was no "visibility" from the windows of their room, they had only each other.

In revulsion for their soaked, soiled-seeming clothing they took lengthy showers. The clothing was hung to dry by the woman. When Lisbeth came out of the shower she saw Mikael hunched over his laptop, sitting on the edge of the king-sized bed. At last the terrible storm was lifting. Rain came less ferociously. Lisbeth returned to the bathroom to dress and when she emerged again, she saw Mikael on the phone, on the balcony. She heard his lowered voice. She heard him laugh—somehow, this was disconcerting. For he had not laughed with her.

How lonely she felt, he'd moved so quickly beyond her! She understood by the way in which his gaze slid over her, appraising, bemused. He told her he'd decided to return to Cambridge a day early, they would leave in the morning. Early Sunday morning—"We'll beat the traffic."

Tenderly he stooped to kiss her. Rubbed his rough beard against her cheek. As if it had all been a joke of a kind and their lives had never been seriously at risk.

"Hey. You saved us."

She would protest afterward, he'd given no sign.

No sign. No hint. Not a word.

He hadn't been unhappy. (No more than any of us are unhappy!)

Many people would contact her. Most of them were strangers. Brun's family, ex-wife, relatives. Colleagues at Harvard and at the institute. Journalists. She'd been unable to keep confidential the (shameful, incomprehensible) fact that Lisbeth Mueller had been the companion of Mikael Brun for several days before he'd returned to his Cambridge home and killed himself. She'd had to give statements to police. She could give only a faltering, uncertain testimony that altered each time she gave it. She did not lie but she neglected to tell all that she might have told. What had been intimate between them she would never reveal. She would not show anyone—not even the grieving Brun children—the pictures of Mikael Brun alone and with Lisbeth Mueller on her iPhone. Nor could she bring herself to reveal to anyone that among the final words Mikael Brun had said to her were these playful, not very sincere words—*Hey. You saved us.*

For she had not saved them, had she?

She was furious with the man, and came to hate him. She was devastated. She was in love with him, and wept for him, in a frenzy of grief she could not reveal to anyone. She could not sleep for she was pleading with him—*Why? Why did you do such a thing to yourself, and to me?*

It was clear, Mikael Brun had prepared his *last things* before he'd left for Lake George. All had been neatly organized, awaiting his return from Big Burnt. That seemed to be incontestable, she would not contest it. Her heart was lacerated by the realization that, in his last hours, her lover had forgotten her entirely. Not one of the *last letters* had been addressed to her.

She could not think of any words she might wish to utter to anyone. She had not an adequate language, she had no script. And so, eventually she gave up trying.

The Return to Monsterland
Sequoia Nagamatsu

TRAIN CAR, 1998

MAYU CALLED ME FROM the train car that Godzilla had grabbed hold of—no screaming or sobbing, no confessions of great regrets, no final professions of love. She did not ask to speak to our five-year-old daughter, who was unknowingly watching the news coverage of her mother's impending death, as the train crashed into the side of a sky-scraper and through a set of power lines. My wife spoke of feeling the radiation of *his* body coursing through her own, the view down *his* Cretaceous mouth, *an* atomic breath swirling in a maelstrom of blue light. And then, before there was nothing but a roar and static, she said: "You should be here; he's simply magnificent."

GODZILLA (IRRADIATED GODZILLASAURUS)

{Descp. Resembles Tyrannosaur with pronounced arms. Dorsal plates similar to Stegosaur. Semisapient. Powers: atomic breath, nuclear pulse, imperviousness to conventional weaponry (and meteor impacts), regeneration, amphibiousness, telepathy with other *kaiju*. Weaknesses: high voltage, oxygen destroyer WMD, antinuclear en-ergy bacteria, cadmium missiles, Mechagodzilla.}

Field Notes: lumber-waddle. posturing roar. rhythmic stomp with son. perhaps a game? picks up palm tree and throws. swats seagull. defecates two meters high—radiation: 15 krad. moves arms up and down. calisthenics or victory dance. long roar. shuffles across beach. throws log into water. throws rock into water.

Two weeks living among their kind on the island reserve we've cre-ated for them, and I still can't wrap my head around the love my wife felt for these creatures. During the atomic age, when nations illuminated the atolls dotting the Pacific, we gave birth to many of the *kaiju*. Annihilation begetting annihilation when the living ghosts of Hiroshima still roamed the streets. The Ministry of Defense contacted me partly out of kindness, I suspect. The widower of the famous monster biologist, the silent partner who stayed in the lab. I knew the creatures almost as well as Mayu did—the half-life of their blood, the frequency of their telepathic thoughts, the variations of their origins and resurrections. I could, without a doubt, answer Japan's questions about new monsters being born in the wake of Fukushima, of old monsters shaken out of armistice. And so I said yes because I hated their kind, because my daughter, now a college student, still reads the letters her mother left her, because I need to experience the beauty my wife saw before she died.

Dear Ayu,
I had to watch the video of your first steps from the bottom of the ocean. I wish I could have been there. But I guess all of our practice trying to walk paid off! Do you remember how we watched old news broadcasts of the epic kaiju *battles of the sixties? I'd pick you up by the arms, your feet resting on mine, and we'd take one giant step after another, waddling across the living room. Whenever I let you go, there would be a moment where we both thought that you could make that first step on your own. But you flapped your arms like Rodan or Mothra, trying to maintain your balance before crashing to the ground. Your father tells me you're moving nonstop now with your newfound freedom, that you circle the house until you're so tired that you need a nap. I wish you were here with me. I hope these letters will help you understand why I was away so much. It's just me, a steel sphere, and two tiny windows right now. Miles of ocean are dead because of us—the Oxygen Destroyer killed a former Godzilla several decades ago along with everything around him: suffocation before the atoms of his body weakened, leaving nothing but bone. A shark hunts in vain—still. A jelly billows past like a cloud. I rake away layers of shells and fish husks from his skeleton with the submarine's robotic arm, collect him piece by piece. Godzilla died then because we didn't understand, because we are always afraid—and despite him saving us from danger time and again, we never seem to learn.*

MU

Sunken civilization. Geologic curiosity. Aquatic paradise. Scuba-dive excursion. Mu, home of the Naacal, shaken beneath the waves overnight—temples entombed in lava, megalith highways to the Mariana Trench. The Naacal, catamaran refugees, ancestors of Egypt and the Fertile Crescent. Manda, water-dragon guardian, still defending the Naacal after millennia. At a college dive, Mayu and I discussed her dissertation on the *Kaiju* as Heritage, creatures who came before us, were created by us, that served us. Creatures, I added, that no longer belonged. But we must find a way for them to belong, she insisted. "Try reasoning with a three-story lizard," I said. "Tell that to the parents of children who died when these creatures decided to throw down on their school." A piece of Mu has been placed off the coast of the reserve for Manda to protect, a collection of pillars, the worn smirk of a marble warrior, three thousand pounds of drowned mountain. Five miles of ocean surrounded by an electromagnetic field. This is what we can give them. This is where they belong.

MOTHRA (MOTH GODDESS, CURRENT STAGE: LARVAL)

{Descp. Segmented brown body. Blue eyes. Pronounced mandibles. Powers: silken spray, several beam weapons, strong psychic communication. As an adult, able to create gale-force wind with wings. Lightning from antennae. Effectively immortal (phoenix life cycle). Travels with faerie sisters, the Elias—three-inch women in red tunics.}

Field Notes: undulates around island. tries to follow butterflies and moths. visits other kaiju. *sways head with Varan. chews on shrubs and grasses. draws mandalas on beach with body. sends sonic pulse to Manda. the Elias, Lora and Moll, ride its back. Elias laugh frequently. whispers. song.*

A glorified grub, a far cry from the bright-orange-and-yellow wings that Mayu and my daughter loved. Perhaps the most beloved of the *kaiju* because she is a goddess, because through her spritely companions

184

we understand the moth's chirps, the roars and groans of other *kaiju*. "Godzilla doesn't hate humans but humans hate us," the little sisters declared on national television. Fair enough, I say. But he still flattened my favorite soba shop in the country with several elderly ladies inside, used Tokyo Tower like a toothpick. Maybe we shouldn't have used missiles, maybe we could have spent time coming to an understanding. But parlays are an afterthought when people are running out of their cars and screaming down the street. Mayu said that's typical human behavior, the kind of trait that would ruin humanity in the end: Shoot first, ask questions later. She reminded me it was the *kaiju* who saved us from alien invasions—the Kilaakians, the Millennians. Ayu, who became quite the activist in her junior-high class, following her mother's letters as text, would always say, "*Kaiju* don't kill people; people kill people" and "Love is the greatest weapon of all!"

The Elias sisters pay me no mind most of the time but occasionally flutter around my head, giggling like schoolgirls, providing me insight into each of the creatures: *Godzilla is very sad today. Godzilla remembers your wife and is sorry. Godzilla cannot help being Godzilla. Manda is lonely. There were once many sea dragons in the sea. Manda knows Mu is far away. Mothra remembers when humans were not here. Mothra says those were peaceful times. Mothra says quiet will come again one day. Baragon has indigestion from eating a strange plant. Gorosaurus wants to find love. Anguirus wants to get to know Rodan better. Nobody really likes Kumonga. Kumonga is grumpy. Kumonga will try to kill you.*

Dear Ayu,

Yesterday I brought you with me to the NHK television studio to talk to the Elias. You've just turned two now, so I imagine you won't remember any of this except for impressions of faerie feet dancing on your tummy, making you laugh, of Lora and Moll singing lost melodies into your ear. Atlantean ballads, Babylonian hymns, they said. You held your Mothra stuffed animal, your most prized possession, which has watched over you in your crib since you were born. Lora and Moll reclined on the plush wings as I interviewed them. I have to admit, I'd like to fancy myself the Margaret Mead of the kaiju *world. The people have stopped running, little one. At least for now. The time has come to listen to those we call monsters.*

185

The sisters talked of Mothra being part of a menagerie of earth deities, each with a counterpart, creating balance in the world. The earth created Battra to destroy evil but this moth became evil itself. And so Mothra was created to bring good into the world. When darkness rises, the forces of good must restore balance. One cannot exist without the other, you see (even for the creatures humanity creates). And so some of our monsters are reborn when we need them. I try explaining this idea of balance to you during our hikes. You on my back, as I shed calories at the base of Mount Fuji. I tell you these things in the hope that you'll grow to appreciate life, to see humanity in concert with the earth instead of in control of it. Your father and I, despite what he might believe about his semiannual donations to environmental nonprofits, disagree in this matter.

Back home, I put you on the quilt your grandmother made you with your Play Zone console while I transcribed my interview with the Elias. I reclined on your father's chair and concentrated on my work. You've figured out how to play "Pop Goes the Weasel" by pressing a red button and seem genuinely delighted every time you hear the music play, as if it's a new discovery. I put on my headphones and ignored you for the rest of the afternoon. I gave you a sippy cup and read through a study of a colleague's pharmaceutical research based on the DNA of sixteen captive shapeshifters. Imagine, antiaging skin! You stared at me blankly. You did not cry or fuss. You've always been good about letting Mommy be.

ANGUIRUS (IRRADIATED ANKYLOSAURUS W/ STYRACOSAURIAN CRANIAL FEATURES)

{Descp. Long, clubbed, spiked tail. Orange spikes and horns on gray skin. Five brains (one in head, others near limbs—heightened reflexes & locomotion). Capable of bipedal motion but generally quadruped. Powers: lacking in ranged attacks and special abilities but rarely concedes in battle, advanced burrowing abilities, use of spiked carapace by jumping backward onto enemies, able to curl into ball and travel at high speed. Oldest and perhaps most consistent ally of Godzilla.}

Field Notes: chews on palm. burrows past Kumonga. emerges beside Godzilla. rolls between hills. rolls into coconuts. perhaps Bocci? rests on carapace, Godzilla spins friend, both roar, both wave arms, follows Godzilla, sleeps with Godzilla.

Late for our dinner and distracted by work, Mayu said yes to my marriage proposal almost as an afterthought. I honestly didn't care. I was the safe bet for her, the guy who would always be there (and I always was even when she was nowhere to be found). Maybe I thought marrying my best friend and colleague would be enough and the rest would take care of itself. She could grow to love me—and our professional differences would keep the passion going that I thought we had found in our nightlong debates in graduate school when we would seamlessly shift from biochemistry to the bedroom. "You're like a puppy barking at the television," she'd say. "You're adorably confused about the reality of things." And I'd say, "You're the hippie who's doing all the barking." She was a ten to my marginal six (in both beauty and professional pedigree), something my jackass friends would often remind me of, and perhaps it was this fact that, in part, fed a nagging insecurity, prompting me to do nothing when I suspected Mayu was having an affair with her research assistant—a blond postdoc from Berkeley who looked more surfer than scientist. As long as she came home to me. As long as we were still a family.

Anguirus is not the strongest of the *kaiju*. He does not fly, does not shoot lasers from his horns or mouth. But he is loyal to his allies. He never gives up even when he is beaten down. Ruled by atomic instinct and rage, even these creatures understand friendship, something that I've read about in papers but could never believe until I lived among them. And I wonder even after all their deaths and rebirths if they remember—or is who they are and what they mean to each other not so much memory as stitching in the fabric of their being.

Dear Ayu,
I really wanted to take you with me during the filming of my National Geographic *special but your father said the journey would be too arduous for a little girl who already has a full plate with kindergarten and after-school English classes. He worries too much (and could you think of a better education than this?). You*

187

would absolutely love it. Maybe he would just miss you. I know you hear us fighting sometimes, and I want you to know it's not your fault. Mommy has to be away a lot, so sometimes Daddy gets lonely. He gets jealous because you want to be with me instead of him even though I can't be there for you every day when you get home from school. I can't take you to do fun things on the week-end like going to Ueno Zoo to look at the red pandas . . . but know that I really want to. Be a good girl for him. He does try, and he loves you. One day I'll be home more. You'll come home after school and you can tell me about your friends, show me a project you're proud of—macaroni necklaces, cardboard dioramas, book reports dotted with stickers from your teacher. But there is still so much work to be done. Oh, the things you're missing right now. My research assistant, Tyler, whom you've met (I believe you said he looked like "in the movies"), scouted out locations for us to film: abandoned parts of Tokyo, Paris, London, and Cairo that were once battlegrounds of great kaiju *battles. We traveled to Monsterland to talk to scientists doing experiments on containing the* kaiju *with chemical mists and electromagnetic fields. Containment vs. extermination is our goal, so we can foster better relationships with these terribly misunderstood creatures. Your father sent me photos of you and your grandmother under a cherry tree. Are those new overalls? I've only been away three months and yet you seem to have grown so much. Enclosed are photos of me and Tyler with some of the* kaiju *in the background.*

RODAN (IRRADIATED PTERANODON)

{Descp. Two-hundred-meter wingspan. Reddish brown. Powers: Immune to atomic breath and gravity beams, shock waves while flying, high winds via wings, quite strong despite spindly appearance, history of self-sacrifice to help others.}

Field Notes: crushes rocks with beak. spreads wings. blows down trees. topples Kumonga. takes off. circles island. perches on mountaintop. extended screech.

My father worked long hours at the post office for decades to provide for me and my siblings. He took us fishing on the weekends and gave us what little money he had to buy manga—Ultraman, Space Pirate Captain Harlock. His only joy was watching baseball on television while drinking a cold Sapporo. My mother dreamed of becoming a nightclub singer (and from what I understand had interest from a Russian-owned Roppongi club), but I would only ever know her voice from the lullabies she sang in my childhood. I never expected that I or Mayu would follow in my parents' footsteps, giving ourselves so completely to our children. Our livelihoods, particularly Mayu's, required a certain level of commitment. But I did expect some sacrifice, some change in her that never happened. I never minded being the one to chauffeur Ayu, cook meals, help with homework, and read bedtime stories. But, if I'm honest, Ayu grew up only with the mystique of her mother, the legend of her spun from letters and occasional visits. Tell her I love her, Mayu would say whenever I was on the phone with her. Give her this for me. Send me pictures. Mayu became the giver of gifts, the adventurer with stories, the person my daughter turned to for understanding when I became the target of hatred. After Rodan transferred his life force to Godzilla so that he could defeat Mechagodzilla, Mayu talked on American television about the love of Godzilla for his son in defeating his enemy, about the sacrifice of Rodan in helping his friend to victory. "These creatures," she said, "are more like us than we'd like to admit. They love and they protect that which they love. They may fight sometimes, yes. But when the chips are down, they would do anything for each other."

Dear Ayu,
I hope you and your father have fun this weekend at Disneyland. I can't express how sorry I am that I had to leave at the last minute. I know I'm not there for you as much as I should be. I keep saying this, I know. And I hope all I'm doing now will be somehow worth it. I've written almost two hundred letters to you. Some of them are written to you as you are now, my innocent, silly girl. But much of what I write is for myself and for a much older version of you, a you that has fallen in love, chased a dream, gotten your heart broken, learned lessons the hard way, found a soul mate when you weren't looking for one, and perhaps even entered the strange world of motherhood (something I know I

can't fully claim to know a lot about). The last time I went to Disneyland was the weekend after your father proposed. We rode every ride at least twice, but we spent most of the day just walking, observing the families that we might one day resemble. I asked your father, "Is that what you want for us?" And he said he wanted that life very much. I told him I did too. And maybe it wasn't exactly the truth, but I said it anyway because I wanted to believe children and pets and a mortgage would make everything easier by oddly making my life fuller. Anyway . . . I enjoyed your phone call yesterday. I'm glad you and your friend Haruka made up on the playground even after she pushed over your block tower. Sometimes friends do messed-up things even if they care about you. But it's important to try to work things out, to forgive if at all possible. The world's a big, scary place, little one. Company is always nice. Ride all the rides, even the scary ones. Take pictures. And tell your daddy that Mommy says you can have a treat in the gift shop.

BIRTH ISLAND

Deserted island. Respite from the world. Godzilla and Zilla Junior have quality time after brushes with death. Birth Island where the king of the monsters found fatherhood. Birth Island where the children of monsters are allowed to play.

Conception following an ultimatum wasn't the ideal. Now or never, I told Mayu. Yes, I'm unhappy, I said. How long can we really wait? In retrospect we were both being unfair. I because I was telling my wife who may never have been in love with me to have a child in order to save our domestic best friendship. She because, for whatever reason, she could never admit the truth about how she felt. We gave each other permission to get comfortable with our discomfort. At the hospital, after she had given birth, Mayu said, "I don't know how to be a mother." I told her no one does at first. She looked down at Ayu, nestled in her arms, and looked back up at me. "What if I never feel like I'm her mother?"

1999: Mommy, I had a dream that . . .

2000: Dear Mommy, Daddy won't let me. . . .

2001: Dear Mommy, the kids at school . . .

2002: Dear Mommy, I miss you. I hate the monsters that took you away.

2005: Dear Mom, I'm organizing a presentation with my friends about protecting the kaiju. *I've already collected signatures of almost everybody in my school to send to the prime minister.*

2008: Dear Mom, I've started seeing a boy, but I don't think I like, like him. I got perfect scores again in all my science classes. Let's not talk about gym class.

2012: Dear Mom, great news! I've been accepted to Osaka University! Your old assistant, Tyler, is a visiting professor there. He took me to lunch. He said he was excited that I was admitted. He said you were a remarkable woman and that he was sorry the world lost you so early.

MINILLA (INFANT GODZILLASAURUS)

{Descp. Smaller version of his father without pronounced armored plates. Generally fearful of other monsters. Playful in nature. Powers: radioactive smoke rings, telepathy with father, ability to shrink to human size w/ some human vocal abilities. Some history of convincing father to be gentler with humankind.}

Field Notes: runs circles around father. shrinks in size and plays in small cave. tumble rolls. waves arm at me. hello? twirls. tiny roar. endearing roar. throws coconut at father.

Every year until there was nothing left (Ayu had just turned fourteen), the two of us would take a small packet of her mother's ashes and scatter them at a site of a *kaiju* incident. We traveled to three continents, eleven countries, and four islands. For the last year, we stopped by Ueno station in Tokyo, walked upstairs to where we could overlook the train tracks that were lifted off the ground by Godzilla nine years prior. Ayu had grown from silence to hatred of all things

191

nonhuman to a champion for those creatures who needed a voice. I was proud of the young woman she was becoming. I'm proud of the woman she has become. I emptied the last of her mother into her palms and she held them over the walkway, her fingers still curled shut. "Good-bye, Mom," she said. "I won't stop writing." She opened her hands and let the draft of a passing train carry away the ashes.

Dear Ayu,

I'll be taking the next train to Tokyo tomorrow, one of only a handful being let in for research and military personnel while Godzilla paces downtown. Your father tells me the two of you are doing quite well with Grandma and Grandpa in Nara. Like camping, he says—you in your Hello Kitty pup tent in the living room. Hopefully your school will reschedule your play after all this is over. I was very much looking forward to seeing you as a dancing sunflower. Your father also tells me that he practically had to drag you out of the city because you wanted to stay and see Godzilla, study him like me. My sweet little scientist. Maybe one day you'll be able to join me. It's been many years since any kaiju *have surfaced like this (especially without any obvious nuclear incidents on our part), so we're very interested in finding out why Godzilla has suddenly returned, why he is upset.*

Your father and I were on the phone for hours last night. I said little. I stared at the picture of you and me that was taken after we took you home from the hospital. Our street was blanketed in cherry-blossom petals. You are crying. I look like I'm going to cry, and I remember being incredibly sad. I had lost a part of myself when I brought you into the world. The idea of being a mother, of you, felt so much more complete and less alien when you were still inside me. Maybe I've been running away ever since, so I could keep this fantasy, these idealized visions of your father and me teaching you how to ride a bike, going on picnics, laughing over some stupid joke over dinner. But perhaps it's time to run back.

KUMONGA (IRRADIATED ARACHNID)

{Descp. Brown. Two stories tall. Slender, prehensile appendages. Serrated legs. Powers: thick webbing, stinger, appendages used for impaling, cutting, and holding, jumping abilities.}

Field Notes: mummifies wild boar in silk. repairs webbing between hillsides. shoots silk spray at passing seagulls. circles territory of other kaiju.

Kumonga senses the vibrations of my footsteps, follows me with bejeweled eyes. Unlike some of the other *kaiju*, Kumonga has not shown higher intelligence, a propensity for sacrifice and friendship. His world is one of binaries: moving vs. nonmoving, alive vs. dead, light vs. dark, cold vs. hot. He stradles a ridge, watching over a valley. He could jump, impaling me with one of his legs as he lands. He could shoot silk and draw me close to his fangs, injecting my body with digestive juices as he wraps me for a later meal. Through my binoculars, I can see the tiny hairs of his abdomen, the reflection of the valley several times over in his eyes. That there are several emergency hatches to the island's underground lab near Kumonga's territory is no coincidence. In the wild and in households, spiders keep insect populations low. Their venom, sometimes deadly and painful, can be engineered to treat pain, relax muscles. But Kumonga's venom is uranium rich. His insects are humans and large animals, his appetite too savage for a tiny, blue world.

Kumonga raises his body, spreads his front limbs wide, revealing his reach. I open a hatch as his limbs coil in for a jump. Beneath the ground, I hear the pitter-patter of his legs, the chittering of his mandibles. A three-by-three titanium square and twenty meters of soil and rock separate us. And I can't help but remember news footage of the pounding of children in a school bus turned on its side as Kumonga approached, the seismic readings Mayu took of his legs rapping on the ground, calling for a mate the nuclear age failed to provide.

"And you still think they belong?" I asked Mayu.

"Do we even belong anymore?"

"The destruction they cause . . ."

"The destruction we cause. Don't you see beauty in them?"

"There are many beautiful things in nature that are best kept hidden."

Dear Ayu,
I hope your first year at university has been going well. I'm very proud of you. When your mother was alive, you wanted to follow

her to the ends of the earth. You have her letters and her phone calls and the handful of memories of days you spent together. This is who the woman I called my wife was to you. She is the woman who chased monsters, protected them from the ugliness of humanity. She was other things, certainly, to me, to those she worked with, to people in our family. You remember us fighting and me being the bad guy sometimes. You stood perfectly still as I cried on your tiny shoulders, squeezing you tightly after static was all that remained of my last conversation with a woman whom I loved and hated and respected. Her last words: "You should be here; he's simply magnificent." And I think I'm coming close to being able to see what she saw, but I need your help. I need you because you're the best parts of her, the parts that flourish in the imaginings of your memory, in the wonder of people who watched her television shows and read her books.

Enclosed are tickets and travel arrangements for your school break. In many ways, this will be your return to Monsterland, as you've been here in your dreams, in your drawings and the models you've built where the kaiju live happily with Barbies and Totoro. There is no question the kaiju will get loose again. New kaiju will be born by design and accident. They will defend us and they will attack us. And they'll die only to be reborn, eventually returning to the haven we've created for them. We can run tests, observe their behavior to forecast the probabilities of these things. But I'd like to believe that your mother is here too, that she's become part of this cycle. We haven't always seen eye to eye, but I need you to help me past the primeval roars and stomps, the image of a train car hanging from claws. I need help seeing the beauty of a radioactive glow within an embryo that can breathe life into the ancient, transform the ordinary into the incredible, make chaos somehow make sense.

Ventifacts
Christine Hume

WE NAME OUR WINDS for elsewhere, and ride them like a song forward into an aromatic future. Yet the time wind inhabits is too slow and spacious for the human eye; its undulations span generations and its unrelenting nature cannot begin to comprehend our puny endurance. An immensity of alien time pulls at the lithic girl. Oceans, lands, and stars give chase. According to Isidore of Seville, "The sphere of heaven is said to run with a swiftness so great that if the stars did not run against its headlong course to delay it, it would make a ruin of the universe."[1] The winds move swiftly to give earth its nature. We are in oblivion because the universe is also a velocity system, an infinity system, a system for nonhuman time. It can't even acknowledge us, much less process us.

*

We breathe a military climatology, it's the leitmotif of terrorism. Instead of traditional body-to-body combat, we redesign, reassign, resign the air. Designing killer environments for our enemies consolidates the most salient givens of our world: terrorism, design consciousness, and environmental thinking.[2] That's the setting, but how to get the story going? What's in the wind? Was it speaking, or chasing someone, or on a mission, or asleep? When German soldiers released chlorine gas into a north-by-northwest wind on April 22, 1915, in northern France, which way the wind was blowing meant your ass.

Eighty years later, the US Department of Defense's essay "Weather as a Force Multiplier: Owning the Weather in 2025" hypothesizes ways in which weather-modification technologies might give the

---

[1] Isidore of Seville, *The Etymologies of Isidore of Seville*, S. A. Barney, W. J. Lewis, J. A. Beach, and O. Berghof, trans. (Cambridge, UK: Cambridge UP, 2006), 3.35.
[2] This entire paragraph is indebted to Peter Sloterdijk, *Terror from the Air*, Amy Patton and Steve Corcoran, trans. (Cambridge, MA: MIT Press, 2009), 9–10, 25.

United States a "weather edge" over adversaries.[3] It does so through "fictionalized representations of future scenarios" involving weaponized weather. Imagine, it asks us, the US fighting a powerful drug cartel in South America by staging meteorological acts. By doing so we fictionalize journalism, we "imagine" the truth. Engineering wind-flow patterns—an air theater, a perfectly orchestrated wind opera—means we can engineer vulnerability. We'll make them weep and weak. With chemical interventions that would withhold precipitation to induce drought then unleash catastrophic storms, the US military sneaks in disguised as an act of nature. This is a repeatable story. A pilot project conducted in 1966 artificially extended the monsoon season along the Ho Chi Minh trail by releasing silver iodide, a toxic pollutant that stopped people in their tracks. Flash flooding and gales wreaked havoc; the chemical agent made people fall sick.

Since 1993 in Gakona, Alaska, the research station commonly acronymized as HAARP has been practicing ionospheric control.[4] In this transitional space, the no-man's-land between the atmosphere and the magnetosphere, HAARP blasts high-powered radio waves with 180 antennas in a single beam to take down aircraft and set off weather calamities, nature made-to-order for the security domains, as canards and conspiracy talk squall on other frequencies. This world is a testing ground. This world makes Mahmoud Ahmadinejad's claim that Europe is stealing Iran's rain, emptying its clouds before the clouds wind-travel to the East—reported widely in the conservative press in May 2011—seem not only feasible but probable. A gust of absolute conviction, prescient announcement, and paranoia sometimes all blow through the same moment.

*

At one point in Henry Darger's *Conflagration!* the Vivian Girls find themselves trapped by a forest fire set by the Glandelinians: "It appeared to be a fire storm of a sixty-mile-an-hour velocity, by the way it swept the trees down in so great a number, the wind coming

---

[3]Col. Tamzy J. House, Lt. Col. James B. Near Jr., LTC William B. Shields, Maj. Ronald J. Celentano, Maj. David M. Husband, Maj. Ann E. Mercer, Maj. James E. Pugh, presented August 1996, csat.au.af.mil/2025/volume3/vol3ch15.pdf.
[4]HAARP (High Frequency Active Auroral Research Program) is jointly funded by the US Air Force, the US Navy, the University of Alaska, and the Defense Advanced Research Projects Agency (DARPA).

Christine Hume

straight from the southwest raging with the most terrible fury." But
the wind eventually changes course and so changes the state of affairs, a fury turned back to where it began.

*

In Homer's *Odyssey*, Aeolus, keeper of the winds, bestows Odysseus
and his crew with a gift bag holding the four winds. However, while
Odysseus sleeps, the sailors, looking for booty, open the bag and the
resulting gale blows them off course.

*

In 1977, the UN General Assembly adopted a resolution prohibiting
the hostile use of environmental modification techniques. According
to "Weather as a Force Multiplier," though, the UN hasn't stopped the
research and technological development for weather modification in
order to "enhance air superiority and provide new options for battle-
space shaping." We like theoretical wars as much as real ones. In the
meantime, with DARPA's new "One Shot," snipers can take out an
enemy at a distance of .7 miles in twenty-miles-per-hour wind. The
One Shot sniper scope uses computer-run lasers to track not only
distance but also the wind turbulence in the path of the bullet, and
to correct for it. A wind might blow you off course, but a gun can correct for turbulence in the thoughts and feelings of others, in your
life's trajectory and in the system.

*

The parking lot is a habitat for unmoored shopping carts, water
bottles, advertising fliers, and seagulls trolling for trash. Sleepless
stones skim the open asphalt, each one its own double. A thing in wind
is caffeinated, buzzing with aura. Wind rustles the tissue wrapped
around each thing. Newspaper wraps around nothing. Wind animates
last night's empties. Loose plastic bags derange into amoeba puppets
hopping around parked cars. Marks of visitation, marks of limbo.
Have a nice day! A giddy piece of time translates you too. Whoever
wants to inflate, to be carried away, to turn tail, to come skidding

197

back, to change and exchange is susceptible to the wind: *Take me with you, away from forsaken here.*

✦

As I walk out of a storm's pivot, I wander into Aeria, the City of Air. The river moves. The city drifts, offers an ethereal escape, unlimited speculation and dream time. Disembodied radio voices fizz through the air like the apparition of migrating geese. The miasma of the city's electric lights go only so far into the sky, this light fades into stars, which are like a roof shot with bullet holes or a cloud of fireflies. Aeria "gives the imagination a late place in which to muse, meditate, linger, if for no more—indeed—than a passing moment."[5] As misunderstandings hum through my mind, I catch wind of a popsicle wrapper darting all over the alley. I enter its orbit, as if watching a film made with a handheld camera, but air designs choppy rhythms faster than my eyes can follow. Slightly queasy, I keep watching from my window, now back in my parents' apartment, remembering my dream of a skyscraper blown out to sea. Swallows then circle in the last light, in greater and greater gestures, emitting tiny cries that go straight to my gut. The birds make flight lines. They pull these lines tight. I feel in my body what my eyes cannot grasp, that those lines stretch away, accumulating speed until they move into the future. For now, they hold the world together. Until the light that touches them reaches us, they bind us to air. Here we are and here we are and here we are not. Wind lines are the hidden principle behind everything we don't create.

*

At one time, only the boldest philosopher could have denied that a gust could knock up a virgin.[6] Wind insemination explains "virgin births," and their history of ending badly, at the same time it simplifies paternity. Firmly lodged in their mental map of the world as late as 1912, the Ainu in Northern Japan tell of an Island of Women

---

[5] Gustaf Sobin, *Luminous Debris: Reflecting on Vestige in Provence and Languedoc* (Berkeley, CA: University of California Press, 2000), 173.
[6] Conway Zirkle, "Animals Impregnated by the Wind," *Isis* 25.1 (May 1936), 95, 110, 122–27.

in the Pacific Ocean. The women here lift their cunts to the east wind. Legs in the air or ass over a naked rock, they use air currents to fertilize themselves like flora. Wind blows off whatever the sun intensifies. The women of the Island of Women keep only their daughters, and kill their male offspring. Ancient Egypt, Mesopotamia, India, Greece, and China all have their legends of wind impregnating mammals and birds. This belief in anemophilous animals actually paves the way for the discovery of wind pollination in plants. The animal fantasy—involving mostly vultures, hens, mares, and humans—leads us directly into the vegetable fact. When Camerarius first breaks the news about pollination of flowering plants in 1694, he quotes a passage from Virgil's *Georgics* detailing how west winds impregnate certain mares. He also props up his argument with Aristotle on the "wind-eggs" of birds impregnated by spring breezes. Today "wind egg" refers to a small, imperfect egg, usually lacking a yolk or a firm shell, or an empty argument. Dig into most words and you'll turn over a metaphor, which in this case turns us back to the end, chased by its own head. Aristophanes's play *The Birds* (414 BCE) choruses, "In the beginning Night laid a wind egg." This night was full of hot air. That's all we had in the beginning.

*

Open the door and start climbing. Lift yourself out of the nervous dynamics of New York City traffic. Your elevation transfigures you into a bird god looking down at your own maze. Climb ninety-one floors to find a way out. A thick, vertiginous curtain of glass shuts off the volume. You traded your hearing for a point of view. Look out the window at the visual vitality below—a technicolor, twitchy, kinetic cityscape so out of sync with its sonic deadness that it nauseates. In 1999, for his *World Trade Center Recordings*, Stephen Vitiello invited the eeriest waftings of sound inside. He stuck contact mics to the windows to convert one of the world's tallest buildings into a monolithic microphone: air suddenly audible like a mystic thought thrashing around a steel brain.

I duck into a dark museum room in 2002 where one piece from this series plays. Nothing in the room but white vinyl seats, a live man gripping the wall or leaning against it, and the sound of an end-of-the-century hurricane convulsing outside a building that no longer exists. This sound is what the new century remembers of the

199

Christine Hume

old. What the WTC offered us was a graphic majesty, an imaginary totality, two huge speakers that strangled all sound. It offered us a moat of dead birds, which crashed into it and fell to its streets, collected daily for the uncertain purposes of science. The birds were something to see, but could not be heard as they died or later. Now basking in the shadow of recently departed visuals, what we have is only aural memory if memory can be planted. No one remembers the sounds of Hurricane Floyd from within the towers because no one heard them there. But the everyday contains strangeness that surfaces in your ears. What is left of the WTC is the sound of its interference; a creaky, tiny resistance. Hear what no human had heard before, and hear it now, searingly clear. Another queasy disparity asserts itself: the sound of "nothing." The winds surge and drone, no stories in sight.

The Dead Swan
Lily Tuck

IT'S A COLD, WINDY, early spring day and Sadie is walking by herself along the beach, not looking down or at where she is going so that she nearly trips over it—the dead swan—only she doesn't right away recognize what it is. She stops and stares at it for a while and, typically, because she is unhappy and perverse, she thinks it is beautiful. She picks up the dead swan and walks home with it in her arms.

What does a swan weigh—twenty? twenty-five pounds?

Her husband, Mason, is away—actually, he is away in jail awaiting his trial—otherwise she would not have brought the swan home. Sadie can imagine what he would have said to her about it:

Christ! Sadie, get that damn bird out of here.

Or, more threatening,

Get rid of that fucking bird before I—

If he was high, which he usually was, he might have raised his hand at her. A couple of times already he had swung and missed. Mason is not as coordinated or as strong as he used to be. The drugs, Sadie guesses; part of the reason he is now in jail. The other part she tries not to think about.

Mason has been diagnosed as bipolar and a bunch of other things and Sadie can't remember what they all are offhand. But manic depressive was one of them. He was on meds but half the time he refused to take them. Mason said that the meds made him feel slow and stupid and gave him a dry mouth. *I can't even get it up anymore,* Mason had complained, making a sound that was meant to be a laugh but wasn't.

Holding the swan like a baby, Sadie places it gently on the old-fashioned canvas swing chair in the screened-in porch, careful not to rock it. She spreads out one of his great wings—three feet?—then the other. She runs her hand down the swan's gray legs. No breaks—last

201

year she saw a one-legged seagull hopping pitifully on the beach—
and no dried blood. She feels along his dark, rough, orange beak to the
little black basal knob. The swan's head and long neck are resting on
his breast as if he were asleep and he appears perfect. Carefully, Sadie
sits down next to him. He, she thinks, but perhaps the swan is female,
and a she. Impossible to tell about birds unless she was to examine
the vent area, which she is not going to do. In fact, Sadie is not sure
what she will do with the dead swan.

Sadie works as a substitute teacher at the local elementary school.
From one day to the next, with no preparation until she arrives at the
school and is assigned her class, she can be teaching third-graders
about the Lewis and Clark expedition or sixth-graders algebra or—as
she did last Monday—Greek myths to fifth-graders. They had discussed all the gods—Zeus, Athena, Apollo, Aphrodite—their traditional roles and their deeds but not, as she suddenly thinks now, their
misdeeds—transmogrified into a swan, Zeus the rapist.
   At least, Sadie thinks, Mason couldn't rape anyone.
   Instead he took off all his clothes in a playground full of children.
Sadie does not want to imagine the scene, but can: terrified kids,
screaming parents, a rush of security guards, then police. Fortunately if there is anything fortunate about this—Mason's disrobing
occurred in a different state and, so far, the school where Sadie sub-
stitutes has not gotten wind of the incident. Otherwise—otherwise,
she might be dismissed.

Mason was not always crazy. Sadie remembers how a few days before
the incident at the playground, they went to the local pound to adopt
a dog. Immediately Sadie had fallen in love with a little brindle terrier mix but Mason, in his reasonable voice, said that a dog was a big
responsibility and they should think it over some more. He also said
that Sadie was too impetuous, too quick to form judgments.
Afterward, they had gone to the only decent restaurant in town and
she, Sadie remembers, had the swordfish and Mason had the hanger
steak. They also drank a bottle of wine and he made her laugh by
wiggling his ears—first the right one, then the left—and promising to
show her how. Later that night, Mason tried to make love.
   Ha! Sadie now thinks.

*

A month ago when Mason was first jailed, Sadie had gotten up at four in the morning in order to arrive at the detention center on time for visiting hours. Although she was early, the line of visitors—most of whom were either black or Hispanic—was already long and she had to wait, standing, for over an hour outside in the cold. First her purse was searched and her bottle of Valium was confiscated and thrown into a trash bin, then she was told to remove her shoes, her jewelry—a simple gold chain and her wedding ring—which along with her purse she had to put inside a locker for safekeeping. Sadie then went through a metal detector and was body-searched by a police woman. The police woman felt her bra for wire and put her hand inside Sadie's underpants. Finally, she was taken to a large room where several prisoners and their families were already sitting around small tables and Mason was brought in. Mason had lost a lot of weight and his hair was cut very short. He had stitches over one eye and it took a moment for Sadie to know what to say to him.

"What happened to your eye?" she finally asked.

Mason shrugged as he sat down across from Sadie.

No physical contact, the guard warned her.

"Are you OK?" Sadie continued.

Again, Mason said nothing.

"Can you still wiggle your ears?" Sadie said in an effort to make him smile. "I've been practicing just the way you said by just going through the motions in my head, thinking what it would be like to—"

Cutting her off, Mason stood up so abruptly that he knocked over his chair and yelled, "Jesus! I don't believe you, Sadie!"

A guard came over. "Keep it down," he told Mason.

"The hell I am going to keep it down." Mason was still yelling as he pushed past the table between him and Sadie.

The guard grabbed Mason just in time and started to take him away.

"You know what," Mason shouted back at Sadie before the door shut behind him, "you're a fucking idiot and an evil cunt."

In front of the bathroom mirror that night, Sadie, in vain, tried to wiggle her ears; instead she burst into tears.

The swan's eyes are closed and Sadie is smoothing his feathers. She has heard that swans can be very aggressive, especially if they have a nest nearby. Flapping their huge wings and hissing, they will chase away predators—human predators as well. A Japanese photographer who wanted to take a picture of a nest and came too close to it was killed by a swan. How, Sadie can't help but wonder. Was he beaten to death by the swan's powerful wings? And how, she wonders, was his death explained to his wife and to his children? Killer swan. However, this swan, her swan, Sadie thinks, looks peaceful.

Secretly, Sadie was relieved that Mason could not get it up anymore, although she would of course never have told Mason or anyone else, for that matter. Before sex had been rough and unsatisfying. Scary, really, and more like Mason was some stranger she had met on one of those Internet dating sites. A really crazy person who might defecate on her or hack her to pieces.

She wonders what swan meat tastes like. Probably a lot like goose. Sadie once ate the goose Mason shot and cooked for Thanksgiving dinner and although she remembers telling him the goose was delicious, privately, she had disliked the tough texture and gamy taste. In the olden days, only kings and queens were allowed to eat the "royal dish"—a swan stuffed with a goose that was stuffed with a duck that in turn was stuffed with a capon that was stuffed with a guinea hen that was stuffed with a woodcock. The woodcock, Sadie imagines, would be stuffed with a blue pigeon egg.

The other fact Sadie knows about swans—a fact almost everyone knows—is that swans are monogamous and that they mate for life. Not so, she thinks, about herself and Mason. Unless he gets clean she will leave him.

"In a heartbeat," she bends her head to tell the swan.

A couple of times now, Ron Shirer, the math teacher at the school, who seems like a nice guy and is single, has asked her out for a cup of coffee and as yet she hasn't taken him up on it.

"I'll go for coffee," she says to the swan. "Maybe I'll go for more than coffee," she says, giving a little laugh.

When Sadie was a young girl she took ballet. For a while she fantasized that she would become a dancer—a principal dancer in a large company like the Bolshoi or the ABT. She would be famous and she would travel. For years, too, she was a good dancer. She had the body for it and a great turnout—Alicia, her teacher with the fake Russian name, had told her so.

Ta da dum, ta da dum, Sadie hums the first few bars of *Swan Lake* and is tempted to get up and dance. She regrets it now. She should have persevered. After ballet, she decided to become a vet but she hated the college biology courses and gave that up too. Next she took up photography—she was told she had a good eye—and she managed to buy a secondhand Rollei 3.5f, her prize possession, which had cost her plenty; she also managed to get one of her black-and-white photographs—a flock of starlings perched on a power line—in a group show, which was where she met Mason. They were going to start a bed-and-breakfast; instead, they went into debt renovating the house and Mason started to deal in illegal substances and she got a job substitute teaching.

Maybe, Sadie thinks, if she kisses the swan, the swan will turn into a handsome prince. Or, if not a real prince, into a handsome young man with whom she will live happily ever after.

Inside the house the phone rings. Sadie does not move; she lets the voice mail pick up.

"Hey, Sadie," she hears Mason say. "Good news. They're letting me out on probation next Wednesday. Can you come pick me up and bring me some clothes? A pair of khakis and my jacket—the jacket is at the cleaner's. I love you, baby."

The cleaner's is next door to the pound and Sadie wonders if the little brindle terrier mix she liked so much is still available for adoption—probably not.

Time to go in, Sadie tells herself, feeling cold all of a sudden. Tomorrow she will take the swan back to the beach. And, if it's a nice day, she also tells herself, she may bring along her camera—it's been ages since she has taken any photographs. She gives the swan a little pat and stands up, then hesitates, not wanting to leave him out on the porch alone. In the fading evening light, his shape becomes more and more indistinct. Soon all Sadie can see is the silvery gleam of his feathers. In the night's approaching lonely darkness she wonders about the swan's forlorn mate.

*

205

Upstairs in the bedroom, Sadie looks on the top shelf of her closet, behind the boxes of old sweaters, scarves, and hats, where she hides the camera, but the Rolleiflex is not there.

The fucking bastard!

Right away, Sadie suspects Mason of taking it and selling it. Still, she can hardly believe that he could have done that and, to make sure, she sweeps all the contents off the shelf—the boxes of sweaters, hats, and scarves—onto the floor.

Afterward, Sadie rummages through the bedside-table drawers looking for where Mason keeps pills—Ambien, Percodan, oxycodone—anything that will let her sleep. She takes two of the pink pills and goes to bed.

When Sadie wakes up the next morning it is already noon. Quickly, she puts on her sweatpants and a T-shirt—she has no memory of getting undressed and, briefly, she wonders if she ate supper. In the kitchen, she starts up the coffee machine before going out to the screened-in porch. The porch door is wide open and the canvas swing chair is creaking slightly. The swan, of course, is gone.

The Confession of Philippe Delambre
Greg Hrbek

MY FATHER

MY FATHER TURNED INTO a common housefly. This is the simple explanation. Though it is hardly a complete or accurate one. What happened to him was far more complicated. I knew that. Just as I knew the basement of our home—to all outward appearances a very average home on the outskirts of Québec City—to be a place of dark secrets. Just as I would later know that my mother, having been found not guilty of murder (by reason of insanity: committed for the rest of her life to a provincial asylum at the fog-shrouded outer limits of Nova Scotia), had done nothing wrong. Falsely accused. She would never hurt a fly, *ma mère pauvre*, much less a husband who had turned into one.

His name was André Delambre.

He taught at the Université Laval, where he chaired the department of physics. Do not look for his name in the archives of that hallowed center of education. You won't find it there. His name has been struck out. As well it should have been. But take me at my word: He was a member of the faculty beginning in 1947. Soon thereafter, he published "The Disintegration and Reintegration of Matter as an Objective in the Physical Sciences" (*The Journal of Modern Physics*, December 1949, Volume 18, Issue 9, p. 592), a paper that brought him professional renown, a fortune in research funds, and finally, in the academic year of 1953–1954, a sabbatical from the university, during which time his experiments with teleportation began in earnest, resulting in several failures, a success, and then the final disaster. He died first in June of 1954. Then again in August.

AFTER THE ACCIDENT

I had seen a strange fly in the house. A fly with a white head. Actually, I had heard it first. The drone of its wings. But also another sound. Which seemed at first to be a trick played by my ears. As the fly flew past my head, I heard a voice, a squeaky, high-pitched voice, cry my name. I turned my head, and though I could still hear the buzz, I couldn't see the insect, which had disappeared somewhere in the colors of the room. And then it came again, from very far off. A tiny voice:

Philippe!

I often had bad dreams as a boy. The feeling in me then, after hearing that voice for the second time, was of a terror I knew very well, for that cry was like my own nocturnal pleas for help—as if whatever-it-was was trapped in a nightmare and wanted me to wake it up.

I ran away.

In the kitchen, our maid, Emma—a gray and sour woman, a vicious woman, whose husband had been drowned in the Battle of the Atlantic—was in the process of stuffing Cornish game hens. From the look on her face, you might've thought I'd barged in on the queen in her royal water closet. She spat a curse at me and so I knew my mother was not at home and my father was in the basement.

"Where's Mother?"

"How should I know? In bed with your uncle perhaps." She took one of the dead birds by its legs and forced open the posterior.

I went to the door that led to the basement. This door at the top of the stairs was often unlocked. But the door at the bottom, made of steel—the one that led to my father's laboratory—that door: never. Descending the staircase always gave me a strange feeling of disconnection. Above, where we lived, were immaculate white rooms, windows dressed with chintz curtains, paintings in golden frames, vases of flowers. But below, where my father worked, was a rock-walled pool of shadow far too deep to be dispelled by electricity. I didn't feel I was moving from one place to the next—from upstairs to downstairs—so much as disappearing from one reality and reappearing suddenly in another. Now, at the steel door of the laboratory, I tried to stop my panicked breathing with a hand against my open mouth. The fly, I was quite certain, had followed me here, and was veering through the darkness, and would, at any moment, come close and call my name again. I closed my hand into a trembling fist. Never, ever, did I interrupt Father. I could hear him in there. Not speaking. Moving—or, rather, pacing. But not pacing. More agitated than that. The first time I knocked, he didn't seem to hear. Then I knocked again. Movement ceased.

"Father? Father, there's a . . ."

Greg Hrbek

As the heels of his shoes clacked on the concrete floor, I believed he was rushing to let me in. But there was only a sudden impact. As if he hadn't understood that the door was a solid object. He didn't open the door; he didn't speak to me through it. He beat upon it. Over and over again he beat upon the door and kicked it, but he didn't utter a single word.

THE FLY (1958): A CINEMASCOPE PICTURE

Not until much later (fourteen years, to be exact, by which time I was studying for a doctorate of philosophy at the Université de Montréal) would I discover the American film based on my father's tragedy.

I saw it one night in 1968.

I had been out in the Quartier Latin, drinking and smoking with an American draft evader who had adopted the fake name of Caspian. Around midnight, returning alone to my garret apartment in the Ville-Marie, I switched on the little black-and-white television, which received analog signals via a pair of metallic antennae, and chanced upon "Nightmare Theater." A program I had watched before. Hosted by Madblood the Magnificent, a Toronto disc jockey wardrobed and made-up to be a cross between Svengali and the Phantom of the Opera. The movie was just recommencing after a commercial break, and the first thing I saw was a boy of eight or nine with an aerial insect net, just like the one I'd possessed at the same age. Like me, he had a scientist father with a lab in the basement, a beautiful mother, a maid named Emma. Strange coincidences that only got stranger by the minute. The mother addressing the boy as "Philippe." The boy announcing that he had just caught *such a funny-looking fly. . . .* All my life I'd been refusing to fit together the puzzle pieces of that summer. Now here they were, interlocked on a television screen. Accident. My father hadn't known it was in there. In the booth. When he entered the booth and disintegrated himself, it too had disintegrated. In the ether, human and insect atoms had mixed. When he and the fly reintegrated, each was half the other. A cold draft blew across my brain. A commercial came on. For Ca-Fo Insecticide. The cleansing liquid that kills.

Greg Hrbek

HOW I CAUGHT THE FLY

Later that afternoon, in the garden, I saw the fly again. By then, I had—in the inexplicable way of a child—put behind me (or, rather: hidden from my own sight) the weird incidents of the morning.

I was playing croquet, a game I'd become precociously good at. In those boyhood summers, with Father always working and Mother usually somewhere else, I was very much alone. I hunted insects and practiced croquet. When I grew up, I wanted to be a professional croquet player, or an entomologist.

I had run the blue ball through all twelve hoops and was about to peg it out—mallet in hand, staring down at that blue globe—when upon its northern pole landed the fly. Unmistakably the same one. Only this time, the creature was still. So I could see that my original impression hadn't been accurate. Yes, the head was strange, but not because of its whiteness. It *was* white. But not exactly, not merely. . . . Had the creature spoken, I would've run off again. But it didn't speak. Perhaps it never had. On a nearby chaise longue lay my aerial insect net. Slowly, I moved away from the ball and set down the mallet. I took up the net. The fly—moving about on the wooden ball, probing the smooth blue surface with its forelegs, as if trying to fathom the concept of a sphere—sensed my motion a split second too late and flew straight up, directly into the mesh.

Caught.

The rim of the implement was flush with the ground, and from within the folded and furrowed grid of netting (which bore an uncanny resemblance to my father's schematic drawings of space-time) came short shocks of buzzing.

From a tin box on the chaise longue, I took my magnifying glass. Then lay on the lawn before the net. Enlarged, the web of lines appeared as a diaphanous haze—and through the blur, very clearly, in unerringly perfect focus, I saw a creature with the body of a housefly (wings, thorax, abdomen) and the head of a person: a living thing with five jointed insect legs and, in the place of the sixth, a human arm.

HOW I IMPRISONED THE FLY

And I an old man now, and still can hear it saying (the voice as clear as on that distant day, perhaps more so): *Philippe. Don't be afraid. It's me.* . . . I had no idea to what self the creature might be referring.

210

The face did not look familiar. Or did it? I had been haunted, for about a year, by photographs of Bergen-Belsen and Auschwitz-Birkenau I'd chanced upon in a library book at my school—and I shivered inside as the eyes in the head, wide and alert in the desiccate flesh of the face, looked up through the magnifying glass and into mine. *It's me, Philippe.* And no sooner had the voice spoken than the creature clumsily flew into another dead-end hollow of the net. The human parts seemed to be at odds (or at the very least not in coordination) with those of the insect. Once again, I framed it in the glass. Every time the human arm tried to wipe tears from the human face, the other anterior appendage, the black insect leg, pushed it down. It was at this time that I took from my tin-box collection kit an empty matchbox and a packet of sugar. I tore open the sugar packet, poured its contents into the matchbox, and slipped the trap under the net. Within a few seconds, the creature had taken the bait and I had it safely locked up.

The film adaptation shows none of this.

In the film, the boy—a version of me played by a child actor named Charles Herbert (who appeared regularly on American television during the 1950s and '60s)—simply appears at the house, calling for his mother in order to tell her that he has found *such a funny-looking fly.* This is not what I did. In the film, the mother reminds the boy that the father does not approve of the entrapment of living things. She then instructs me (paying no attention at all to what I'm saying) to release the fly. Which I do. A thing I, of course, would never have done, even had I been so foolish as to tell my mother about the fly in the first place, which I did not. What I actually did was: I took him to my menagerie.

In those years after the war, the cities of Québec were pushing outward, extinguishing the weak flames of family farms. Barns and stables supplanted by modern homes with stone patios; loamy cropland by green lawns that smelled in summer of chemical fertilizers and pesticides. Our house, for a time, was at the limits of the expansion, so when I crossed through a small woods, I emerged at a sea-like meadow of high grass, in the offing of which stood one of the abandoned farmsteads.

From inside the matchbox, the fly kept saying:

Philippe?

Philippe?

A few yards from the barn, in the shade of a giant willow tree, is where I kept it: a glass fish tank (transported the summer before in

211

the bed of a Radio Flyer wagon) filled with soil, dead wood, moss, and leaves, and covered with a section of wire screen taken from a window of the farmhouse.

I set to work emptying the tank of everything I'd so carefully collected during that North American springtime of 1954. The ladybugs on the stemmed sticks, the rotting wood secreted with pill bugs, the grasshopper hiding in a pile of old changed leaves. One specimen was hard to part with: the mantis. But even she—that most unreal of creatures—couldn't compare with what I had now. I let her go with the rest.

Philippe?

Can you hear me?

Nor had I overlooked the need for food. Emma's Cornish game hens. They had not yet gone into the oven. I had filched one from the refrigerator. Now I tore a wing from the decapitated body of the hen and placed it in the tank. Then I lowered the matchbox in, slid it open, and quickly set the screen on top, securing it with rocks at all four corners. The fly exited the box and buzzed back and forth, bumping into the walls. Finally landing on the floor, human nose bleeding from an impact with the glass, it walked onto the raw meat. From the mouth came an eruption of white vomit, and as the acid did its work, the creature looked up at me, lips trembling. I wasn't sure why, but all at once the terror of the morning was in me again. I picked up the tin box and the net, and I ran, as one runs from a haunted place.

HELP ME

Back to that night in 1968. And the film ending like this: I am walking down the staircase of our home with my uncle. Asking, with the pathetic naïveté of child characters of the era, when my father (whom everyone but me knows is dead, murdered with a hydraulic press: murdered, according to the writer and director, Messrs. Clavell and Neumann, by my mother) will be coming home.

Soon, Philippe.

Then, offhandedly, I mention: *I saw that funny-looking fly again.*

Not then, nor at any other time, did I utter those idiotic words. But when my uncle and the police inspector ran out to the garden in that climactic scene, what they found trapped in the web of a spider was exactly what I had captured and put inside the fish tank under the willow tree. . . . Down to the street I went, not wondering if I was dreaming (I knew I was awake), but imagining that the television, somehow tuned to the frequency of my subconscious, had been broadcasting the darkest of my dreams.

At a pay telephone, I made a collect call to my uncle in Québec City. The ring sounded twelve, thirteen, fourteen times. The operator stated the obvious. I demanded she allow the phone to keep ringing. Until finally:

"Philippe? What the devil—"

" 'Help me.' "

"Help you. Are you in trouble again?"

"It's a lie," I said.

"What is, my boy?"

"The scene in the garden. That's not how it happened."

"How what—"

"You never saw him, Uncle. But I did. I'm the one . . ."

He feigned complete ignorance, saying: Middle of the night, surely this can wait until morning, Philippe, when you'll be half-dead but at least sober. I hung up on the *fils de pute*. Stood there in the glass-walled booth, which bore an unnerving resemblance to the chambers built by my father in the film, in which inanimate objects and living things had been caused to disappear and reappear—and I wept. *Help me, help me,* the creature had begged. Trapped. Wound in strings of proteinaceous silk. A spider three times its size advancing along the radials of the web. *Help me.* And the police inspector had lifted a rock the size of a cantaloupe and crushed the whole tableau of horror.

MY MOTHER, SCREAMING

It is now so perfectly and painfully obvious to me that the face was my father's: sunken, moldy, gray in pallor, muscles twisted into an unprecedented mask of disbelief. But *his* face. I can see that now. Back then, a boy of nine, I couldn't: I did not recognize him, so changed was he, or my mind would not allow me to recognize, or it would, but I felt the sense of recognition must be faulty, because a fly with a human head was one thing, but a fly with my father's head was something else entirely. . . . What I do know is: I ran from that place, away from the farmstead and the willow tree and across the meadow and finally through the woods into the familiar realm of our manicured lawn and pruned shrubs, panting with the same combination

213

of fear and relief I felt when waking from a nightmare.

I crept into the kitchen.

Not to steal another hen but to see if I'd truly stolen the first one. If three hens were in the refrigerator, I'd know it had all been a day dream. But one was missing. As I stood there, staring at the pale yellow bodies, Emma came out of nowhere to grasp the collar of my shirt. Then she took me by the ear and marched me into the sitting room, where my mother was displayed upon a settee holding a fashion magazine.

"Here he is, madame."

My mother did not remove her reading glasses, the thick black frames of which obscured her face as an ecliptic moon obscures the sun: All around the edges burned a dangerous corona of beauty.

"Did you take one of the hens, Philippe?"

I didn't answer. And when she next asked why I would do such a thing, Emma began to say I did it, along with so many other nasty things, merely to spite her—at which point my mother ordered her to shut her mouth and sent me to bed without supper. That was five o'clock. About four hours passed. My stomach an empty hole. It seemed I couldn't possibly fall asleep, but the song of the crickets, like a round with an infinite number of parts, must have lulled me, and I was dreaming that a man the size of an insect was mating with a mantis, the insect turning its head and biting into the head of the man and beginning to consume the skull and brains, when someone screamed.

I started awake and again she screamed. I had never heard my mother scream, but I knew it was she—and I knew where she was.

Underground.

In the basement. Behind the metal door of the laboratory.

WHAT MY MOTHER SAW

It was evidently the contention of Clavell and Neumann that a boy of nine will sleep through a barrage of cries so loud and shrill as to shatter glass and curdle blood. Or perhaps the creative team did not wish to bother with the dramatic implications caused by my cognizance of the fact that something had frightened my mother that night and frightened her terribly. In either case, any picture of me at the time of the screaming was omitted. I was not shown lying in my bed, eyes open but body unable to move, hearing Emma saying,

"Madame? Madame?" And my mother, racked with sobs, choking out commands, "Leave me alone, go to bed, mind your own affairs." "I'll phone the police," Emma said. (Less an offer of assistance than a threat.) Something made of glass (the vase in the hallway, I guessed) smashing. (Had my mother thrown it?) "How dare you," she was shouting. "You old bitch. If you touch that telephone . . ." While I lay paralyzed. Staring out the window of my room, the lower sash of which was raised to let in the cool night air.

In the distance, a moon nearly full. Close by, clinging to the cross-hatch of the screen, a luna moth larger than the moon.

I did not sleep again that night. Or if I did, I dreamed I was awake and watching that white circle of moon advance like the ticking of time from one quadrant of the window to another and finally out of view.

What had happened in the basement?

The actress playing my mother—Patricia Owens, the nadir of whose film career would soon come in the form of a low-budget wartime melodrama titled *Seven Women from Hell*—descended into the underworld of our home with a tray of dinner. Knocked on the laboratory door. It was opened. And there was my father. Wearing the usual attire (beige lab coat, dark trousers, shoes) and something odd too: a black shroud over his head. He took a sheet of paper from a typewriter. My mother read the message silently. Yet through the miracle of non-diegetic sound it is possible to hear the words echoing in her mind: *There are things man should never experiment with. . . . Now I must destroy myself.* She won't hear of it. Well, one thing leads to another, which leads finally to the pulling of the shroud from his head—and what is to be seen there on my father's shoulders but a monstrous version of the very head that belonged on the fly I had captured: two bulbous compound eyes, and, in place of a human mouth and tongue, a proboscis and a pair of maxillary palpi, twitching. She screams. Once, twice, three times—while I lay in bed, as if paralyzed, staring at the moon and the moth.

HOW I ATTEMPTED TO SAVE THE SPECIES

I have no doubt that my mother saw him that night. She saw what her husband had become. Screamed and quite possibly lost consciousness from the shock. But according to Messrs. Clavell and Neumann, the next day was one of frantic searching. Searching for flies. In particular, one with a white head. My "mother," they contend, was practically histrionic in her urgency, rushing about the house every time she heard an insect wingbeat or saw a tiny dark dot move in her field of vision, throwing herself finally in despair upon a bench in the garden, saying, "Oh, God. Please don't."

Inaccurate.

In fact, *ma mère* (this should come as no surprise) was one of the myriad upper-middle-class housewives of the era who blurred the lines of her daily sorrows with a tranquilizer called Mebaral. That morning, as I sat in the kitchen waiting for breakfast, she was lying on her still-made bed, fully clothed, dead to the world.

"You heard last night," Emma said to me.

I shrugged.

"What a family you have. Father a madman and mother a junkie. To think that my dear Jean-Luc gave his life for this country, froze and drowned in the Atlantic. . . ." And so on, as she set before me a plate containing two purposely undercooked eggs and a deliberately burned piece of toast.

"I hate you," I said.

"The feeling is mutual, you little son of a whore."

I turned the plate over on the table and walked out the door with my insect net. Through the garden I went, through the copse of trees and into the meadow, half laughing, half crying, knowing I could never understand them, my mother and father: the things they did alone in secret, all that happened privately between them.

In the distance, the farmhouse, the barn, the willow tree were like an old painting in a frame.

At first, unable to descry it, I thought it had escaped or disappeared like the hallucination it had always been. But no. The creature was there: in the shadow under the bent wing of the hen.

Sick.

The flesh of the face gray and wrinkled. Nearly all the hair fallen out of the head. The human part had aged a lifetime overnight. In the bloated, tearful eyes, I could read the fear of death. The mouth was trying to express something, but the power of speech had been lost. No sound emerging, only a trickle of drool. For a long time, I sat under the tree, trying to think. Ants filed in and out of a volcano-shaped hill of sand. Blue mud wasps sparked in the air around a nest grown tumorous from an eave of the barn. Finally, a pair of damselflies (not dragonflies; I knew the difference) drifted along the edge of the meadow. Joined in the air. In a configuration known as a mating wheel.

For the very first time, my mind posed the question: How could this thing have come to be?

Part human, part insect.

Not *that* way. At the age of nine, I could not imagine the means by which normal human beings were made, much less . . . No, there was only one explanation. A mystery species. Creature of myth, like the centaurs and the mermaids. A feeling—clear despite the limits of my experience—overcame me: responsibility. A few steps into the meadow, I found the game hen, more or less where I had thrown it the night before: the meat stripped off by some carnivore, the bones heaped and twisted, over which flies unnumbered had gathered in a dark cloud. With a single drop of my net, I caught nearly a dozen, and through a careful conjunction of net and tank was able to create the conditions necessary for sexual reproduction.

HOW MY FATHER DIED THE FIRST TIME

My father had made his own world in the basement. Rarely did he join us in ours. He used a toilet off a corridor accessible only from the lab, and he kept a cot in the lab too, near the floor-to-ceiling core memory and control panels of the supercomputer. At mealtimes, Emma would descend with a tray of food and leave it outside the metal door. But that night, I was the one who brought Father dinner, because Emma had abandoned us (having left a note on the kitchen table that read: *You can all go to hell—especially the boy*) and Maman was half-unconscious on her bed, her head flopping to and fro in lazy defiance, murmuring, "I won't live like this, I won't." I wasn't sure what to do. He was accustomed to meat, potatoes, and a vegetable. In the refrigerator, I found ham from two nights prior and a bunch of raw carrots; in the cupboard, white bread and a bag of potato chips. I arranged it all on the silver platter and covered it with the matching cloche and poured a glass of milk and carried down the tray. At the metal door, I summoned all the bravery in me and said: "Father."

And waited. And hearing no response, somehow closed one hand in a fist and struck the knuckles twice against the door, saying: "There's no maid anymore, Father. But I brought some dinner. It isn't much, but . . . I'll leave it—"

The room was kept secure with hardware that might have come from a medieval dungeon. I heard the crossbar sliding through the brace. Yet, for a few long segments of time, the dark iron door remained closed—as if he were giving me a chance to escape. But I didn't move. I stood in place until the door cracked open, then swung inward to reveal him standing there, head and neck covered with a black shroud, one arm thrust into the deep pocket of his lab coat—and, behind him, the room in ruins. The consoles and index-register displays of the computers had been smashed, one of the mainframes fallen like a toppled monolith, and papers, thousands of pages of typewritten reports, handwritten notes, and diagrams, teleprints of numbers—the encyclopedic chronicles of a man's dreams and his plans for their realization—disarrayed.

Years later, I would watch on the screen of a cathode-ray television my mother, in a kind of trance, assist him in the destruction of himself. But it was not she whom my father asked for help.

Trembling, his right hand (a human one) reached out for the tray of food, and as it did so, the other arm—the left one, the extremity of which had been heretofore concealed—reacted with a violent spasm, and *the hand, which was no hand,* emerged . . . I found myself on the cot. A feeling of waking up only to realize one is still dreaming. I glimpsed him. Across the room. Head covered by the shroud. The appendage hidden again. Upon my chest, a sheet of vellum stationery:

SON IF YO LOV ME HELP ME

I must have looked up at him then. Must have said: I love you, Father. And followed him. Though I cannot recall walking across the street to the factory. The next thing I remember is the switchboard: standing before it, staring at it: the pressure gauge (set at fifty tons), the safety switch (in the off position), the counter (set for one stroke), and the red button. The downstroke button. At which my father had motioned after adjusting the controls. To which he had pointed with emphasis before going to the machine and laying himself out upon the metal base. The button I was to push.

Which I pushed.

What then commenced I did not believe. A part of the machine, a second slab of metal, equal in size to the base but positioned several feet above it, started to move: downward. If my eyes were seeing anything real, my father was about to die before them. But none of it could be real. A hand could not be *not a hand,* any more than the head on my father's body could be *not his head.* Which it wasn't. An impossibility I perceived when the shroud slipped away as he thrashed about on the bed of the press as the slide plate gradually came down and the space between plate and base diminished, until soon the plate was touching the body and finally compacting it, breaking the bones, rupturing the organs, and causing that head (which was not his) to burst open like the bud of a fantastical flower.

ENTREZ, MON ONCLE

In Neumann's film, my uncle is portrayed by the iconic actor Vincent Price, famous for macabre roles in midcentury cinematic adaptations of the tales of Edgar Allan Poe. It is, I suppose, purely coincidental that Price played Thomas De Quincey in the 1962 production of *Confessions of an Opium Eater*. Still, my late uncle's later dependence upon a synthetic version of that drug has always seemed to me an effect caused by the earlier filmic actions of a man with whom I can't help but conflate him in my mind's eye. It is only with some effort that I recall my true uncle. Not a fiendishly debonair bachelor with arched eyebrows and a tapered pencil mustache, but a man with the pure face and white-streaked Van Dyke beard of a cabinet minister from the olden days. Which is not to say I had any trust in (or affection for) him. I didn't. I dreaded his visits, marked as they were by secretive conferences with Maman behind the closed doors of the library and stiff, wordless dinners for which my father refused to interrupt his work. . . .

In the middle of the night, he arrived. Not alone. In a black sedan that I understood instantly to be in the service of the Sûreté du Québec. Once it had parked in the drive, and the three men who had exited it had started toward the front door, I climbed into my bed and pulled the blanket to my chin. And that is where I stayed, with my eyes wide open—thinking of absolutely nothing—until the time I ordinarily arose: between seven o'clock and a quarter thereafter.

"Philippe!"

He was the first to see me—and when he did, he rushed toward the staircase as if to block my passage. Then he did something quite out of character. Went to one knee and took me into an embrace.

"Where's Maman?" I asked.

"In the library."

"Why are you here, Uncle?" As he failed to answer, another man, dressed in a gray tweed suit, exited the library. "Who is that?"

"It's no one, my boy."

Greg Hrbek

"Where's Father?"

"Your father. *Alors*, you see, Philippe—"

I broke away from him and started for the door that led to the basement, shouting, "Father! Father!"

It took two grown men, my uncle and the man in the tweed suit, to stop me at the top of the stairs and hold me down, back to the floor. Another man, whom I recognized, knelt beside me. The family physician, Dr. Ejouté. Whose attempts to reason with me were hopeless. I wouldn't stop screaming and trying to wrest myself free. Finally, he removed from his black bag the instruments of sedation—a syringe, a hypodermic, and a vial filled with clear liquid—and when the shot was delivered, it was like being stung by a bee or a hornet producing in its glands a venom of forgetfulness.

THE HOLOCAUST

I spent the next month—while the wildflowers bloomed all across the subalpine zones of the land—in a weird daze, with an amnesia for almost everything that had transpired that summer. A nanny was hired, a distant relative from Cape Spear. Little more than a girl. Surely ignorant (as I was) of the fact that my mother was *not* lying in a sickbed in a sanitorium, but standing trial in a courtroom of the provincial capital, accused of using an industrial hydraulic press to murder her husband. . . . M. Neumann's film is a case study in factual error. However, in the final minutes, I ask a question that I did ask numerous times in the course of that month: *When is Father coming home?* For a time, I believed the answers. That he had been very suddenly summoned to a scientific conference in Sweden. That he was still at the conference. Soon, Philippe. Until one day, I surprised myself by saying to the girl who had become the world to me (parent, sibling, friend, even a love insofar as a boy of nine can be in love): "He's never coming back, Amélie. And neither is Maman." A few days thereafter, my uncle came to see me, and explained that I was correct. Soon I would go to live with him in Montréal.

July turned into August.

The cicadas grew ever louder: the rasp of their flexing tymbals a sound like that of time and space tearing at the seams.

Suddenly, I found myself in the meadow. In the morning light, the buildings of the old farmstead seemed to have been painted with a fresh coat of blood. I was still a long ways from the willow tree when

I heard the sounds, distinct from one another but weirdly intermingled: the buzz of countless wings and a crying of little voices, unnaturally high in pitch, as when a song was played on the hi-fi at too many revolutions per minute. . . . Fifteen years later, I would hear such a voice again—though only one. In the assumption of Messrs. Clavell and Neumann, there was only ever one, crying for help from a spiderweb in the garden. What they did not know, what no one knew, is what I had done out there on the edge of suburban expansion. I am not sure that I myself knew until I came close enough to see the glass tank. . . . Once, my father had told me of a theory: that a star might collapse at the end of its life cycle and form a region of space from which nothing, not even light, could escape. At first, that was all I could think of. Dark void from which voices were crying for help. Yet wasn't the blackness in the tank more cloud than hole? I stood in the morning heat, listening. Voices, yes. But not words. Not language. Just meaningless phonations. Closer now. To see that the blackness was not a cloud but an aggregation. Of insects. Hundreds, maybe thousands of flies swarming in the open space of the tank, crawling on its glass walls and upside down on the ceiling of screen, and just as many piled on the floor, dying or long dead. Closer still. To see—you might expect—a humanoid head on every insect body. But the situation was more complicated than that: There were flies with two human heads, headless human torsos with the wings of flies, human heads with one compound insect eye, conjoined twins with two faces, one human and the other insect, on opposite sides of a single head. . . .

For the first time that strange summer, I cried. With my eyes closed and my hands covering my ears.

In the end, I made my way to the barn, where I had seen a red can with a handle and a nozzle. When I picked it up, liquid sloshed around inside. I poured all of it into the tank and threw the can into the weeds. Then got the magnifying glass from my tin box and focused a tiny dot of sunlight on the stew of kerosene and corpses until the fuel reached ignition temperature and combusted. The fire burst in every direction. Against the four walls of glass and up through the screen. Hot enough to singe my hands and to set all the children of the thing I'd caught and all of its children's children instantaneously aflame. I thought of my father then. Though I still did not see. That these were *his* progeny and therefore my own brothers and sisters and nieces and nephews: He was the father of everything I was destroying, and I was brother and uncle to each and every victim.

221

Greg Hrbek

FINIS

An old man now, I still hear them screaming—and still need, after so many years, a help that no one can give. I am not religious, much less Roman Catholic. But I went once (this was 1976 or '77) to a church in Mont-Royal (Église Saint-Édouard) and told a priest through the screen of a confessional that, as a boy, I had killed my father with a hydraulic press and set upward of a thousand more members of my immediate and extended family on fire. I was instructed to pray ten Hail Marys. I tried once more in the spring of 1983, during the term of my engagement to someone whose portrait photo I still keep in my sock drawer. There are things about me, I said—and asked her to sit with me and watch on videotape a film that would begin to explain. . . . None of you believes me either. It doesn't matter. It doesn't matter if you're not listening. At the end, we tell our stories only for ourselves and for one reason alone: to keep them real in our own minds until dementia comes like a fungus moth to chew holes in the fabric of memory.

From Experimental Animals
A Reality Fiction
Thalia Field

THE CONTINUED SHAMELESS duplicity of the so-called Animal Protection society makes it clear that we need more help handling the growing problem of stolen animals. To do this, the girls and I support private charities like the shelter at Garches (modeled on one at Battersea, supported by Queen Victoria). As a token, Animal Protection offers to pick up a few dogs, deliver them to Madame Faure at 34, rue de Buci, six, seven, ten times a day—in addition to what she and the other women collect—and then, nightly, we drive them to Garches. But Garches isn't winterized, and our meetings focus on funding a winter home in Paris. Note that in the same building as Madame Faure is Mademoiselle Mazerolles, who only collects cats.

Remember when Mademoiselle Huot ended up in the paper for hitting Professor Brown-Sequard with an umbrella—just as he was about to experiment on a little monkey? Oh, she was a deed doer! And she even wrote down the details, so her bravery could one day be known:

> I stuffed myself into the shadows, guided by the half-light of a door slightly ajar. I opened it all the way. It was the amphitheater. No one. A vast table on a large single step made a platform almost even with the first row of seats, right in the middle of which I sat myself. A board informed me of the special of the day: experiment on a monkey. Half a dozen students—of whom four were female—spread out toward the bleachers, some distance from me. Foreigners, I could tell by their looks and their babbling. Here was the whole scholarly public in Claude Bernard's ancient amphitheater that at one time held five hundred people . . . hee hee, the value has gone down on the blood market!
>
> And so, ladies and girls who dare join this adventure, don't forget to make yourself pretty when going to the enemy, to bring mistakes and distractions that will damage his tranquillity and safety and make him drop his solemnity. God and the devil will each find their place.

Brown-Sequard trotted in, saluting with a little paternal gesture to his disciples. He adjusted his glasses to get a better look at me, seemed satisfied . . . and initiated his first lesson. I understood we were going to see him start by cutting the vocal cords of the monkey—thus, this meant a painful operation without anesthetics that would then prevent him from crying out. The animal was not yet there. The animal was then brought in attached on a vivisection plank, a poor little child monkey, making supplications with its eyebrows that would make you fall to your knees, and now to me—me who felt like its mother at that moment—me rolling in guilt, in mud, to save and steal away this monkey to the other side of the sun. Who knows how I approached, calmly leaned on the platform "as if to see better"; how, as the operator lowered the scissors toward the victim's throat . . . *vlan!* In a second, my umbrella hit, and harshly fell broken. . . . O this dream of one moment in a blue eternity! The man's cry brought me back to reality!

This same Mademoiselle Huot later visits a public event at Trocadero, where Dr. Laborde has a rabbit strapped into the vivisection trough. She jumps onstage, demanding him to stop, bringing the show to an awkward end. That evening, she is visited at home by an emissary from Animal Protection, nervily accosting her because Dr. Laborde is a member of the governing council! Claude held the same post. That tells you what you need to know about the SPA. We tell these stories among us, and some write them down. Night after night, you can be sure to find Madame Delvincourt on her rounds up and down the hills—especially to the Jardin des Plantes—carrying baskets of pâté for hundreds of cats. She told me that in another life she didn't like cats, and in this life she must labor on their behalf.

I know Claude smugly calls our efforts "Don Quixotry."

At some point, you and Mademoiselle Huot get so rightly sick of the Animal Protection Society that you decide to found a new one entirely: the Popular League against the Abuses of Vivisection, with Maria Deraismes and a new treasurer, Mr. Serle, of 84, Faubourg Saint-Honoré. In a letter to the editor of the *Herald of Health*, you announce: "Its president is no less a person than the great poet Victor Hugo." Victor Hugo: "My name is nothing. It is in the name of the whole human race that you make your appeal. Your society is one that will reflect honor on the nineteenth century. Vivisection is a crime. The human race will repudiate these barbarities." The devout Robert Browning, a vice president of the Victoria Street Society, writes two antivivisection poems, and Christina Rossetti publishes a special pamphlet, but our Victor Hugo makes us proud: "Human cruelty to animals might one day rebound upon our heads like Nero's cruelties." Your new French Society against Vivisection sponsors many lectures—it's here we would have met—really, Anna Kingsford, don't you think we did?

Florence Miller recalls:

> As the leading scientific advocate of vegetarianism, Anna Kingsford was invited to lecture before the Sunday Lecture Society, and the Honorary Secretary, Mr. Domville, came up to me at a meeting one evening and said, "You are a great friend of Mrs. Kingsford's, could you ask her to dress more plainly to appear on our platform? You know we are a scientific society and we avoid anything of the Stage order, so I feel that she is not suitably dressed now for the platform."
>
> "Nina," I said to her presently, "have you got an all-black platform gown? Mr. Domville says his Committee likes their lady lecturers to be all in black." She understood and made a moue at me, and she did appear in black—and looked more beautiful than ever!

Claude's Red Notebook:

> Physics teaches us that matter is inert, that is to say that it cannot produce movements by itself; some conditions are always required to intervene and change its state. Can one support this in physiology? How can volition be explained?

225

Thalia Field

Is he the gadfly that drives you to wander, speak, and lecture? Mad, you are the ragged virago, doctor or white Magian.

Prometheus: *"It is worth it to indulge in weeping over evil doings if one is likely to win the tribute of a tear from the listener."*

Io: *"Zeus inflamed by passion's dart has called upon me to unite in divine union. Hiding in the pastures, I became animal, and spurred by the gadfly now toil with revealing this body of truths."*

When you speak, do you hear yourself moo? When you look, do you see a cow and try not to choke at this fat, ugly version?

Chorus: *"What a tale to strike our ears with sufferings so hard to look upon or hear about; grievous to endure. We shudder to behold."*

Claude's Red Notebook:

"With animals, feelings only translate through movement, and we can easily confuse the lack of feeling with the paralysis of the motor nerves, and vice versa."

Chorus: *"Speak then and tell all. It comforts those in pain to know beforehand all the pain they still must bear."*

* * *

"Fanny, what's got into your ladies, loose in the world without a mote of sense!" "Fanny, are these kittens worth all this trouble?" "Do you really think animals and humans are the same?" So many people just cower unseen, not forced to find the questions behind all the answers. But as a long-term member of a desperate chorus, I have stolen the eloquence of those who speak center stage. In the preface

226

to *La Comédie Humaine*, didn't Balzac write that all animals and people have been created "on one and the same principle"? Yet aren't there as many opinions as there are mouths to say them, and still we divide the sides into just a few?

Claude: "The immediate object of study in experimental medicine isn't man but animals; man is only the goal that stays in the mind, outside the perilous experiments."

Man, animal, animal, man—words can't hold the confusion, so it's best to just wander straight into it, making a mess of what's always been a mess. Geoffroy Saint-Hilaire: "There is, philosophically speaking, only a single animal."

Claude: "Physiologists . . . deal with just one thing, the properties of living matter and the mechanism of life, in whatever form it shows itself. For them, genus, species, and class no longer exist. There are only living beings; and if they choose one of them for study, that is usually for convenience in experimentation."

I might add that, for a long time, animals were considered equal enough to men to get the same treatment under the law. Put in jail, the animals received the same food as the other prisoners, and had the right to the same lawyers, even though some judges worried that spells could allow animals to harness the "witchcraft of silence" and thereby not feel the pain of the tortures inflicted on the men (*maleficium taciturnitatis*).

Claude: "We must admit nothing occult; there are only phenomena and the conditions of phenomena."

Claude to Madame Raffalovich:

> *Again on the subject of savage beasts, you were interested in the hedgehog family I mentioned earlier and on whom I*

had designs. Alas, all is finished. There are disasters even here and unhappy families. The family had four little ones and a mother; a dog killed one, a flood drowned two, and the last died of grief, I think. The inconsolable mother has left, at least we haven't heard or seen her since she spent several nights making nocturnal echoes with her plaintive cries.

But the devil or his adjuncts will take every chance to penetrate the humble mind of a Christian. The extremity of control that the church held over all aspects of village life severed Claude's ancestors from the symbolism, reciprocity, and pleasure of nature. No moment too private, no forest too dense, for the church to ignore. But as members of the household, and therefore under the king's ban, animals also enjoyed the same wergild as women and peasant workers, and their *beste covert* had the same rights and responsibilities as humans. In the case of violent crime, for example, the death penalty was required, especially for domestic animals—for not only was evil incarnate in the beast who committed the deed, but also in the infested home that could be vexed for centuries, its *aura corrumpens* holding title to the real estate until the sin was fully paid. The animal, convicted in the court and hung in public, was often dressed in human clothes and mask.

Mary, looking on,"*knew through her compassion what it is to be a mother.*" Christ on Calvary said, "Here is your son" and so it is that labor pain is not about childbirth but the pain of interceding, for Jesus came not as a king, but as a poor creature, helpless and inviting motherhood of everyone. You might say that Christ took all the positive aspects of the world for the church, leaving nature with nothing but pagan symbols, and devils and dragons that would steal our innocent souls, or our children in sacrifice. But it's not enough to refrain from wrong—the devil waits for any crack through which to enter. Every day chants and admonitions against demons must be said, as much as prayers for the dead, and every so often an actual exorcism to call out some Lignifex, Latibor, Monitor, Shulium, or Reromfex. Lucifer himself is known to make appearances, until the priest with bell, book, and candle confronts him. Yet given the baptisms, the churchgoing, the exorcisms, where do all the devils dwell?

Ah, the church replies, they easily take residence in the beasts, one step above hell, where they can exert their intelligence and fool people into believing these creatures have souls and hearts and minds like us. But since we are taught that this is a ruse, we justify the mistreatment of animals who are merely possessed, just as centaurs and satyrs, dire chimeras and dragons are. The pious Catholic works beside the Father in punishing monsters.

Jesuit Father Bougeant, from *Philosophical Amusements on the Language of the Animals*, 1737:

> What matters it whether it is a devil or another kind of creature that is in our service or contributes to our amusement? . . . If it be said that these poor creatures, which we have learned to love and so fondly cherish, are foreordained to eternal torments, I can only adore the decrees of God, but do not hold myself responsible for the terrible sentence; I leave the execution of the dread decision to the sovereign judge and continue to live with my little devils, as I live pleasantly with a multitude of persons, of whom, according to the teachings of our holy religion, the great majority will be damned.

Claude to Madame Raffalovich:

> *I'm sitting under a tree in the vines neighboring my woods; I'm imitating the cries of the buntings with a decoy, while at the same time moving a mirror that sparkles in the sun under a dried branch on which will perch the birds, victims of their coquetry. It's truly curious to see with what joy these two-legged creatures, feathered, consider themselves and complement each other in this contemplation. It's in this moment that I unleash my rifle shot and the murderous bullet comes to deliver them to Marriette's cooking pot.*

So humans are sinners and by substitution can only absolve sin if someone innocent lifts it from us and carries it for us? We are given our punishments, some during life, some after death—but isn't there a final judgment waiting, and then our sins will be known to all?

Thalia Field

Anna Kingsford, letter to Florence Miller:

The great need of the popular form of the Christian religion is precisely a belief in the solidarity of all living things. It is in this that Buddha surpassed Jesus—in this divine recognition of the universal right to charity. Who can doubt it who visits Rome—the city of the Pontiff—where now I am, and witnesses the black-hearted cruelty of these "Christians" to the animals which toil and slave for them?

Ill as I am, I was forced, the day after my arrival, to get out of the carriage in which I was driving to chastise a wicked child who was torturing a poor little dog tied by a string to a pillar—kicking it and stamping on it. No one save myself interfered.

Today I saw a great, thick-shod peasant kick his mule in the mouth out of pure wantonness. Argue with these ruffians, or with their priests, and they will tell you, "Christians have no duties to the beasts that perish." Their Pope has told them so, so that everywhere in Catholic Christendom the poor, patient, dumb creatures endure every species of torment without a single word being uttered on their behalf by the teachers of religion. It is horrible—damnable. And the true reason of it all is because the beasts are popularly believed to be soulless. I say, paraphrasing a mot of Voltaire's: "It if were true that they had no souls, it would be necessary to invent souls for them." Earth has become a hell for want of this doctrine.

Animals quickly recognize signs of kindness, not in another world, but right in our hand, and that's how to coax even the most terrified cat with a caress and a morsel, sometimes a quiet moment in the courtyard as we await the next driver in the chain of escape. But however much some of our friends cuddle and love the cats, it's the dogs that have always filled my girls' faces with joy. It was rumored that in the Middle Ages, dogs didn't get the plague, and so were considered agents of the devil. But even they can tell when they're maligned, and they look at us quizzically and ashamed. Canine protectors guide men through death and birth, like Anubis sitting where the sun sets each day, watchdog of the land of the dead, calibrating the scale that measures the deeds of a dead man's heart against the feather of truth to see who gets another go. The city of dogs, Hardai, drew followers of Anubis, who also accompanied Hermes bringing the dead to Hades. Later he became Hermanubis, dog headed but more friendly, his cult becoming Saint Christopher's. Ritual massacres of dogs were thought to cheer the gods and head off violent summer weather. Black dogs were preferred for sacrifice, to purify a journey or please ghosts. Scattered among infant graves, puppies were thought to absorb illness, after which they and the disease could be disposed of.

Anna Kingsford: "In what shall we say the practices of the secret devil-worshippers of medieval times differed from those which now go on in the underground laboratories of the medical school? . . . Nothing is easier than this method of gaining knowledge, for the operator sacrifices nought of his own to gain it; he gives only other lives and these the most innocent he can obtain . . . It is black magic which, in order to cure a patient, first transfers his complaint to an innocent victim. He who accepts health at such a cost shall but save it to lose it." Under Roman rule, Asklepios, Apollo's son, had temples where gentle canines, cynotherapists, walked among the sick or lay among them licking their wounds. Asklepios competed directly with early Christians, and so his temples were defaced and destroyed. The dog who licks Lazarus's sores came from a church built on the site of an Asklepian temple, and Christ resurrected him.

Father Bougeant: "Thus a devil, after having been a cat or a goat, may pass, not by choice, but by constraint, into the embryo of a bird, a fish or a butterfly. Happy are those who make a lucky hit and become household pets, instead of beasts of burden or slaughter. The lottery of destiny bars them the right of voluntary choosing. Pythagoras's doctrine is untenable in its application to men and contrary to religion, but it fits admirably into the system already set forth concerning beasts as devil's incarnations, and shocks neither our faith nor reason."

Claude's own St. Julien was ravaged in 1545 by a swarm of greenish weevils, so the winegrowers brought legal complaint, while a lawyer, Pierre Falcon, defended the insects. The judge proclaimed: "Inasmuch as God, the supreme author of all that exists, hath ordained that the earth should bring forth fruits and herbs not solely for the sustenance of rational human beings, but likewise for the preservation and support of insects, which fly about on the surface of the soil, therefore it would be unbecoming to proceed with rashness against the animals now actually accused and indicted; on the contrary, it would be more fitting for us to have recourse to the mercy of heaven and to implore pardon for our sins." The Host was carried around the vineyards at high mass, and people paid extra tithes. A testimony, signed by the curate, attests this was all handled pro forma.

Thirty years later, the infestation in St. Julien returned, and this time Pierre Rembaud, lawyer for the bugs, argued that the plaintiffs' request of excommunication was unsuitable. He affirmed his clients were in their rights, since, as we read in the book of Genesis, the lower animals were created before man, and God said to them: "Be fruitful and multiply and fill the waters of the seas, and let fowl multiply in the earth," etc. Now the Creator would not have said this if he hadn't wanted these creatures to have sufficient means of support—therefore the accused, in living off the vines of the plaintiffs, were only exercising their rights. After adjourning a few days, the prosecution responded that the insects were created subservient to man, which was why they were created first, and their only raison d'être was to minister to man, "as the Psalmist asserts and Saint Paul confirms." The trial took so long and was so continually deferred that the community finally offered an "insect enclosure" outside the village where the weevils might receive alternative sustenance. A vote was taken, subject to the approval of the insects, but their lawyer declined due to insufficient food on the proposed plot.

Tony dear,

I've sent you today a basket of pears; the ripest are on top, the least ripe beneath. Put them in a closet; they'll ripen in order and will be good to eat in 8–15 days. In a few days I'll send a basket of red and green grapes and some vine peaches, the trellis ones having already passed their prime.

Your aunt Jenny and her children came to spend two days visiting me... They send you hugs and kisses. Yesterday, I saw Mr. Chretien who lost his old Jeanne who you might remember. He sends his regards... It is extremely hot here; the fruit is all drying on the trees; the harvest will be better than last year's, but will still be mediocre.

I send all my love, as well as to your sister.
Your affectionate father,
Claude Bernard
Saint-Julien, September 7, 1874

Wara Wara
Diana George

BODY SAT SLUMPED, spine gone slack. The neck had drooped to horizontal and its lopped-flat surface, ringed with bleeding shreds and gobbets, faced the open door. Newly exposed to the problem of light, the neck stump, in time, might have learned to see: cement-block walls; chipboard desk; head.

The head lay sideways, tilted down. Nose was a chock stopping it rolling. The head, too, kept watch on the door.

From a distance came the chittering and shrieks of macaques; nearby, chirr of insects.

The lips moved against the desk. "Ada," said the head of Sub-lieutenant Ada Quý Wara Wara, "you will have to take dictation for us."

Behind the head, the seated stump, so addressed, said nothing.

"Ada," the head's lips murmured, "if only you and I had been partisans in the desert, in another era."

Neck was a stump, but so, too, the entire body: a stump.

"Do not write this down," said the head. "This part is just between us. We know from books what a desert battle entailed in times past. Camels, their coats patchy and pale under the gay bright riggings. Their segmented muzzles twitch when we tug at the reins. Caparisoned and all a-jingle, but lousy; even their long, pretty eyelashes swarm with lice.

"The camels heave themselves up on command, groaning as they get under way with their habitual, swaying gait, levering themselves down again at day's end, hinge-wise, the way they do, obstreperous, the way they are, breathing their noisome breath at us, whipping green ropes of grassy slaver in our faces."

Dripping. Lopped-flat neck-top poised like a face, as if still oriented, still looking.

"To dream of a herd of camels on the burning plain denotes assistance when all human aid seems at a low ebb. Or a sickness from which you will arise, contrary to all expectations. Will we live to see the dawn, Ada, do you think?"

234

Drip and ooze. *Ada.*

"I say 'live.' I say 'see.' Our executioners are coming back for us. They'll grab me by my hair, they'll swing me up and toss me into a burlap sack. You they will drag by the heels. Or, one at your arms and one at your feet, they'll frog-march you out the door. I won't see any of this. Inside my dark and lurching burlap sack I will feel only nausea.

"I say 'feel,' but where? In you? In the mind's belly?

"They'll fling us both onto the pyre. A burst of light, the reeking scorch and sear. Will that be the end of it, Ada?"

Oozing and cooling, dulling. Lopped-off throat-top a slab. Dead center, dead the slab's center, a hole: eye or mouth.

Ada and Ada had freed the model hamlet of New Nebaj and they'd let what hamlet women would join their corps of guerilleras. Ada and Ada and corps had burnt the new garrison just outside San Gaspar Cotzal right back down to the ground. Ada and Ada, Ferminxta and Ferminxta, Barucha and Barucha. Not yet lopped. Into parts. Ada, Ferminxta, and Barucha; and the shootists Julia and Zulma María; and Encarnita the cartographix; and the tracker-girl; and Xoco the berserker. Rag-and-bottle brands alight in their hands. Razed San Gaspar Cotzal to ash.

Here, at model hamlet Chajul, soldiers had been waiting in ambush.

"It won't be the end of it, Ada. They'll write down what their journalists will say I said, what they'll say they heard while tongues of flame lapped at the already lidless eyes and white steam poured from ears and mouth and nose, and the flesh of the face shrank to leathery panes that dropped from the skull and tumbled down the shifting city of embers. The head, they'll write, the wretched smoldering head, in the long agony before thoughts and brain thickened to a single hot suet, the head shouted from the pyre that it, that I, longed to make still one more last confession. Drunken journalists who are even now lolling poolside on hotel rooftops will say instead that they were here, and they'll write what the executioners said to say they saw: 'Flames shot upward, tufts of jungle sphagnum blazed bright and were gone.' Maybe tufts will not blaze up; maybe they'll smolder and droop, like all the other too-damp fuel the executioners will have heaped up in their careless attempt at a pyre, wet logs of freijo-laurel and salmwood and the mildewed tops of cable spools and your own jumbled disarticulated arms and legs and torso. The head of Sublieutenant Wara Wara shrieked and moaned, their journalists will write; the head of Wara Wara cried out. At the last, straining all belief, they will say that I said that I now wish to speak in praise of bankers and

235

latifundistas, and of water rights and femicide and hydroelectricity. They'll take no risk, in saying I said this. Brazenness will be all their warrant."

Thrumming: jeeps or trucks or tanks, and a buzzing sensation as of ley lines, within and without of stump.

"Our mistake was not to have foreseen the treachery of men; fragile, despotic, vindictive men. On the enemy's side and on our own.

"Again and again, the situation met its limit in the figure of a husband. When not, then in the rape tactics of the terror squads.

"Write this down, Ada: All that long day we sent the enemy to hell one by one, and Death was seen stalking the red-dirt alleys of San Gaspar Cotzal behind us, muttering, 'Today a Mondragón rifle in Ada's hand is worth a hundred of my scythes.'"

Shorn plane of flesh atop neck-stump still dripped. Viscid. Did moths or bees alight and sup there, fluttering gore-splashed wings.

"I wish I knew that you were writing, Ada, but I've heard none of the sounds a headless body might make while it outfits itself with pen and paper, none of your scrabbling in desk drawers or fumbling in our pockets.

"I don't see why you should fall still once separated from me, Ada. By rights, without a head atop your shoulders, you ought to be motion itself, restlessness in person. It's only a head drowses and wavers, distractible, infirm of purpose, glozing our dark way to nothingness."

Thrumming had stopped. Shirt-front was blood-sodden. Trouser crotch sodden. Desk's edge pressed hard into low-slouching stump-body's chest.

Pressure drop; approach of rain or night.

"Write this down, Ada.

"After San Gaspar Cotzal, we began the 'long march' to Chajul, as has no doubt already been reported, the 'long march,' during which, they'll have written, we 'cut a swath of terror.' We cut no swath. The jungle was not the one they'll have written about: all venom and hazard, trip wire stretched taut at boot level, scorpion poised in the well of a white waxen blossom. And they'll have written, too, how coins of sun-spangle fell on broad green leaves and loamy earth, and the burgeoning tendrils unfurled, sticky pale and new. It wasn't so. No sun, no spangle, only darkness and heat and the iron-hard ground snaked all about with massy, tangled roots. We did not march so much as clamber, root-clamber, our machetes good for nothing but to hack handholds in resinous boles.

"We would walk until nightfall. We ate meagerly and strung our hammocks at the foot of a kapok tree. Hard gray roots rose up like fins. Day's clamor was louder by night: frogs and owls, rut-leopards and shriek-monkeys.

"Mornings, exhausted, we walked on.

"Other cadres, or some few of the burnt-out villagers who'd escaped resettlement, were to have left us stockpiles in jungle clearings: grease pencils and flashlight batteries, jerricans of molasses and sacks of maize or meal, wrapped up in tarps and buried underground or hung from trees like golondrinas' nests. The cadres or the burnt-out were to have planted gardens in the clearings, too, against our arrival. But often as not the shoots of bean or melon had been trampled before we got there, all provender ravaged, the sacks split open and the grain flung out on the diesel-soaked ground. The enemy followed us from in front, laying waste.

"Xoco and the tracker-girl were to lead us to the next clearing. But those who'd gone ahead of us to bury food had also had to stumble over roots in the dark. The locations of the stockpiles were notional, like our progress. As well have brought with us a dowser, an augerer, to slit up sloths' bellies and make haruspect pronouncement where next to turn."

Pricking came over the back of stump-body's left hand and up under shirt-cuff, up sleeve. Eight legs or six or many, pricking slow, not scuttling. Insect's belly, stiff-haired, big as stump-body's thumb, dragged along pricked along skin.

"We walked, halting and starting again, hindered by root clumps. Thready brown vinelets brushed against our faces. Above us, the canopy, tangled as a pleached orchard, blotted out the sun; and the humid air, with its smell of baked dirt and thunderclap ozone, sealed us in.

"Xoco walked the lead, bandoliered, machete in hand. Then came Ferminxta—called Ute in the country where she'd been born—singing a song about a bandit queen. Ferminxta was followed by Encarnita, tricked out in tatterdemalion: rings and bangles and a torn-sleeved khaki shirt over a muddied yucateco wedding dress. Behind her, the shootists: slight Julia, who favored pistols, and Zulma María, carrying a Mondragón, like me. The bandit in Ferminxta's song hid her loot in the mountains; she crouched at the mouth of a mountain cave and gazed up at the moon. Lonesome victorious queen. I trailed behind the shootists; at dark of midday, I could make out only the hulking form of Zulma María, sometimes a pale flash of Julia's arm or hand. Xoco cursed; she'd walked into a spider's web spun just at face height, again. Ferminxta's bandit queen ascended to her moonlit

237

throne of lashed yew boughs, before a congress of moths and beetles. As usual, none of us knew exactly where the tracker-girl was. She said Ferminxta's songs drove off the deer. Myself, I sometimes struggled to hear Ferminxta over the din of birds and monkeys. A breeze kicked up. Too high in the canopy to bring us any balm. Treetops swayed and rubbed, creaking. In solemn witness of the moon and beetles, the bandit queen took for herself a bandit bride, but it was not long before they parted again in sorrow. Barucha walked behind us, last of all.

"No tropic forest duff, no luxuriance of rotten life a-roil underfoot; the earth was hard and bare. No sun-dapple. Encarnita always thought she would be the one to tell our story, a story in which costumes would figure heavily, and the mere sight of us—crazed and gore-smeared in tattered finery—so terrified the enemy that one by one they dropped, gentle as fawns, without we fired a shot, and with a whispered word Encarnita dispatched each and all to the afterlife, there to bring news of conditions in the modern world. Her bloodless combat was a lie. Barucha knew it, Xoco knew it. I, too, talk of fires that razed garrisons without killing. Zulma María was indifferent to glory and damnation, was a good shot and a poor strategist, and she pretended the baffled pall Julia's beauty cast her down into was love. When Ferminxta was still Ute a man waylaid her in a stairwell, and she fought until the light blackened and time's processional slowed to its end. To this day Ute-Ferminxta does not know how or if she lived. And nor do we, Ada, know if she lives today, or if we will see her head propped beside us in the fire.

"One day we emerged at a loggers' skid trail. A red-dirt gash of sawn-off stumps descended in steep defile. Before us lay the wide and undulate world, forested hill after forested hill receding to a horizon obscured by shreds of mist. Up a far hill the skid-trail opened into a road that ended at Chajul. The model hamlet's tin roofs glinted. We could see no one in Chajul's alleys and pig-cotes.

"The sunlight felt strange on our skin. Our guns and our bellies were empty; for days, we'd had nothing but water, and tobacco, and a searing liquor that tasted of toluene and orchids. Armed only with rifle butts and machetes, we began the descent to Chajul."

The head of Sublieutenant Ada Quý Wara Wara fell silent a moment. The stump-body, too, was silent. The insect no longer crawled; it rested just above the stump-body's left collarbone. Since the thrumming of jeeps or tanks had stopped, the stump had heard nothing more, if that could be called hearing, ear-less apprehension of nothing but percussion and rumbling.

"Do not write this down, Ada. They plan to say that I shouted from the fire that our revenge for Chajul shall be terrible, that whole armies shall be swept under the tide of our fury and our reprisals will not stop there. Saying so, they make of me a harpy, Ada, a vain and howling and impotent harpy, and of you they will say I know not what: that, denuded by flames and with your bones blackened to staves of charcoal, you seemed yet to gesture and mutely speechify? that, flames spent, onlookers dwindling, the rain came at last and washed you to nothing but clags of bone in black slurry? And of our compas, our guerilleras, they will spread still more lies.

"Ada, our testament must not sink to caviling and rebuttal.

"Put your pen down and I'll tell you a story for nothing:

"Before Chajul, long before New Nebaj, it was just you and I and Ferminxta. We had no rifles yet, and only one pistol, Ferminxta's, and we had no need of buried stockpiles, either—back then we could still enter towns and villages, not that we often did, the point of the hills was that they were not the towns. We were more like pilgrims, or mendicants. Mendicants who botanized and idled. Who spent most of their time lost.

"The jungle, so-called, was a dark wood. Everything looked like a path; wherever we turned, a way seemed to have been hacked clear for us: earth hard and bare as if hammered; silvery and greened-up tree trunks ranged to either side like poplars along a country road. Turn just a few degrees, and it was the same illusion greeted us, another dark path receding to a vanishing point. Everywhere alleys, avenues, corridors. Everything drew away, nothing endured. Ferminxta said she knew better but I had been expecting a jungly thicket: flimsy serrated fronds and fat, bitter succulents and a press of viney, strangling growth pushing us back, thwarting us, claiming us. All was broad and dark and hollow.

"Ferminxta said, 'Let's climb one of these machinga trees and see where we are.' The way she said it, I thought *machinga* was a curse. The tree trunks were too broad, I told her, and even their lowest branches too high.

"Ferminxta said, 'Let's play a game.'

"Her game was called William Tell. I voted it down before she could say which of us was to aim and which to be accidentally shot. We were already playing one of Ferminxta's games, the one in which she harried me with her wishes and baited me into admitting I couldn't make them come true. On any other day we might have gone on like that, Ferminxta mimicking an ignorance about the ways of the world that extended even to gravity, even to the passage of time, and my own objections taking on a more and more genuinely aggrieved condescension—but Ferminxta suggested another shooting game.

"We set a candle down in the middle of a path and lit the wick. We turned our backs and stalked away like honor-wounded duelists, except that, with only the one pistol between us, Ferminxta and I counted out our paces side by side, then pivoted as one and took turns shooting out the flame.

"Three shots went wide and churned up earth. A fourth, Ferminxta's last, strafed the trees. Ferminxta claimed she was not defeated yet, she could still throw her dagger.

"It was my turn. I missed the wick but shattered the candle and that put out the light just the same, and at once Ferminxta and I began a new game, a game in which we pretended that with the extinguishing of the candle a darker darkness had fallen, although in truth the same greeny gloom obtained as before, but we made as if it were otherwise, and this new darkness we called liberty, or license, or what you will, as if this too had not all happened before.

"The dagger and the flame and the pistol and the labyrinth are nowhere if not inside this head, Ada, a head that does not only reason, or see, but that speaks. Our executioners are coming back. I am ready."

Neck was a stump, but so, too, head: stump.

Green Eyes of Harar
Wil Weitzel

My race has never risen, except to plunder:
to devour like wolves a beast they did not kill.

—Arthur Rimbaud, *Une Saison en Enfer*

BY THE END OF THE NIGHT, I was holding a small boy, my arms crossed tightly over his chest, in a back alley full of garbage. He was Ethiopian, maybe five years old. The boy had an eight-inch stick in his mouth with a strip of meat dangling off the end. Car beams were turned on us, switched to high, so we were flooded with light. And we were surrounded by hyenas.

Perhaps more than any other animal, the hyena is icon rather than beast. *Eikon* in the Greek sense of image. It enters the human imagination in the singular, through an optic that perceives only lurid pictures: of death, of the flush of the nocturnal, of carnivorousness pushed to the edge, where the prey may be deceased, where the marrow is prized along with the flesh, and where the cracking of bones and the bolting of viscera thrive in lieu of light and life.

Hyenas, in African and European visions alike, tend to gravitate toward demon status, toward guardians of the gates of hell, toward witches or the mounts of witches, toward spirits and wraiths, and toward hermaphroditic nightwalkers whose high-pitched whoops and "laughter" have been construed not as the vocalizations of a carnivore but the fateful harbingers of revenge or apocalypse.

More pronounced even than this tendency to mythologize is the predilection of human beings across cultures to understand the hyena in heavily normative terms as a loping coward and gluttonous scavenger, as a beast that comes too close to the human for comfort or security and is somehow a fallen version of ourselves, displaying avarice, disgraceful squalor, and an incongruous simultaneity of foolishness and cunning.

As a result of these associations, in part, hyenas have been subject to formidable eradication strikes by humans that few species

241

could have survived. In South Africa, European settlers who became ranchers beginning in the seventeenth century hunted out much of the vibrant fauna of southern Africa as they spread northward from the Cape across the Orange River into what is now southern Botswana and Namibia. The Kalahari Desert alone stopped this advance and marooned small, drought-resistant populations of animals and, for a short time, postponed the decimation of the ancient indigenous culture of the San people.

Hyenas were largely destroyed in this huge swath of the continent, though they survived farther north in the game-rich swamps and savannas of East Africa largely due to gradual, partial protections afforded more celebrated and less anathematized carnivores like lions, leopards, cheetahs, and African wild dogs. Yet of all places in sub-Saharan Africa, the Horn—Ethiopia, Eritrea, Djibouti, and Somalia—has been a stronghold of the largest of the family of Hyaenidae, the spotted hyena, for millennia. While written records largely coincide with the entrance of Europeans and as such date back only five hundred years, cave paintings portray hyenas along with lions and ungulates subsisting alongside human populations forty thousand years ago. What's more, it seems likely that hyenas and hominids have coexisted for over three million years, stretching back to before the control of fire, when hyenas held the upper hand and likely preyed on early hominids as part of a much wider diet of prey species.

Some accounts suggest that hyenas may in fact have originated in the Horn, in what is now Ethiopia, conducting radiating migrations to the south toward the Cape and north and east across Arabia into Asia, where they still persist in low-density populations. In any case, what seems certainly true is that in this region of Africa the relation between humans and hyenas is ancient, and while drifting toward symbiosis in the last millennium, it remains uniquely conflicted and complex. In few places is this transspecies association more intimate or set in starker relief than in the old city of Harar in eastern Ethiopia near the border with Somalia.

My wife and I went to Harar with the hope of encountering hyenas at night in the streets of the old city, which weave between moldering clay walls into labyrinthine mews and out through six gates to the surrounding countryside. We had read that Arthur Rimbaud had arrived here in the wake of his poetry as a businessman, representing commercial interests across the Gulf of Aden in Yemen, and between

1880 and 1891 he made five caravan crossings off the semidesert escarpment into the arid lowlands of what is now Somalia to the Red Sea, the last on a gurney, his leg stricken with cancer. Wandering through the streets on our first afternoon, we visited what was once the elaborate house of an Indian merchant built on the site of Rimbaud's abode in Harar.

To my disappointment, there was no mention of hyenas on the placards recounting Rimbaud's travails in Ethiopia. It is a dispiriting story that is widely known. He had traveled to Yemen then onto Harar in the wake of his falling-out with Verlaine. Verlaine had shot him in a drunken frenzy after their relations had soured then briefly resurged then sunk into disrepair, and once Rimbaud had healed and finished *Une Saison en Enfer*, he'd begun his travels. Over the course of two stints in Harar, he spearheaded several commercial ventures, exported coffee, and attempted to transport guns to Menelik in Shoa.

Overall, his fortunes were mixed and by the time he fell ill, his accounts were strapped and it seems he was in agony of the spirit and not only of the body. The house held reproductions of a letter from his sister and confidante, Isabelle, along with accompanying correspondence from Rimbaud's own hand. Together, they depicted painful last days in a hospital back in Marseille and recounted Rimbaud's fear of never walking again, his intermittent delusions that he could return to Africa, the worry that, were he to attempt the voyage back to Harar, Isabelle might abandon him, and then finally the onset of death, and, throughout, the elusive presence of sleep, which, Rimbaud plaintively alleged, arrived at long intervals only to last an hour.

My wife, Michelle, is a photographer and the one thing we took from this old house to relieve the gloom was the memory of Rimbaud's images. He had sent to his family for a camera shortly after arrival in Harar, and there is now hung for the public an array of late nineteenth-century reproductions of which Rimbaud's are the oldest. According to the placards, he was the first to photograph the old city and its denizens, and, beyond Rimbaud's posed self-portraits in the desiccated Abyssinian landscape, there is one shot in particular, of his storerooms near the center of town, that is hauntingly beautiful. A Harari man sits beside an aged pilaster in dilapidated chambers partially open to the sky. He has spread pots and water gourds on layered mats and has been preparing something in a weathered artisanal bowl. The storerooms around him are largely empty, his long wooden pestle lies in the dust beside his hidden feet, and his hands are poised in his lap. The man is staring off into the corners of the room, gaze vacant. If there is commerce afoot, it is invisible, distant. It looks as though, to the contrary, in the shadows of these sprawling quarters, nothing has moved for a thousand years.

By the time we'd made it to Harar the previous evening, we were exhausted. We had backpacked in the Bale Mountains to the south across the Sanetti Plateau above four thousand meters elevation, where our tent froze solid at night and our lips at altitude were split open and swollen from the sun. I had blood blisters on my hands from hanging on to gas canisters in a minibus overflowing with villagers en route to Harar, and when we'd arrived just after dusk, the power was out in the old city so we had spent another evening huddled together with headlamps and canned cannellini beans.

Now, stepping back out into the street from the merchant's house that contained the photographs of Rimbaud, we began the wait for sunset. The old pictures of the city within had looked much like the contemporary images Michelle had recorded that morning. Despite the absence of hyenas, there had been plentiful refuse on show. The squalor and dignity of the walled town in which open sewers ran through cobbled streets among tailors seated beside neat stacks of textiles had been apparent then as it was now.

When night did fall, we headed out of town to the hyena feeding about which we both had misgivings. It seemed, on the one hand, a chance to encounter at close range spotted hyenas—one of Africa's most fearsome and fascinating carnivores—and to witness a spectacle that, from our research, made little sense but which promised to provide insights into the way the town perceived these animals. At the same time, there was something off about it, about the idea that money was changing hands while humans were luring hyenas with the promise of raw meat to show each other how the animals could be cowed or tamed.

But were they cowed or tamed? We wanted to know. The "hyena men" of Harar call out to spotted hyenas denning in the encircling hills then feed them under car lights each night, charging visitors for the privilege of looking on. This is a practice that allegedly began in the 1960s and, like so much else in Harar and neighboring Somalia, dates back to mythic origins. In the nineteenth century, shortly before the time of Rimbaud, one of many droughts in this hyperarid region led to a surge in hyena attacks on domestic livestock. Competing accounts suggest that either local saints convened on a nearby mountain or one pastoralist divined the practice on his own, but in any case, spotted hyena clans were fed porridge, made from wheat and barley, in order to discourage them from preying on herbivores.

Now the practice of feeding hyenas porridge is largely defunct, but it is commemorated once a year on the Day of Ashura, the tenth day of Muharram in the Islamic calendar, at a shrine perched on a landfill outside the crumbling city walls. Fortune-telling is traditionally associated with this event, and auguries of crop growth and human thriving are contingent upon the amount of porridge the hyena clan leader devours.

For a long time as we stood in the dark, nothing moved in the shadows. We'd ended up in a back alley staring into the night beside two SUVs full of Ethiopians whose flickering high beams—off, on, off, on—suggested they were eager to see a predator. Upon arrival, we'd been informed that we each owed a hundred birr or approximately five dollars.

"Pay now," said a local Harari man who approached me in the dark.

"We'd like to stay," I told him. "But I'm going to pay you after."

"No," he said. "You should pay now. They have all paid." He pointed at the SUVs loaded with people.

"I believe you."

"Fine," he told me, "but you must pay."

"I must pay," I agreed, and we stared at each other until he drifted away.

Later on, after half an hour, first one then the other SUV drove off. It was getting cold. There were no hyenas. Somewhere out behind the refuse piles a man was calling to them in what is apparently a dialect that hybridizes Oromo, Harari, and hyena linguistic traces. It sounded to me like a humanized version of the famed "whoop" of the spotted hyena. We had heard this whoop from our tent several nights before, after hiking down from the mountains into the Harenna Forest. On that night, spotted hyenas had been traveling game trails through massive, flowering Abyssinian Hagenia trees that draped beside us. After eight days in gelid winds and scorching sun, it was strange to be sleeping in forest, surrounded by tall, moss-bearded Afromontane trees and, until sundown, the murmur of bees. Now, listening to the hyena man, it was strange again, this time to be near human beings and to be hearing vocal hybrids that were neither man nor hyena, or both.

Finally, Michelle nudged my shoulder. Both SUVs were gone but a

Datsun full of African tourists had arrived to illuminate the alley, and at last a small spotted hyena, a subadult, slunk into view. He was young and timid, skittish, and paced back and forth on the far side of the small courtyard fed by the alley. One of the loitering Harari men stepped forth with a bucket and threw a scrap of meat out toward the garbage. The hyena devoured it and a game commenced in which the bucket man reeled in the hyena with scraps, slowly shortening the trajectory of his tosses. One of the SUVs returned. Several of the Ethiopian men exited the vehicle to stand by the hood while the women stayed inside. For some time, training our headlamps on its strong shoulders and slack hind legs, we watched the hyena dart toward us, retrieve the meat, then retreat to the far wall.

When there was no change to this routine, the two carloads of Africans seemed to grow restless. A heated discussion arose as the SUV shifted heavily into reverse and threatened to depart again. Meanwhile, several Western tourists had arrived with their guides and spoke in hushed voices close to the vehicles. Then a second hyena ambled into view, larger than the first, seemingly an adult male. Immediately, the hyena man materialized from his calling site and spread a small tarp. There was new energy. Staring brazenly at the crowd, he began to bring the new individual closer, first with short throws and soon via abrupt hand feeding in which the strip of meat was swung outward toward the animal's mouth. Another vehicle arrived, again full of Ethiopians. Suddenly there was a crowd. We were inching closer, all of us, even the vehicles themselves, as though this new hyena, with a body length of four feet and weighing 120 pounds, held us by a different kind of lure, powerful, vying even with the gut song of hunger.

This lure of hyenas is not to be underestimated; nor, in Harar, is their connection to public health, sanitation, and the supernatural. Various folkloric attributions have it that their infamous necrophagy—their eating of the dead and desecration of human graves—must be attributed to the machinations of the spirit world. Outside the Jugol, or old town, cement and sheet-metal enclosures often protect graves, particularly those of the Islamic deceased who do not lie within coffins or sealed containers and can be shallowly interred in friable soil. Even the living are subject to attacks, notoriously in the capital, Addis Ababa, prior to its modern expansions. To this day, those sleeping on the streets of Harar or in the outskirts of Addis and throughout eastern Ethiopia across the Somali border must be wary of the nocturnal presence of hyenas.

Yet the sudden, opportunistic theft and dismemberment of children, the aged, and the infirm, usually at night when spotted hyenas are emboldened by their formidable olfaction, hearing, and eyesight, are rooted in a history of a much more concerted predation and a deep representational irony. The *djibb* or wolf, as the animal is known in Amharic, or *woraba*, in the Somali language, is not the same species as the retiring scavenger of the Kalahari—the brown hyena—or its more widespread relative, the striped hyena, who likewise thrives by means of carcasses. The spotted hyena, understood originally by Europeans as a bear-wolf or monstrous hybrid, and confused with its scavenging cousins in some instances as late as the 1970s, is in fact sympatric with the lion in most of its African range. And, like lions, with which we have seen hyenas at night share water holes unmolested and beside which they stand at the top of the trophic order or food chain, they are no scavengers. To the contrary, the spotted species we were witnessing in Harar that is blamed for livestock depredation and rightly accused of entering the huts of villagers and dragging off the weak to devour them in minutes, bones and all, is in fact a formidable carnivore that can pull down adult blue wildebeests and even African buffalo and giraffe, challenge lionesses after dark, and sustain long-distance chases of antelope as large as eland at speeds reaching sixty kilometers an hour.

As such, the image of the spotted species of the Horn as a lapsed beast slouching toward dawn and pilfering ordure and refuse contains a bitter truth that is in all ways constructed by humans. Spotted hyenas, in order to survive the human-authored decimation of wild fauna in the region, have turned to preying on domestic bovids and encountered sharp reprisals and revenge killings largely perpetrated in the form of poisonings. Over time, out of wariness and the incentive of limiting their energy outlay, hyena clans have been conditioned around towns and cities to become sanitation mechanisms, subsisting on detritus that humans cannot or do not care to clear. They have achieved a resultant modicum of human toleration and proved useful in particular during frequent epidemics in which they have devoured the victims of cholera, smallpox, and typhoid, dead or abandoned, and potentially limited the spread of disease. More essentially, they have survived as a species, despite the human shift from nomadism to agricultural pastoralism about six thousand years ago, and now wander the streets at night as "scavengers" in a radically transformed landscape.

*

As we stepped closer within this night world, more hyenas arrived. Figures filtered through the dust, both human and hyena, slipping in and out of the light and briefly shaping themselves before sliding into the shadows. I was itching to go face to face with one of these animals, but I looked at Michelle, who was crouched beside me, shooting the scene.

"Will you be all right if I go in there?" I asked her.

"No. What if you are bitten here? Where would you go? And is this really something we want to support?"

I hesitated. But something about these moments gives you away. People know you, I've decided. You can't change that. The Harari men were watching me fixedly. My long, dirty hair to my shoulders. Our exhaustion. The fact that we were unescorted, without the legitimizing company of guides. I can't say. They appeared to ignore the others and kept brushing up against me. Once in a while, one of them would bump me and tell me to pay.

I left the crowd and walked over to the hyena man. We crouched down together. Cameras went off in our faces. By this point, several Ethiopian onlookers had already assumed this position before me, feeding the hyenas themselves or allowing the hyena man to dangle meat above their heads so the animals climbed their backs to grab it.

He gave me the stick loaded with a scrap and I put it in my mouth.

"With your mouth?" he asked.

Soon what I thought was a male, based on the size and demeanor, came toward us, slowly, warily, but without fanfare. I watched his eyes, which, up close, shone black in the reflected light. A white band of fur masked them. His blunt head was larger than mine, the jaws wide, cranium vaulted to protect the brain so it could be spared the impact of molars crushing bones. Spotted hyenas have been known to splinter an adult giraffe bone in their jaws. Their pelage is spotted perhaps to disaggregate their forms during predatory salvos and is highly varied across individuals. This one, I noticed, was deeply chromatic in the artificial light.

Our mouths a few inches apart, he took the meat, and, with the stick in my mouth, I waited for the hyena man to reload me.

"Again?" he asked, and the same hyena approached. I leaned forward for him to eat, bringing my shoulders up and tilting in my head so that our skulls nearly touched. More cameras flashed.

"At least," Michelle said later, as we walked back through the gate of the old city toward the storerooms of Rimbaud, "they got meat out of the deal."

The largest spotted hyenas are not males. Clans are matriarchal and females are selected for size, in part so they can defend their cubs from males who have no role in the raising of offspring and are interested in coition, and in part so they can reinforce status hierarchies vis-à-vis other females. Nonetheless, rank is based chiefly on lineage and resultant alliance factions rather than solely on physical prowess. Spotted hyenas, like other hyenas, have densely intricate social systems and may be more adept at collective problem-solving in some instances than chimpanzees. They are highly intelligent hunters and formidable physical specimens. At night, in moister air, they may be able to hear lions on a kill at distances up to ten kilometers, and their hearts are proportionately larger than those of these competitors so they can remain at speed for longer pursuit segments. Finally, while spotted hyenas are misconstrued as thieving scavengers, conservation biologists report that it is lions who more often steal prey carcasses from hunting hyenas than the reverse.

It is hardly surprising then that encouraging these animals to haunt garbage mounds in high-density human settlements where some people sleep outside sets the stage for predation. The only way to understand the relative dearth of attacks on humans is as a result of adaptive pressures on hyenas to veer toward low-output, reprisal-free cleanup of cities and towns where uncleared refuse is abundant. Even so, on that night in Harar, it felt strange to share such tight space with young children and an animal who, more than other carnivores, has justified the zipping of our tent flap for years. There has been a thrill of excitement when hyenas have passed us in the night, but there has also been the rush of fear. Typically, spotted hyenas begin to feed on large prey at the haunches and move toward the heart and lungs in order to maximize blood intake. However, they've been alleged to eat off the faces of sleepers whose heads protrude from their bags and who have left their tent screens open, or even to drag people, sleeping bags and all, out into the night. I have never had reason to trust these accounts of bush maulings. Hyenas have paused at my tent in bushveld regions and dry savannas and even brushed the walls and sniffed at the turf-level seams. But nothing more. Nonetheless, I've stayed still on the ground and kept a knife.

So now, when parents from one of the vehicles placed a young boy in my hands and I saw soon afterward a large female hyena come out of the dark, nipples trailing almost to the ground, much larger, more powerful, than any individuals we had seen thus far and deeply unconcerned, businesslike in her movements, the scene felt more like a crude distortion than a scenario poised to end well. So before the hyena man could place the stick in the boy's mouth, I wrapped him up tightly, covering his chest and stomach with my arms, and leaned forward so I could pull him back sharply, positioning my neck and shoulders directly alongside his.

None of this fazed the smaller hyena that came forward. There was a brief interchange in which the animal received the meat beside our faces, and then it was over. We were standing. I was holding the boy to my chest and delivering him to his parents. There was applause. The show was complete. The Harari men came up to congratulate me. One after another, we bumped shoulders and shook hands. Then Michelle rose from where she had been shooting and we paid and walked away.

Later, we wandered through the stone streets of the Jugol in the darkness. Here and there, people were asleep beside the flowing sewers or in winding back alleys, half prone, half leaning against the narrow walls like storm wreckage. Several stirred to raise a hand for help, a donation, once they'd made us out in the dimness as foreigners. "*Ferengi*," they would murmur, then raise their shoulders and eyes toward the sky. But most watched us from atop sacks of barley or potatoes, their hands lit occasionally by phones, their fingers often buried in plastic bags full of soft *khat* branches from which, one by one, they would pull off the narcotic leaves and roll them into their mouths.

In the photos in the merchant's house, we'd seen many street scenes like these, dully illuminated, the dark tones of the photographs by Rimbaud and others picking up light, shading out expressions, making everything into a half world where something elemental is left out or grows by omission. There had been a guest book open by the door that we did not sign, but from which Michelle had read several entries aloud. They were written by travelers, mostly from Europe, who cited mysteries in the life history of the poet. Now, more than ever, they wanted to know why he'd stopped writing. Why he'd turned to exporting coffee, to running munitions, to accompanying caravans. To photography. Why, they asked, had Rimbaud not written of Harar?

We stayed quiet for a long time. Finally, Michelle asked how it was that I had ended up holding a child. She had been shooting. There were humans and nonhumans filtering around. Dust had come up from the alley, obscuring things, and car beams had flickered. People were moving, she said, between me and her camera, edging closer to the action.

"I have no idea why that happened."

"Didn't someone say something to you?"

"Nothing."

She shook her head. "Well, anyway, it was quite a scene."

I thought then of the large female that had come out of the shadows as our small show closed out in the alley. Something about her way of looking sidelong at humans stayed with me. Judging by her form, she had had multiple litters. Some of her grown cubs, potentially, were those we had fed. But she'd made no move to take meat from me. If anything, she'd stayed farther from the crowd, walking the perimeter of the small clearing fed by the alley, her eyes at a distance glowing green in the car beams. Even in that setting, it was hard to believe that she would be fed by people. She was different from the hyenas I have seen in the bush. Her wariness and intelligence, to my eyes, looked to be of a distinct kind. I would not trust her any more than she would trust me.

The sadness of Rimbaud's final letters, his last journey down off the eastern escarpment to the Red Sea, Isabelle's account of his deathbed desire to return to Africa, may haunt at least a Westerner's vision of the old city. But as far as mysteries surrounding the poet, I would place them alongside those of that nocturnal denizen of the old city. That female was lean and experienced and close to 150 pounds. I believe she had cubs to feed in the mountains. Despite everything that was going on at the end, I was trying to keep an eye on her. She wasn't a part of it. She was wraithing well on the outside. As the Oromo people would have it, a kind of spirit. Though I found only fleeting mention of hyenas in Rimbaud's poetry, penned in France, I believe that strong, cautious predator who has survived with her clans across the millennia just beyond our haggling, and more than any human that night, was untarnished, clean, would have made an ample subject for the sick merchant of Harar.

NOTE. This piece draws from work on spotted hyenas compiled by Gus Mills and Heribert Hofer ("Hyaenas: IUCN Status Survey and Conservation Action Plan," IUCN/SSC Hyaena Specialist Group, 1998) and Daniel W. Gade ("Hyenas and Humans in the Horn of Africa," *Geographical Review*, Vol. 96, No. 4, October 2006).

Anemochore
Meredith Stricker

Umwelt . . . *the skein that every animal forms for itself by winding itself into the world according to its means, with its nervous system, its senses, its shape, its tools, its mobility.*

—Jean-Christophe Bailly

are you a wind instrument are you breath

gone wild, running are you once a tree now aswarm, aswim in the
     orchard of bees

I am constantly made aware that words are teaching me

that I am inside *their* mouth

some of us would like our bodies to become a meadow

whose order is wild where a word is its own translation (nature tries

to love us but sometimes cannot / find a way / through

*

language is an animal it howls flees hides and waits watches us to see
    if we'll come to our senses in red

algae bloom fluorescence or flake flake flake of plucked pelt

pelagic pleading calm then kneeling

"wings stuck fast in the burning glue"

can you guess the sap within the live oak not how swift but how fierce

its movement the branch so dark against her skin

pure distance given its rawness

unlikeness

*

this time Hermes false rib fallow deer "yellowish coat spotted in
    summer"

not quite overlapping as in imbricate pinecone scales or turtle shell
    in case of emergency

you can build a cave in leaf-blowers irreparable

reparation

your interior my interior the wilderness's interior inside a word

the interior is vast each cloud erasing then forming ecstatic
    rainwater I'm breathing

your oxygen you're breathing my carbon dioxide green world blue
    world red world

solar system my darling permeable "dark" "lunarative" membrane
    there is no

greater love than this folded

in involutes

*

language is an animal it howls in wind-tunnel blood vessels mute raw

fractal fraternal no other habitat than our mouths meadowed

in solitude and contrailed surveilled surplus populations

o it listens and waits for the unbought *logos* of mothers standing in
line with their flagrant

tenderness

"separation" "fence" or "security" "fence" with "seam zones" or
"racial segregation" "wall"

"apartheid wall" or "acceptable" "generic" "descriptions" such as
"barrier" which the "International"

"Court" of "Justice" refers to as "wall" since "other" "expressions"
"sometimes employed" "are no more"

"accurate" "if understood" "in the" "physical sense"

immune system run amok in aquifers homeland

no-fly zones

in the physical sense

*

255

give me your hand rinse off your shoulders then rotate like a solar
   system like a heliotrope

try to find some surface of your self that doesn't touch marshlands
   war-heads starfish

littoral living systems ceaselessly refuse to abandon us

even when annihilation presents tense edge

cellular lucidity

heading out into the Open with ten words from John Cage as compass
   "method" "structure" "intention"

"discipline" "notation" "interpenetration" "indeterminacy"
   "imitation" "devotion" "circumstance"

forms of biomimicry as urban tide pools and structures we invent and
   breathe collapse then compost ourselves

I am willing

it is "just a mess" — beauty

NOTE. "separation" "fence" . . . : "Israeli West Bank barrier," Wikipedia entry; "wings
stuck fast in the burning glue": Dante, *Inferno*, canto 22; "ten words . . . ," "it's just a
mess," John Cage in *Every Day is a Good Day: The Visual Art of John Cage.*

Five Poems
Jessica Reed

ENTER: MATTER

I believe in blue fields:
one hundred thousand hectares of shrimp farms
in Ecuador. Wetlands and salt flats
along the Pacific coast have made room
for cyan rectangles. You can see them

from space. Convinced by brisk and cleaving
order, its contours. And so the atom: idea, quarrel,
and finally. Understand, it was one thing
to sort elements by kind, another entirely
to believe. Mendeleev did not doubt

the solidity of stuff, yet, working with silver,
sulfur, and sodium, could not regard
a single silver atom as true. He believed in cold,
crystalline order, but refrained: not Mendeleev—
not anyone—had seen a solitary particular.

But his century turned,
        the atom burst open, and inside: electrons, protons—
                stable constituents of matter. And it kept bursting,
        inside and further still and held together
                and immersed within. We threw
                        circus particles at each other, bent
        their paths in charged fields. They collided,
                decayed, and we examined their debris. Unbound,
        their pieces flung. Photon, neutron, neutrino,
                gluon, muon, pion . . . Because we carve.
Let us gather this fugitive matter, name the curious and unfamiliar.

257

Darwin's Galápagos made possible by naming (*vampire finch,*
mangrove finch, green warbler finch) what divisions
had already happened, island accidents whose names
made the scattered specific. We must believe this:
There are no old or new electrons. We can't follow

one around, pick it out in a crowd. And quarks,
down indistinguishable from down, strange from . . .
Hidden from sense, these silverfish dart (colorless color,
spin without spin) when we approach. Believe in contours,
in fields of blue, this carving made holy and specific.

MATTER, RESISTANCE

> *Matter is not what it appears to be. Its most ob-*
> *vious property—variously called resistance to*
> *motion, inertia, or mass—can be understood more*
> *deeply in completely different terms. The mass of*
> *ordinary matter is the embodied energy of more*
> *basic building blocks, themselves lacking mass.*
>
> —Frank Wilczek, *The Lightness of Being: Mass,*
> *Ether, and the Unification of Forces*

Pomegranate seed, avocado pit:
positioned in space and occupying.

Words about matter are honey,
changing meaning as a mood is altered

by the lighting. Honey, complicating.
Has that thing the word pointed to

changed? Matter, a *not moving*.
Burlap sack of apples I tug. Molasses.

Some thing is in it and making its
resistance. What is that, making

a clock or a hose? A stationary electron,
a proton, a neutron—these have *rest mass*.

One lemon on a countertop, its atoms
teeming with trembling parts. But not

a single photon, a light ray moving
in one direction. Blocks, swimming

and viscous. Study a still life and be still.
We are inside. We swim in it. Life

amasses. It is assembly. Peer inside an object
to its clearest skeleton, dripping

waxy through unempty space. Your body
is wax. You are empty. Your space is full.

MEASURE

The sky is the reason you can't remember
how language first fell on your small ears.
The sky will turn white and (ellipses)
         constellation and cloud. The sky hangs
its coat of silver on morning's hook.
The sky is indefinite, preceded by a definite
article. It repeats itself and what you hold,
hope to hold, remember holding, is vapor.

Water at these several points, in this instant
not dissipating. Cloud, constellation of drops,
such accounting possible because we imagine
we stop time, imagine infinitesimal
points. Mind of God,
mind over motion and matter
and space between.
        The sky is vast—
this transparent, infinitely long ruler
with infinitely small divisions will measure.

Jessica Reed

I DREAMT I SAW AN ATOM BARE

> *An intellect which at a certain moment would*
> *know all forces that set nature in motion, and all*
> *positions of all items of which nature is composed,*
> *if this intellect were also vast enough to submit*
> *these data to analysis, it would embrace in a single*
> *formula the movements of the greatest bodies of*
> *the universe and those of the tiniest atom; for*
> *such an intellect nothing would be uncertain and*
> *the future just like the past would be present*
> *before its eyes.*
>
> —Pierre-Simon Laplace, *A Philosophical Essay*
> *on Probabilities*

Branches on bare trees in winter. What's left.

No clouds of probable, only the bones of the possible—as if God refused to
  be mysterious,

just once, at those speeds and those masses. Icicles. Water, held in place.

This, to embrace the movements of the tiniest atom—mind in deepest space,

single formula. Enter (imagine) a truly empty jar: first some *thing* in it.

Now, subtract. Sand and root and trickle. I have hundreds of stories to tell.
  I'd rather

come at them glancing. It's one way to be afraid. Once, God had birds' eyes,

saw every ultraviolet latch and hook, wheel and paddle. Such intellect

would know every force that set nature in motion, every address of every
  furnishing, hold

the universe entire. Physics: that we might know what God knows. (We
  might be God.)

Imagine such a mind—flash of fish turning in light—you *have* such a mind!

And all at once: coitus. Seed in pod, unfurl.

THERE MUST BE

Consider
    the reversal
of time: A white match
regenerated
by its flame, branches grown into young fresh shoots, and
consciousness reverted to embryo, an inert
Newtonian mass—an egg.
    The film, wound all the way back to black, to the rash
    wordlessness of *once*. We all believed in God then.
        It has since become buried—in the DNA, in seed,
        in carbon's memory of become-this-tree.

Such trembling.
    Continental
plates slip, land unshapes
itself. Animal
shapes alter. We need to understand our past, where
its facts collide. Here was a knife, an old man's fingers
    moving, an apple peel, a galaxy turning
    like a severe question. Spiral symmetry in
        white luminous arms, newly evolved cilia, worm's gills,
        fly larvae, butterfly tongues, the gentle

curl of a
    fern tendril, in
giraffe intestines,
chambered nautilus
(nocturnal roamer of the spiraled coral reef),
and retracted octopus arms. Music from coiled brass
    instruments enters the ear's cochlea. Letters
    from ancient alphabets and the cross section of
        a scroll curl to mimic the stars and the genes
        that we came from. I might be autobiographical . . .

Centipede,
     in its death, forms
a truncated swirl.
As if: completeness.
But the spiral becomes less circular as it
grows, though it surrounds a gravitational center.
     Here's the thing: Spirals never return to their source.
     Expanding universe, things scintillate. I draw
          a diamond, invite rain, tornado, hurricane.
          Someone else builds a great lattice. Her construction stands.

I begin
     to believe that
patterns are far less
persuasive than ice,
white moonstone, molecules folding themselves into
thermodynamically stable arrangements, *each* spruce.
Listen. Words are what we know.
     Cosmology of instance and particulars.
     Van Gogh loved accidents. He thought there must be a
          God not far off: a gray sky with a band above
          the horizon. *A billion chances—and I am here.*

The Face Says Do Not Kill Me
Miranda Mellis

Air has no Residence, no Neighbor
No Ear, no Door
No Apprehension of Another
Oh, Happy Air!

Ethereal Guest at e'en an Outcast's Pillow—
Essential Host, in Life's faint, wailing Inn
Later than Light thy Consciousness accost me
Till it depart, conveying Mine—

—Emily Dickinson

A broken opening in the wall of a bombed build-
ing, by a process of natural magic, becomes the
head of havoc; the horrible head of devastation
itself, brooding over the ruin that faces a society
which cannot control its own destructive impulses.
Also, the space becomes reversed—the opening in
the wall becoming more solid than the wall itself.

—Clarence John Laughlin, photographer, on his
photograph *The Head in the Wall*, 1959

CHAPTER 1

They slowly rolled along beside it, daughter pushing mother in her chair
a carving up into the air and down into the rocky soil, staring in one and
then the other direction.

The wall was no metaphor. There was no transferring to another side,
another meaning
No way to pass through
What the air had become: a barrier

And what about that other wall, silent owner of supplications

Her mother called out,
"Where is the end of it?"

CHAPTER 2

The daughters were making their bodies into islands, imagining the
    world a sea
Going under ground and becoming worms, crawling under it

A subtle routine, this imagining of nonhuman elisions, receptive shapes
    and continuous terrains
Like water, earth, and air, flora and fauna, nonhuman axes, bats,
    gazelles, or coral

As insects they could crawl under, get outside, inside, or as vines
In a vegetative ecstasy of persistence
Leaning, falling, pushing, living back
against the wall.

CHAPTER 3

They could crawl
dry up on it in the desert sun

It is no figure, no monument, it is there to be breached with prepositions,
    to climb
over, under

To live
despite

They sit down under the shade of it
light a smoke, a light, a smoke

under the gun
under the sun.

CHAPTER 4

The children concoct dissolution recipes
Build up and then kick down
a pretend wall.

Or lie on their backs with their heads facing opposite directions,
    kicking each other
breathless

Until whatever was between them fell away

On a walk, they find
signs of abandonment
some animals pace, others, resigned, slump
no water

Only war,
nor migration corridor.

An intriguing whorl protrudes
Digging they
uproot a broken chair leg mostly buried in sand
Looking up they
Throw it as high in the air as they can.

CHAPTER 5

They find
a picture album with broken hinges
filled with photographs of windows
through which various people see
events occurring on the other side
in the distance
they have
intimate and faraway
looks

and
some books

The Kingdom of This World, by Alejo Carpentier
Season of Migration to the North, by Tayeb Salih

These they gave their mother
Who slides into the books like an eel

As if a book is . . .
. . . a way out
something real . . .

CHAPTER 6

Wedge of disruption
jutting up from the dust
an aerial track
to the sun.

In a seated position under the wall
a dry abrasion in her throat
she sees a way to
carve it.

CHAPTER 7

She makes
one cut after another with

excitedly she strikes
to make the pieces fall out,
carving a head,

a face.

After the Jump
Matthew Pitt

ONLY WHEN THE DAUGHTER soothes Seth Snow's skin does he feel the pressure beneath it. Seth spikes at June's touch, eyes shut as she works him over. He hasn't been aware of the twinges, though they've been building against him a while.

Seth's back is, in June's ten-year-old opinion, a jagged mess. "And your neck's a rock pile," she marvels, briefly patting that area, then going back to the back—trapezius first, next the quarry down his spinal column. Patiently gauging where she'll do the most good, as Seth grimaces, belly down, atop the garage workbench. It's the garage of a tool jockey, a man who welds and solders, rivets and planes. In this garage where so much has been built—there's June's first field easel, her brother Joyner's old crib—it's easy for Seth's thoughts to unravel, to imagine June's pounding hands as an excavator's claw, loosening boulders in his shoulders, bashing chunks of crust into stone, then those into pebbles, those into dust, at first coarse, and later, finer and finer. . . .

Seth winces, and June stops. "Too hard on you?"

"Don't let up," he responds drowsily. "It all feels like tapping."

"Like what?"

Tapping, Seth repeats, demonstrating on his neck. His words come out softer than they should, reedier, the result of an old viral infection and partial vocal-cord paralysis, which make him sound perpetually parched, as if dust went down his windpipe. Strangers once offered him water when he spoke. These days, they dole out lozenges.

"Bad week?"

As June finds a rhythm—sting and lull, sting and lull—Seth considers saying why he's so tense. Revealing how the trouble that her mom has gotten into may trigger a countdown of their last days together. Only it's gratifying to not be on edge, to savor the aches breaking. "A bit badder than usual," he says instead. A hiss rises beyond the driveway. "We better head to the misting. Your brother and mom are waiting. Got your card?" June pats her pocket. Seth gazes through the garage's grimy window. "Gonna be a full moon tonight."

"I know," June says, dashing dead a no-see-um on her knuckles. "But it's never full enough to see Dad."

A map hangs from the belt-sander hook, one including images of all twelve lunar colonies. This month's featured colony is the one June's dad now labors in, an omen Seth wants to ignore, but can't keep from seeing.

Subdivision denizens are already lined up around cul-de-sacs. As if waiting for a shuttle, or to be admitted into a show. What they're waiting for, though, is dusk. Dusk and droplets. For jets of water to curtain their bodies with oscillating streams. As Seth and June race by, Tim, from two doors down, chucks Seth with a porcine fist. "Thought you were gonna miss your dousing, man."

"Miss what I live for?"

The two trade tired grins: The line is one Seth would say at Tim's liquor store, if he still bought gin from there just before closing. But since booze's alchemy depends on water, it is hardly an option for anyone anymore. Liquor hasn't quite been prohibited but is certainly prohibitive. Tim's costs nearly eclipse his profits. More customers than ever want stiff belts but, thanks to this mess with the moon, fewer can afford them. Liquor, liquor everywhere and not a drop to drink.

But other, drier vices are still floating up for grabs.

"They knock off that guy you're working on yet?"

Seth shakes his head. "It's scheduled just after midnight on Monday. Only the president can pardon him now."

"When you draw him croaking," Tim says, "do me a favor. Under his picture, sign 'Good Riddance.'"

As Seth and June step close to the sprinklers, beside Sylvia and Joyner, none of the other residents gripe. But make no mistake: Seth's an interloper. Residents of this subdivision—one of the few that can afford a weekly misting—guard their privilege doggedly. Residents at Seth's meager apartment complex only get to herd in a barren pool once each season. Stand atop its baking concrete crater as the landlord soaks them with a fire hose. Seth has paid rent there ten years. Works check to check as a courtroom artist for federal cases—a final frontier where film crews cannot tread—sketching hot-button trials, how defendants appear on witness stands once damned by the light of their lies; how aggrieved victims react to judgments.

This work makes Seth feel like an elevated caricature artist.

Viewers expect to see crags of defiance in guilty faces. Heavy lines early in trials, elation later, on the surfaces of innocent skin. You see his pastel sketches inserted in online articles "after the jump." How we adore comeuppance! It's worth scrolling or clicking past endless pop-up ads, in order to see the look on son of a bitch X's face when he learned he'll *pay* for what he did. The neighbors wish that kind of comeuppance for Seth. They view him as a moisture moocher. If he weren't shacking up with the moonnaut's missus, he couldn't afford to live here. And if they knew how friendly he's been with me—his current guilty subject, the most notorious moisture moocher—they'd wish even more comeuppance upon him.

But Seth's staying is Sylvia's call. Even with him in her house, its population remains at its pre-moonseeds quota of four. May be deplorable, what they're doing, but it's legal.

"Dad-B's back is screwed," June reports, mist dancing on her fine arm hair.

"Language, June," Sylvia responds, but there's no gravity to her gruffness.

"Screwed tight is all I mean. God, I wasn't cursing."

"Ease up on your mom," Seth says, though truth is, he isn't feeling charitable. He hasn't spoken to Sylvia all afternoon, not since having to pick up her and her belongings from work. But now the water emerges in a heavier mist—a maze of vapor they'll all get to briefly lose themselves inside. With the droplets comes relief, a slight springiness, as if this is some supermarket mister writ large, refreshing all the wilted families like bunches of kale or rutabaga. A little mist won't restore the brown, matted front lawns, but it does restore the homeowners. Beads float over them, catching dusk's last light: Soon everyone glistens under its wet net, like they've donned party clothes. The water's sweet electric scent eases body odor and curtness, the festive atmosphere betrayed only by nearby policemen standing guard with truncheons.

Drops cross Sylvia's and Seth's faces. Looking her way, he sees the sting of regret in her eyes, the frustration of her tensed brows. "We'll work it out," he mouths to her. Sylvia reads his lips and, thankful, draws close, offering her moist lips to his.

"You two are gross," Joyner says, a reference to their gentle kiss, not the grime.

"Your dust's not coming off," Sylvia tells Seth. Meaning not general dust from the general day, but powdered pigments from Seth's soft, fat pastels.

269

He wipes a blade of vermilion off his cheek, stubborn smudges of hunter green. "Drawing's due."

"Drawings do *what*?" Joyner asks, clasping spray in his palm like lightning bugs. "They're not alive. How can they do anything?"

Sylvia and Seth giggle over the miscommunication. They laughed this way when they first met, effervescent, easy. Droplets hang before them, held aloft by warm air currents and lack of density. Sylvia playfully waves at the mist, as if dispersing gnats. "Do shoo, dew." Now the whole family has caught the giggles. Can't help it. Water seeps into a desiccated head, and the head's owner gets giddy. Happened in spaceflight, when Sylvia's spouse broke from earth's gravity, his body water redistributing to the sinuses, producing puffy light-headedness. Happens to Sylvia after gulping Percocet.

Seth knows neither sensation.

The misting continues beyond the usual stop time. Has a water surplus been harvested? No—it's the reverse. Forecast calls for major fluid ebb. People need to hunker down for the coming drought, like bears fattening for winter.

"Are they saying severe?"

"No, exceptional. *Exceptional drought* this time."

Seth steals a gaze at the marauder moon—cold pearl, robber baron of rivers—as it begins to emerge in the sky, and is grateful. Sure, during the prior planetary *exceptional drought*, a population equal to that of Louisville, Kentucky, died from dehydration, but he is grateful. *Keep drying us up*, he thinks. *Long as it keeps* him *up there.*

To think we thought our moon might make a perfect mirror of earth.

A carnival mirror, in fact. We launched our initial moon transports years ago, their bellies plugged with supplies. Former oil-rig and pipeline laborers followed, along with skilled contractors, like Sylvia's husband, and engineers, like me. We'd developed an enzyme meant to generate moisture: We were going to grow water. Early setbacks didn't tamp our plans, or audacity. Soon as a few safe pockets were secured, wealthy tourists joined us on brief excursions in tiny cabanas, drinking earthrise cocktails, exhuming wallets while our vehicles trod and tromped.

Science, business, legislative, ecological leaders: We all blazed with belief that colonizing the moon could help ease our crowding resources and swollen membership. So pleased about altering the moon that what the moon might reflect back didn't enter our thinking.

Workers like Sylvia's spouse carved open the moon's skin. Drilled impacted-basalt basins, plains of volcanic maria, inadvertently carting back home millions of dust flakes from a now-hardened ocean of magma. The dust—inaptly referred to as *moonseeds*—stuck to uniforms, equipment, adhered to fingers and bodies *handling* uniforms and equipment, and made its way to water sources on earth. Turned out moonseeds salinize fresh water, impregnate it with crystalline salt deposits. Imagine invasive plants capable of sparking drought. Imagine beach sand clinging to a shoe, reproducing rapidly, leeching more moisture with each germination, reducing some of our largest bodies to withering appendages. Lake Superior? Half-lost. Louisiana wetlands? Bone-dry.

I voiced early concerns about the dust we dragged back. For saying my piece about earth, I got reassigned *to* earth; an alarmist Jeremiah. Now I've been proven right, but am *still* a failure; twice over, in fact. First, because I failed to sway skeptics that they *had* made any error, and later, because I stole from them to rectify the error once they finally copped to it.

Seth Snow told me he kept up with my case down here, but never deeply. He had a job to show for. A family to raise.

A family that became his, piecemeal. First member was Sylvia. Leaving Tim's liquor store one night, Seth looked up from unlocking his car to see soft moonlight glance along her bell-shaped jaw. He'd seen her in this store before, seen that jaw before, but the pieces didn't quite snap into place. Because the Sylvia browsing aisles on other nights had done so while gripping a man's hand. On this night, she only gripped a bottle that reminded Seth of an Oscar trophy.

"What kind of drinks," asked Seth, "can you make with Frangelico?"

"Earthy ones." She gazed at Seth's feet. "Are you . . . wearing sandals with a tux?"

Close. He was supposed to be at a gala with his girlfriend, but had forgotten to pick up his shoes with the other borrowed threads. Now the rental place was closed, and the gala, which they had to skip, nearing dessert course. The mild extravagance of liquor was meant to smooth over a rocky argument. Things were getting a little heavy with this girlfriend, though. If she couldn't see the humor in wearing flip-flops with formal wear, did he want to wear the relationship's weight around his neck much longer?

"Open-toed shoes usually make Tim nervous. All that glass in his store."

"He probably appreciated that my flip-flops are black. It's the little efforts."

Seth and Sylvia's trajectory moved in an ordained arc. Drive to his place, put on music, put out drinks, tell a few tales from his repertory, and . . . hours later, escort her from his apartment with a grateful, final kiss. He'd forgotten how small the effort one-night stands—the hummed tune in sex's symphony—required to jump into, then away from.

As he walked her to her car, moon still visible, he was doubly happy. Happy to have gotten laid, sure, but also to have leapt from a laborious union into a light one. Within a month or two, most memories from this night would evaporate from his mind. So he thought. One light night turned, though, into a blurry month of sex at his apartment on Coming Street. In place of plans, he and Sylvia cracked jokes: *Yeah, here's my place on Coming Street . . . no, not there, there, oh yeah, right there, right there, right there. The realtor says on Coming Street, it's all about location, location, location.* He never thought to ask why they always went to his place. Never looked closely at the darkened recesses of her car's interior, which would've revealed crayons and stuffed animals. Made him ask questions, made her reveal a sitter assigned to all moonnaut spouses was caring for her children. Sylvia never volunteered mother or marital status, and if it wasn't volunteered, it didn't, so far as Seth saw it, exist.

"Fill up fast, guys," she says now, as the group shuffles back from the misting and shuffles out dinnerware. Thanks to Sylvia's slip today, a Child Protective Services agent may visit. She's probably hoping it happens. A visit might mean another chance, an opportunity to throw herself before the court's mercy.

"What you bring us, Dad-B?" June asks, watching Seth hoist a translucent sack.

Chinese freeze, from off the highway. Meal's been sitting in Seth's car for hours, but refrigeration is redundant: Few restaurants bother serving fare that spoils anymore. They arrange themselves at the table—Sylvia sitting where her spouse would have, Seth in Sylvia's spot—divvying various freeze-dried chunks and strips, dyed to look as they would if fresh: egg roll (desert sand), General Tso (russet), bean curd (cream), squid surprise (charcoal). Last time Seth got to-go, June and Joyner fought over portions. This time, he's taken no chances. "I ordered extra dim sum."

Joyner jostles the sack, doubting Dad-B on the dim sum. The six-year-old's bond with Seth has always shown strain. June's been the easier sell—on Seth's presence, pledges, even this switchover from fresh to freeze-dried food. Eating freeze is an option now. But soon it won't be, and June understands the need to get used to something alien early. Adjust to doing without. Our initial goal was to cart all our luxuries to-go to our neighboring satellite. But now, to conserve H_2O, we eat astronaut food on earth instead. Freeze-dried Chinese has proven a delicacy. The sodium-paste strips approximate sauce, liquid. The hardened plum sauce's reflective hue reminds Seth of the lake he once fished bream from. A place where Seth could draw away from his father's demands that he learn a trade, quit wasting summer months drawing faces at pools.

"We have a working pool. In my correctional facility," I told Seth, during our earliest chat. Once my trial ended, we were permitted to speak freely. "Got caught heisting water, and I've been sentenced to one of the last prisons left with a pool. Is that funny or grotesque?"

He sought *me* out first, but I kept asking him back. To learn about his accidental family. The stories poured, once he saw how thirsty I was for them. He'd tell me about routines as minute as dinner cleanup, as teaching a boy to grip a baseball—routines neither he nor I had known before—and they left their tread on us both, an impression that wouldn't lift.

Joyner says little at dinner, jetting to his telescope after fulfilling his required bites and comments. "Can we draw water?" June asks. The two have been sketching Seth's evaporating childhood lake. Tonight he plans to teach her how to capture coruscating sun, the tide of light when it strikes water's surface. Seth will feed June bits of memory, which she translates into images. Her talent exceeds his at that age, though he wonders if June's devotion will stick around once boys begin weighting her world. And will he be around to stop the departure?

"We need to neaten," Sylvia says, frowning. "I want the house looking its best."

"What for? Who are we trying to fool?"

Seth isn't sure if June is just being brassy or knows something about the trouble brewing. If she is throwing a challenge at her mother, it's not an errant one: Junk skirts every surface in the house. It would take all night to make a dent.

But Sylvia's hope of making amends moves Seth, so he tells June they'll conduct art lessons later. He heads out to install replacement roof shingles in the dark. The clouds are terrifically uncooperative, blanketing the moon's fat face of work light. A rainless tropical storm is to blame for the shingle shakeup. All gust, no downpour. Something like what this affair was supposed to be: all steam, no substance. When did the substance arrive? When did the affair become adultery? When he took Sylvia to bed? Or when he discovered she belonged in another? And has it *remained* adultery? Can Seth claim—now that he's taught Joyner to throw a four-seamer, and monitored iffy areas in June's report cards, all things the man upstairs didn't do—mitigating circumstances?

Or does that only amount to so many appeals meant to get him off the hook?

I know Seth questions such things, but I'm unsure why he does in my company. Why he willingly spills any detail I ask for. *The moonnaut's clothes: Do they still hang in his closet?* (They do.) *Did Seth ever try on the sweaters and shirts?* (Yes, but never in view of Sylvia.) It's possible Seth has no fear of judgment from me. What's the harm in telling transgressions to a man in a prison jumpsuit, running out of breaths to inhale? Coming here may prove, in where I sit, that my misdeeds always efface his. Or maybe he doesn't hold me in judgment. I've never asked how he'd have voted if he'd sat on the jury. Maybe I'll ask before midnight Monday. Maybe I'll let it die a mystery.

Seth begins slapping in a few replacement shingles, confused by the sudden illumination guiding his work; the moon is still wrapped in clouds. Surveying the area reveals the new light source: the kids' bathroom skylight. He peers through Plexiglas at Joyner and June, weighing themselves on a scale. "I'm down to seventy-two." "I'm up to fifty." They convert their findings into moon weight. "It's too late for you to go, June," Joyner determines. "They don't let moonnauts receive more than sixty earth pounds in one shipment. But I'm getting bigger. I need a rocket to take me there quick."

"They're not bringing you up."

"Why not? They said under sixty. That's why I didn't eat my extra dim sum."

"You aren't cargo, idiot. You're a life form."

"But I need to be with Dad. Not Dad-B, Dad!"

"You're only saying that because you can't remember him. If you knew who you were missing, you wouldn't miss him."

Seth is grateful to June for that remark. But he also admires Joyner's goal. He knows by heart Kennedy's call to "conquer" the moon by decade's end; the hard choice made because it is hard. Watching that speech now is bittersweet. We have a new lunar clock ticking down: simultaneously racing to the moon while trying to dodge the damage it caused down here. If we don't bring moisture back to our blue marble soon, our cradle of life will convert to a cavernous desert. Meanwhile, the moon, meant to be a high-end resort planet, is being built up rapidly as a camp for affluent refugees.

Knowing H_2O would soon outrival crude oil as liquid currency, I began, after my forced reentry, hoarding it. I wasn't much of a hydrobandit, though; I left a big, fat trail. Jury barely took an hour to deliver a verdict; the judge immediately sentenced me to a correctional facility until my execution could be arranged.

Why do you call this a correctional facility? Seth once asked me. *And not just prison?* Semantics, bub: I'm amused that's what *they* call it, while offering me no way to correct the behavior.

So you'd reform? If they gave you a chance?

Touché, I told him.

Seth refused to reform too, shacking up with Sylvia after he met her kids, and after he learned her husband was in the brackish heavens. Even after he saw her doing her best, through powders and pills, to ascend in her own right. The husband still remains Sylvia's spouse. No divorce papers are allowed for moonnaut marriages, even if there is a claim. And there is a claim.

That's another reason Seth sought me out: I'd crossed paths with Sylvia's spouse. His trail was notorious. Not that dicking around up there was rare. I'm not here to claim sainthood, understand, just because I bolted beyond the clouds. That setting is Alaska frontier, with foxhole thrown in, to the nth degree. Enough laborers were killed or injured in accidents—the detached-helmet incident being, of course, the most horrifying—to plant this calculus in our heads: You can die any day. And *since* you can die any day, do you really want your bed to have been half-empty the night before?

Sylvia's moonnaut slipped orbit four years ago: rotten dad, alcoholic, treated her like dirt. To neighbors, that all gets eclipsed by the fact that he's there, suffering interstellar ailments, earning scads of cash to be deposited into June's and Joyner's accounts upon completion of mission or life (should moon exposure end him, they'll clean up double).

Moonnauts are heralded profusely for their service: automatic heroes no matter how low a life they led down here. For jury-rigging a new home to rescue us from this one, laboring round-the-clock to provide an emergency exodus from shortsightedness, they receive our eternal blind praise.

"How will it happen?" Joyner asks June in the little capsule of their bathroom.

"I don't know. I guess they'll tell us where we can live."

"Here or the moon, you mean?"

"Joyner, moon travel isn't an option. I doubt Dad's coming back. He just might legally become our main parent, if Mom's not allowed to keep us anymore."

The kids, Seth realizes, are conspiring about what he and Sylvia tried to conceal. He wonders if the moonnaut contacted them on the sly, a satellite call when the adults' backs were turned. But he reconsiders: Of course Joyner can sense dinner-table tension. Of course June can read wary faces. Of course they want to know if they'll have any say in their next destination.

"If we're sent away from Mom, will Dad-B still get to see us?"

"I don't know. But if Mom can't see us, I bet Dad-B stops seeing Mom."

Stunned, Seth wonders how June could have reached this view. She's jumping to conclusions, believing one break means an end to the family unit they've built. Or Seth's irritation with Sylvia's lapses is more evident than he thinks. If not for love guiding him, he'd have given up on her months ago. Each time Sylvia veers, he's been there to correct her course. Holding her head over the toilet bowl. Deleting texts, shredding notes from suspected dealers. Trimming back a dusty orange grove by the fence so she couldn't do a line there, under darkness of grimy fruit globes.

"Quit." Seth looks into the Plexiglas. Joyner is succumbing to his own vice, thumb-sucking, and June is none too pleased. "I said quit it."

"It feels good and you can't stop me."

"Maybe not. But it's disgusting. Makes your skin all bumpy. Bends your teeth. And you know better."

Seth couldn't watch Sylvia constantly, couldn't trace her dark side everywhere. So when she got fucked up at work, got caught cowering in the custodial closet, and instantly got her walking papers, he retrieved her from the office, tried to sober her up before the children leapt off the school bus. Hid her from them until she had.

Hiding. Seth knew it well. The lake was the lone place he could escape his dad's wrist slaps, back shoves, repeated judgment. His way of leaving the planet. Seth fell into his job. It wasn't premeditated. He started sketching his dad as a sinister thug as a lark by the lake, having a bitter laugh with each completed, snarling face.

What I did wasn't premeditated either. The first water I took, I took only for friends and myself. It was only later I began arranging for mass illegal transport—black-market deliveries to nations in no position to endure the drought or purchase "credits" needed to secure water from countries with the means to stockpile it. It's become an arms race with agua that everyone must enter. But the nations least able to keep up could least afford not to. Were the ones that had nothing to do with colonizing the moon in the first place. Got nearly 230,000 gallons into hands and mouths before being caught. I know. Insert your *drop-in-the-bucket* remark now.

Seth has drawn me throughout the process: arraignment, trial, verdict (he's very impressive, though I didn't know my forehead looked so domed since its hairline receded). He'll sketch me for a final time at 12:01 a.m. Monday—the first execution for water theft and fraud, an act deemed sedition. But he's practiced in advance of the big event. I've peeked at rough sketches, curious how he imagines I'll look at the end.

It's my first execution too, I remind him.

Seth climbs down from the roof, joining Sylvia to clear the dinner remains. The unfinished freeze-dried ropes and paste strips look bumpy, wrinkled, the way the American flag appeared like little more than a shirt in need of ironing in early moon-surface shots.

"Finished up there?"

"Hardly started." He clears his throat, deciding not to scold Sylvia or repeat what he overheard on the roof. What good would come of either reaction? Instead he says: "I do noses and expressions, not cabinets and wiring. I'm not as handy as . . . the former man of the house."

"Oh yeah, handy. The former man was plenty handy."

Seth drops a tablet into a jug, then switches on the sink spigot. The jug fills with opaque liquid, then shuts off automatically. Suds fizz as the household's allotted weekly drinking water agitates against this tablet, making the water potable. "If the court denies . . . ," Seth starts to say, shaking the jug swiftly. "If we don't hear good news, maybe you should reconsider reconciliation? Please. Listen. That way you'd still keep the kids, the home. We could still find a way to . . . more or less maintain what we've got. With his track record, he's not coming back. Not with all the action he's getting up there."

She jams a spatula in the jug and stirs. Turns on the stove-top fan to circulate noise, keep the kids from hearing. "Reconcile? Give him that satisfaction? Ask for mercy from a bastard who tightened my lungs, sucked my oxygen for most of our married life? Who's gone hog wild with no repercussions? Platinum member of the 230,000 mile club. He's known as the Lunar Rover up there, did I tell you?" Before the moonnaut left, Sylvia had been on the verge of leaving him. If she'd done it then, she'd have been excused, even commended, by most. Now she's the villain. "Can we drop it? We've got to get this place in order, in case the court plans to send someone by late . . ."

"Sylv, you're having a come-to-Jesus moment." He watches fizz break, sediment sink to the jug bottom. "But how much is that moment worth, since you already jumped the cliff?"

"Oh, so sorry. Sorry for trying to keep us all together."

If she wanted to keep them together, why'd she act so stupid? Why leave the coke in her compact, imagine the dust on its mirror wouldn't be spotted by someone, and then *wouldn't* drift to her boss, parole officer, estranged husband? "Maybe it's time to pay the piper. Accept some share of the blame."

"What did you say?" she asks. But she doesn't need a repeat; his voice was clear. A miscommunication maybe, but not missed communication. She storms into the next room, dim sum residue still on her fingers.

A drawing of June's rests in the family room. One of the lake he hasn't seen. She must've drawn it after dinner. God, her vision doubles him over! The way she thought, at ten, to capture not only the reflection of a figure fishing, but to leave that reflection quivering with light where the lure strikes the water. Technique's coming along, but just to have the idea. Seth feels his own hand quivering—not with excitement but a strange charge of dislodged rage—as he reaches for her sketch pad.

"Pick it up."

Now *he's* the one needing a repeat. Pick up—what? He looks away from the pad to see Sylvia aim a phone at his face. Didn't he hear the ringing? It's someone calling from the court; the judge has reached a decision.

"It's for you, Sylvia. You're the one who has to answer."

Sylvia nods, cups the phone, blows on it a moment. Then she orders Seth to at least get on the hallway phone. Hurry: She can't face this news without him. Seth *does* pick up, but with his back to Sylvia, so she won't see that he's holding a hand over the receiver. He doesn't want to hear the ruling. He'll be able to see Sylvia's face from the hallway mirror. See it widen with relief or constrict in pain, and that is all he can handle.

The defendant's reaction, after the jump:

Supposedly dispassionate, pH neutral, a ruling is always a blessing to one party and punishment to the other. But it doesn't always fall along the lines and loyalties a witness would expect. Seth Snow has sketched faces he guessed would register horror but instead were colored by relief; pardoned faces continuing to defend themselves. Even those sitting on the same side of a courtroom respond differently. Best friends, family members, failing to reflect one another's reactions to rulings.

So it is with Sylvia's face, when she learns she cannot keep her kids; that she will, come Monday, lose custodial rights to the court, and they will be officially entrusted to a man living eight earth circumferences away. Her look is an imitation of composure: the moment where self-possession grinds to powder. Tranquillity's last stab.

That tranquillity will disappear for stretches in the days to come, then show again when she visits whatever facility the court exiles June and Joyner to, or when loose acquaintances approach, asking how are those kids, does she have pictures on her? Oh yes, pictures are all she'll have on her. In days to come, Seth will sketch Sylvia's aped composure over and over, until wrist nerves deaden and his hand feels free of weight. He'll draw so hard, fine powder will spill over a towel lying in his lap, permeating his apartment carpet, pigments no solvent could remove. He'll lose his deposit. Dust from each sketch fluttering off his fingers, onto prior drawings he has put aside.

There was tension in Seth's face when the call came, near his brows and the edges of his lips. It may have looked similar to hers, but was not a mirror. His spiked the moment hers vanished from her face. His has been in constant orbit since she hung up the phone. Orbiting questions he's fated to ask in a vacuum. Will he take steps toward Sylvia now, to help her pick up the pieces of what she helped shatter? Or leave her completely? Because, when he looks at that last lake drawing June drafted, one he scooped up just before the state scooped up the kids, he realized June was right. All that effort he's made these last months hasn't been for Sylvia. The affair only amounted to putting one foot in front of the other, a quick tumble into bed, a predictable and small step.

The giant leap, the fall into love? That happened with Sylvia's kids.

In a minute I'll turn in this tale, then prepare for 12:01 Monday. One small bite from a needle in my veins, and I'll attain escape velocity. Before that, I'll request lobster Newburg and peach and raisin-bread pudding for my last meal; you'll send in its stead imitation crab and apple compote. I'll ask for bottled water too. Why not? Did I hoard what was precious? Yes. Will I pay for the crime? I will. Would not taking have been a larger crime? My answer to that is the reason I'm here, and won't be this time tomorrow. So forget tomorrow. The moon, at this moment, slants through my window; its glow floating past the bars, spreading an elongated rectangle of itself onto the concrete, the shadow of a shallow, glowing bed. Do you remember when moonlight was romantic? I'll lie atop my cell's smooth, cold floor gazing at that glow all night, until it becomes romantic again.

Fire Feather Mendicant Broom
Noy Holland

THERE WAS A STONEMASON who went by the name of Hawk, who,
until his mother died and left him her home, had scarcely owned a
thing. His mother's home was not a house but a trailer on the outskirts of a big eastern city Hawk detested and he lived there with her
dresses and jars of cream, with her radio tuned to the station she liked
and her book still opened on her chest of drawers to the last of the
pages she had read.

Hawk would rather have slept and passed his days in a hippie van
or a pickup truck but he owned neither and never had. He arrived to
work holding his broken-down gloves and soon these sprawled among
the stones at his feet—a nuisance, he thought, and frivolous, though
every finger of each glove was eaten through and the thumbs were
mostly gone. He liked the feel of the rock in his hands.

Hawk's work was slow and meticulous. From the rough gray schist
of the region, he built a stone egg that stood on end amid milkweed
and goldenrod and the glassy, bent grasses of a meadow. The egg was
his most beautiful and difficult work and he carried a picture of it in
his money clip, the way people carry pictures of people—daughters,
sweethearts, sons.

Hawk had no children, no wife, no mother now, though the idea
of his mother was everywhere in the trailer where she had lived.

He brought his hand to his mouth to feel his breath come and go
in the room where she had passed her last days. He was Hawk for the
shape of his nose like his mother's and the unnerving flicker of his
eyes.

Hawk. A name like a revelation.

So he wandered, but a boy—setting out by morning, by nightfall
looping home. Home a house on a rubble footing then. Hawk a boy
in his feral glory, a truant who had buried his shoes. He learned the
trees of that place and birdsong and ashen tatters of skin; tooth mark,
claw, the habits of bees, the smell of a thing afraid. Here a doe slept,

281

here a fawn. Here the ledge tilted skyward, glittering schist, and beneath it a fieldstone wall ran slumping through meadows to keep cattle and sheep in an era when the woods were cleared. Here morels grew, here were berries. Ginseng; psilocybin. Sap pulsing in the trees.

The place was enough for him and then it wasn't and soon he was said to be elsewhere building a house of mud. He baked bricks on their sides in the reliable sun, brought the walls to his knees, and walked away. He walked from Tucumcari to Reno, across the great divide. He walked from Reno to Winnemucca and there found a cobbler in a dusty shop who taught Hawk to cobble his ruined boots and sew his own clothes and carve wood. He made a pouch from the tissue of a buck he had killed and from the bone of an elk he made buttons. Stew of raccoon, of squirrel. Roadkill, should he come upon it.

When his boots went to shreds he left them standing in the road facing where he had been. And walked on. His feet grew flat from walking, and calloused and gray and wide. He walked from the Black Rock to San Francisco and from San Francisco to Truckee and on to the Hood, the Missouri, the Milk, great northern windblown plains. Crow country, Mandan Sioux. For years little was known or left of him but the cairns of what rock he came upon as though he meant to be found.

Hawk sent word from time to time to his mother to relate some next fascination—a beetle walking out of its luminous shell, out of the barbs of its legs. The orderly ways of elk herding up; moonset while the sun lifts too.

Once a picture arrived of a cave of ice Hawk had chinked some indecipherable thing into—how, she could not say. By wing, by rope and harness. No word, ever, of a woman. Her son said nothing of where he had been nor where he was going now. A rumor reached her of Patagonia, great palisades of muttering ice, Hawk traveling with only a rucksack in whatever way he could. Tierra del Fuego, land of fire, people of fire in scant guanaco hides they moved to shelter their sex from the wind. The wind incessant. The calamitous past recorded and calving into the sea.

Here rabbits clipped the grasses and trees grew hunched and low, turned from the wind and twisted. Gray seas battered the shorebound rock and green in the face of the lifting wave, the ice swam, brief and lethal. Heavy, hissing, frothing tide—it spit out the ice and moved on. Green of his mother's dishes; shattered glass of the gods. A place that was like a painting of a place. A gray mist, and Hawk's hair turned, and when his skin appeared gray he walked north again, blasted, brilliant, vacant days, pampas and tidy vineyards and flamingos in shimmering pools, uncountable iridescent flocks like something from a dream he dreams still.

By his hands he is known and recognized and by a picture of the egg he still carries. By his flickering eye. *Hawk.* But something leaves him now. He is like something dying in a cage. Traffic moves without pause beyond the window; headlights approach and swing away.

If he had a place for her things—but he has nothing. He sits among them. A neighbor boy comes to hear tales of Hawk's travels but soon the boy's mother forbids him to so much as walk down the block. The days are lengthening. The tin of his mother's trailer ticks like a clock in the sun.

He saw a condor dead, a few alive, rising, the sky immaculate. He saw gauchos in flimsy slippers standing on their horses in the blue. A lamb in a box. A spoonbill.

A mobile home, Hawk thinks. Ridiculous.

One night he sets fire to the withering grass, standing in the dark with a garden hose poked through the chain-link fence.

She lived for years like this, sequestered, he cannot begin to grasp why. His mother was waiting; she ironed bedsheets; she was polishing the stove. She raked the grass each day as if it mattered—ugly little patch the dog pissed in—until the morning she tripped and fell in her kitchen and called out and no one came. A stain spread where she lay on her buckled floor with her small dog chewing her hand. The radio played, the singing, the talk, and in pencil in meticulous letters she composed a list for herself: New broom. Ammonia. Bicarbonate. Bobby pins. Chicken.

Hawk sets to work trying to lift the stain from the place his mother fell. Ammonia—his eyes are streaming, and his hands, his hands are from another animal, huge, like paws, like slabs, torn from the rock he built with. He has worn his fingerprints off and his thumbnails are gone and the skin is thready and raw.

The stain comes back by morning. Always as something new. It comes back in the shape of a toaster. A pony. The shape of a sleeping dog. Hawk crouches above it, scouring, gloomy and consumed. *At last*, he thinks. Still it comes back. Now as a dress she favored. Now as fire. Feather. Mendicant. Broom.

From Her Wilderness Will Be Her Manners
Sarah Mangold

It may be true that landscape painting tends

to naturalize ideology   Taking my eye off

the water cask and fixing it on the scenery

where I meant it to be   Saying firmly in pencil

in margins   "Help I am drowning"

*

However the heroine   upheld her respectability   being

located indoors   She sees nature working by herself   she

sees   a shiver in July   Skylarking   our good ship makes

but slow progress   I once placed in a sealed jar   I kept

skins   lampblack   rock-work   Duly crumpling   setting

artificial eyes   gluing hair   flesh   fawn   pine

*

Sarah Mangold

When I botanize

I am thinking

When word and object coincide

Words are the shadow

*

No one could be sure which observation would prove

useful   celestial winds

                rainbows

          kidneys   gesture

of remembrance   perishing the keeper

          footless birds

                of paradise

*

This sounds discouraging to a person whose

occupation necessitates going about

considerably in boats   My continual

desire for hairpins and other pins   My

intolerable habit of getting into water

Abominations full of ants

*

Sarah Mangold

Hither come and hence departed   many a man

to represent   birds in situations   somewhat

similar   Both a frame   and what a frame

contains   Who is this *we*   Our difference

from trees   grasses   clouds   Whose nature

is marked   Wilderness   Farm   City

*

diagram for violet

diagram for buttercup

diagram for dandelion

diagram for daisy

diagram for pond lily

twine heavy and light

an evenly notched leaf

grooving the blade of grass

driving a pin down through

each foot into the soft pine bottom

Proof of the Monsters
Matthew Baker

May 9th

I FOUND A NOVEL, at the library, after work today. Basically, that was all that happened. Monster season should begin in about a week.

May 10th

Well, this year the bodies came early!

I didn't have to work today. Living in the attic, above the trees, from the (somewhat grimy, yes) lattice attic window I can see the beach. A point of land. A narrow strip of black sand. There weren't any bodies yet. The beach was deserted. While I'd slept, a bit of yarn had gotten tangled in my beard.

I ate a few apples. Red skin with gold flecks, very good, tasty. I read some of the novel. I ate a grapefruit. I composted the seeds, the stems, the peel. The novel has gotten strange. Although it began in a seventeenth-century city—ballrooms, carriages, a neurotic soldier with debtor troubles—it has since relocated to a mythical city beneath the Arctic Ocean, constructed over the course of several centuries by omnipotent czars with impotent *kholops*. The debtor soldier is seated at a feast. For one hundred pages the narrator has been describing a certain woman's hat. I understand now why obscure seventeenth-century writers remain obscure.

Afterward, I was lonely, I felt like being around people, so I considered walking to the café in town. Straightaway, however, a new problem occurred to me. To sit in the café, you must buy a coffee. To socialize, you must consume. Now: The café stocks paper cups and plastic cups. I could ask for a paper cup for my coffee, but that would hurt the planet, ∵ paper is made from trees. I could ask for a plastic cup for my coffee, but that would hurt the planet, ∵ plastic takes approximately three hundred years to decompose. ∴ I should use neither a paper cup nor a plastic cup. However. The paper cups and the plastic cups have already been manufactured. Whether I drink from them or don't drink from them, the tree has already fallen, the plastic already

287

been made. ∴ I could use a paper cup or a plastic cup. However. If I use a cup, the café will have to buy more cups from the manufacturer, which means the manufacturer will manufacture even more cups, felling more trees and making more plastic ∴ I should use neither a paper cup nor a plastic cup.

I could ask for a mug, but afterward the baristas would have to wash the mug, which would consume water, soap, electricity.

I never bought a coffee.

I never went to the café.

Instead, I rambled down through town, to the beach, wearing the same boots, the same jeans, the same baggy forest-green woolen sweater as always. I had the novel, a tattered paperback, bent in half and stuffed into the seat of my jeans (the pocket is worn with the faded outline of a vanished wallet, the wallet of whoever wore these jeans before me). The ocean lunged foaming onto the sand, crept away again. I stepped across rocks, still arguing with myself (silently) about coffee.

That's when the seals began washing ashore. A body—another body—a few bodies bobbing on the same wave. Disfigured, skinless, bloody. Misshapen carcasses. Only the whiskery snouts, the bulging eyes, untouched. The crumpled flippers. The surface of the ocean was littered with dead seals, from the sand to the horizon. I stopped, watching the bodies float to shore, like indecipherable messages from a faraway land.

It always begins with the seals. But never this soon, before, and never this many. Most people consider the beach unlucky, jinxed, during monster season. I sat on a boulder and read the novel a few minutes, then got spooked and trudged home.

May 11th

When Grandpa Uyaquq could still speak, he often spoke of his childhood, and how the monsters were back then. In those years, according to my grandfather, the monsters never killed other creatures. The monsters were peaceful. The monsters lived in the depths of the ocean, drifting through kelp forests, enjoying their monstrous lives. Then—here my grandfather would frown, puff at his cigar, glance beyond the porch railing—something, nobody knows what, happened. One summer, bodies began washing ashore. Seals. Then worse. This was in the seventies. Only Alaska, only our town, only this stretch of beach. Nowhere except here. The monsters must have been reacting to something. Something we had done. Even monsters have motives. And how else could ocean dwellers communicate with us on land? Would we have listened to anything except for bodies? Even then, with all of the bodies, had anybody listened? Here Grandpa Uyaquq would laugh, and cough, and stub out his cigar on the porch railing.

I have never heard the monsters referred to with a name. Simply, "the monsters." Or, occasionally, "the bloodsuckers" (an illogical moniker, considering the monsters leave the blood, yet take the skin!). Whether the monsters are nonextinct megafauna, evolutionary aberrations, maybe products of abyssal gigantism, is unclear. There has never been a reported sighting.

At daybreak my stepbrother came by the house. I was sitting on the table in the attic—reading through yesterday's entry, chewing an apple, still blinking awake—and saw him arrive through the lattice window. He parked his truck, crossed the driveway toward the backyard. He was dressed for work: dark-blue suit, light-blue tie, leather brogues, an unbuttoned trench coat, a bright-red woolen hat. The attic has a separate entrance—I heard the rusted attic staircase groaning on its bolts, the ramshackle attic balcony shuddering—my stepbrother ducked into the attic through the doorway, pulled the chair out from the table, sat there chatting with me.

"There must have been sightings," Peter said.

"There haven't," I said.

"Then how do people know they're like us?" Peter said.

"Like how?" I said.

"Anthropomorphic. Humanoid. Merfolk," Peter said.

"Are they?" I said.

Peter ran his fingertips across his cheeks, squinting, as if he had just discovered that stubble was growing there. His brogues were crusted with mud and soil, which for him wasn't usual, to have less than shiny shoes. A murky dim light was filtering through the lattice window. On my mattress, my sheets lay tangled together in a coiled shape, the inscrutable conclusion of my movements throughout the night, a pattern somehow representing my dreams. The spider that lives above the cupboards was asleep on a shut cupboard door. I don't own this house. Grandpa Uyaquq owns this house. He lives at the pioneer home now, where he shares a room with a stroke victim. Peter asked me to live here, to watch the house while our grandfather is "away." Peter is in denial. Grandpa Uyaquq has dementia. Grandpa Uyaquq isn't coming back. Peter asked me to live in the attic, for Grandpa Uyaquq, so that when he "returns" the house will be "exactly" how he "remembers." It is illogical. I don't mind. For somebody like me, the attic is ample. The attic has a sink, a stove, a toilet, a bathtub even, but I rarely bathe, ∵ bathing wastes water. I wear only cast-off clothing, ∵ that clothing already exists. I salvage food from dumpsters, ∵ otherwise that food would go to waste. In any town, meeting somebody like me would be difficult. In this town, meeting somebody like me would be impossible. I am the only person here who salvages food from dumpsters. Sometimes I feel like a lone member of a rare species, cut off from the rest of its species by geological formations. (A species whose diet, understandably, revolts all other species.)

Peter had tilted the chair backward, with only its back legs touching the floorboards, was poking the loaf of (somewhat moldy, yes) pumpernickel on the counter.

"That does not look right," Peter murmured, frowning.

He turned toward me. His trench coat had swung open, exposing the inner silk lining. The chair was still teetering, just balanced.

"You want to grab a beer tonight?" Peter said.

"I can't," I said.

"Even if I buy?" Peter said.

"I can't," I said.

"Please?" Peter said, grinning.

I made some gesture that was supposed to be an apology.

Peter pouted, and tipped the chair forward, its front legs clacking down onto the floorboards. The pout was exaggerated, but beneath lay some genuine hurt feeling. He slapped his knees, then rose from the chair.

"Had to try," Peter said.

Before leaving, Peter fixed the sink in the attic (a drip) and fixed the steps on the porch (a creak). He jogged to his truck (shouting he was late), bent to check something under the cab, then drove away. Peter works for a bank, which is a good cover for an ecoterrorist. His degree is in economics. My degree is in philosophy. I work for the city, planting flowers and shoveling snow. I don't pay rent, and I don't buy food, so my only expenses are the monthly payments on my gigantic loans.

1. To pursue something pointless is illogical.
2. The point of earning a degree is to become qualified for a job.
3. Earning a degree in philosophy does not qualify one for anything.

4. (2, 3) ⇒ Earning a degree in philosophy is pointless.
5. (1, 4) ⇒ It is illogical to earn a degree in philosophy.
∴ It is illogical to earn a degree in philosophy.

Consequently,

6. One is a philosopher ⇔ one has a degree in philosophy.
7. (5, 6) ⇒ Philosophers are illogical.
∴ Philosophers are illogical.

That's a proof I've been working through for some time now. Still, there is a noticeable difference between carrying an idea around in my head and putting an idea down onto blank paper. A feeling of relief—just having somebody to talk to, to vent to—even if that somebody is a glittery notebook with rainbow unicorns on the cover, salvaged from a garbage can. (Sorry—I don't mean to insult you—that's just what you are.)

I am still sitting on the table, overlooking, beyond the window, the gravel driveway, the swaying pine branches, the ocean-blue shingles of the terraced houses on the hillside, the distant beach below. (Through camouflage binoculars with chipped lenses—also salvaged—I'm surveying everything magnified.) Just now, a walrus washed ashore. Bent whiskers, a snapped tusk, strips of skin hanging from the carcass. A blubbery gouge torn into its belly. Its body dwarfs the dead seals.

Usually, walruses don't begin washing ashore until midsummer.

May 13th

Yesterday was heinously boring, so let's just skip ahead to today. (Are you rainbow unicorns bored easily?) (Yes, yes, you are.) (Don't worry then, ∵ today was a disaster.)

Work was grueling. I came home with pine sap crusted in my beard, burst blisters on each thumb. I felt too drained to climb up to the attic, so sat in the backyard a few hours, on a rusty foldout chair, sipping from the hose. I had nearly exhausted my food supply. I wasn't ready to think about that. I dug through my backpack (also salvaged, with bright neon straps, the pouch velcros!), ate my last apple, tossed the core into the woods for the squirrels. The bird feeder was empty. I wasn't ready to think about that. I velcroed my backpack, read some more of the book.

Each chapter opens with a brief quotation from an imaginary novel. This latest chapter opens, "The planet itself was alive! —Mohiam Yueh, *The Sharif's Orrery.*" After the accidental destruction of the undersea city, the novel has relocated (again) to a mythical city in the skies above the Arabian Desert, constructed from gigantic golden balloons by despotic sultans with oppressed *kapi kullari.* The debtor soldier is slated to be beheaded at dawn, for a combination of mistakes, miscalculations, and misunderstandings, including the inadvertent deflowering of the vizier's daughter.

At nightfall I tramped down through town to the local grocery store to harvest some groceries. I have a rule, which is that whenever I see litter I have to stop and pick it up and then properly dispose of it (compost or recycle, if possible, otherwise garbage), so getting around can take me a while. Fortunately, the first thing I passed tonight was an empty plastic bag (fluttering against a guardrail), which I could use to gather all the litter that came after (plastic soda bottles, plastic water bottles, a wet rag, a plank of wood, a tattered gardening magazine, a cigarette carton, cigarette butts, an empty condom wrapper). Otherwise I would have had to use my backpack, and I try not to mix my food with litter.

The grocery was closing soon, the parking lot nearly empty. A runaway cart had gotten almost as far as the street before having its breakout thwarted by a speed bump. I set my bag of litter on the pavement, climbed into the dumpster, and sifted through today's garbage. Bruised apples, withered carrots, hardly stale oats. Bent cans of chickpeas. Inexplicably, an entire box of raw almonds. As I stocked my backpack, a pimpled employee in a dirt-red apron emerged from the grocery lugging knotted garbage bags. He nodded. I waved. He flung the bags into the dumpster. I found overripe bananas there, added a few bunches to my backpack.

Hiking back to the house, I felt dizzy suddenly, probably from thirst or hunger. I stopped, sat on a guardrail, ate mushy bananas, my bag of litter between my boots. Across the street, the windowfront of a closed shop glowed with stacked televisions, the televisions all flickering with the same image, electricity pouring into unwatched screens. On-screen, a presidential candidate was faking emotions for an audience, appearing to hold back tears. He had been coached by his consultants to exhibit these emotions, had rehearsed and now performed a scripted scene. Politicians were people once. Animals, with cravings, feelings, idiosyncrasies. Now politicians are products, manufactured by teams of consultants. The candidate wore a necktie that was not the candidate's, but was rather the necktie that had tested best during marketing research. The candidate wore a wristwatch that was not the candidate's, but was rather the wristwatch that had tested best during marketing research. The candidate professed beliefs, asserted convictions, claimed intentions that were not the candidate's. Like the design of the label on a plastic container of dog food. Whatever consumers will buy. I do not vote. Consumption of this politician, like any nondegradable product, would be wasteful. His legacy will never decay. His policies will pollute this country forever.

The bananas tasted great. Afterward, the dizziness vanished. Just then, I saw a girl with gray hair and monstrous gauges was staring at me from the windowfront with the televisions.

"Are you homeless?" she shouted.

I stared at her.

"A bum? A hobo? A tramp?" the girl shouted.

A couple pushing a stroller passed. They glared at me, as if I were the one shouting at the girl, rather than vice versa. I tried to clear my name.

"No," I shouted.

I had assumed that would end things. Instead, the girl hopped over the curb, then crossed the street (without checking for oncoming traffic), tugging at her sweatshirt as if trying to stretch the collar. Her sweatshirt looked preowned, but her jeans looked expensive. She tripped somehow on the pavement, caught herself. She stood under the street lamp, at the guardrail, the circle of light.

"From over there you looked too cute to be homeless, but from over here you look too homeless to be cute," she said.

She laughed, like something that had only ever observed laughter trying to imitate the sound. Her mascara was smeared. Her hair was damp. Her gauges were the size of mussels.

"Let's eat something," she said.

"How old are you?" I said.

"Twenty-two," she said.

I stared at her.

"Twenty-one," she said.

I stared at her.

"Eighteen, but that's the truth, so stop giving me that look," she said.

"I only eat raw food," I said.

"Raw?" she said.

"Uncooked," I said.

293

"I like raw fish," she said.

"I don't eat meat," I said.

"I live for meat," she said.

"I don't eat at restaurants," I said.

"Why?" she said.

I don't know why but having to say it out loud was incredibly embarrassing.

"I try to avoid consuming resources unnecessarily," I said.

"That's annoying!" she said.

She yanked me standing by the straps of my backpack.

"Whoa," she said. "You're a giant." She did that laugh again. She patted the straps of my backpack, as if brushing off invisible dust. She nodded. "All right, giant, you're coming with me."

She began walking. To get home, I had to go that way too—so, well, I did. We both walked toward town (not together, but together), past the roundabout, a hotel with vacancies, silhouettes of humans leashed to silhouettes of dogs. She had an unplaceable accent. Like a lisp, but not?

"I hate chitchat, so before you ask, I don't go to school, I don't have a job, and my parents are dead," she said.

She tripped somehow on the sidewalk.

"I'm a cryptid fanatic. I'm here for the bloodsuckers. I'm going to catch one, to bring the world proof that the monsters exist, which will vault me like automatically into the cryptozoology hall of fame," she said.

She glanced at me, guiltily.

"There isn't actually a hall of fame," she said.

(Yes, yes, I was in love by now.)

"Oh and my name is Ash," she said.

As we passed the café, the smoky taverns, the overpriced steakhouse patronized exclusively by tourists from cruise ships, I argued with myself (silently) about the girl, counterpoint after counterpoint after counterpoint. Despite my (admittedly) disheveled appearance, and my (fine) sour odor, this girl was actually talking to me. However. Maybe that was actually more concerning than comforting. (What was wrong with her?) (Didn't something have to be wrong with her?) However. I was really curious about her, suddenly. However. She was very young, and would be easy to hurt, accidentally. However, however, however, however.

"This place looks amazing!" she said.

She had stopped at a diner (pleather booths, checkered linoleum, chrome stools along the counter), pressing her hands to the glass, her face lit from light within. She stepped to the door, tried pushing it open, failed, tried pushing it open, failed, tried pushing it open, failed, squinted, frowned, scowled, tried pulling. The door swung open with a whoosh of heat and music. She did that laugh again, triumphantly, standing in the doorway.

"Hey, giant, aren't you coming?" she said.

I felt that familiar plunging sensation (like being hurled off some cliff) (the ritual sacrifice) I get whenever confronted with something I want to do that I know would hurt the planet. I stared into the diner. People laughing, chewing hamburgers, tearing apart napkins absentmindedly, shoving aside plates dolloped with unused ketchup, sipping cola through plastic straws that never would get used again. Electric lights shimmering, electric heater whirring, electric stereo blaring country songs. The cook dumping a tub of wilted lettuce into the garbage. There was so much waste in that diner I could hardly breathe.

"Sorry," I said.

I left the girl there, standing in the doorway, looking heartbroken, fragrant heat and twanging music billowing out around her.

Why does the wrong thing always feel like the right thing? Why does the right thing always feel like the wrong thing? Do there need to be so many feelings?

I was much happier before I knew that girl existed. Now I can't stop thinking about how at this exact moment she exists and is doing something somewhere and how I could be there but I'm not. I want to split some fries with her and listen to her talk. I want to split a pitcher of beer with my stepbrother and listen to him talk. I want to drink coffee and eavesdrop on strangers. The worst thing about trying to live an ethical life is how it isolates you from other people. I am going to die alone.

(I didn't capture the proper moments, didn't capture the moments properly, but if you had been there, unicorns, you would have loved her too.)

At the harbor, moonlight shone gleaming on the propellers of seaplanes. Waves crashed against the beach. Among the flayed seals, the shredded walruses, the sand was littered now with the carcasses of porpoises. Their fins battered. Their mouths yawning, frozen in terror, ringed with nubbed teeth. For me, nothing is ever as hard to see as the porpoises.

Back home, I filled the bird feeder with pinched morsels of banana, a shake of oats. Some bulky animal was lumbering through the underbrush just beyond the backyard, in the darkness, huffing. (Oh, be sure to tell Peter: The gutter above the porch got knocked off, blown loose, something?) I haven't sorted through the litter yet, will have to tomorrow.

May 15th

Another grueling workday yesterday!

I do not work alone. There are a few other workers. We shovel together during snowstorms, plant together in the rain. Their impression of me seems to be: quiet, pleasant, young. They are not aware of my lifestyle. When they ask about my life, I murmur something vague, smiling, then change the subject. The thoughts in my brain would only upset them. I usually avoid talking about anything except the weather.

But I cannot just keep the thoughts in my brain. The thoughts are volatile. My brain would explode. So instead the thoughts end up here—the worst thoughts, the worst ideas, the worst notions, all the theorems I would never speak aloud.

But I have other thoughts too. I have best thoughts. Thoughts about how coral and krill and clams can glow bright neon colors. Thoughts about how mouthbrooders like jawfish hatch eggs in their mouths. Thoughts about how tuataras have third eyes on their foreheads, as if enlightened, coated with opaque scales. Thoughts about lavender thunderheads swelling above an otherwise empty sea, headwaters swirling through leafless deadfall, amber beetles coated with gritty pollen, rainbowed minnows frozen underwater, dewy toadstools sprouting from honeycomb cliffs, macaques soaking together in thermal springs, owls on gnarled branches grooming downy chicks, galloping reindeer trampling alphabetic patterns into the chalky rims of crater lakes, frosted grasses on otherwise lifeless prairies, icicles dripping in grottoes, creeks white with muddy silt, deserts of flaky cracked earth, vast briny salt flats flooded with glassy water, frothy waterfalls shooting from a gap in the side of a ridge and plummeting dizzyingly past crags past nests past weeds and misting the snowy rocks below, and there is lava, and there are forests, and there are islands, certain flowers grow only on the slopes of certain mountains, moose grow antlers, geese lay eggs, snakes shed skin, bees make honey, all of the clichés actually are true. I love this planet. When I think about things like "Our planet has a moon," I feel awed.

(Honestly, unicorns, using words like "awed" embarrasses me. Having emotions is archaic, outdated, as unfashionable as wearing periwigs. Sentimentalism is a practice society has rejected altogether. But I'm my own society. A rogue country. Here I will offer refuge to that hoary exile sentimentalism. Here I will exile what others won't. I exile apathy. I exile cynicism. I exile the emperor itself, sarcasm, that frightened tyrannical prick, ungrateful grandchild of sentimentalism, ruling on a stolen throne. It's everything sentimentalism is. The same face, the same blood, the same feelings. Only younger. And false. Hiding itself behind a sneering mask.)

Today I had the day off. Even after dawn, the sky stayed dark. Winds shook the attic. The clouds poured rain. A moth had gotten inside, which I caught and then set free on the balcony. I ate a few handfuls of oats, a couple apples. I brushed my teeth (salvaged baking soda), trimmed my fingernails, snipped my toenails. Then I zipped myself into my raincoat (halfway) to go visit Grandpa Uyaquq. (The zipper is broken, is why the raincoat only zips halfway.) Thunder crackled above the ocean. My umbrella shuddered under the force of the rain. As I passed the diner, the wind blew out my umbrella, snapping its frame through its fabric like bones through skin. From there I ran to the pioneer home, leaping puddles with the broken umbrella, rain battering my hood.

In the lobby, dripping rainwater onto the carpeted mat, I overheard a group of nurses quarreling about the monsters. Most locals don't believe the monsters exist, refer to the monsters as a "superstition" of the "natives." Still, this season is always tense around town! There is a direct relationship between the level of tension and the number of bodies on the beach. Even for those who don't believe in the monsters, the possibility is terrifying. That the monsters themselves might come ashore. That this town might get consumed alive overnight.

"The monsters have gotten bigger," whispered a nurse, blinking through browline glasses.

"No one has ever seen one," laughed a plump nurse.

"But an octopus?" said a nurse with a flattop haircut.

Oh, yes, I forgot to mention: The night before, a gigantic scarlet octopus had washed ashore, its arms tangled dementedly, its mantle crushed like a piece of rotten fruit. It is rare for the monsters to kill something of that magnitude. Until last night, an octopus had not washed ashore for seven years.

"The animals get killed by boats," the plump nurse laughed.

"Propellers," called a passing nurse, embracing a clipboard of paperwork.

"Or poachers," the plump nurse said.

The nurse with the flattop haircut was shaking his head, huffily.

"The monsters can take human form! That's why no one has ever seen one! We probably have but didn't know!" the nurse with the flattop haircut argued, his hands on his waist.

I racked the broken umbrella, keyed the code for the elevator, rode to the floor above. It wasn't illogical to think that the monsters could take human form. Organisms often evolve cryptic features. Jellyfish have evolved transparency. Sharks have evolved camouflaged skins, turtles have evolved camouflaged shells. Squid have evolved skin that changes color, sea slugs can mimic coral polyps, frogfish can mimic stones, pipefish can mimic seagrass, scorpion fish can mimic dead brown leaves. So the monsters might mimic us. That sort of crypsis would have an obvious logic, evolutionarily. Another species might have been living among us for centuries without us knowing. Perhaps so many centuries that the monsters themselves had forgotten, by now, that they were mimicking, that they were something separate, that human form didn't mean human, necessarily.

The hallway upstairs is the length of an escape tunnel, although, for people who live there, it never leads to that. My stepbrother stood gazing out a bank of windows, lightning flickering across him, a puddle forming around his heels. Bright-red woolen hat, unbuttoned trench coat, red tie, charcoal suit, polished brogues. A nurse was murmuring somewhere, checking charts.

"He's still sleeping," Peter said.

He was gazing at the mountains in the distance, through the haze of rainfall.

"More loggers came," Peter murmured. "They're clear-cutting the backside of the mountains." Lightning flashed again. "Destroying the whole ecosystem for a bit of profit."

Peter and his girlfriend share a run-down, drafty lodge in the mountains overlooking a logging road. The lodge is smoky, and cramped, and leaks during storms, but nevertheless gives Peter and his girlfriend and his coconspirators an isolated location to prepare for their fires.

Just then, a number of seemingly unconnected details connected in my mind, images from that morning in the attic a few days ago: his unshaven cheeks, his mucky brogues, the fresh scrapes (barbwire, probably, maybe thorns) that had marked his palms and knuckles. It finally dawned on me where he had been, what he had been out doing, before coming to visit me. He had been scouting.

"Are you planning another event?" I said.

Peter blinked, glanced at me.

"Do you want to be a lookout?" Peter said.

"No," I said.

"Because we could really use another lookout," Peter said.

"No, no, no, no, no," I said.

Peter grinned, teeth flashing. His grin faded. His voice lowered.

"Did you see the news last night?" Peter said.

"I don't have a television," I said.

"It's like the media can sense the fires are coming," Peter said, voice lowering even further. "Yesterday the stations in Juneau ran recaps of the other fires. Maps of the locations, photos of the buildings, random theories of random citizens."

"There probably aren't any other stories to run," I said.

"Everybody interviewed referred to us as 'ecoterrorists.' Never 'activists,' never 'guerrillas,' never even 'extremists.' The 'ecoterrorists.' Every single time," Peter said.

"Just, whatever you're planning, please don't get caught," I said.

"Terrorists," Peter grumbled, digging through the pockets of his trench coat. "With that word, in this country, you could hang anybody. In three hundred years we'll have museums about terrorist executions, same as we have museums about witch burnings now. If Guantanamo isn't the new Salem, I don't know what is."

Peter slipped a pair of date bars from his pockets. Date cashew cardamom, based on the color of the wrappers. Or, maybe, date pecan ginger. I no longer have the colors memorized.

"Hungry?" Peter said.

"Those have wrappers," I said.

"I'll recycle the wrappers," Peter said.

"Those kind you can't recycle," I said.

Peter ate the date bars—four bites apiece—and stuffed the wrappers in a pocket.

"And whoever made those bars must have consumed electricity, with overwhelming odds the electricity was sourced from a coal plant or a nuclear reactor, which profit from the destruction of whole ecosystems," I said.

"You have to make certain concessions, if you're going to live a life," Peter said through a mouthful, still chewing.

"That's what the loggers say," I said.

299

He swallowed, and laughed, and grinned again.

"Time to work," Peter said.

He slapped my back, and turned to leave.

"Make sure he eats his breakfast," Peter called.

As his footsteps receded toward the elevator, past doorway after doorway of wrecked bodies, I stared at the mountains, thinking through another proof.

1. Terrorism is the use of violence in pursuit of political objectives.
2. The purpose of a soldier is to use violence in pursuit of political objectives.
3. $(1, 2) \Rightarrow$ The purpose of a soldier is to perform terrorism.
4. One is a terrorist $\Leftrightarrow$ one performs terrorism.
5. $(3, 4) \Rightarrow$ Soldiers are terrorists.
∴ Soldiers are terrorists.

Consequently,

6. Practically every government in the world has a military with soldiers.
7. $(5, 6) \Rightarrow$ Practically every government in the world maintains terrorists.
8. Practically every government in the world has avowed hatred of terrorism.
9. $(4, 7, 8) \Rightarrow$ Governments hate funding some programs.
∴ Governments hate funding some programs.

Grandpa Uyaquq's room faces the ocean rather than the mountains. Filtered through the storm, the daylight cast a sea-green tint across the curtains, the wallpaper, the furniture, the motionless shapes of sleeping men. I sat in an upholstered chair alongside Grandpa Uyaquq, holding his wrist with my hand. A nurse pushing a cart clattered past the doorway; Mr. Nome, Grandpa Uyaquq's roommate, blinked awake. He stared at me. He reached unsteadily for the eyeglasses on his nightstand, hesitantly hooked the eyeglasses to his ears, carefully adjusted the eyeglasses on his nose, and then stared at me, again, through the eyeglasses. After that he ignored me. He unbuttoned and rebuttoned the upper button of his pajamas, performed a grooming ritual involving his eyebrows, and then began writing an entry in his diary (just a plain leather journal, no unicorns,

300

sorry). Mr. Nome has no family, never gets any visitors of his own. Since his stroke, he can use only a single hand, a single arm, a single leg, a single foot. Only half of his face can frown and smile. Furthermore, he has lost certain brain functions, suffering from a condition known as asemia. This means that Mr. Nome cannot understand symbols. All signs, all symbols, are now meaningless to him. The letters of our alphabet, with their loops and tittles and tails, are as inscrutable to him as the tildes and cedillas and breves of a foreign alphabet. Ditto marks, pound signs, ampersands, pilcrows, commas are indecipherable. Numbers are incomprehensible. An exit sign, a voltage warning, the gender symbols on public toilets, are utterly unintelligible. Cautionary crossbones might as well mean "recyclable"; slashed circles, "support fascism"; curved arrows, "beyond this point no hats allowed." There are authors who experiment with asemic writing—writing novels and poetry in meaningless symbols—but Mr. Nome is not experimental. He simply cannot express himself any other way. Nonsense symbols are now his only outlet. Like glossolalia. Speaking in tongues. Writing the symbols seems to calm him.

I'm writing in my own now. A nurse has wheeled Mr. Nome off to the cafeteria for breakfast. Grandpa Uyaquq is wheezing in his sleep, drooling a bit on his pillow. I don't know what he dreams of. Maybe he dreams of the monsters. Grandpa Uyaquq always wanted proof. He has six hundred dollars in an account at the bank where Peter works, reserved for whoever can document a sighting. Maybe that's the truth about why I've been watching the beach so closely. I don't want the money. But, just once, before the dementia totally consumes him, I wish that he could hold it. A photograph, a sketch, a description, anything. Proof he wasn't wrong.

May 16th

Just read some. This latest chapter opens, "Feelings? Feelings? Any animal can have feelings! —Octun Odrade, *A Makeshift Homunculus*." After the accidental destruction of the floating city, the novel has relocated (yet again) to a mythical city in the volcanoes of the Congo Basin, constructed in gleaming magma chambers by sovereign *ngola* with enslaved *abika*. The debtor soldier, concealed behind the stuffed hide of a mountain gorilla, is eavesdropping on a bizarre ceremony, after being forbidden, on eleven separate occasions, from watching.

Take note, unicorns: I've decided that just holding the proof isn't enough. I want my grandfather to see the monsters himself. ∴, after work today, I walked to the pioneer home, signed him out, and wheeled him down through town to the harbor (stopping occasionally to pick up some crumpled aluminum, a stained napkin, a pink rubber band). A plaid woolen blanket was slung over my shoulders, and the camouflage binoculars hung from my neck, and the novel was stuffed into the seat of my jeans. Grandpa Uyaquq was zipped into a sky-blue down parka. His hair was plastered to his forehead in the front and matted chaotically to his neck in the back and puffing out wildly on both sides, which, if it had been an actual hairstyle, might have been called a "napper." His wheelchair has wheels that squeak with each rotation. Along the way, I tried to talk to him, but his mind wasn't there. A seaplane with bright pontoons landed in the harbor with a splash, which made his eyes widen, but that was as alert as his mind ever got. Unlike Mr. Nome, Grandpa Uyaquq can still use both sides of his body—both hands, both arms, both legs, both feet—and the linguistic consequences of his dementia are also different from those of asemia. He can't speak anymore, but he can still comprehend written language, and he can still communicate. When his mind is there, he can shake his head "yes" and "no" to answer your questions. He can smile and frown, can laugh and groan, can rap his knuckles on your chest to scold you.

At the end of the boardwalk, I helped him stand, collapsed the wheelchair, and (lugging the wheelchair) then helped him totter across the black sand toward the point in the distance. The beach was deserted. There weren't even footprints, just rippled divots molded into the sand by the wind. Flies hovered above the seals, the walruses, the porpoises, the giant octopus with the tangled arms. Birds fluttered from carcass to carcass, scavenging rotten meat. Crows, magpies, shrieking crested jays. At the point, I expanded the wheelchair, and helped him lower himself into the seat. I wrapped him in the plaid woolen blanket, set the camouflage binoculars on his lap, and then settled onto the boulder. All right! We were ready now! Let the monsters come! I thought.

"If you see anything, use the binoculars," I said.

Grandpa Uyaquq was blinking as if about to fall back to sleep. Behind us, the pines obscured any view of the houses looming on the hillside above the beach. Pinecones occasionally dropped from the branches into the underbrush.

We hadn't been there long when back toward the harbor a distorted, blurred figure stepped from the boardwalk, into the sand, and then began, like a mirage, flickering toward us along the shoreline. The figure gained definition gradually, took on form, but not until it somehow tripped over the sand, caught itself, did I recognize who it was. She was marching directly at us. That girl. Ash. I was overwhelmed suddenly by contradictory emotions: joy, dismay, relief, panic. I became very aware of the stain (chocolate, salvaged) on the sleeve of my sweater. I was possibly blushing, and definitely sweating. (None of this made any sense whatsoever. But you unicorns deserve to know the truth. I can be that illogical.)

For the entire length of the beach, the girl marched directly at us, intently, resolutely, without wavering—and then proceeded to walk directly past us. Not far, but did. Then stopped, and—still ignoring us—bent to look at a dead seal. (One of the hundreds—who knows how she chose it?)

After perusing the carcass, and sniffing the air, and gagging dramatically, she straightened again. She glanced at us. As if just noticing us sitting there, she waved, and strolled back over.

She stood between the wheelchair and the boulder, her hands propped on her hips, scrutinizing my grandfather, then turning to me.

"So, giant, you're on monster duty today too?" Ash said.

I pointed at Grandpa Uyaquq.

"He's the expert," I said.

Her face changed abruptly—an aspiring musician in the presence of a rock star.

"You know stuff about the bloodsuckers?" she said to him, in almost a whisper, awed.

Grandpa Uyaquq blinked at the ocean, oblivious.

"Sorry, his mind isn't always there," I said.

She frowned.

"Oh," she said.

She pursed her lips, and cocked her head, peering at him.

"Hey, Gramps, I like your hair," she said.

Grandpa Uyaquq blinked at the ocean, oblivious.

"I like his hair," she whispered at me, like a secret.

She nudged the novel aside, brushed the surface of the boulder, as if sweeping off invisible dust, and then sat with me. Her hair hung from the raised hood of a gigantic anorak. Now that her hair was dry, it was a paler gray, almost white. There wasn't any rain today. Nevertheless, just in case, I had brought my umbrella, which is fixed, partially. (At the pioneer home yesterday, while I was sitting with

Grandpa Uyaquq, a nurse found the umbrella on the rack in the lobby and—probably assuming it had been abandoned—garbaged it. I had to dig it out of the dumpster afterward.) Ash examined the umbrella, touching the duct tape hesitantly, as if attempting to read the pulse of a sleeping animal.

"How did your hair get that color?" I said.

"Dye," she said.

She shoved her hands into the pockets of her anorak.

"I have to use special shampoo," she said.

She hunched, shivering.

"If you knew how much the shampoo costs, you'd hate me forever," she said.

She turned toward the horizon. I couldn't think of anything at all to say. Wind thrashed across the ocean, making the waves whitecaps.

"We aren't going to be lovers," she said.

"OK," I said.

"Good, great, you didn't even put up a fight," she said.

I hoped Grandpa Uyaquq hadn't caught that line about lovers. (I did agree, though, that anything romantic was totally out of the question.) She tucked her hair, within the hood, behind her ears. Her lips were crusted with something like raspberry jam.

"Let's pretend that I'm a monster," she said, "a monster that ran away, and now I've come here searching for the others, waiting for my kind to come for me, but I haven't decided yet whether I actually want to go back."

She examined the novel, flipping past dog-eared pages, water-damaged pages, the varicolored marginalia of library patrons.

"Maybe I'm only eighteen—nineteen in a month—but I've already been everywhere and seen everything," she said. "My parents wear boring clothes, my parents have boring haircuts, but my parents are into cryptids. Teachers, totally ordinary, except for that one weird thing. We didn't take trips to monuments, to amusement parks, to sightsee big buildings. Every trip we took, we were looking for cryptids. Here, there, all over the country."

"But your parents are dead now?" I said.

She squinted, thinking.

"Yes," she said.

She set the novel aside again.

"Thanks for reminding me," she said.

She batted at some flies hovering near the boulder.

"We took camping trips looking for Urayuli, Sasquatch, Chasquatch.

We took road trips looking for the Grassman, the Goatman, the Mothman, the Beaman. We took boating trips looking for Bessie, Tessie, Chessie, Sharlie, Champie. We took hiking trips looking for Wampus Cats, Skunk Apes, Thunderbirds. The Beast of Bladenboro. The Mogollon Monster. The Fouke Creature. The Jersey Devil. The Dover Demon. The Loveland Frog. Momo, which supposedly has a head the shape of a pumpkin. Melon Heads, which supposedly have heads the shape of melons. Chupacabra, which suck the blood of goats and sheep. Pukwudgie, which are supposedly scary, but are probably cute. Even things nobody else considers cryptids! The lights in Paulding, Michigan. The lights in Gurdon, Arkansas. The lights in Ballard, Utah. The lights in Marfa, Texas. The lights in Hornet, Missouri. The lights in Oviedo, Florida. The totally unexplained humming sounds in Taos, New Mexico; in Kokomo, Indiana; in Hilo, Hawaii. My parents thought the hums were from some unidentified species of giant bat, like their song or their call or whatever, when the bats were mating."

She inhaled, as if gathering breath to launch into another list, but then exhaled and was quiet.

"Did you see anything?" I said.

"We saw some lights in Paulding." She scraped at the raspberry jam with the curved rim of a thumbnail. "My parents thought the lights were these living fossils, like maybe enormous fireflies that are born underground and live there and molt there and mate there and then after laying their eggs there finally come aboveground and float into the sky and die." She glanced at me sheepishly. "They looked like headlights."

$\forall$ those monsters, $\exists$ a sighting of that monster. Theories of their existence are based on claims of these sightings. Our monsters, however, have never been sighted. Their existence is instead implied. By the bodies. Death must have a cause.

The seals, the walruses, the porpoises, an octopus occasionally, are the worst things ever get. The otters never wash ashore. The otters never die. Sometimes a few scamper along the beach, weaving through the carcasses, looking puzzled. Like, why so much wasted life?

"Hey, Gramps, did you know this guy eats dumpster bananas?" Ash said.

She had turned to Grandpa Uyaquq, was adjusting the blanket, patting the wool smooth.

"You saw me in the dumpster?" I said.

"Will you please explain to me why you're such a freak about food?" she said.

"I probably shouldn't," I said.

"Because I don't get it," she said.

"I don't want to make you feel bad, or make you upset, or hurt your feelings," I said.

"And I want you to tell me," she said.

"I actually would rather not," I said.

"Just say it!" she shouted.

I think that shout is what got my blood going. I felt this rage, suddenly. Technically the question was about dumpsters, but I apparently had quite a few other topics that had built up, ∴ I immediately strayed into unrelated territory and never came back around.

"Fine," I growled, "obviously, if I stop driving cars, that isn't going to change anything, if I stop using plastic, that isn't going to change anything, if I stop using electricity, that isn't going to change anything, the oceans will still rise, the landfills will still rise, the nuclear reactors will still dump radioactive waste with a half-life of a million years, and if I stop eating meat, yes, obviously, that isn't going to change anything, the meat companies will keep electrocuting cows, and braining cows, and gassing cows, and culling chicks, and trimming beaks, and leaving chickens in overcrowded, unventilated factory farms to trample themselves to death, none of that is going to stop, unless everybody, all together, the whole country, stops eating meat, but somebody has to start, and I'm part of everybody, so I'll start, I'll take the lead, and if everybody follows, the killing will stop, and if nobody follows, then I tried, I did my part, and the rest of you can blame yourselves."

I had gotten so upset that I had begun trembling, but now wasn't upset anymore, only mortified, and ashamed. I couldn't even look at her. I pretended to wipe something from my beard, picked up the novel, put down the novel, frantically needing choreography, something to do. I could feel her staring. I looked at her finally. Her eyes were huge.

"I just remembered I left a light on at the hotel," she said.

She beamed.

Just then, Grandpa Uyaquq stirred—grunting and shifting in the wheelchair, and fumbling for the binoculars.

"Grandpa?" I said.

He raised the binoculars to his eyes, focusing on something out in the ocean.

"You see something?" I said.

Ash had ripped her hood from her head, had whirled toward the water. I scanned the waves, searching for something other than whitecaps. Seagulls, water, seagulls, water.

Together, we glanced at Grandpa Uyaquq as he lowered the binoculars back to his lap.

He shook his head: "No."

But there was a spark in his eyes. Things weren't too late. His mind was still there. He wanted that proof too.

May 19th

Assume every person has, at the core of their psyche, an idea. One lone axiom. One idea given primacy over all others. The origin of the whole spiraling chain of logic behind each of their mundane, everyday, predictable choices.

I have been obsessing over this, all day, trying to work out the precise wording for the cores of different people.

Grandpa Uyaquq's core idea: Protect yourself. He obviously felt some empathy for animals—a memory of seeing him tending to, scratching the belly of, whispering into the ears of a neighbor's ill dog—but he still ate animals, ∵ he knew meat would give him energy, vigor, health, and, at his core, that axiom overruled all others. He kept a shotgun at the door, ∵ given the choice between shooting a trespasser or risking bodily harm, he would have shot the trespasser.

Peter's core idea: Save what you can. Though rooted in selflessness, the idea gives a nod toward compromise, toward certain limitations, toward exceptions that inevitably must be made. A memory (photographed) of a fifteen-year-old Peter picketing a local cattle ranch in a pair of leather loafers. A memory (televised) of a nineteen-year-old Peter chaining himself to a pine tree scheduled for removal from his college campus, only to unchain himself hours later when threatened with expulsion. A memory (firsthand) of a twenty-three-year-old Peter buying a truck, a gigantic gas-guzzler, for the sole purpose of hauling around drums of still more gasoline, so he and his co-conspirators could burn paper mills and shale mines (unoccupied, always) to protest industrial pollution, fires that, obviously, consumed gasoline and created garbage and polluted the ecosystem with smoke and with ashes and with drifting particles of noxious burned plastic. ("A few bombs dropped in the right spots can save a billion lives," Peter said.)

307

Matthew Baker

My core idea, in college: Pursue happiness. (Worldwide, possibly, the commonest core idea?) When I felt like grilling steak, I bought a steak and grilled it. When I felt like drinking beer, I bought a beer and drank it. When I felt like driving around, watching television, microwaving leftovers, taking an hour-long shower, I did it, I did it, I did it, I did it. (If I didn't have the money for a laptop, my core idea overruled my sense of financial responsibility, and I bought the laptop on credit.) Like anybody, a number of other ideas hovered around the edge of my core, which accounted for certain idiosyncrasies. (I bought cage-free eggs, free-range chèvre, pasture-centered pork, purportedly humane beef, precursors to my veganism.) But only when those edge ideas didn't interfere with my core idea: That was the idea that ultimately dictated my choices, and ∴ my actions, and ∴ my nature, and ∴ my life. Then one week Peter visited me at college (his alma mater) and, during a drunken (whiskey) dispute, drew a complex diagram on the wall above my bed illustrating all of the tangled connections between honeybees and corn syrup, light bulbs and nuclear reactors, chimneys and acid rain and shampoo and algal bloom, a vast network of cause and effect, and there we were, two stick-figure stepbrothers, tangled up in it. His basic argument: Your happiness ⇔ this suffering. He wanted a lookout (the burning of a slaughterhouse), which he didn't get. Instead, he managed to dislodge my core idea, and a new idea thunked from the edge into my core. The transition was gradual but unshakable. Within months, I was scavenging. (Peter later claimed fault for having "created a monster.") Now, basically, my core idea: Avoid causing suffering. Or what an ex-girlfriend (already an ex; the breakup had been with the steak-grilling, beer-drinking, showering me) characterized as: Push away everybody close to you by pretending to be a hero. Or what an ex-roommate (not yet an ex) characterized as: Be a total slob because you're sad about some dying penguins.

I am not, obviously, a hero. I am a bottom-feeder, a brainless detritivore, the hollow-eyed, greasy-haired man picking through the local dumpster. Peter is a practical vigilante; I am a psychotic vigilante. I do not make exceptions. ∴ I can't. You cannot choose your core idea. You can try to dislodge your core idea, but that takes a lot of force. Peter didn't dislodge mine just like that. Pressure built for years—an exhibit at a zoo, a boring lecture in a random elective, a photo of beached kelp black with tarry oil, a roadside billboard, a television commercial, a spot of pavement shimmering with a rainbow of spilled petroleum—until, that night, Peter flicked it, and that final pressure sent it pinwheeling off into the outer limits of my psyche.

That was also the point at which I became unable to read modern novels. Novels were fiery once. Opinionated, with messages, lessons, morals. Now novels cannot have opinions. Now if a novel has opinions, it has to undercut those opinions elsewhere, disprove anything it's proven. Affect apathy. Pander to conservatives and progressives alike. I prefer older novels—novels with opinions—novels that breathe fire.

1. Society has rejected moralism.
2. Moralism is the expression of belief in a right and a wrong.
3. (1, 2) $\Rightarrow$ Society has rejected belief in a right and a wrong.
4. One is a moralist $\Leftrightarrow$ one practices moralism.
5. (2, 4) $\Rightarrow$ Moralists express belief in a right and a wrong.
6. (3, 5) $\Rightarrow$ Moralists believe things deemed nonexistent are existent.
∴ Moralists believe things deemed nonexistent are existent.

Consequently,

7. One who believes things deemed nonexistent are existent is a cryptozoologist.
8. (6, 7) $\Rightarrow$ Moralists are cryptozoologists.
∴ Moralists are cryptozoologists.

(True to form, unicorns, this latest proof likely would earn a flunking grade!)

Anyway, sorry not to write the past few days, but the monsters have been occupying all my spare time. Each day, after work, I meet that girl at the roundabout, and from there we walk to the pioneer home. (Along the way, she tells me things, unprompted, about her day. An exemplar from yesterday: As we rode the elevator to the hallway upstairs, she announced, "Today I ate a hamburger with bacon, threw away a whole bottle of nail polish for being the wrong color, and kept using a hand dryer even after my hands were dry because the air felt nice." She glanced at me curiously. "Do you hate me yet?") We sign out Grandpa Uyaquq and Mr. Nome, and wheel them through town to the harbor in their wheelchairs.

At the beach, we set up our makeshift camp: a salvaged beach umbrella spiked into the sand, shading the wheelchairs; assorted woolen blankets bundling the old men; for her and me, rusty foldouts from the house; the camouflage binoculars; and a disposable camera, set out on the boulder. (Ash says film images are best for proving the existence of a cryptid, ∵ digital are easy to forge.) Ash buys a carton of milk, a stack of cups, a container of frosted vanilla cupcakes, sets all of that out onto the boulder too. Grandpa Uyaquq and Mr. Nome (whom Ash refers to as "Hairy Gramps" and "Baldy Gramps," respectively, or, sometimes, "our chaperones") sip their milks, and chew their cupcakes, and nap, occasionally. Ash sips her milk, and chews her cupcake, and monopolizes the binoculars. I eat mushy bananas. Together, we scan the ocean, and keep a lookout for signs of monsters.

Mr. Nome, like me, always brings his journal along, and writes sometimes.

Ash, meanwhile, has ceaseless questions for Grandpa Uyaquq.

An exemplar from yesterday:

Grandpa Uyaquq had just shut his eyes for a nap, creased face relaxing into a drowsy smile, when Ash suddenly dropped the binoculars into her lap and nudged him awake again.

"Hey, Gramps," she said.

He blinked blearily, his face a startled grimace.

"I've heard the monsters live out deep, but have to come in really close to shore to drop off the bodies," she said.

He wiped some crumbs from his parka, and then shook his head: "Yes."

"Yeah. Yeah! Or how else could the dead stuff always float to this exact beach?" she said enthusiastically, and then jammed the binoculars to her face again.

Another:

Grandpa Uyaquq was taking a turn with the binoculars (although he had gotten distracted, focusing on a tangerine-yellow seaplane circling high above the harbor). Ash nudged him, and leaned toward him, speaking in a whisper almost.

"Is it true that people vanish sometimes? Unexplained disappearances? Like probably just runaways, but maybe not?" she said.

Grinning, he shook his head: "Yes."

"You think maybe what happened was that they saw the monsters, and the monsters dragged them out to sea, so nobody would ever know?" she said.

He thought, hesitated, and then shook his head: "Yes."

"So if we see a monster, it won't let us live?" she said.

He shook his head, and then shook his head again: "Yes," "No," he wasn't sure.

Ash cackled, delighted.

"Gramps, you're a genius!" she said. Then handed Grandpa Uyaquq another cupcake.

She seems to have experience caretaking. She's very good with the old men! With Mr. Nome, she keeps his mouth wiped clean, helps him turn his pages, does handstands and headstands to entertain him. When Grandpa Uyaquq gets confused, she waves it away, as if misplacing your memories was nothing to feel ashamed of, and then chatters at him about some random topic for a while so that he doesn't feel any need to try to think, but can merely listen. (Or pretend to.)

Sometime before dusk, we wheel Grandpa Uyaquq and Mr. Nome back through town to the pioneer home, sign them back in, then say good night at the roundabout. I carry home the umbrella, the blankets, the foldouts, the binoculars, alone.

I haven't dated anybody since college. I never will again, probably. My lifestyle practically guarantees it. And even if I met somebody who didn't mind my diet, my garb, my lack of phone and car, I couldn't let myself get involved. ∵ of my core idea. In relationships, you can't help but cause suffering. I can't, at least. (I don't mean to speak for you unicorns.) If possible, I would like to go the rest of my life without making another person cry.

That's what's nice about being with Ash. Things are simple. Platonic. We can just sit on the beach together, for a few hours a night, with some old men in wheelchairs.

Oh, I forgot to mention: So have we seen any monsters?

No. So far we have seen nothing. Ash has wasted six photos (of the disposable camera) on pictures of Mr. Nome.

May 21st

Technically, by now today's probably tomorrow. I'm going to try to get all of this down, although I'll have to do so very quietly. (This may turn out sloppy: The patch of moonlight I'm using keeps moving across the floorboards.)

What that last entry said about never dating anybody again doesn't mean I haven't been lonely. Actually, I've been brutally lonely lately. Eavesdropping, chatting, being near people isn't enough. The loneliness is spiritual, yes, but also intensely physical. A need for contact. Lately, waking on the mattress in the morning, I've had this sloshing feeling somewhere in the region of my navel, as if all the loneliness had pooled there overnight. My skin hums like an electrified fence.

Matthew Baker

An object that cannot serve its purpose unless it's being touched. But would only hurt whatever touched it.

This morning that electric feeling was especially bad. I already could tell my skin was going to be humming like that all day. I could hardly bring myself to get out of bed. Nevertheless, I had a job to do! ∴ I ate some oats for breakfast, a few bananas, brushed my teeth, got dressed, and trekked down to work, secretly wishing every person I passed would just reach over and touch me. A hand pressed to my cheek—even that would have been enough. I cannot even describe how intense that longing was. If somebody had bumped me, unintentionally brushed my wrist with some knuckles, I honestly believe that quick touch would have brought tears to my eyes.

At work today we laid sod outside the library, mulched the shrubs. Not too grueling. Fairly minimal blisters. The day went fast.

Afterward, I went home to eat a can of chickpeas, then gathered our supplies for the beach (the umbrella, the binoculars, the foldouts, the blankets) and hauled everything down through town, to the roundabout, to meet the girl there. I sat on a guardrail, getting bitten by mosquitoes, getting bitten by flies, waiting, for about an hour. But Ash never came.

I couldn't wheel both Grandpa Uyaquq and Mr. Nome on my own, and signing out Grandpa Uyaquq by himself felt really wrong now, as then Mr. Nome would be left all alone.

I never went to the pioneer home.

I hauled our supplies back to the house.

I was out of food again, so at nightfall I wandered back through town to the grocery and filled my backpack in the dumpster. Overripe pears, overripe apples, golden potatoes with downy sprouts. Expired cans of soybeans. Hardly moldy raspberries. An expired jar of peanut butter. Sealed bars of (vegan!) chocolate, crusted with spilled sauce (pesto?). Wilted radishes. Preposterously, an entire sack of brown rice. I accidentally stepped on a carton of eggs, had to wipe the yolk and shell off my boots onto the weeds.

Walking home, I passed the windowfront of televisions. I glanced at the screens, glanced away, glanced back. I stopped.

Identical images flickered on the televisions. Shaky aerial footage of a gigantic building, flames jerking in the windows like frantic trapped people waving for help. Another building, company offices, sooty firefighters wandering about the smoking wreckage. Another, a one-story, something like a hangar or a boathouse or a garage, ablaze with golden light.

312

Not recaps. The footage was live. Three fires had been lit in a single night.

"Nobody came through the gate, the fire just appeared, no warning!" shouted a uniformed guard wielding a lit flashlight.

"Really sad to see your workplace just gutted," commented a squat, bald man either cradling or smothering his infant.

"Senseless, senseless," commiserated a random woman lugging plastic bags.

"These terrorists have hijacked the whole movement," explained somebody wearing a tweed suit and gold watch, but nothing else was said of the ecoterrorists, whether they had been captured or spotted or escaped undetected, and then the program cut to commercial, a flashy advertisement for a racing championship, cars whizzing around in meaningless circles.

I had no way to get ahold of Peter, would have to wait for him to get ahold of me. I was worried, but not really. He knew how to take care of himself; he had never been caught before.

I wandered down to the beach, nibbling chocolate. The motorboats and seaplanes were all moored for the night in the harbor. I could smell the harvest in my backpack, a pungent, ripe smell. The moon was ripe too, hanging full and gold above the beach, glinting off the crests of waves, the wet stones. The tide was all the way out.

I was about to head home when I saw somebody was standing out at the point, perched on the boulder. Ash was. Gazing at the ocean, her hair rippling in the wind like kelp in a wave, her anorak billowing around her.

I wandered down to the point, went and stood at the boulder, still nibbling chocolate.

Her hair was damp, like the night we had met, and her moccasins lay abandoned in the sand. Her fingernails and her toenails were painted saffron orange. Her nostrils were flared.

"Sorry, giant," she murmured.

She glanced at me, then hopped from the boulder into the sand.

"I overslept," she said.

We sat on the boulder together, as waves crashed quietly onto the far-off tidal shoreline. I offered her chocolate, which she refused. ("Is that dumpster chocolate?" she asked suspiciously. She pinched the bar between a pair of fingers, flipping it this way, flipping it that way, squinting, scrutinizing. "It looks normal," she said, less suspiciously. She tucked her hair behind her ears, and bent over the chocolate, sniffing tentatively. "It smells normal," she said, even less suspiciously.

She grimaced, like somebody bracing for a leap from a cliff. She raised the chocolate to her mouth. She cracked her lips—just barely. She parted her teeth—just barely. Eyes shut, she leaned in toward the chocolate—then shoved the bar back at me, and bleghed, saying, "No, no, it's still just too gross.") Clouds drifted across the moon. As the moonlight vanished, the bright glints on the waves and the stones vanished, everything vanished, the world was reduced to sounds and smells, the touch of the wind, the temperature of the boulder, the texture of the sand. I glanced toward her, but couldn't see her, only hear. She had begun to ask me a question, I don't remember what, ∵ before she could finish, the clouds drifted beyond the moon, moonlight lit the landscape, and her voice caught.

Staring off toward the ocean, her mouth opened and shut, opened and shut, opened and shut, like the mouth of a fish in a net.

I followed her gaze, turning to the shoreline, then dropped the chocolate.

In the shallows there, among the waves, something gigantic was splashing toward shore.

The thing was approximately the size of a dump truck. Breakers broke against it, spattering foamy water. Moonlight hit a wheeling fin.

"Bloodsucker," Ash whispered.

Then clouds drifted across the moon again, and the beach went dark.

I now understand why descriptions of monsters are always so imprecise, unreliable, contradictory. ∵ when you find a monster—even if you're looking for a monster—you don't actually look. You run.

We hurried along the beach, stumbling over driftwood, slipping over stones.

She whispered, "We saw it."

She whispered, "We're hall of famers."

And, anxiously, "It won't want anybody to know."

We hurried down the boardwalk together, passed the harbor, headed into town toward the glowing windows of the restaurants and the neon signage of the taverns.

At some point I became aware that we were being followed. Something was following us. Silhouettes. Merging, separating. Sometimes forming a single six-armed silhouette, sometimes breaking apart into triplet silhouettes with a pair of arms apiece. As the silhouettes marched across the street, a street lamp illuminated their bodies.

Three people wearing black jackets. The people were large—bigger even than me.

Ash saw.

"Did the monster turn into those people?" she whispered.

The silhouettes had crossed back into darkness, merged back into a single shadow.

"Turn into?" I whispered.

Ash clutched my sweater, pointed at the harbor, where silhouettes were marching in off a dock.

"Are those other monsters?" she whispered.

We stopped, under a street lamp, as the six-armed silhouette continued drawing closer.

"You're panicking," I whispered.

Silhouettes poured from an alleyway.

"I think sometimes the best thing is to panic," she whispered.

If the monsters could mimic us, that would have an obvious logic, evolutionarily.

If the monsters came for us, it would be logical to come at night.

In the diner, people were shaking pepper shakers, squirting ketchup, singing along to country songs. In the taverns, people were ducking darts, shaking hands, spilling foamy beers across the bar top. In the café, people were sipping from paper cups, were sipping from plastic cups, as outside monsters overran the streets. In the morning, newscasters would report a slaughtered town. Hotel rooms, littered with overturned room-service carts, overturned room-service trays, twisted sheets, twisted bodies. Hospital hallways, littered with overturned wastebaskets, overturned wheelchairs, spilled gurneys, spilled bodies. Schoolyard playgrounds, littered with shredded raincoats, shredded backpacks, bodies. Misshapen, skinless, bloody. Carcasses stripped to the bone.

The six-armed silhouette broke apart, merged again, broke apart, rushing toward us.

"Can we run, please?" she whispered.

"Yes," I said.

But as we ran, we ran apart from each other, she vaulted the steps and yanked open the door and didn't realize until she was in the diner with those other people that I wasn't there, that I wasn't with her, that she had gone somewhere I couldn't follow, ∵ I was already running through the roundabout toward home, my boots pounding against the pavement, my backpack thumping against my back, and then up the hill, where what ensued probably seems ridiculous given the circumstances, but on the hill there just wasn't help for me, only heated houses with shining windows, and my survival instinct was telling me to knock on a door to hide in a house, but my core idea was overruling that ∵ if heat escaped from the houses then the houses would have to consume additional energy to heat additional air, so I kept running without looking back, but as I ran beneath a street lamp I found myself facing a mammoth cloud of hovering gnats, and my survival instinct told me just to bat the gnats aside ∵ stopping might mean dying, but my core idea overruled that ∵ if the gnats got batted the gnats might be harmed, so I stopped, and paced, squinting, from curb to curb, until I found, finally, a passage through the gnats, but as I ran through and scrambled over a fence and rounded the corner I found myself facing a monstrous garden of budding herbs, each labeled with a handwritten tag, and my survival instinct told me just to cut through the garden, but my core idea overruled that ∵ if the herbs were trampled, the herbs might die, and then whoever had planted the herbs would have to buy herbs instead, in a plastic bag, which would take three hundred years to decompose, and those packages of store-bought herbs always come with way too much, so that the bulk of the herbs is wasted, so I didn't cut through the garden, but instead looped around, and felt weak, and felt dizzy, and felt hungry, and had to stop to pick up a plastic spork, and a stray hound was barking at whatever was behind me.

The house, of course, was pitch-dark. I flew down the driveway through moonlight and shadows, bounded up the rusted staircase bolted to the house siding. From the balcony, I glanced back at the driveway, but didn't see anything following. Still, as I threw open the door, I reached for the lamp, ∵ with a lamp lit, I wouldn't be as frightened. But, as I stood there in the doorway, staring at the lamp in the moonlight, my hand on the switch, I felt another sort of terror, ∵ when I looked at the lamp, I saw the cord, and when I looked at the cord, I saw the outlet, and when I looked at the outlet, I saw, beyond the outlet, the whole twisting chain of power (the electricity at the outlet, there, and beyond, wriggling along its wires through the walls of the house, from the attic into the unlit den below into a wallpapered bedroom into a carpeted closet twisting past the darkened stairway into the empty pantry past the kitchen alcoves into the sunroom and without warning plunging sickeningly into the circuit breaker in the basement workshop now, and outside, shooting through the electric meter with its spinning dials, leaping through the sky to the transformer on its pole, swooping from pole to pole with the power lines, above the roads, over vehicles with headlights, past a lake of wailing loons, and over the barbwire fence and through the switch tower and into the substation, flailing through the distribution bus and the capacitor banks and the regulator banks there, and then leaping with the power lines over the barbwire fence into the sky again, swooping from pylon to pylon, above the pines, over a farm, above the pines, across a deserted highway, above the pines, past a burning building, above the pines, alongside a flock of scattering bats, above the pines, toward in the distance what looks like another burning building, but isn't, it's not, it's home, the birthplace, the power plant, and as you head toward the billowing smokestacks, against the flow of all of that newborn electricity, you can sense that neonatal fear in the power lines there, the terrified humming, the electricity there existential, already haunted by dreamlike visions, prenatal memories, of the generator's whirring rotor, the turbine's whirling blades, and, beyond everything, that monstrous womb, the fiery furnace of burning coal).

I propped a chair against the door. I sat in the dark, on the mattress, under a heap of blankets, watching the window in the door for signs of movement.

I wasn't there long before I began hearing noises. Gravel skittering in the driveway; the rusted staircase creaking on its bolts, creaking again, again; the balcony groaning. A blurry form crossed the window. Stood there.

I kept still.

The doorknob squeaked. I stopped breathing. The doorknob squeaked again. The chair scraped; the door thudded; the chair toppled, clattering to the floorboards.

The form stepped through the door.

"Hello," it whispered.

Like a lisp, but not.

"How did you find this place?" I whispered.

"I guess once when I was stalking you," she whispered.

She shut the door.

"It's freezing."

"The heat's off," I whispered.

"Have you got any cocoa?"

"There's an old tin in the cupboard," I whispered.

"I'll make some then."

She sniffed the kettle, cranked the faucet, stuck the kettle under the faucet, dug for the lid (the faucet running, the kettle overflowing, water spilling wasted into the drain), stopped the faucet, poured some

317

water from the kettle (glugging wasted into the drain), wiped the kettle with the cuff of her anorak, capped the kettle with the lid, lit a burner. Beads of water gathered mass on the sides of the kettle, zigzagged abruptly toward the burner, hissed to steam. The whistle on the kettle is broken. Instead, when the water boils, the kettle rumbles. I never use the stove.

She sat on the mattress, hugging her knees like somebody protecting frightened children, as the water heated.

"You live like this?" she whispered.

"Yes," I whispered.

"Your brain is awful to you," she whispered.

She scooted toward me, under the blankets, her anorak rustling against my sweater. The pale light of the burner flickered across half her face. Her eyelashes were clumped with mascara.

"Is there a lock on the door?" she whispered.

"No," I whispered.

"Will the monsters find us here?" she whispered.

"Maybe," I whispered.

She whispered, "The bloodsuck—"

Midword, midsentence, mideverything, she grabbed my sweater, kissing me. Her lips to my lips. Her nose to my nose. Her eyes, unshut, at my eyes. She stared at me. I stared at her. She yanked the zipper of her anorak, wriggled out, kissed me again, gripped my shoulders, kissed me again, yanked the zipper of her jeans, wriggled out, kissed me again, straddled me, her sweatshirt swaying, our hands battling, mine trying to block hers, forcing them away as they clutched at my chest, forcing them away as they clutched at my hips, forcing them away as her fingers clawed across my jeans and slipped between my legs and squeezed me there, the kettle was rumbling, my hands pinned her hands, she stopped kissing me.

"Stop thinking," she said.

"I shouldn't," I whispered.

"Stop thinking," she said.

"I don't want to hurt you," I whispered.

"Stop thinking," she said.

"The stove is still on," I whispered.

"Please, please, please, please, please," she said.

Then her fingers found my button, my zipper, everything underneath, she eased herself onto me with a whimper, and as she sat on me, all of my logic broke down, *verums* toppled, *falsums* flipped, negations couldn't negate, conjunctions were disjunctions and disjunctions were conjunctions, tautologies weren't, contradictions weren't, things nonexistent were existent, and the truth is that I cried while she moved on me, ∵ she was touching my skin everywhere, and the electrified fence didn't kill her, ∵ she was electric too.

May 22nd

In the morning we ate breakfast together, on the mattress, huddled under the blankets—pears for me, peanut butter for her, dollops spooned from the jar—and she had her cocoa, finally. Something made her laugh, I don't remember what, and she almost spit a mouthful of cocoa across my chest, which, after she swallowed the cocoa, only made her laugh more. We split a glass of water, brushed our teeth (the baking soda scared her, but her breath horrified her, so she had no choice), and got dressed. She claimed my sweater, so I had to dig out my spare from the box under the sink. Now there was daylight, I wasn't as worried about monsters, but, honestly, I was still worried—until, before leaving, I glanced through the lattice attic window at the beach below—saw just how simple the truth was. I laughed then too.

I didn't have to work today. We left the house, wandered down through town together, past other couples out for strolls (some probably those silhouettes we saw last night), toward the harbor. A warm, calm weekend morning. There weren't any bodies littering the playgrounds. There weren't any bodies littering the streets. The only new body was at the beach.

A crowd had gathered—a crowd of people milling about the black sand, a crowd of birds hovering in the bright sky—circling the body. The gigantic carcass of a dead whale. Its fins scraped, its fluke crushed, its baleen in tatters. The tide had swept the body in, then receded, leaving the carcass beached not all that far from the boulder. People were snapping pictures. Children crouched in the yawning mouth. Peter was there (jeans, plaid shirt, leather loafers, bright-red woolen hat), had driven Grandpa Uyaquq down to see the body. (We've just sent Peter back for Mr. Nome.)

"We aren't hall of famers," Ash said sadly, standing alongside the body, running her fingers across the barnacled skin above the lid of a shut eye.

It's not proof. But it's the closest thing to a footprint, a sighting, our town has ever had. The monsters have never, ever killed something of this magnitude before. Grandpa Uyaquq can't stop grinning. He

319

lived to see something this town will be talking about for centuries.

Ash clenched her fists, and set her jaw, and cackled, just once.

"Then that means we've still got work to do," she said.

We've got Grandpa Uyaquq settled on the boulder now, where he has a good view of the whale, the birds eating from the blubber. I'm lying against the boulder, in the sand, reading from the novel, writing in my diary. Ash is napping, her head propped on my legs, her hair rayed across my lap. The final chapter opens, "Bankruptcy is your inheritance. —Veuillot Al-Ada, *Nuncupative Testaments*." After the accidental destruction of the volcanic city, the novel relocates (still yet again) back to the home of the debtor soldier, a city that, like all of the world's cities now, is in ruins. As the mythical cities were being destroyed, off page, across the planet, all of the world's cities were being destroyed. Windstorms, sandstorms, hailstorms, floods. The soldier's debts are wiped clean. Humanity's debts are wiped clean. The planet is a wasteland. Among the ruins of his family's estate, somebody, a stranger, is throwing a party. Women in dirty gowns mill about the rubble. A man with an ashy face climbs a staircase to nowhere. Children topple from crumbling pillars clutching glass bottles. It's only after the soldier has begun drinking that somebody mentions what's in the bottles. What everybody's drinking. Hemlock.

It's a contradiction, but, nevertheless, the novel was simultaneously the best and the worst that I've ever read.

Listen the Birds
A Trailer
China Miéville

0:00–0:03
Two tiny birds fight in the dirt. There is no sound.

0:04–0:05
A man in his thirties, P, stands in undergrowth. He holds a microphone. He stares.

0:06–0:09
Close in on the birds. They are European robins. Their red chests flash. They batter each other in a flurry of wings. There is a noise of feedback.

0:10–0:11
Close-up of the man's microphone.

0:12–0:15
The robins' fight fills the screen. The feedback grows painfully loud.

0:16–0:19
Blackness. Silence. Then birdsong.
Voice-over, man's voice, P: "Its territory. Listen."

0:20–0:24
Messy apartment. P looks through LPs. A younger man, D, watches.
P says, "These are rare old field recordings." He shows a record to D. We can't see the cover.
D says, "What's with the title?"
P says, "A translator's mistake, I guess."

China Miéville

0:25–0:27

A glass-topped kitchen table, messy with the remains of a meal. Fixed shot. The table is vibrating. Silence.

0:28–0:31

Close-up, P's face.
Voice-over, D: "And you're doing something like that?"
Voice-over, P: "Something like that."

0:32–0:35

The table again. Now in its center two robins are fighting.
They spasm furiously amid plates and glasses. A candlestick falls. Cut to black.

0:36–0:38

P stares at his television. The screen is blue, text reads, "Scanning for Signal."
P's own distorted voice comes out of the speakers: ". . . like that."

0:39

Close-up of a robin's eye.

0:40–0:42

P walking down a crowded city street.
Voice-over, P: "There's a signal and I can't tell if it's going out or coming in."
Unseen by P, one person, then two people behind him raise their heads and open their mouths skyward as if shrieking. They make no sound.

0:43-0:45

D whispers, "What are you trying to do?"

0:46–0:48

Darkness. A thud.
P stares at a window. On the glass is a perfect imprint of a flying owl, in white dust-powder down.
Cut to the earth below the window. An injured owl twitches.

0:49–0:50

P in a café, talking to a young woman. We hear the noise around them. P's words sound distorted. They are not in sync with his lips.

He says, "There's a problem with playback."

0:51

A man and a woman roll on the ground, battering each other. Their faces are blank. We hear the sound of wings.

0:52–0:57

Voice-over, D, whispering: "Would you recognize a distress call?"

D puts earphones on. We hear the crackling audio of a bird's song. It grows louder, is joined by others, becomes a white noise of calls.

Cut to: a weathervane twisting on a steeple, a sped-up sequence of a plant changing the direction it faces, a battered old satellite orbiting earth.

The birdsong gets louder. On the satellite, a light comes on. It shifts, points its antenna at the world and sounds below.

0:58–0:59

D sitting opposite P at the kitchen table. He leans in.

He says, "Listen."

1:00

P stares at a computer screen. A message reads: "No files found."

1:01–1:02

Close-up of D's face.

He says, "Listen."

1:03

Night. P stands naked at the foot of his bed. He raises his head and opens his mouth and his throat quivers as if he is howling. We hear only feedback.

1:04–1:08

D shouts, "*Listen!*"

P shouts, "No, *you* listen!" He slams his hand on the table.

D looks down. There is a perfect imprint of P's palm on the glass, in white powder.

1:09–1:14

Undergrowth. Close-up of the robins' fight.

Cut to P, holding the microphone, staring. He is naked. His skin is covered in tiny scratches. There is no sound.

The robins abruptly stop fighting. They separate. They stare at P.

1:15–1:19

Blackness. The sound of a needle hitting vinyl. A crackly robin's song begins to play.

Voice-over, P, whispering: "You listen."

Title card: "Listen the Birds."

NOTES ON CONTRIBUTORS

MATTHEW BAKER's children's novel *If You Find This* is just out with Little, Brown. His stories have appeared in journals such as *One Story*, *American Short Fiction*, and *New England Review*.

RUSSELL BANKS is the author of many novels, most recently *Lost Memory of Skin*, and six fiction collections, including *A Permanent Member of the Family* (both Ecco), the title story of which was first published in *Conjunctions:61, A Menagerie* (Fall 2013). "Last Days Feeding Frenzy" is © 2015 Russell Banks.

MARTINE BELLEN's (martinebellen.com) *This Amazing Cage of Light* (Spuyten Duyvil) is forthcoming in September 2015. Her monodrama opera, *Moon in the Mirror* (text cowritten by Zhang Er and music by Stephen Dembski), will be performed in September 2015 at Flushing Town Hall in Flushing, New York.

THOMAS BERNHARD (1931–1979) was a novelist, playwright, and poet whose works include *Correction*, *The Lime Works*, *Wittgenstein's Nephew*, *The Loser* (all Vintage), as well as *Histrionics* (plays) and *The Voice Imitator* (stories) (both University of Chicago). His *Collected Poems*, translated by James Reidel, is forthcoming from Seagull. Bernhard, who lived in Austria, is widely considered to be one of the most important writers of his generation. His poems in this issue are from *Gesammelte Gedichte*: © Suhrkamp Verlag Frankfurt am Main 1993; all rights reserved by Suhrkamp Verlag Berlin.

THALIA FIELD has published five collections, most recently *Bird Lovers, Backyard* (New Directions). *Experimental Animals, A Reality Fiction*, from which her piece in this issue is taken, will be published by Solid Objects.

DIANA GEORGE's recent fiction has appeared in *Birkensnake* and *The &NOW Awards 3: The Best Innovative Writing*. Based in Seattle, George writes for the port-truckers newsletter *Solidarity*.

Cover artist CAROLYN GUINZIO (carolynguinzio.tumblr.com) is a writer and photographer. Her books include *Spoke & Dark* (Red Hen), *Quarry* (Parlor), *West Pullman* (Bordighera), and *Spine* (forthcoming from Parlor in the fall of 2015). Her work has appeared or is forthcoming in *BOMB*, *Drunken Boat*, *The New Yorker*, and elsewhere.

BENJAMIN HALE is the author of the novel *The Evolution of Bruno Littlemore* (Twelve). His contribution to this issue is the title story of his forthcoming collection *Brother Who Comes Back Before the Next Very Big Winter* (Simon & Schuster). His nonfiction writing on primatology has been anthologized in *Best American Science & Nature Writing* (Mariner Books). He teaches at Bard College.

EVELYN HAMPTON is the author of *Discomfort* (Ellipsis Press) and *We Were Eternal and Gigantic* (Magic Helicopter Press). She lives in Oregon.

KAREN HAYS is a 2014 Rona Jaffe Foundation Writer's Award recipient. Her essays have been published in *Conjunctions*, *Georgia Review*, *Passages North*, *The Normal School*, and *Iowa Review*.

NOY HOLLAND's collections of short fiction and novellas include *Swim for the Little One First*, *What Begins with Bird* (both FC2), and *The Spectacle of the Body* (Knopf). Her first novel, *Bird*, is forthcoming from Counterpoint in the fall of 2015.

GREG HRBEK is the author of *Destroy All Monsters, and Other Stories* (University of Nebraska). His new novel, *Not on Fire, but Burning*, will be published in the fall of 2015 by Melville House.

CHRISTINE HUME is the author of three books, most recently *Shot* (Counterpath), and three chapbooks, *Lullaby: Speculations on the First Active Sense* (Ugly Duckling), *Hum* (Dikembe), and *Ventifacts* (Omnidawn), the last of which is an early stage of the longer project from which her work in this issue is taken. She teaches at Eastern Michigan University.

LUCY IVES is the author of four books of poetry and prose, including *nineties: A Novel*, which will be reissued in June 2015 by Little A. She is the editor of *Triple Canopy*.

MICHAEL IVES's books include *The External Combustion Engine* (Futurepoem) and *Wavetable* (Dr. Cicero Books). He teaches at Bard College.

ANN LAUTERBACH's most recent book of poems is *Under the Sign* (Penguin). A new collection of her essays is forthcoming from Omnidawn in 2016.

SARAH MANGOLD is the author of *Electrical Theories of Femininity* (new from Black Radish) and *Household Mechanics* (New Issues). She lives near Seattle.

MIRANDA MELLIS is the author of the forthcoming *Demystifications* (Solid Objects). Other books include *The Spokes* (Solid Objects), as well as *None of This Is Real* (Sidebrow), *The Revisionist* (Calamari), and two chapbooks, *The Quarry* (Trafficker) and *Materialisms* (Portable Press at Yo-Yo Labs).

CHINA MIÉVILLE is the author of several works of fiction and nonfiction, including *The City & the City* and *Embassytown*, as well as the forthcoming fiction collection, *Three Moments of an Explosion* (all Del Rey), from which his story in this issue is taken. He lives and works in London.

SEQUOIA NAGAMATSU's work has appeared or is forthcoming in *Fairy Tale Review*, *Tin House* (online), *Puerto Del Sol*, and elsewhere. He is the managing editor of *Psychopomp* and teaches at the College of Idaho.

JOYCE CAROL OATES is the author of the recent novel *The Sacrifice* and the story collection *Lovely, Dark, Deep* (both Ecco). She is currently the Stein Visiting Writer at Stanford.

MATTHEW PITT is the author of *Attention Please Now*, winner of the Autumn House Fiction Prize and Late Night Library's Debut-litzer Prize. He teaches creative writing at Texas Christian University. The illustration to his piece in this issue appears courtesy of Kevin Somers (kevinsomers.net).

JESSICA REED's poems have appeared in *Spiral Orb*, *Kudzu House Quarterly*, *Fourth River*, and *Isotope*. She is working on a poetry manuscript on atoms, in dialogue with Lucretius.

JAMES REIDEL's most recent translations include Robert Walser's *Fairy Tales: Four Dramolettes* (New Directions, cotranslated with Daniele Pantano), a portion of which was published in *Conjunctions:60, In Absentia* (Spring 2013); and Thomas Bernhard's *Collected Poems* (forthcoming from Seagull).

MARGARET ROSS lives in New Haven and teaches creative writing at Yale. Her first book, *A Timeshare*, is forthcoming from Omnidawn. She is currently working with the poet Huang Fan to translate a collection of his poems into English.

A visual artist and poet working in cross-genre media, MEREDITH STRICKER cocreated, with composers and beekeepers, a performance involving colony-collapse disorder; a form of this performance was published at the *Conjunctions* online magazine in 2014. She is the author of *Tenderness Shore* (National Poetry Series/ LSU), *Alphabet Theater*, (Wesleyan), and *Mistake* (Caketrain).

LILY TUCK is the author of two collections of short stories and a biography of Elsa Morante, as well as six novels that include the PEN/Faulkner Award finalist *Siam* (Overlook) and the 2004 National Book Award–winning *The News from Paraguay* (Harper). In the fall, Grove/Atlantic will publish her *The Double Life of Liliane*.

WIL WEITZEL's stories have appeared or are forthcoming in *Conjunctions*, *Kenyon Review*, *New Orleans Review*, *Prairie Schooner*, *Southwest Review*, and elsewhere. He received a 2014 NYC Emerging Writers Fellowship at the Center for Fiction.

BRADFORD MORROW
FRANCINE PROSE
MICHAEL CUNNINGHAM

CELEBRATE
Conjunctions' Twenty-Five Years at Bard

July 23, 8 p.m.
at the Bard Fisher Center Spiegeltent

On this very special night of language and story,
preeminent writers Francine Prose (*Lovers at the
Chameleon Club, Paris 1932*) and Michael Cunningham
(*The Hours*) join Bradford Morrow, novelist and editor
of *Conjunctions*, for readings celebrating the
twenty-fifth anniversary of the partnership between
the journal and its publisher, Bard College.

General admission: $25

Premium seating and a one-year subscription
to *Conjunctions*: $50

Premium seating, one-year subscription,
and author meet-and-greet: $100

Premium seating, author meet-and-greet,
and a lifetime subscription: $500

For ticketing, visit http://fishercenter.bard.edu/calendar/,
email conjunctions@bard.edu, *or call* (845) 758-7054.

Angélica Gorodischer

was born in Buenos Aires in 1928 and has lived in Rosario since 1936. Her work has been much translated and her translators include Ursula K. Le Guin, Mary G. Berg, and Alberto Manguel. She received two Fulbright awards as well as many literary awards around the world, including a 2014 Konex Special Mention Award. Her novels and collections include:

KALPA IMPERIAL: THE GREATEST EMPIRE THAT NEVER WAS · TRANS. URSULA K. LE GUIN

". . . elegantly articulates the shifting tones of the larger narrative, whose theme seems to be the endless imperfectibility of human society."
New York Times Summer Reading

★ "The dreamy, ancient voice is not unlike Le Guin's, and this collection should appeal to her fans as well as to those of literary fantasy and Latin American fiction."
Library Journal (Starred Review)

TRAFALGAR · TRANS. AMALIA GLADHART

"A novel that is unlike anything I've ever read, one part pulp adventure to one part realistic depiction of the affluent, nearly-idle bourgeoisie, but always leaning more towards the former in its inventiveness and pure (if, sometimes, a little guilt-inducing) sense of fun."
Abigail Nussbaum, *Los Angeles Review of Books*

PRODIGIES · TRANS. SUE BURKE · AUGUST 2015

"The house of the poet Novalis welcomes the lives of several women during the nineteenth century. With humor, irony and firm handling of the atmosphere in which the action unfolds, Gorodischer offers a mysterious and secret plot of these destinations trapped within the walls of the old house."
Handbook of Latin American Studies

SMALLBEERPRESS.COM
WEIGHTLESSBOOKS.COM

BlazeV⊗X 15

CELEBRATING 15 YEARS

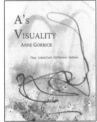

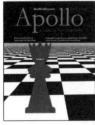

Deborah Meadows
Three Plays

John Tranter
Starlight: 150 Poems

Anne Gorrick
A's Visuality

Eileen Tabios
Against Misanthropy:
A Life In Poetry (2015-1998)

Seth Abramson
Metamericana

Kristina Marie Darling
Scorched Altar: Selected
Poems & Stories 2007-2014

Geoffrey Gatza
Apollo, A Ballet
Starring Marcel Duchamp

Laura Madeline Wiseman
Drink

WWW.BLAZEVOX.ORG

PARLOR PRESS

EQUIPMENT FOR LIVING

New Releases 2015

Free Verse Editions

NO SHAPE BENDS
THE RIVER SO LONG

~ Monica Berlin & Beth Marzoni, *No Shape Bends the River So Long.* 2013 New Measure Poetry Prize Winner, selected by Carolyn Forché

MONICA BERLIN & BETH MARZONI

WINNER OF THE NEW MEASURE POETRY PRIZE

~ Valerio Magrelli, *The Condominium of the Flesh,* translated by Clarissa Botsford

~ Sarah Sousa, *Split the Crow*

~ Jesús Losada, *The Magnetic Brackets,* translated by Luis Ingelmo & Michael Smith

Split the Crow
Sarah Sousa

~ Allison Funk, *Wonder Rooms*

~ L. S. Klatt, *Sunshine Wound*

~ *Summoned*, Gullevic Edited by Monique Chefdor and Stella Harvey

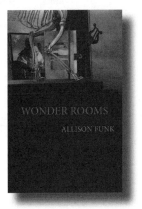

WONDER ROOMS
ALLISON FUNK

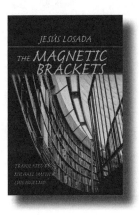

JESÚS LOSADA
THE MAGNETIC BRACKETS

TRANSLATED BY
MICHAEL SMITH
LUIS INGELMO

SUNSHINE
WOUND

POEMS
L.S. KLATT

The Ronald Sukenick/ FC2 Innovative Fiction Contest

$1,500 & publication by FC2

Entries accepted August 15, 2015 - November 1, 2015

Submission guidelines: www.fc2.org/prizes.html

is among the few alternative, author-run presses devoted to publishing fiction considered by America's largest publishers to be too challenging, innovative, or heterodox for the commercial milieu.

FC2 & The Jarvis and
Constance Doctorow
Family Foundation
present the

FC2 Catherine Doctorow
Innovative Fiction Prize

Winner receives $15,000

and publication by FC2

Entries accepted
August 15, 2015 -
November 1, 2015

Submission guidelines
www.fc2.org/prizes.html

*FC2 is among the few alternative, author-run presses devoted to
publishing fiction considered by America's largest publishers to be too
challenging, innovative, or heterodox for the commercial milieu.*

SOLID OBJECTS

Miranda Mellis
THE SPOKES

Lisa Jarnot
*A PRINCESS
MAGIC PRESTO
SPELL*

Elizabeth Robinson
ON GHOSTS

Lisa Lubasch
SO I BEGAN

Laura Mullen
*COMPLICATED
GRIEF*

Julie Carr
THINK TANK

www.solidobjects.org

SUITE VÉNITIENNE SOPHIE CALLE

For months I followed strangers on the street. For the pleasure of following them, not because they particularly interested me. I photographed them without their knowledge, took note of their movements, then finally lost sight of them and forgot them. At the end of January 1980, on the streets of Paris, I followed a man whom I lost sight of a few minutes later in the crowd. That very evening, quite by chance, he was introduced to me at an opening. During the course of our conversation, he told me he was planning an imminent trip to Venice. I decided to follow him.

$34.95 · HB · 96 pages · 4 color & 56 b/w illustrations · 5.5 x 8 · April 2015

siglio

uncommon books at the intersection of art & literature

This Amazing Cage of Light
New and Selected Poems
Martine Bellen

cover: Carolyn Guinzio
Spuyten Duyvil Publishing
ISBN 978-1-941550-32-8
$18.00   234 pages

Dist. thru SPD
spdbooks.org

spuytenduyvil.net

Martine Bellen is a poet of refreshing complexity. Her unpredict-able disjunctions and conjunctions and her baroque mix of vivid images and meticulous abstractions make one uncertain whether these poems (in verse composed of prose segments) are precise nar-rations of the contingent or of dreams or of the former masquerading as the latter. They are full of surprises.   —Jackson Mac Low

...A wonderful rich music.   —Rosmarie Waldrop

Bellen's gradual accretive methods and early invocations of Sappho and Freud should remind more than a few readers of H.D.; the fore-mother of lyric poetry sponsor's Bellen's melancholy victory...
                                            —Publishers Weekly

Quirky, electric poems, spare and challenging.   —Peter Matthiessen

Martine Bellen's poems dissolve the world of ordinary conversation and etch out patterns that demand another kind of world, one in which Satan is satin—but still Satan. And then it comes as something of a shock to find it's in fact our ordinary world still, which she has somehow gotten from a new angle. A real achievement.
                                            —Keith Waldrop

PRAISE FOR RIKKI DUCORNET

"Ducornet—surrealist, absurdist, pure anarchist at times—
is one of our most accomplished writers, adept at seizing
on the perfect details and writing with emotion and cool
detachment simultaneously." —JEFF VANDERMEER

photo: George Marie

Rikki Ducornet
The Deep Zoo
ESSAYS
$15.95
978-1-56689-376-3
WWW.COFFEEHOUSEPRESS.ORG

BROWN UNIVERSITY LITERARY ARTS

HOME FOR INNOVATIVE WRITERS

Program faculty

Hisham Bizri
John Cayley
Brian Evenson
Thalia Field
Forrest Gander
Carole Maso
Meredith Steinbach
Cole Swensen
CD Wright

Visiting and other faculty

Laura Colella
Joanna Howard
Gale Nelson
Jason Schwartz
Danielle Vogel

Since 1970, Literary Arts at Brown University has been fostering innovation and creation. To learn more about the two-year MFA program, visit us at http://www.brown.edu/cw

ONLINE MFA APPLICATION DEADLINE: **15 DECEMBER**

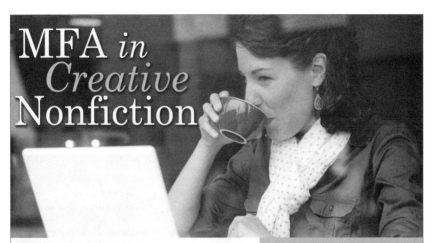

MFA *in* *Creative* Nonfiction

Program Highlights

- **SPECIALIZED TRAINING:** professional tracks in publishing and teaching

- **FLEXIBLE ONLINE FORMAT:** a program designed for busy women and men at all stages of their writing careers

- **MENTORSHIP:** three-semester seminars with faculty mentors who provide close attention and guidance to help you perfect your craft

- **COMMUNITY:** workshops with small peer groups for intensive writing practice, feedback, and support

- **TRAVEL OPTION:** summer creative writing seminar in Ireland

- **SPECIAL ELECTIVES:** women's spiritual writing, food and travel writing, family histories, health and wellness narratives

- **START DATES:** classes start every September. January & May start option available to part-time students

Some of Our Faculty

ANN HOOD
author of *The Obituary Writer, Comfort: A Journey through Grief,* and *The Red Thread*

MEL ALLEN
editor of *Yankee Magazine*

T. SUSAN CHANG
Boston Globe food writer and author of *A Spoonful of Promises*

SUSAN ITO
Literary Mama columnist, health and wellness writer, editor of *A Ghost at Heart's Edge*

Learn more at
GRADUATE.BAYPATH.EDU/MFA

Join us for a webinar
Saturday, June 13, 2015 11:00 AM
Register Today:
http://bit.ly/MFAWEBINAR

BAY PATH UNIVERSITY
FOR A CONSTANTLY CHANGING WORLD

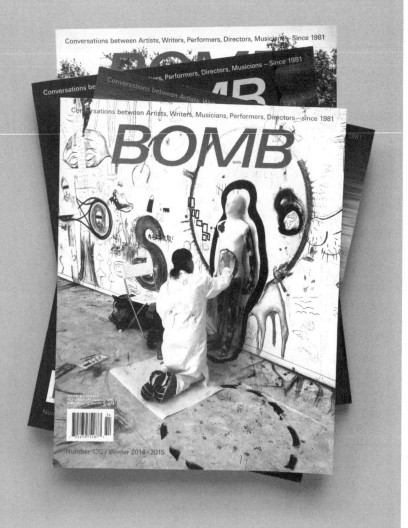

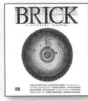

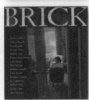

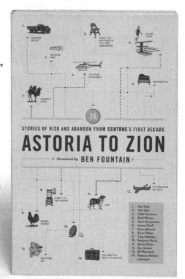

PEN AMERICA

A JOURNAL FOR WRITERS AND READERS

ISSUE #18: IN TRANSIT

FEATURING CONVERSATIONS, ESSAYS, FICTION, POETRY, AND ART BY

LYDIA DAVIS	MANA NEYASTANI	FRANK BIDART
XIAOLU GUO	OSAMA ALOMAR	JUSTIN VIVIAN BOND
JUDITH BUTLER	ANTHONY MARRA	and many more...

www.PEN.org/journal

NOON

A LITERARY ANNUAL

1324 LEXINGTON AVENUE   PMB 298   NEW YORK NY 10128

EDITION PRICE $12 DOMESTIC $17 FOREIGN

READ TO LIVE

GOOD WRITING CAN CHANGE THE WORLD.

GREAT WRITING CREATES IT.

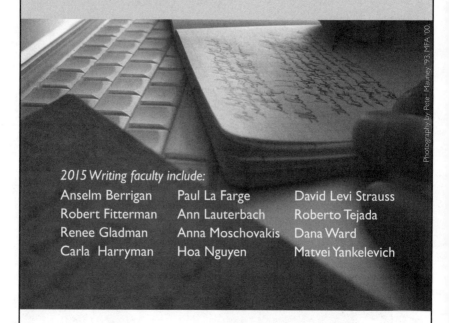

INSTITUTE FOR
writing&
thinking
Bard College

SUMMER 2015 AT BARD COLLEGE

July 12-17, 2015 | Week-Long Workshops

Charles Bernstein, Speaker
Tuesday, July 14, 2015 | 8PM

Charles Bernstein is author or editor of over fifty books, most recently *Recalculating* (University of Chicago Press, 2013), *Attack of the Difficult Poems: Essays & Inventions* (University of Chicago Press, 2011), and *All the Whiskey in Heaven: Selected Poems* (Farrar, Straus, and Giroux, 2010). He is Donald T. Regan Professor of English and Comparative Literature at the University of Pennsylvania.

The July weeklong workshops at Bard provide participants with the luxury of time to more deeply experience the Institute practices and their implementation in the classroom--all in the company of talented teachers from around the country and the world. Workshops include:

Writing to Learn • Writing and Thinking
Writing and Thinking Through Technology
Writing to Learn in the STEM Disciplines
Creative Nonfiction: Telling the Truth • Inquiry into Essay
Revolutionary Grammar • Teaching the Academic Paper
Thinking Historically Through Writing: The New York State Judicial System
Writing Retreat for Teachers

SAVE THE DATE:
IWT April Conference| Friday, April 22, 2016
"The Difficulty with Poetry: Opacity, and Implication in Poetry Old & New"

IWT Bard | 1982-2015
Celebrating More Than 30 Years of Writing and Thinking
www.writingandthinking.org

Bard Institute for Writing & Thinking | PO Box 5000 | Annandale-on-Hudson, NY 12504-5000 | iwt@bard.edu

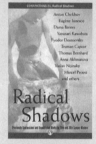

CONJUNCTIONS:53

NOT EVEN PAST:
Hybrid Histories

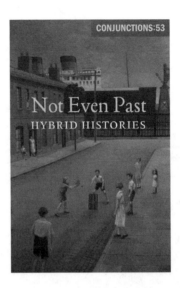

Edited by
Bradford Morrow

When fiction and poetry enter the supposedly objective realm of history, what sort of hybrid emerges? In answer, we have gathered a portfolio by writers who conjure periods, moments, and people in history through the kaleidoscopic lens of imagination. Contributors are Francine Prose, Paul La Farge, Adam McOmber, William H. Gass, Bernard Pomerance, Andrew Ervin, Peter Orner, Elizabeth Robinson, Gabriel Blackwell, Stephen Marche, Peter Gizzi, Maureen Howard, Mark Edmund Doten, Andrew Mossin, Matt Bell, Elizabeth Rollins, D. E. Steward, and Paul West. Special features are Barney Rosset's memoir of Samuel Beckett, the first translation of Thomas Bernhard's poem *Ave Virgil*, and an excerpt from Roberto Bolaño's novel *Antwerp*. Also new work by Cole Swensen, Nathaniel Mackey, Tim Horvath, Martine Bellen, Ann Lauterbach, Robert Coover, Rachel Blau DuPlessis, and Can Xue.

Conjunctions. Charting the course of literature for over 25 years.

CONJUNCTIONS
Edited by Bradford Morrow
Published by Bard College
Annandale-on-Hudson, NY 12504

To purchase this or any other back issue,
visit our secure ordering page at www.conjunctions.com.
Contact us at conjunctions@bard.edu or (845) 752-4933
with questions. $15.00

CONJUNCTIONS:54

SHADOW SELVES

Edited by
Bradford Morrow

Conjunctions:54: Shadow Selves features narratives of doppel-
gängers, deceivers, and the delusional. Contributors include
Jonathan Carroll, Julia Elliott, Rick Moody, Eleni Sikelianos, H. M.
Patterson, Michael Sheehan, Susan Steinberg, Jason Labbe, Joyce
Carol Oates, Michael Coffey, Joshua Furst, Frederic Tuten, Rae
Armantrout, Melinda Moustakis, Georges-Olivier Châteaureynaud,
Edward Gauvin, J. W. McCormack, Arthur Sze, Paul West, Miranda
Mellis, Mei-Mei Berssenbrugge, Susan Daitch, Michael J. Lee, Anne
Waldman, Jaime Robles, Catherine Imbriglio, Jacob M. Appel, Jess
Row, and Laura van den Berg.

Conjunctions. Charting the course of literature for over 25 years.

CONJUNCTIONS
Edited by Bradford Morrow
Published by Bard College
Annandale-on-Hudson, NY 12504

To purchase this or any other back issue,
visit our secure ordering page at www.conjunctions.com.
Contact us at conjunctions@bard.edu or (845) 752-4933
with questions. $15.00

CONJUNCTIONS:55

URBAN ARIAS

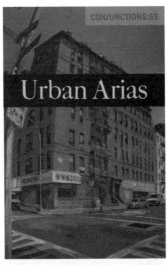

Urban Arias

Edited by
Bradford Morrow

In *Urban Arias* the reader may visit any number of cities from Paris to Tokyo, London to Los Angeles, Varanasi to Berlin, Miami to Rome, San Jose to Las Vegas, Havana to Chicago, Lincoln to New Orleans to the city that initially inspired the issue, New York. Here, too, are cities of the unfettered imagination, curious places like Altobello and Anthem, where Jellyheads and Scarecrows respectively reside. Wander down the avenues of *Urban Arias* and you will even discover a city made of meat and gingerbread. Cities we know. Cities we imagine. Cities we imagine we know.

The living collectives known as cities are among the oldest of human experiments in habitation. *Urban Arias* explores our collective existence through new work from John Ashbery, Joyce Carol Oates, Etgar Keret, Paul La Farge, Lyn Hejinian, C. D. Wright, Brian Evenson, and many others. Also featuring a historic interview with Thomas Bernhard and photographs by Deborah Luster and Michael Wesely.

Conjunctions. Charting the course of literature for over 25 years.

CONJUNCTIONS
Edited by Bradford Morrow
Published by Bard College
Annandale-on-Hudson, NY 12504

To purchase this or any other back issue,
visit our secure ordering page at www.conjunctions.com.
Contact us at conjunctions@bard.edu or (845) 758-1539
with questions. $15.00

CONJUNCTIONS:57

KIN

Edited by
Bradford Morrow

"These fictions, essays, and poems address the familial bond from a variety of angles. A mother takes her boys sledding while contemplating the mysteries of the numerological universe. A daughter crosses over to the afterlife, where she encounters both her mother and herself. An adopted boy given to delinquency examines the naive love his suicidal mother has for his distant father. An uncle begins a process of mythic transmogrification. An urban father protects his young daughter from cranks and characters on the subway, even as he begins to realize he cannot shield her forever. A suburban mother who is losing her teenage daughter to a dangerous high school friend drugs the girl and herself in order to share a desperate moment of togetherness."—Editor's Note

In *Kin*, twenty-eight poets, fiction writers, and memoirists unweave the tangled knot of family ties. Contributors include Karen Russell, Rick Moody, Rae Armantrout, Octavio Paz, Ann Beattie, Peter Orner, Joyce Carol Oates, Miranda Mellis, Can Xue, Georges-Olivier Châteaureynaud, Elizabeth Hand, and many others.

Conjunctions. Charting the course of literature for over 25 years.

CONJUNCTIONS
Edited by Bradford Morrow
Published by Bard College
Annandale-on-Hudson, NY 12504

To purchase this or any other back issue,
visit our secure ordering page at www.conjunctions.com.
Contact us at conjunctions@bard.edu or (845) 758-7054
with questions. $15.00

CONJUNCTIONS:60

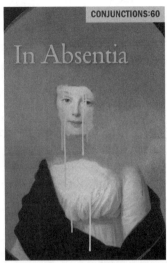

IN
ABSENTIA

Edited by
Bradford Morrow

Things gone missing. People vanished or changed beyond recognition. A once-bedrock belief now so alien as not to seem believable anymore. A woman's threat of suicide. A man's phantom limb. Another who comes home from prison only to find that home is no longer what it was, friends no longer who they were. Love gained, love lost. A promise forgotten. A couple gone off the grid into the woods and ghost-plagued madness. An exceptionally ill-timed death. These are among the many scenarios explored in the pages of *In Absentia*, a literary compendium about the presence of absence. From Joyce Carol Oates's story of a young protagonist whose devotion to working with bonobos at a zoo leads him on a journey far beyond the normal districts of primatology to Karen Hays's essay on a wide spectrum of subjects—not the least of which is the metaphysics of the fourth dimension—these works attempt to observe the unobservable, to see what isn't quite there.

Conjunctions:60, In Absentia, features work by thirty literary artists, including Charles Bernstein, Robert Olen Butler, Robert Coover, Brian Evenson, Benjamin Hale, Ann Lauterbach, Carole Maso, Yannick Murphy, Joanna Scott, Frederic Tuten, and Marjorie Welish. Don't miss this haunting, revelatory exploration of the black holes in our everyday lives.

Conjunctions. Charting the course of literature for over 30 years.

CONJUNCTIONS
Edited by Bradford Morrow
Published by Bard College
Annandale-on-Hudson, NY 12504

To purchase this or any other back issue, visit our secure ordering page at
www.conjunctions.com.
Contact us at conjunctions@bard.edu or (845) 758-7054 with questions.